STEVEN HOPSTAKEN & MELISSA PRUSI

STOKER'S WILDE WEST

This is a **FLAME TREE PRESS** book

FLAME TREE PRESS
6 Melbray Mews, London, SW6 3NS, UK
flametreepress.com

US sales, distribution and warehouse:
Simon & Schuster
100 Front Street, Riverside, NJ 08075
www.simonandschuster.com

UK distribution and warehouse:
Marston Book Services Ltd
160 Eastern Avenue, Abingdon, OX14 4SB
www.marston.co.uk

Publisher's Note: This is a work of fiction. Names, characters, places, and incidents are a product of the author's imagination. Locales and public names are sometimes used for atmospheric purposes. Any resemblance to actual people, living or dead, or to businesses, companies, events, institutions, or locales is completely coincidental.

Thanks to the Flame Tree Press team, including:
Taylor Bentley, Frances Bodiam, Federica Ciaravella, Don D'Auria,
Chris Herbert, Josie Karani, Molly Rosevear, Mike Spender,
Cat Taylor, Maria Tissot, Nick Wells, Gillian Whitaker.

The cover is created by Flame Tree Studio with
thanks to Nik Keevil and Shutterstock.com.
The font families used are Avenir and Bembo.

Flame Tree Press is an imprint of Flame Tree Publishing Ltd
flametreepublishing.com

A copy of the CIP data for this book is available from the British Library
and the Library of Congress.

HB ISBN: 978-1-78758-196-8
US PB ISBN: 978-1-78758-194-4
UK PB ISBN: 978-1-78758-195-1
ebook ISBN: 978-1-78758-198-2
Also available in FLAME TREE AUDIO

Printed and bound in Great Britain by Clays Ltd, Elcograf S.p.A.

STEVEN HOPSTAKEN & MELISSA PRUSI

STOKER'S WILDE WEST

FLAME TREE PRESS
London & New York

WHITE WORM SOCIETY ARCHIVIST'S NOTE

This collection pertains mostly to the California Incident of 1882. The exhibits here are for the most part in chronological order, with needless passages and multiple entries on the same subject removed.

Most items were legally acquired or given freely to the White Worm Society in aid of our efforts to contain the supernatural forces that threaten our world. However, in some cases we resorted to more underhanded methods of acquisition.

See the collections 'The Greystones Hunt' and 'The Black Bishop Incident' for more information on Stoker, Wilde, Irving and the other narrators in the materials to follow.

At this point in time, Bram Stoker's attentions have turned from vampire hunting and are focused solely on his marriage to Florence Stoker and his job as the manager of the Lyceum Theatre, where he works for the actor/vampire Henry Irving. Oscar Wilde has just returned from his lecture tour in America and has become famous on both sides of the Atlantic.

The White Worm Society was well aware of Henry Irving's activities in seeking a cure for his vampiric affliction, and his reasons for travelling to America. While we sympathised with his desire to become mortal again, we were wary that any attempted cure that involved 'the Realm' had the potential to unleash more destruction into our world. We did, however, realise that his research could unearth valuable information on the occult, and so we thought it best to let him proceed, to a point. To ensure we were kept apprised of his endeavours, we planted operatives close to both Irving and Stoker.

Wilde appeared to be fully occupied with his burgeoning career and newfound fame, and we saw no reason to tie up valuable operatives to keep an eye on him, though in hindsight perhaps this decision was unwise.

Viewing of this collection is restricted to members of the White Worm Society. Removal of these materials from the Society's library is strictly prohibited.

FROM THE JOURNAL OF BRAM STOKER, 13TH OF MAY 1881

Archivist's note: These entries are from one of the seven journals believed by Stoker's wife, Florence Stoker, to have been burned upon his death. They were saved from the fire by one of the White Worm Society's operatives, embedded as a servant in the Stoker household. Mr. Stoker's nearly perfect memory recall makes him a reliable, thorough and graphic narrator. Unlike Mr. Wilde, Stoker is less likely to exaggerate in his descriptions, particularly of his own heroic actions.

11:37 a.m.

Oscar came to the door of the Lyceum yesterday evening. As we are between productions, the theatre was closed, but we were having a small get-together with the actors and staff to celebrate the announcement of next year's tour of America. Henry had just given a toast, and the assembled company was babbling excitedly to one another about the trip and all we had to do to prepare when Oscar barged in.

"Bram, thank God you are here...." he exclaimed, but paused when he saw the small crowd gathered on the stage, drinks in hand. "A party? Why wasn't I invited?"

"Because you do not work here," I said. "What is the matter, Oscar? You look a fright."

He was dressed in his typical regalia: a purple velvet waistcoat, silk britches and black stockings. (Honestly, I sometimes have trouble remembering he is a fellow Irishman, what with his absurd taste in clothes and his affected London accent.) He was clutching his purple top hat and fidgeting with it like a schoolboy in front of his headmaster. He was sweating profusely and kept glancing over his shoulder at the door, as though he were either expecting someone or anxious to be on his way again.

Florence and I hadn't seen him since he returned from Paris, and before that he had spent a year in America on a lecture tour. This had been a smashing success, apparently, and Oscar is now quite famous. (As if his ego wasn't bad enough when he was an unknown.) The Americans had obviously fed him well, as he has gained quite a bit of weight, I'd say at least two stone.

Florence joined us. "Oh, Oscar how nice to see you!" she said, kissing him on the cheek. She could see that he was frantic, however.

"Hello, Florrie dear. I am frightfully sorry to interrupt your party, but I'm afraid it cannot wait." He lowered his voice. "It's Willie. He is...off his leash."

"What?" I exclaimed, more loudly than I intended, for the cast and crew turned to look at me. "Let's go upstairs to my office."

As we climbed the stairs, Oscar said, "You see, I have this almanack that tells me when the full moons are, and there seems to be a misprint." He pulled out a book from his waistcoat pocket. "You can clearly see here it say it is tomorrow...."

"He is loose?" Florence asked. "Here in the city?"

We entered my office, and I shut the door for privacy.

"Yes, not far from here in fact. I lost him in St. James's Park. That is why I thought to come here, hoping against hope that you would be here, Bram. And look, you are!"

"How fortunate," I said, with an irritation that I immediately regretted. It is not Oscar's fault his brother is a werewolf, and I know that Willie takes care to restrain himself during the full moon. This is the first time, to my knowledge, that he has failed in this, and if I could help Oscar recover him before he hurt anyone it was my duty as a friend to do so. I quickly retrieved my coat and hat, and a pistol that I have taken to keeping in my desk drawer.

"Oh my, we shan't need that," Oscar protested.

"Only to slow him down," I said, checking the revolver chamber for silver bullets. "I will shoot him in the leg if need be." Left unspoken was my uncertainty about my own ability to aim with such accuracy.

"I have chloroform and his chain," Oscar said. "If you could just use your voodoo powers to track him, I'm sure we can make quick work of bringing him in."

I hadn't used my second sight to sense anything supernatural in quite some time. Richard Burton and his men, with some assistance from the White Worm Society, has taken on the job of clearing out the remaining vampire nests in London, so presumably there has been nothing about to trigger the visions, but I was gripped with a sudden anxiety that my ability had waned. However, now wasn't the time to express doubt in my powers.

As we exited, I said, "Leave the hat!"

"Oh, yes, good idea," he said, handing it to Florence. "Wouldn't want it to get ruined."

"You two be careful," Florence said. "And for heaven's sake, don't get bitten!"

"Where did you lose him exactly?" I asked as we hurried down the road.

"It is hard to say, it is terribly foggy out tonight. I think he stopped to eat a cat on Downing Street. I heard him snarling and a cat screeching, so there was at least a scuffle. Fairly close to the prime minister's residence, I would guess."

I hoped it wasn't the prime minister's cat. More importantly, I hoped the prime minister hadn't looked out of his window to see a werewolf running by; it could be the end of old Willie.

"Take me there. I'll try and work up my second sight," I said.

Oscar was right, the fog was very dense; probably a good thing. It was eerily quiet, too, for central London, and as we hurried through the misty streets, I could almost think we were alone in the city.

This illusion was destroyed as we crossed The Mall near Charing Cross. We were stepping up onto the kerb when a tram rattled past mere inches behind us. My heart pounded and Oscar clutched my shoulder for support. The driver clanged his bell in a warning that would have been too late if we'd been unlucky enough to have crossed the street a few seconds later.

As we approached Downing Street, I caught the first glimpse of the telltale green glow that signifies traces of the supernatural to my eyes. It was oddly exhilarating to see it, considering how often I've cursed my power and the complications it has brought to my life. The glow continued east.

"He went towards the river," I said, and we hurried in that direction ourselves.

We had just reached Victoria Embankment when we heard a woman scream. We looked about, trying to determine from which direction the sound had come. The scream was soon followed by running footsteps, then a woman careened out of the fog and slammed right into us. She was young, a housemaid to judge by the uniform I glimpsed under her coat. She grabbed hold of my lapels to steady and pull herself up.

"Run! It's a rabid dog!"

Willie came out of the fog, all fangs and growls, but stopped short when he saw us. The woman pushed past me and disappeared into the fog behind us.

Willie gathered himself into a crouch, in preparation to give chase.

"Stop!" I commanded. To my surprise, Willie obeyed momentarily. He stopped and sat down, like a dog listening to his master's command. I forget that my occult affliction gives me some powers over supernatural creatures.

This was the first time I had seen Willie in his wolf form. He was larger than a regular wolf, with a lustrous grey coat and a great bushy tail. His hands were not transformed fully into wolf paws and resembled the hands of an ape. I had a fleeting memory of being held by the throat by a werewolf's hands when I first encountered one in Greystones.

Willie's teeth seemed bigger than a real wolf's and saliva dripped from them as he sized us up. His head tilted, as a dog's might when it is looking closely at something. Did he recognise us, even with his wolf brain?

As he looked me over Oscar was moving slowly around to the side. I raised my hand in a pacifying gesture, hoping to keep Willie mesmerised long enough for Oscar to get the chain around him. Willie whimpered and backed up a bit, as if confused.

"Stay, Willie," I said. He stayed. This was going to work!

However, at that moment a boat on the river blew its horn, breaking the spell. Willie shook himself, as though he were shaking off water, and bolted away back into the fog.

We gave chase, my second sight proving useful again. I could see a green glow through the fog I knew was the werewolf. He was moving at an incredible speed. If he hadn't stopped now and then to sniff things or snap at the occasional pigeon, we would have lost him outright.

"Stop, Willie!" Oscar commanded. His voice can be quite booming when he wants it to be, which, I suppose, contributes to his appeal as a lecturer.

We caught up with Willie at Cleopatra's Needle, where his leg was up and he was relieving himself.

"Oh, Willie, not on an historic monument!" Oscar exclaimed. "Bad dog!"

I hoped Willie wasn't taking on an additional Egyptian curse for his blasphemy. He already had quite enough problems to be getting on with.

He turned and ran towards us and I raised my pistol. He veered off at the last second, almost going over the railing into the Thames, but bouncing off of the railing instead.

We once again lost him in the fog, but we continued the chase, wanting to at least keep him moving to distract him from attacking a person.

Oscar was becoming very winded and was falling behind. He was not only out of shape, he also had the extra weight of the large chain and manacles he was carrying.

I followed the green glow ahead. The river to the right of him and carriages to the left thankfully kept him pinned in and going straight down the Embankment. Werewolves, you see, don't like horses and naturally avoid crossing their paths. Ah, the things one learns when one is friends with the Wildes.

I, too, was becoming winded, and it was getting hard to keep up with Willie. Often I lost sight of the green glow. Occasionally we would hear a scream from the fog, but Willie was not stopping to kill. I couldn't help but think of how many people were seeing him. At least it was dark and foggy and he would be easily mistaken for an enormous dog, but the White Worm Society was bound to get wind of this, and if they found out it was Oscar and I who were in pursuit, they would make quick work of deducing that the werewolf was Willie Wilde.

When we reached London Bridge Road Willie was blocked by a building to his left and a long row of carriages waiting for passengers. The horses bucked and whinnied.

Willie slowed and stopped, hiding himself in the shadows.

It gave me a chance to catch up with him. I pulled my pistol.

Oscar finally caught up with us. "No, Bram, don't!"

Willie took advantage of this distraction to run out onto the bridge.

"I have to stop him, he is bound to kill someone!" I yelled as I followed the werewolf into the fog.

To my consternation, Willie was scaling one of the lampposts. This not only brought him out of the fog, but the light also made him visible for all to see. A throng of people behind me were rushing to find out what the commotion was and would surely spot him in mere moments.

I reluctantly climbed the lamppost too, with Willie snarling and taking swipes at me. I knew it only took one scratch and I too would become a werewolf.

"Sorry, old friend," I said, taking aim. I was too slow, however, and he kicked out with his hind leg, knocking the gun out of my hands. I heard people gasping and shouting. I had no choice but to grab his leg and try to pull him down. We both fell from the lamppost, and not in the direction I intended. We tumbled into the river! The journey down was long enough for me to feel the free fall and to curse the Wilde brothers for getting me into yet another life-threatening situation.

We plunged into the water. When I surfaced moments later, I could hear people on the bridge shouting as we were both swept along downriver.

The Thames was bone-chillingly cold even in May and smelled putrid. However, I am a strong swimmer, and apparently, so are werewolves. Both Willie and I made our way to a set of stairs that extended into the water.

Willie dragged himself up the steps, which were moss-covered and slippery. His wolf paws and legs were having difficulty navigating the steps, and he slipped a few times. At least this distracted him from attacking me, though he turned and snarled in my direction to keep me from advancing.

Suddenly, Oscar appeared at the top of the stairs with, of all things, a roasted chicken. Where he got it, I still do not know.

"Here, Willie," he said, waving it about. "I have a lovely chicken for you." Willie, with this new incentive, redoubled his efforts and made it to the top. I hurried up the steps after him and emerged at the top to see him in a pool of gaslight, slowly stalking Oscar and the chicken. Oscar tossed the chicken to the side and Willie greedily pounced on it. As he tore into it, Oscar took out a rag and soaked it with chloroform.

Willie made quick work of the chicken and turned to Oscar, his mouth dripping with saliva. The chicken was only an appetiser and Oscar was to be the main course.

"Willie!" I yelled. "Down!"

He turned to me and then, to our surprise and relief, he sat. Oscar sneaked up behind him and quickly put the chloroform to his muzzle. It does take some time for chloroform to work, but Willie did not fight it. In fact, he seemed to enjoy it and breathed deeply. Somewhere in the wolf was the Willie I know so well, who enjoys being sedated much of the time.

"There, there, Willie," Oscar said. "Let's take a little nap."

Luckily, at the top of the stairs where we had emerged was a fishmonger's shop, closed and vacant for the night. It was a place most people would avoid because of the smell, and we found ourselves quite alone in the fog.

We secured our wolf, and I went back to the theatre to get a carriage. Willie is now safe in his cage in Oscar's cellar, sleeping off the chloroform with a belly full of chicken. I wonder if his human skin and hair will smell of Thames water in the morning.

I can't help but think about the first werewolf hunt I went on, that horrible time in Greystones, when I first discovered my supernatural second sight. How innocent I was before that day! At least Willie, unlike that werewolf, did not commit any real violence that I was forced to relive through my visions.

What would my life be like, I wonder, if I had not gone on that fateful trip with Captain Burton and the Wildes. Would I still be in Dublin, clerking at the castle? I do not like having these brushes with danger thrust upon me, but perhaps it was only that adventure that made me bold enough to leave my comfortable position and take the job with Henry, or to pursue Florence, for that matter. Perhaps her life would be better if that were the case. Would mine?

On the other hand, Henry would have still sought me out, for the connection between us was forged years earlier, though I did not know it at the time. In that case, I would have come to London a single man. I would have met Ellen Terry as a single man, with no wife to be hurt by the love that grew between us.

It does not bear thinking about.

Noel just ran, giggling, past my office door, his nanny in pursuit. Without those choices in my past, there would, perhaps, be no Noel. If that is the case, then I have no regrets.

FROM THE JOURNAL OF FLORENCE STOKER, 14TH OF MAY 1881

Archivist's note: These journal entries were purloined by a White Worm operative. She was able to steal the journal in the aftermath of the California Incident, the details of which follow.

The monstrous man who was the Black Bishop is dead, yet his horrible deeds continue to haunt us, as is evident in poor Willie Wilde's curse. Bram tells me the Bishop's efforts to open a portal to hell directly led to Willie being bitten by a werewolf and becoming one himself.

I shudder to think how close that madman came to destroying all we hold dear. He cared nothing for the harm he caused in his quest for power.

Last night was a full moon, and Willie would have normally been restrained. However, he escaped, and it is only through Bram's and Oscar's efforts that he did not kill anyone or, worse yet, turn someone else into a werewolf.

Though he drinks too much and is somewhat irresponsible, Willie is a dear friend and frequent guest in our home. His monthly transformations take a great toll on his health and mood, and I always try to invite him for dinner in the days following a full moon, to raise his spirits and ensure he is eating enough. He usually appears at our door looking gaunt and moody, and I count the evening a success if we hear his laughter ringing through the house at least once. I wish we could do more for him as he is a good man. We have talked about his affliction, and I know that last night's events are his greatest fear. If he had hurt someone, I don't think he could bear it.

The Bishop's actions have left scars on the Stoker family as well.

Bram has left out many of the lurid details of what happened at Stonehenge, but I have heard from others that he and Oscar came close to losing their lives.

Since then, Bram often has night terrors and there are times it is hard to wake him.

The only comfort I can take from that dreadful time is that Bram's brush with death renewed his devotion to our marriage and family.

This does not mean, however, that everything is as it was between us. Maybe the fault is mine, as I still bear resentment over Bram's brief infidelity with Ellen Terry. I'm sure he senses this, and it keeps us from being as intimate as we could be.

He also fears that his 'demon blood' may cause him to lose control in times of lust, to the point that he might harm me. I have not seen this to be the case, and he has remained gentle and decent.

My hope is that the change of scenery and routine we'll find in our upcoming travels will help us rekindle our intimacy. I am so looking forward to touring America with the Lyceum company. Henry tells me he will cast me in several parts and at this I am elated.

Of course, my joy is dimmed by the presence of Ellen Terry, who will be the star in all the productions. We are surprisingly civil to one another. I suppose we must be for the good of the company. I do see regret in her eyes and she often tries to reach out to me as an acting mentor, but I cannot bear to have her teach me anything that she hasn't already.

Oh, how I wish we could all be French and not have these things matter to us so much, but alas we are not. We are British and so pretending nothing has happened is the best we can do.

TRANSCRIPT OF THE WHITE WORM SOCIETY COUNCIL MEETING

Presiding: Mr. Errol Hammond, Director

Council members present: Lady Alene Stewart, Mr. Lawrence Lambert, Mrs. Viola Knight

Agenda: Report on the matter of Mr. Bram Stoker and Mr. Henry Irving, presented by Agent Philippa D'Aurora

Director Hammond: Agent D'Aurora, we are here to discuss your briefing report on these fellows, Stoker and Irving, which I read with great interest, and considerable astonishment. I am struggling to understand how my predecessor allowed this situation to continue.

Agent D'Aurora: I'm not entirely certain what you mean, sir.

Hammond: Let me state some facts gleaned from your report, Agent, and do correct me if I misstate anything.

D'Aurora: Certainly, sir.

Hammond: Mr. Henry Irving, owner of the most prestigious theatre in London and the most acclaimed actor of our time, is a vampire.

D'Aurora: Yes, sir.

Hammond: Do you not see a problem with this? The last time I checked our bylaws, they clearly stated that disposing of vampires is one of our aims.

D'Aurora: He does not appear to be dangerous, sir. In fact, we have numerous reports, including from our own operatives, that he himself kills vampires. We have no evidence that he has ever killed a human in Britain.

Hammond: When I was a young operative, we didn't look for evidence that a vampire killed humans, his mere existence was enough. But we'll return to that later. Your report also states that Mr. Bram

Stoker, the manager of the Lyceum, has blood that can open the gates of hell.

D'Aurora: Well, sir, that's not exactly—

Hammond: That's taken directly from your report, Agent. This Black Bishop scoundrel used Stoker's blood to open a crack in the earth from which a dragon and a giant worm emerged! Is that not true?

D'Aurora: Yes, sir, but it's—

Hammond: My God, what if he cuts himself shaving and unleashes fiery Armageddon? We could see demons strolling along the Thames. Are you prepared to deal with that?

D'Aurora: If need be, sir, but it will not happen, at least not by Stoker's hand.

Hammond: And what makes you so certain?

D'Aurora: Observation and research, sir. Our own Occult Ceremonies Division has ascertained that the ritual employed by the Black Bishop needed to occur in a specific place on a specific night – in this case at Stonehenge on Saint George's Day during a full or nearly full moon. There is also some rigamarole involving the alignment of the planets or some such. I don't fully understand it all, to be honest, but the significance is that the likelihood of these circumstances occurring again – with Stoker there to cut himself shaving – are beyond miniscule.

Hammond: Ah, but Stonehenge isn't the only gateway about which we need to worry, is it? And they don't all demand such complicated conditions to open.

D'Aurora: That is true, sir. Nor do they all require the blood of—

Hammond: It is our sworn duty to prevent the opening of the Realm, is it not? And yet Stoker and his dangerous blood are permitted to roam free, with no regard to security, and to consort with a known vampire. I tell you, I am strongly inclined to order that both men be taken into custody if not eliminated entirely.

D'Aurora: Director Pryce felt—

Hammond: Former Director Pryce.

D'Aurora: Yes, former Director Pryce felt that as both Stoker and Irving had proven themselves useful, it was worth the risk to let them continue on with their lives as usual.

Council member Knight: If I may interject, Director.

Hammond: Certainly.

Knight: It was not just Pryce's decision. The council weighed the evidence, discussed the matter and concurred. Any threat posed by Stoker and Irving is negligible compared to the services they have rendered. They both risked their lives to stop the Black Bishop. In fact, they did far more than we did.

Hammond: Well, just because Director Pryce wasn't up to the task that doesn't mean—

Council member Lambert: Former Director Pryce. In any case, we are keeping an eye on Stoker and Irving. Since the incident, they are, by all appearances, just an actor and a theatre manager. Though I will say that I have no doubt that if they were to encounter dark forces again, both men would rise to fight them.

Hammond: I see. And Lady Stewart, you feel the same?

Council member Stewart: I do.

Hammond: Very well. We'll let the situation continue for now. But Agent D'Aurora, I shall expect a report immediately should anything occur that is at all out of the ordinary.

D'Aurora: Yes, sir.

Hammond: You are dismissed.

LETTER FROM DR. VICTOR MUELLER TO HENRY IRVING, 28TH OF MAY 1881

Archivist's note: Not much is known about the mysterious Dr. Mueller. Public records show he purchased the scientific library and laboratory of Dr. James Lind, who died in 1812. Lind was a pioneer in anatomical research and a mentor to Mary Shelley and was said to be the inspiration for Dr. Frankenstein in Shelley's novel Frankenstein or The Modern Prometheus, *written in 1818. Mueller, it appears, is fascinated with Lind's research into resurrecting the dead and that alone makes him of interest to the White Worm Society.*

Dear Mr. Irving,

I regret that I am no longer in possession of the map I promised you.

Earlier this week, my laboratory was seized by Captain Burton's men and I was forced to flee Scotland.

I regret the part I played in the Black Bishop's plans. Working with him was merely a means to an end. He possessed valuable information I needed for my own research, and I was not aware of his larger plans.

It saddens me that I am now a wanted man and have lost much of my research. I was so close to achieving my goals, so close to making one of the greatest breakthroughs in the history of science.

A setback to be sure, but I shall press on.

Although I no longer have the map, I might be able to point you in the proper direction. The map itself was cryptic and needed some deciphering, and I did not fully glean its secrets. I do remember the opening was somewhere in the southwestern United States, in what is now California. I know that does not narrow it down very much, but the information came from the natives in the region and perhaps you can consult a local shaman for more information on your upcoming trip to America.

I hope this helps you find the entrance to the Realm and a cure for your affliction.

Sincerely,

Dr. Victor Mueller

REPORT FROM DR. NEIL SEWARD TO HENRY IRVING

Date: 30 May 1881

Subject: Properties of your blood

I have concluded my experiments on using vampire blood to cure diseases in humans. The results are not promising.

While I had success using your blood, none of the other vampire blood samples we have tested have worked. In fact, sometimes there have been disastrous outcomes for the patients who receive vampire blood, including madness, necrosis and sudden death.

Your blood has different magical properties that science as of yet cannot explain. Perhaps it is because you were given free will by the original proto-vampire. Maybe it is your advanced age as a vampire. The other samples sent by the White Worm Society were from recently created vampires and might, therefore, be weaker.

In any event, I am afraid the idea of using your blood as a panacea for all human diseases is looking doubtful at this point. You could not possibly give enough to cure everyone who needs it. I am also reluctant to employ this cure in all but the most dire cases as we still don't know its long-term effects.

Mr. Stoker is a case in point. His 'inoculation' as a child by your vampire blood may have cured his childhood ailment, but it also changed him in unexpected ways. Even studying the blood sample Mr. Stoker willingly provided did not help me to understand scientifically why he can't be turned into a vampire or why it has given him power to sense the supernatural.

While you have offered anecdotal testimony that Stoker's blood can stop someone from becoming a vampire if given before the human changes over completely, for ethical reasons which I'm certain you understand we have not tested this in laboratory conditions.

I am sorry that I have been unable to achieve the result you hoped for, but this has been a fascinating study nonetheless and I thank you for trusting me to undertake it.

Sincerely,

Dr. Seward

LETTER FROM HENRY IRVING TO DR. NEIL SEWARD, 13TH OF JUNE 1881

Dear Dr. Seward,

I sincerely thank you for your experiments with my blood. I did hope to help humanity in some way and am disappointed my blood cannot be more useful.

Yes, I believe I am a rare and different kind of vampire. When my free will was restored by the vampire king so many years ago, I felt a change come over me. It was as though I was awakened from a dream and at the same time plunged into a nightmare. I suddenly felt remorse for the murders I had committed as a vampire. It was like my soul was pulled back into this demonic vessel. I have spent the decades since trying to atone for my actions.

Though I understand your reluctance to continue your experiments involving vampire blood as a cure for human disease, I still hope that scientific study can eventually lead to a cure for vampirism. I find it harder every day to keep my humanity from slipping away. The incident with the Black Bishop and being around so many of my own kind has made this even more difficult.

Oddly, it is when I am on the stage pretending to be other people that I feel the most human. It is a nightly tonic that restores my human vitality as blood restores my vampire nature.

I too worry about the long-term effects, as you say, of my inoculation of Bram as a child. It did save his life, though I did it for selfish reasons. I needed him to fulfil the prophecy: creating a man whose blood could open the door between worlds. I had hoped that opening the portal to what the vampire king calls 'The Realm', a strange world from which vampirism originates, would provide a cure for my affliction. In doing this, however, I almost unleashed an unspeakable evil on the world and burdened Bram with his own demon. This I did not intend to do.

I not only seek a cure for my own affliction but for Bram's as well. I will continue to fund your research and would like you to turn the focus of your study on Bram's blood.

In the meantime, I will continue to seek a safer way to enter the Realm and search for a cure there. These evil things come from that place and there must be a way to send them back there for good.

Thank you for your work so far and for being someone in whom I can confide.

Sincerely,

Henry Irving

FROM THE JOURNAL OF BRAM STOKER, 22ND OF JUNE 1881

10:04 p.m.

My preparations for the Lyceum tour of America continue. There is much to do! Sometimes I despair that I will ever reach the bottom of the lengthy list of tasks to accomplish. I must secure lodgings and transport for 60 people. Sets must be shipped across the ocean. Arrangements must be made to rent theatre spaces across the American continent. Such is the life of a London theatre manager!

Still, even with all the aggravation leading up to it, I toil happily, knowing it will be a grand adventure, and not of the supernatural kind for a change. Florence and Noel will be coming along and I feel it will be good for all of us to get away from this rainy, gloomy island.

And though I will have duties to perform, I am also hoping this will serve as a honeymoon, of sorts, for Florence and me. We never had one, as we married so soon before I took up my position at the Lyceum. Perhaps some romantic evenings on the deck, in the moonlight, on the journey over will rekindle the feelings that swept both of us up and led us to our rather impetuous marriage. I want Florence to see that I have redevoted myself to our union and am striving to make a happy life for her and Noel.

I know this will be more difficult with Ellen on the tour. I must devote my every spare moment to Florence, so she sees she has no rival for my affections. Ellen understands this, I know, and will behave with professionalism.

Coincidentally, I hear that Oscar will also be returning to New York City to mount his play, *Vera*. Since his first tour of America, he has become something of a celebrity there, and that renown has even spread over here. Apparently, he has become famous for just being famous, as he has yet to produce any critically acclaimed work. I hope his play is a success, I really do. I have read it and it is quite good, if a bit overly dramatic, much like the playwright himself.

The acclaim, as one can imagine, has all gone to his head. Any ounce of humility he may have possessed is surely gone now. The upper class of London are now falling at his feet, worshipping him as the high priest of aestheticism – for that movement was the subject of his lectures.

While in America he participated in a new form of journalism called 'the interview', a question-and-answer format where the one being reported on can choose how they are reported upon. That does not sound like journalism to me, and Willie, a journalist himself, says it is just a passing fancy in the newspaper world.

It is, however, extremely suited to Oscar's nature. He tells me he gave over one hundred interviews and plastered the country with photographs of himself and this has somehow led to his being a household name over there. He often filled thousand-seat lecture halls at one dollar a ticket.

Merchants are even using his image to sell everything from cigarettes to ladies' bosom cream. (I am not sure I know what bosom cream is, but I have a difficult time imagining how Oscar's image could help sell it.) As you can guess he is over the moon with delight at this as he has always been a fan of all things Oscar.

Not all of America is enthralled with him, however. Some have taken to calling him an 'Ass-Thete'. This does little to perturb Oscar, for he says, "There is no such thing as bad publicity."

All I can say is that we of the Lyceum will fill theatres the old-fashioned way: by performing works that have edified and entertained audiences for centuries. Aestheticism may be today's fashion, but Shakespeare is eternal.

Here is one of the reviews George Whistler sent me, typical of most of them:

OSCAR WILDE
The Appearance of Utterly Too Much Art
Quite a large audience assembled at the opera house last night to listen to the apostle of aestheticism. It is probable that the larger portion were attracted by curiosity rather than an idea of a literary feast. Oscar made his appearance

up on the stage without introduction. He was dressed in purple silk velvet, wide sleeves, cutaway coat and knee-breeches. One hand was encased in a white kid glove and the other sported a lace handkerchief. A long lace necktie encircled his neck. His hair was parted in the middle and hung down upon his coat collar, even partly covering his cheeks and completely concealing his ears. His eyes had a dreamy, languid look and as he commenced his lecture he had the general 'Aw, this is a dreadful tiresome country', air.

His style of delivery was merely a plain sort of talk. He had a roll of a manuscript which he occasionally took in his hand, but spoke without referring to it. There was almost no gesticulation beyond fumbling with his watch seal, which was evidently less exhaustive than more violent motions.

The subject matter of the lecture was 'art', consisting of a sort of lament that there was so little 'art', especially in this country, and depicting the art that had existed centuries ago in the old world, and the progress now being made in art cultivation in England. He spoke in a decided English dialect, and his accent gave no trace that he was an Irishman.

He was shocked by our buildings, by the mud in the streets, and especially by the rooms and furniture in the hotels.

The lecture was well worded, and at times poetical. It was certainly harmless and does not entitle Mr. Wilde to either abuse or ridicule. It was simply the smooth sentences of a languid poet that strike the ear somewhat melodiously without arousing any overwhelming enthusiasm or creating sufficient excitement in the listener to cause him or her to burst a blood vessel.

There is undoubtedly room for a great deal of advancement in 'art' in this busy country, and if Oscar succeeds in accomplishing anything in this direction, he will have done no harm. In fact, he is an entirely tame and harmless young man, on the rostrum at least, and it probably pays him to devote himself to 'art'.

FROM THE JOURNAL OF FLORENCE STOKER, 24TH OF JUNE 1881

I am trembling. I feel terrified, foolish and ashamed. I nearly died today and almost got Bram and Noel killed as well.

Not that I'm making excuses, but when one is busily going about the daily activities of life, it is difficult to remember that we are surrounded by supernatural evil.

I was getting ready for our trip to America. We will be gone for almost a year and I was busy with making all the arrangements and packing, which requires planning on the scale of a military campaign.

To compound my frustrations, our nanny has fallen ill. I suspect she really just doesn't want to make the journey and is faking – or at least exaggerating – her illness to get out of it. But in either case, she will not be coming with us. So, in the middle of planning and packing, the household is short-staffed and I am interviewing nannies.

I was quite distracted and detecting vampires was the last thing on my mind, especially when Captain Burton has assured us that he and his men have destroyed most of the nests in London and that vampires would not dare show their faces in the day. The fact that it was a very cloudy day never entered my mind.

When there was a knock on the door and a distinguished, well-dressed woman was standing there presenting herself as a nanny, why would I doubt her?

She had references and a letter of introduction from the agency. She was much too pretty, with lustrous blond hair neatly coiffed, and a shapely figure her demure blue dress could not hide. I don't mean to sound catty about it, but it can be distracting to have someone so attractive around all the time. I do not worry about Bram these days, for I trust his commitment to me and Noel. I am thinking of the other male members of the theatre company, for there are long, lonely hours on the road and between shows. Enough fights break out over our few female cast members; I don't wish to throw fuel on the fire by introducing a single, attractive nanny to the mix. Besides, I like a good sturdy nanny who can wrestle children into bed and chase them around the garden. This one looked like she had never broken into a sweat.

I already had it in my mind to pass on her, but it was the least I could do to invite her in and interview her over a cup of tea.

Yes, I invited her in! Stupid of me, I know. When she refused a cup of tea, that should have been a second clue. Although I am not sure that vampires can't drink tea. I think they can without milk or sugar, as I think I have seen Henry drinking tea.

As I sat across from her in the parlour, I looked her in the eyes, which was another mistake. Again, had I known she was a vampire I would not have done so.

"I was the governess to a military captain's family. I took care of three children and we travelled quite often all over Europe," she said.

She had the most beautiful blue-green eyes, and I felt myself falling into them, a feeling I shook off with an effort.

"Uh, travel, you say?" She was winning me over. She had experience travelling with children, and I myself am from a military family.

"All over Europe," she said, looking directly into my eyes.

Again there was a momentary disruption in my thoughts as I tried to ascertain the colour of her eyes, green-blue or blue-green.

"I think we are going to be friends," she said. It was more like a command than a statement. My heart started to race as I instinctively knew something was off with her.

"Yes," I said. I was very much locked in now. I could feel my will falling away. I dropped my teacup. Not even the sound of the cup shattering on the floor broke my gaze into her eyes.

"Where are your servants?" she asked.

"It is the maid's day off and our cook's shopping day," I said unwillingly. It just spilt out. I wanted to say, 'They are upstairs and will be down any minute, wearing large silver crosses and carrying wooden stakes,' or something to that effect, but only the truth would pass my lips.

"And your husband?" she asked. Her voice was low and seductive, as silky smooth as her skin.

I tried to resist with all I had but the more I fought, the more I gave in. "He's at the theatre but he often comes home for lunch." Now I was giving her information she wasn't even asking for. I just wanted so much to please her.

"Very good."

She stood and crossed the room to sit next to me. Then she leaned in and kissed me on the lips. I melted into her and I felt all my will slip away.

She leaned back and said, "Draw all the shades, then go upstairs and get your baby. Bring it to me."

I do not remember drawing all the shades in the house. I do not remember going upstairs or lifting Noel from the crib. I was suddenly downstairs, and she was nestling Noel on her lap, cooing. He is not a shy child, and he was still sleepy and seemed perfectly content to rest his head on her shoulder. The room was darker with all the shades drawn.

"What a sweet, sweet boy." She rocked him gently and told me to sit down, and I obeyed. Inside I was screaming for her to put him down! I remembered the night vampire Lucy visited me with a baby she had stolen. To her, it was just food!

The vampire slowly lowered her head towards Noel's, her eyes locked on mine. I remained still but inside I was frantic, fearing that her fangs would emerge and she would drain the blood from my precious child. Instead she kissed him gently on the head and turned him to face her. "We are going to wait for Daddy to come home and then we will be one big, happy family," she said, looking into Noel's eyes. He giggled as she tickled his toes.

She stood and placed Noel in the crib we keep in the sitting room. "Sleep," she commanded, and he did. "Don't you wish you could do that when he cries?" she asked me.

She sat down next to me, a malicious grin on her face. Though I was still in her thrall, inside I loathed her.

"Now, what should we do until that husband of yours comes home?"

She pulled me to her and buried her face in my neck, kissing me gently. Waves of ecstasy rippled through me. I knew if I gave in completely it would be my death, but I had no will left to fight. I lifted a fist to strike her, but she just gently grabbed it and put it on her breast.

Her fangs sank into my neck and the pain that emanated from the wound turned into intense pleasure that radiated throughout my body. Her hand was up my dress, violating me, penetrating just like the fangs in my neck.

Then by some miracle, we heard a key in the door. Bram was home!

She broke off her attack on me. "We'll have to finish this later," she said, pulling a handkerchief from her pocket and wiping my blood from her red lips. She stood to face the door. "Stay here and be quiet," she commanded, but she was distracted and I felt her grip on my mind loosening.

Bram opened the door, and I tried to scream, but no sound would come.

Bram entered the sitting room and saw her standing there. He was stunned, with a look of recognition in his eyes.

"Good afternoon, Mr. Stoker," she said, standing by Noel's crib.

"Le Fey!" Bram said. He reached into his coat for the silver cross he always keeps with him.

"Careful," she warned, placing her hand in Noel's crib and on his neck.

Bram dropped his arm. "Let them go. It's me you want."

"Who says I want you?" she said. "I'm here to take your family like you took mine. Seems like a fair trade to me."

I felt her slip completely away from me as she talked with Bram. It seems her mesmerism had its limits. She couldn't control me and talk to Bram at the same time, and my mind was my own again. But I could do nothing while she had her hand on Noel. I just sat there pretending to still be dazed, looking for an opening to make a move.

"You stopped the Black Bishop from making this our world. A world that we could run better than you, and why shouldn't we? We are the superior creatures. You and Wilde also killed the vampire who sired me. I am alone. I want you to be alone!"

She yanked me up off the sofa and got behind me as Bram lunged for her. "Back! I'll snap her neck. You know I will! Though I would rather make her my slave."

He stopped sharply and held his hands out. "Please, I'll do whatever you want."

"I know you will," she said. She then licked the wound on my neck, making Bram watch and squirm.

"If you hurt her, I'll rip you apart with my bare hands!"

She just laughed. "Then let's make a trade. You get Mr. Wilde here and I'll kill you both, and then, maybe, I won't kill your wife and son. Maybe."

She squeezed me around the neck with her hand.

"There's a boy outside waiting to trot off and deliver a message. Tell him to fetch Wilde. Send word that it is an emergency, and he is to come here at once. It won't be a lie." She laughed again.

Bram complied and talked to the boy who was waiting on our steps. He told him Oscar's address and gave him the message. "And tell Mr. Wilde it is an emergency that concerns Mrs. Stoker and our son...his godson, little Oscar."

Clever Bram! Oscar would surely know something was amiss as he is not Noel's godfather, nor do we call Noel 'Oscar'. Bram was gambling on le Fey not knowing our son's name and it seemed to have paid off for she didn't react to it as the boy ran off to deliver the message.

Bram shut the door and returned to the drawing room.

"It's only a matter of time before Burton and his men track you down, le Fey," Bram said.

She threw me onto the sofa and commanded Bram to sit in a chair to wait for Oscar.

"We aren't down and out yet," she said. "You may have won the battle but not the war. There are places all over the earth where we can open the gates of hell. It's only a matter of time before we find them. And as we are immortal, we have all the time in the world."

And then we waited, while she wondered aloud whether to kill me, turn me into a vampire, or let me live as a human to mourn my husband.

"After all," she said with a smile, "I can always come back and kill you later if I change my mind."

Bram and I sat silent, but I could tell he was alert and ready to rush her should she make a move toward me or Noel.

Within the hour Oscar was knocking on our door with the top of his walking stick. "Bram, Florrie, I am here!"

It started to rain and le Fey ordered Bram to open the door and invite Oscar inside.

"Bram, I got your message. Whatever is the matter?" Oscar asked, taking off his top hat. He saw le Fey standing there. "Oh, hello," Oscar said to her as if meeting her for the first time.

"Oscar, this is Carolyn le Fey," Bram said, as if it were just an ordinary introduction.

"We've met before, Mr. Wilde," she said warmly.

"We have? Surely I would have remembered meeting such an exquisite beauty as yourself."

"You were preoccupied. It was at Stonehenge. Mr. Stoker was tied to a stone table about to have his throat slit."

"Oh, yes, I remember now," he said, quite jovially. A shot rang out, and I saw a flash come from the derringer he had hidden up his sleeve.

Le Fey took the silver bullet to the stomach, and it knocked her back, but she did not lose her footing. She made a move towards the crib and I knew she wanted Noel as her hostage. I picked up an ashtray from the end table and struck her on the back of the head. It did not bring her down, but she turned, raising her hand to strike me, and Oscar got off another shot, hitting her in the hip.

Bram tackled her, yet even having been shot twice, she still had the strength to push him away and bolt out of the room into the hallway and to the kitchen.

Oscar was reloading his two-shot derringer as Bram gave chase.

I was checking on Noel when I heard the back door shatter!

Oscar and I ran into the kitchen to see she had broken through the door and into the garden, disappearing into the pouring rain. Bram came back into the house; pursuit was useless. He pulled me to him and wrapped his arms around me.

"Burton's men are on their way," Oscar said. "I sent word before I came here."

"Thank you, Oscar," I said, my voice muffled in Bram's chest.

"Smart giving me that message, Bram," he said. "Once again, Oscar Wilde saves the day."

Bram forced a shaky laugh. "Add it to my tab, Oscar."

The house is now under constant guard, thanks to Captain Burton.

After such a terrifying day I am glad we are going far from here, and to a land where we will have little chance of running into anything supernatural.

As I said, I feel foolish. I am ashamed I did so little to save myself. I feel weak for letting her into my mind and not being able to push her out!

I promise myself this much: never again.

LETTER FROM EAGAN RAYNE TO CAROLYN LE FEY, DATE UNKNOWN

Archivist's note: After learning about Carolyn le Fey's attack on the Stokers, Captain Burton's men tracked her to a country house which had been owned by her late sire, Lord Alfred Sundry, only to find that she had fled. We had thought we'd searched all his holdings after the collapse of the Order of the Golden Dawn, but this property had escaped our notice and le Fey had been using it.

She appeared to have escaped in haste as several people were found still alive, chained in her basement, along with the remains of several who had died. Apparently, she found it prudent to capture victims when the opportunity presented itself and keep them alive until such time as she needed them — much as humans might preserve fruits and vegetables in jars for the winter months. We have rarely seen this type of organised planning by a vampire before.

This letter was found in a pile of papers near a fireplace. She had apparently been burning incriminating records, but had not had time to finish. Several books once in the Order of the Golden Dawn's library were also found, and it is believed she had stolen powerful artefacts once housed at the Order's headquarters.

My dear Miss le Fey,

I am sorry to hear of your troubles, but I am in a position to help you.

The Black Bishop's plan to open the doorway and bring the magic from there to our world was foolish. This world is already corrupt with sin and trying to save it is futile. I am more certain than ever that we need to go into that unspoiled world and make it ours. This has been the Order's true mission from the beginning: return the worthy to paradise.

My research tells me there are easier ways to enter the other world. Places on earth where you merely walk through as one walks into a valley.

Come help me in my work! I offer you safe passage to America if you can bring me what I seek. I need my father's sceptre that was stored in the Order's vault. Should there be any dragon's blood left it would be of great benefit to our quest. (The sacred goblet used to serve it would also be welcome, though not strictly necessary.) Procure me these things and a ship awaits you in Liverpool for safe passage to America. Go to the Adelphi Hotel and await further instructions.

I have found a wealthy benefactor who can help carry on the Black Bishop's work. I have also located a possible second Vellum Manuscript that could be the key to everything.

E.R.

Archivist's note: Not much is known about Eagan Rayne or how he came to wield powerful blood magic.

His mother, Edith Giles, was said to be a Gipsy queen. His father, Nigel Rayne, was an Egyptologist and relocated the family to Egypt in 1850, where Eagan spent his formative years.

We know that both Nigel and his son were members of the Order of the Golden Dawn and that Nigel would later become the Order's expert on all things Egyptian, and eventually took on the duties of head librarian of their Middle East and Asian collections.

In 1870, Edith and Nigel were murdered, their throats slit in an apparent robbery. Eagan relocated to the United States where he briefly became a Mormon before being excommunicated in 1878 for his obsession with the occult.

FROM THE DIARY OF OSCAR WILDE, 3RD OF JULY 1882

Dear yours truly,

I am so sorry, diary, that I have neglected your secret pages, but as you know I have been quite busy becoming famous and writing down witty things about art and America, two subjects which, aside from their first letters, have very little in common.

I am very happy to announce that my play, *Vera*, is to be produced in New York. The noted actress Marie Prescott has purchased the rights and will be taking on the title role. She desperately wants me there as they get the play 'on its feet', as they say in the theatre, and so I leave within the month. Though I am dreading another tedious crossing of the Atlantic, I am very much looking forward to my successful debut as a playwright.

If I am honest with myself, there is another reason why I wish to be abroad just now. If you remember, dear diary, I am courting the lovely Constance Lloyd. Mother is thoroughly enamoured with her and is becoming increasingly vocal in her opinion that I should ask for her hand in marriage. The other day she said, "You let Florence slip through your fingers, Oscar, and I would hate to see the same thing happen with Constance." I told her if she were going to reopen old wounds the least she could do would be to supply the medicine, and promptly poured myself a substantial glass of her best whiskey.

However, in private moments, I do concede Mother's point. Constance is a lovely, intelligent, lively woman. I could ask for none better. And I do care for her and can certainly envision a life with her by my side.

But should I marry her? I am reluctant to do so, and the reasons for this are not flattering to my favourite subject: myself. The truth is, I am preoccupied with my newfound fame and career. I am certain that those around me think it has all gone to my head, and to that I say, "Of course it has." I have always thought I had something to say, and now that people are actually listening, my passion must be poured into saying more.

In addition, I have made a tidy sum with my tour and can finally enjoy being a sought-after bachelor. At long last, I am a good catch and hate to think of myself as already caught.

Mother points out that I also do not wish to be seen as a 'confirmed bachelor', or as an unstable genius who is unable to settle down in polite society. (Though as long as the 'genius' part is established, does the 'unstable' modifier matter so much?)

In any event, I think this trip is happening at exactly the right time. I can mull things over while I am abroad and come back to Constance with a clear view on the matter. She is happy and proud of my upcoming debut, and has not taken offence that I will be gone for an indefinite period, nor shown any jealousy or insecurity about my impending absence.

Does that not make her sound absolutely perfect for me?

I would tell only you, dear diary, of my misgivings, just as you are the only one with whom I can converse about the supernatural and all things Stoker. Fortunately, there is nothing of note to report on either of those topics at the moment. I am studiously avoiding the occult, though when one's brother is a werewolf, there is only so much one can do.

Though, speaking of the occult, the White Worms are pestering me to join their ranks again. No doubt they wish to use my fame to root out supernatural fiends among the rich and famous, as well as among the Americans, where they would surely go unnoticed quite easily. (Why, on the frontier, I several times spied men I initially mistook for werewolves, only to find that they were simply bearded, burly and unwashed. It is a peculiar country.)

As usual, I declined the Worms' request to become an operative and again assured them I would continue to keep my eyes and ears open. They once again thanked me for closing the gates of hell and foiling the Black Bishop's dastardly plans, something for which I would surely be granted a knighthood if it weren't all so secret. Ah, well, I will just have to earn one in a more above-board fashion.

I would like to think I won't run into monsters in America, but Bram informs me that Robert has put down several vampire nests over there. Apparently many of them emigrated after the fall of the Black Bishop. (I suppose they have Columbus to blame as there were no vampires or Irishmen over there until he accidentally found its shores.)

I am more troubled by this than I logically should be. After all, even if vampires are there, what are the chances that I should encounter one? It is a vast country, after all, and I had no such problems on my lengthy tour. And yet, I can't stop worrying about some fanged fiend jumping out at me from some dark New York alleyway. They do have quite a lot of alleyways.

Even here, I find myself constantly on guard, particularly after sunset. I keep my sword cane with me at all times, and the sound of footsteps behind me in the street can set my heart racing. I have even taken to drinking less in order to keep my wits about me — what a bore!

I don't even need darkness or the unprotected outdoors to set my nerves on edge. Several times now I have worked myself into such a panic that I thought I was near death. Any tight space can trigger it. For a short time I could not even ride in an enclosed carriage, and that severely limited my mobility.

I am embarrassed to admit that I had to hire a valet to help me dress because I was unable to go into my clothes cupboard to pick out clothes. Upon entering such a tight space I could no longer breathe and my heart felt as if it would explode.

I am certain my condition had something to do with being swallowed alive by a giant worm. Inside that creature I did, in fact, see my life pass before my eyes and often relive the entire event in nightmares.

I was finally persuaded by Frank to see a special kind of doctor called a 'psychiatrist'. (Frank, by the way, has almost fully recovered from his mental breakdown.) He referred me to a Dr. Benjamin Ball, an English doctor living in Paris. I do like an excuse to visit Paris, but my condition was making travel difficult. To my great fortune, he was visiting London and agreed to see me.

It seems I have a condition called 'claustrophobia', a fear of tight spaces. When Dr. Ball asked me if I had experienced some sort of confinement that may have caused this to develop, I made up some story about being accidentally locked in a small wine cellar for several hours, without even a corkscrew. (I couldn't tell him the truth, after all.) But I told him that it happened several years ago and that these symptoms had only recently developed. He explained to me that often the more time passes without an examination of the psychological effects of an event, the more they can be felt in odd ways.

Fortunately, he has been able to help me.

I began doing a series of exercises that involved stepping into smaller and smaller spaces to get reacclimatised to them. It seems to be working, as now I can travel in carriages.

This relieves much of my anxiety about my upcoming voyage. On my last trip, the sponsors of my lecture tour paid for the largest cabin on the ship, but the travel budget for *Vera* is more limited and I will have to make do with a smaller one. I am not sure I could have faced it without Dr. Ball's help.

He also prescribed laudanum should the panic become too much to bear. It must work as a medicine as Willie is drinking it by the cup to treat his own horrible affliction.

We all have our crosses to bear, diary, yet we soldier onward.

I will be off soon to invade the colonies once more with my wit and sensibilities. They do love me there, which proves that good taste and discernment can be found in even the most unlikely of places.

FROM THE JOURNAL OF BRAM STOKER, 22ND OF JULY 1882

12:15 a.m.

We are in St. Louis starting the final leg of the Lyceum tour. It has been a grand adventure, but I will be relieved to see it come to an end. We are packing up and tomorrow we travel to the last theatre on our tour in Salt Lake City.

Robert Roosevelt joined Florence and me for dinner tonight at our hotel. After a delicious meal of oyster pie and mutton stew, we ordered dessert and coffee.

Robert told us he has been tasked by President Arthur himself to investigate reports of vampires in America.

"My nephew Theodore ran across a nest in Utah," he told us. "A big one, fourteen vampires. Seems just two fled here after the Black Bishop incident. That was all it took. They spread like smallpox. There's no telling how many there are now."

"How did they end up way out west?" I asked.

"Just hopped on a train in New Jersey and took it to the end of the line," Robert said. "The West is a big place. Easy to hide and feed in without being noticed. In any event, now that the president believes us, we are putting together special vampire hunting units. We don't want to spook the populace, so we are keeping it hush-hush for now."

"Maybe we should educate the public," Florence said. "People could take precautions."

"It might come to that," Robert said. "But it's hard enough to get people to believe cholera comes from bad drinking water. Telling them vampires are real would get us laughed out of town."

"Knowledge is our candle in the darkness," Florence said.

"I think the president is following England's lead at the moment,"

Robert said. "And on that note, there is something you should know." He lowered his voice a little. "We have reason to believe a vampire named Carolyn le Fey is in America. Richard Burton sent word about it and said you should know."

I set down my coffee cup with a thud, and Florence went pale.

"I take it you've heard of her," Robert said.

"She attacked us in our home. Nearly killed us," I said, taking Florence's hand. "Are you sure she's here?"

"We're not certain, but Captain Burton tracked her to her hideout where he found a letter. Someone was offering her passage to America. She must have gotten word they were coming for her because she took off in a hurry, leaving a rather gruesome scene. He sent me a copy of his report. Le Fey is not to be trifled with."

"What did they find?" Florence asked. Robert seemed uncomfortable thinking about it.

"She had people chained up in her cellar like she was saving livestock for later. Some had starved to death. Some were already drained of blood. Luckily Captain Burton was able to save some of them. They said le Fey had been there just the day before and had stormed down to the cellar in a rage. She had quickly drained several of them, sucking each person dry and casting them aside before moving on to the next. Finally, she had just bitten into a victim when she must have decided she was full. She stalked off, leaving him crumpled, bleeding, on the floor."

"Were they able to save him?" I asked.

"Yes, he'll recover. Physically, at least. I can't imagine he'll ever be the same, though. None of them will."

That night Florence tossed and turned in her sleep and I could tell she was having a nightmare. I woke her and held her.

"I can't stop thinking about that woman. What she did, how she almost killed us," she said. We spoke quietly, as Noel was sleeping in our room. With the stories about le Fey so fresh in our minds, Florence felt better having him nearby.

I cradled her in my arms, thinking again of how my curse had done this to my family.

"Do you ever wish you had married Wilde instead of me?"

"Heavens, no, don't even think such a thing."

"I've done nothing but put you in danger," I said.

She sat up and looked at me in the moonlight. "And you saved England, probably the world – the entire world. I would have been put in danger either way. I am so proud to have you as my husband and so happy to be the mother of your child."

With that, we lay quietly and soon she fell back to sleep. Then it was my turn to worry. A feeling of dread came over me like some dark premonition that the world would again be put in danger.

FROM THE JOURNAL OF OSCAR WILDE, 28TH OF AUGUST 1882

I am despondent, dear diary. The Americans have turned on me!

I would have scarcely thought it possible, after the rapturous success of my lecture tour, but *Vera* has been rejected by the theatre audiences of New York City, as well as the philistines who call themselves reviewers for many of the major newspapers. In fact, the production has closed after only one week of performances.

I poured my soul into this play, and my heart soared when I found a collaborator as worthy as Marie Prescott.

In Miss Prescott I found a kindred spirit, and our correspondence in the months leading up to the opening filled me with confidence. I felt that together we could move and inspire our audience, perhaps even change the world for the better. When I returned to America to oversee the production, I thrilled to her performance and that of the supporting cast. No expense had been spared in producing scenery and costumes that would immerse the audience in the Russian milieu of the play. I could not imagine anything but success for our venture.

Opening night did nothing to dissuade me from that sentiment. Every ticket was sold, and the crowd was animated and engaged. During the act breaks, there were calls of 'author' to which I at first did not respond, but after Act II, I appeared briefly for a modest bow. (Yes, diary, modest. I *can* be modest at times, you know.) The reaction to the final act was troubling – there were a few jeers as my heroine and her lover expressed their feelings for one another. I suppose this scene is a bit sentimental, but I could surely fix that.

Still, I thought the evening a triumph.

Then the reviews appeared.

Some were good, diary. The *New York Mirror* said it was "the noblest contribution to its literature the stage has received in many years."

(Not even I would have said as much, but it is appreciated nonetheless.)

But the *New York Times* called it "unreal, long-winded and wearisome." (Wearisome? Me?)

And the *New York Herald* brands it as "a coarse and common kind of cleverness." (I am many things, diary, but coarse and common? Never!)

Miss Prescott and her husband, Mr. Persel, entreated me to appear in the play, or rather during the act breaks, to perform part of my lectures, but I declined, feeling this would distract from the work itself. Indeed, many of the critics seemed to have expected a light comedy, full of the wit and cleverness that became my hallmarks during my previous tour. Inserting myself into the proceedings would have only provided a starker contrast between what the audience seems to have wanted and what was on offer.

In addition, the theatre owner wanted me to make some changes to the script, but who am I to tamper with a masterpiece? (In reality, yes, I would have done so, but one needs time to do such a thing.)

In *Vera*, I attempted to express, within the limits of art, the desire of all people for liberty, to live and breathe without the yoke of tyranny upon them. One need only read the daily newspaper to see how this universal longing is threatening thrones and destabilising governments from Spain to Russia. Of course, as any good dramatist would, I depicted this not through a political treatise but as a story of passionate men and women fighting for a better future, as I fought with my comrades against the despot who would have imposed a vampire ruling class upon England and the world.

Alas, this is not what audiences want from Oscar Wilde.

When the news broke that we were closing, several of the cast members and I went out to a nearby bar to commiserate. They are all experienced actors, accustomed to the ups and downs of theatrical life, and accepted the end with good humour. They will soon find other roles. But I was a virgin, both to playwriting and to failure, and have not their confidence that I will be able to move on to a new project so quickly. (How long will it take me to write another play, diary? I shudder to think and am not sure I should even make the attempt.) The company tried its best to cheer me up, and I tried my best to be cheered so as to not disappoint them further. But despite all our best efforts it was not working, though we all pretended it was.

One by one, they all wandered off for home. All except one – Walter, who plays one of the nihilists working to overthrow the czar. Eventually, he and I were the only ones left, and we talked at length about the theatre, the world, our lives, our art.

He is a passionate young man, committed to his craft and uncompromising in his belief that theatre can be a transformative art for artist and audience alike. Our conversation was exhilarating, and I felt a connection with him I haven't experienced since the early days with Derrick. At long last words were not enough, and I reached out and grasped his shoulders in emphasis of some point I was making, which was quickly forgotten. Our eyes locked and within moments we were leaving the bar. I had taken a small flat near the theatre and soon enough we were at the threshold, then inside away from prying eyes, and our connection reached another new level.

During the night I had another nightmare. I was reliving the night Derrick visited me. I woke up crying. It was nice to have someone next to me. I felt safe and was able to get back to sleep.

This morning he was gone. I don't know if I'll see him again. I don't know if I want to. I do know that I shouldn't. I still have an understanding with Constance, and it was exactly this sort of behaviour that doomed my relationship with Florence. Do I want the same to happen with Constance? But if this is the sort of man I am, should I end things with her now to spare her future pain? I am still uncertain about so many things, diary.

LETTER FROM MR. WILLIAM DRUMPF TO THOMAS DRUMPF, 1ST OF SEPTEMBER 1882

Archivist's note: William Horatio Drumpf was a wealthy mining baron whose considerable holdings included silver, lead and gold mines throughout the American West. This is the earliest letter we have from him in our collection. Here we can see the beginnings of his dastardly plan.

My dear Tom,

You are to leave university and come home at once. The dean has written to me about your carousing ways and lack of discipline in your studies. I will not throw good money after bad.

This is not what I sent you to college for. To say you are a disappointment is an understatement. But maybe we can make a man of you yet.

Perhaps it is my fault. You were raised with a silver spoon in your mouth and I am the one who put it there. I never went to college. I made my fortune through hard work and my own shrewdness and tenacity. But I wanted better for you. I wanted you to have the advantages I never had: an education, enough money to start you off in life without the struggles that were my lot. I see now that what you really need is experience in the real world, and to work hard to build something of your own.

When I was a young man, I went west with only a single silver dollar in my pocket and the clothes on my back. I had a frontier to conquer, new lands to explore and find my place in. You never experienced the thrill of embarking on a journey into the wilderness and making your own way in the world.

As I look around me, the frontier is no more. But what if I told you we could open a new frontier? There is a new unexplored world that is ours for the taking. A land bigger than all of America, with virgin lumber and untapped mines. We can be pioneers, you and I, of an undiscovered country. Pioneers and profiteers.

This will be your proving ground, son. You will embark on this adventure with me an immature boy, but you will emerge a man, with a fortune at your command and a new land at your feet.

Join me. Your mother and I await you.

Sincerely,

Your father

INTERNATIONAL NEWS SERVICE ARTICLE

Archivist's note: This INS article went unpublished; it was stopped by the news agency's editor-in-chief under pressure from the United States government. By 1882, it was becoming increasingly difficult to keep the existence of vampires from the public. President Arthur did not want to cause a panic that would stifle western expansion and trade, and thought the vampire threat could be eradicated. Other vampire massacres around that time were attributed to Indian attacks, smallpox outbreaks and cannibalism caused by famine situations, as was seen with the Donner Party in 1847.

MYSTERIOUS ANIMAL ATTACKS IN NEVADA

By Carl Kolczak – September 16, 1882

At least 15 settlers are dead after attacks by unknown animals that completely drained the blood of their victims.

The first such attack happened in Fallon, Nevada, on the Peterson ranch. Three ranch hands were found dead in the bunkhouse with puncture wounds on their necks and their bodies totally drained of blood. Two more ranch hands are missing, possibly dragged off to be eaten elsewhere.

The second attack was on a farmhouse in Silver Springs, Nevada, where a family of four was found dead outside their barn with the same type of puncture marks upon their necks.

The third was in nearby Silver City. In contrast to the isolated locations of the previous attacks, in this case six cowhands were found dead in the Big W Saloon. There were no surviving witnesses to the attack, although a woman working upstairs heard a fight break out the night before.

"I do not come downstairs in these situations," she said. "I thought nothing of it at the time as there is a fight here most every night."

She later came down to find the bartender, piano player and four patrons dead and drained of blood with the telltale marks on their necks.

The local law has no theories to go on. While vampire bats that live in the area are known to drink blood, they rarely feed on humans and would be incapable of draining entire bodies. Others claim it is the work of rabid dogs, but they usually tear out the entire throat of their victims. Furthermore, no unusual animal tracks were discovered at any of the scenes.

A Silver City doctor, who wished to remain nameless, told this reporter, "I think it is the work of vampires. What else could it be?" He packed up his wife and child and headed back east that very day.

For those who don't know, a vampire is a creature of eastern European folklore. Legend has it that vampires are people who have died unbaptised and risen from their graves. They walk by night, feeding off the blood of the living.

"Preposterous!" said Silas Smith, the mayor of Silver City. "If it's not wild dogs, these are clearly victims of some disease or tainted food. The marks on the neck are merely hives. The bodies are pale but to say they are drained of blood is a wild exaggeration."

The Silver City doctor refutes this claim and said the bodies were 'as dry as toast'.

It remains to be seen if this plague will continue its spread across the West or if it has run its course.

FROM THE JOURNAL OF FLORENCE STOKER, 19TH OF SEPTEMBER 1882

The Lyceum tour of America has ended and cast and crew are heading 'back east', as the Americans say, to catch a ship back to London.

Bram, Noel, Henry and I have stayed behind for a little well-deserved holiday. And I have to say I am looking forward to time alone with Bram and Noel.

Also staying with us is Noel's nanny, Annabell. We hired her when we arrived in New York and she has travelled with us since without complaint. (I gave up looking in London after the Carolyn le Fey incident. I simply couldn't face it.) She is a sturdy, sensible girl, French in origin. Though younger than I would have preferred, she is up to the travel and very experienced, having helped to raise six of her siblings before emigrating to America and becoming a nanny for a wealthy New York family. Noel took to her right away and they are the best of friends. I have been most pleased with her and wonder if she would consider returning to England with us. She would be nearer to her French family there, so I am hopeful that I can persuade her.

The tour had its ups and downs, but overall I think it was a success. We played to sold-out theatres many times, and the audiences were quite appreciative. Oh, how I loved playing Nerissa in *The Merchant of Venice*, my most challenging role to date. Working with the great Henry Irving has certainly improved my acting. I sometimes – often, in fact – forget that he is a vampire. One would not think it to look at him, or to see how he dotes on Noel.

He continues his quest to become fully human again. Tomorrow he is travelling into the wilderness to consult with an Indian shaman and last week he went out to examine an ancient ruin. He has discovered nothing and has become very discouraged. I hope that he is able to find what he is looking for one day.

For my part, I am just happy to put an ocean between myself and Ellen Terry. As most of my scenes included her I strived to maintain a civil and professional relationship, but her behaviour made it difficult. Several times on the tour she had men fighting over her, often disrupting rehearsals and even performances. Drama is as drama does, I suppose.

Today we are in Salt Lake City in the Utah Territory. We had the good fortune to attend Buffalo Bill's Wild West show, and what a spectacle it was!

We were guests of Buffalo Bill Cody himself, sitting in his special viewing box high above the outdoor arena.

It was quite comfortable, kept us above the dust that was kicked up during the show and, luckily for Henry, was well-shaded. He had little need for the tinted glasses and wide-brimmed hat he has been forced to wear whenever he has to venture outdoors. Exposure to the sun cannot always be avoided when exiting trains and stagecoaches, but as much as he complains about it he has yet to catch fire.

The show was simply marvellous. There was first a 'Wild West parade' featuring the entire cast of cowboys, Indians, horses and buffaloes. There must be over six hundred people in the production – can you imagine? (And Bram feels put-upon shepherding our relatively small company about!)

This was followed by an exciting bareback pony race, a demonstration of the Pony Express by real Pony Express riders, an Indian attack on a Deadwood mail coach, the roping and tying of Texas steers by cowboys and the lassoing and riding of a wild bison! And, my absolute favourite, a demonstration of Indians conducting a grand hunt on the plains, in which we saw how they tracked, killed and prepared buffalo, elk and wild boar.

Noel was delighted the entire time and never once cried. I think he wants to be a cowboy when he grows up, an aspiration that is reinforced by the miniature Stetson hat purchased for him by Henry. He is very big for a three-year-old. He walks mostly on his own now and can be very stubborn like his father.

Earlier tonight we had supper with Bill Cody and some of his friends, the most interesting of whom was a woman named Calamity Jane.

At first I took her to be a man. She dresses and looks the part and even speaks like one, letting out strings of obscenities at the drop of a hat like all the other cowboys. But she is a woman and even had a child once, I am told.

She regaled us with stories about travelling the frontier as a young girl, the adventures she'd had and famous people she'd known. She grew somewhat emotional as she told us the tragic tale of her friend Wild Bill Hickok, who was shot in the back while playing cards.

"I went after the coward what shot him with a meat cleaver, which was the deadliest thing I could lay my hand to at the time," she said. "If folks hadn't've stopped me, there'd've been two men dead on that floor." She took a big gulp of her whiskey. "He was executed, eventually. Woulda liked to do it myself, though."

After that, she grew somewhat quieter, and Mr. Cody entertained us with anecdotes about the Wild West show and soon we were all laughing again.

As the party broke up and we were leaving the restaurant, I found myself walking beside Jane. "It was a pleasure to meet you," I said. "I do hope we will see each other again before we leave town."

She thanked me and said, "I just wish I'd had a chance to see the show that you folks did. I've never seen much Shakespeare myself. But I hear tell some of it has ghosts and witches in it. I'd surely like to see that someday."

"I hope you will, Jane," I said, as we parted.

Later that night Bram and I tried to become intimate. It did not go well. I just tense up when he touches me in that way. I cannot help it and he claims to understand. Having almost died giving birth to Noel, I cannot help but think of all the blood and pain whenever I am even slightly aroused. It is frustrating. I want to feel what I once did and just cannot. I was making strides towards more intimate relations with Bram, but being assaulted by that vampire le Fey undid all my progress. I feel closed off again. Damn that horrible creature to hell!

I did some things for Bram that Captain Burton's wife Isabel had pointed out to me in the *Kama Sutra* and that seemed to please him. It made me happy as well. We are both grateful to just hold each other and talk about our future. And I can honestly say I do see a light at the end of the tunnel. I must be patient with myself.

LETTER FROM EDWARD DRINKER COPE TO WILLIAM DRUMPF, 19TH OF SEPTEMBER 1882

Archivist's note: Edward Drinker Cope was a noted palaeontologist known for his feud with Othniel Charles Marsh. Their competition with each other became known as 'the Bone Wars'. Cope's need to outdo Marsh is most likely what led him to accept financial assistance from Drumpf. Had he known Drumpf's true motives, it is unlikely that Cope would have helped him acquire the Vellum Manuscript.

Dear Mr. Drumpf,

I regret to inform you that our finds from the dig in Wyoming have been stolen by the most unscrupulous of paleontologists, Charles Marsh.

I am outraged at Marsh's audacity, as I am certain you are. With your generous financial help, I had achieved something extraordinary. The dig was one of the most productive I have ever undertaken. Not only did I find a perfect specimen of a previously unknown dinosaur, but also several of the most curious artifacts heretofore unearthed by any archaeologist.

The Vellum Manuscript, in which you were so keenly interested, is the most mysterious of these. It was preserved in a golden reliquary but found embedded in ancient rock, among dinosaur bones. How these items existed side-by-side in the same dig is a puzzle that could revolutionize current thinking on the prehistoric age.

I have it on good authority that Marsh plans to sell the manuscript to Brigham Young, who believes it to be holy scripture of Mormon origin.

I'm hoping you can use your resources to help me recover my dinosaur and your book. I am sending you the information I have on Marsh and his last known whereabouts.

Sincerely,

Edward Cope

LETTER FROM LILLIE LANGTRY TO ELLEN TERRY, 19TH OF SEPTEMBER 1882

Dearest Ellen,

At long last, I have the opportunity to repay you for all the gossip you've shared with me while I've been in America! I'm in St. Louis, Missouri, performing in *She Stoops to Conquer*, and yesterday I had a visit from none other than Oscar Wilde.

You may have heard through the press that he recently made his debut as a playwright in New York City. If so, you will have also heard that it did not go well at all. The play, *Vera*, was not well received and closed after only a week.

As you can imagine, Oscar was devastated by this. He decided to spend some time travelling around the United States, perhaps in an effort to relive the glory of his American tour of last year. He really has become quite famous over here and was recognised many times as we moved about the city seeing the sights (such as they are) and stopping for lunch or tea. Sometimes I noticed people discreetly pointing him out to their companions. Others approached him directly to ask for an autograph or tell him how much they'd enjoyed his lecture. A few also recognised me, but overall, I'd have to say that my ego suffered in comparison. Why, you'd never know that I appear on stage here six nights a week and twice on Saturdays!

Of course, Oscar did nothing whatsoever to blend into the crowd. He appeared at my apartment in head-to-toe lavender linen, with an ornate walking stick, a delicate pink boutonniere, a deep-purple cravat and a broad-brimmed felt hat to match. (How many trunks does he travel with, one wonders?) Nobody has ever accused me of simplicity in my attire, but somehow Oscar has a way of making me feel underdressed for a simple day out in the last somewhat-civilised city before you reach the American frontier.

But I forgave him, as he was excellent company despite his own troubles. He entertained me with stories of his tour, the latest news about mutual friends in London and anecdotes from the production of *Vera*. The conversation did turn serious then. I tried to convince him that theatre life is a series of triumphs and defeats. I've appeared in plays that have failed. I'm certain you have as well, though of course I only remember your many stunning successes! But he is convinced that he will never recover from this and that he will always be remembered as a failed playwright. (I thought it best not to say that *nobody* remembers failed playwrights.)

I hope you don't mind, but I also let him know that you had shared with me the stories of your adventures together hunting the Black Bishop. He was a bit shocked to hear this, but I assured him that I could be relied upon for the utmost discretion. I have not told a soul, I swear to you. I'll confess, your stories were so thrilling that I felt compelled to confirm their veracity with Oscar. He assured me that all you had described really did happen. (I did not tell him of the more personal details you'd shared with me, about you and Mr. Stoker.) I reminded him that what you, he and the rest of your party did was far more important to the world than any play, even if it must be kept secret.

I have to say that part of me hoped that he was here on a monster-hunting mission. I should have liked to join such an adventure, but that is not the case. He claims to have put all that behind him. Just my luck.

But speaking of Mr. Stoker, Oscar did share with me some interesting gossip about him and his wife. He has been in correspondence with both of them and is under the impression that their marital relations are still on somewhat shaky ground. They both seem determined to salvage their marriage, but if I were to guess I would say that Bram Stoker still thinks of you with something more than professional respect. Perhaps I shouldn't have told you that, but I feel that if I were in your position, I would wish to know.

Oscar attended the play that evening as my guest. As we waited for the curtain, our stage manager informed me that he had caused quite a stir with his arrival, and the audience was still whispering and craning necks to look at him. This irritated me a bit, I'll confess, but then I thought that the publicity this was sure to generate could be quite good for future box office receipts.

In any event, the crowd did manage to settle down as the performance progressed, and Oscar led the ovation at the end, bless him. Our producer, seeing an opportunity, coaxed him onstage to say a few words. He trotted out some tidbits from his lectures, about art and about America. He praised the play, and (I blush to disclose) me in particular, saying, "I would rather have discovered Mrs. Langtry than have discovered America." The crowd applauded, the curtain was closed, and a fine time was had by all.

We were to go out together for a nightcap, but he begged off, saying he had met an old acquaintance. This turned out to be a handsome young man. Not surprising, knowing Oscar, but somehow I don't think all was as it appeared there. He did not seem particularly eager to go off with the man.

I must sign off now, Ellen, as it is time to go to the theatre, and I wish to post this on the way. I do hope all is well with you, and that you will write soon and tell me all about your travels across America. I can't imagine what it must have been like for you to share close quarters with the Stokers for so long. I do hope our paths will yet cross while you are here, but I know we theatre vagabonds must go where the audience bids us.

All my love,
Lillie

FROM THE JOURNAL OF OSCAR WILDE, 19TH OF SEPTEMBER 1882

I cannot escape my past, diary, try as I might. Even here in America I am haunted by reminders of all I have lost.

Forgive me for the ink smudges on your pages, but my hands are shaking!

I spent the day yesterday with Lillie Langtry – who knows far too much about my supernatural adventures, courtesy of Ellen Terry, the naughty girl – and in the evening attended her performance in *She Stoops to Conquer*. (Quite brilliant, and so well received. Perhaps I should have debuted *Vera* here in St. Louis where crowds are not so jaded.)

As Lillie and I were leaving by the stage door on the way out for a nightcap, she stopped to sign autographs for a crowd of admirers gathered there. A few wanted my signature as well, but this was her night and after a while I stepped away to wait patiently on the edges of the lamplight for the crowd to disperse. It was then that a young man approached me. He was nicely dressed, and I smiled warmly in anticipation of another autograph request. But that is not why the man was there.

"Mr. Wilde," he said. "I have been looking for you."

"And here I am," I responded, hoping the encounter would not turn into a debate on aesthetics, as occasionally happens when young intellectuals approach me. That can often be invigorating, but it had been a busy day and I was simply not in the mood.

"Merrill Prentice is my name. We have a mutual friend," he said. "Or, should I say, 'had'."

This was starting to feel like a conversation I would not enjoy, and I was instantly on my guard. "Oh? Who might that be? Or should I say, 'have been'?"

"Derrick Pigeon."

It was as if a dark shade had been drawn over all my surroundings save the man in front of me. He was all I could see clearly. I do not have Stoker's second sight about monsters, but even I could clearly see that here was a malevolent creature, and he had not sought me out to share pleasant memories of an absent friend.

I tried to keep my voice level as I asked, "Oh? And how do you know Derrick?"

"Well, you might say he made me the man I am today," responded the man – or, rather, the vampire. For he smiled then, revealing gleaming fangs. I gripped my walking stick more tightly, my mind racing to think of how to escape or fight him off should he attack.

"What do you want?" I asked.

"Oh, just a little chat. A private one, if you please," he said. He nodded towards Lillie, who was finishing with the last few autographs for her admirers. "Unless you want me to…involve your friend Mrs. Langtry. It makes little difference to me, though she would likely prefer to be left out of things."

I drew a deep breath and nodded curtly. "Give me a moment," I said and turned to Lillie.

"Careful what you say to her, Mr. Wilde," Prentice said in a quiet singsong. "Wouldn't want to raise any suspicions."

I nodded again and approached Lillie. "My dear, I am terribly sorry, but would you mind if I bow out on our nightcap? You see, I've just run into an old acquaintance and as it is his last night in town, it is our one opportunity to catch up. I would invite you along, but I fear it would be quite dull for you."

She looked at Prentice, then back at me, her eyebrow raised. Surely she suspected something, though probably not that he was a vampire. But she only said, "Of course, Oscar. Have a pleasant evening." Then she turned and left, and I was alone with the fiend. This monster, who had known an intimacy with Derrick that I had refused.

"Well done, Mr. Wilde. But if you are longstanding acquaintances, no doubt she's not surprised at being cast aside for a handsome young man."

A bit arrogant, that, but I had to admit that he *was* handsome. In fact, well, he looked a bit like me. Tall, with wavy dark hair and eyes that would probably be described as soulful if he were still in possession of a soul. Now they gleamed sharply, but I knew from experience that when he revealed his true vampire nature they would turn black and dead.

"Well, go on then," I said, trying to sound cool and contemptuous. "You wanted a chat. What will we chat about?"

"Why, Derrick, of course. He always had so much to say about you."

My heart throbbed. How I had failed him!

"Well, the only thing worse than being talked about is *not* being talked about." I again tried to sound casual, but my voice cracked and he smiled cruelly.

"Indeed. Do you know why he chose to sire me?"

"Your sparkling personality, one supposes."

He glared at me, but the smile never left his lips. "In a way. He chose me because I reminded him of you."

My throat tightened, and I did not trust myself to speak. I wanted to look away but did not dare relax my vigilance.

"It's true. We look a bit alike, you must have noticed. Well, I'm quite a bit slimmer," he said, with a contemptuous glance at my midsection. (I took some offence, diary. One eats so much rich food while travelling.)

"We have a similar education," Prentice continued, "though I'll admit I was not as ambitious a student as you. Still, I'm a clever fellow. I can converse competently enough on the arts, the theatre, whatever book I happen to pick up in idle moments, stray bits of gossip. And, of course, I was able to satisfy his baser instincts. Yes, that was where I really shone. I could show you if you like." He looked me up and down with bold, lascivious glee.

"I think not," I managed to say.

"Suit yourself." His grin faltered. "But it wasn't enough. None of it. He wanted the real you. Went looking for you, in fact. Never returned."

I shrugged. "Perhaps he was waylaid. I did not see him."

"You're lying," he said, in his quiet, singsong voice. "You killed him. It's the only explanation. He would have come back to me otherwise."

I thought back to the night Derrick had appeared at my flat. How he had tried to turn me. How I had nearly let him. But in the end, I could not renounce my humanity without a fight, and I won, killing Derrick in the process. I sobbed as I plunged the wood into his heart and watched him die before my eyes. It was the hardest thing I have ever done, but I saw it as a mercy, releasing him from life as a vampire. I suspected Merrill Prentice would not see it that way, however.

Besides, my final moments with Derrick were ours alone; this creature did not deserve to know them.

"Perhaps he found another to sire, who would be a closer facsimile to me, and decided to leave well enough alone. Have you checked news reports for stories about a missing young man, with dark hair and literary aspirations?"

Prentice sneered at me. "He still would have returned. Derrick was greedy. He wanted you and me both, and if he'd found another, he would have wanted all three of us."

Was that true? Maybe about the vampire Derrick. My Derrick would have wanted only me. I found my heart hardening to the creature I had killed in my flat that night. He was not the man I had loved and tried to save.

But now I had to save myself.

"You miss him," I said. "So do I. I think about him every day."

Prentice was growing emotional. "You killed him," he said again, advancing upon me.

I backed away, forcing myself to remain calm. I shook my head sadly. "No. I would not have been able to, had he come to me. I would have succumbed. How could I not? I loved him."

Prentice was stalking me, slowly. "He wanted you to join him! He told me. You refused."

"So did he! He told the Order that he did not want to join its ranks. He was taken by force from my flat. That was the last time I saw him. But once he had turned, once that was my only chance to be with him, I would not have been able to resist. The temptation to spend eternity with him would have been too great. You must know that. You must have felt the same."

He stopped, searching my face.

"Yes," he whispered. "It was the best feeling in the world, being sired by him." His eyes, which I had earlier thought soulless, now looked anguished. I found myself feeling pity for him, despite my better judgement.

But not so much pity that I could let him live.

I took a step closer to him.

"You must have been afraid, at first."

"Yes. But that…. That was part of what made it so…."

"Delicious?" I finished.

"Yes." He did not speak the word so much as sigh it.

"We've both lost so much. We're the only ones who can understand each other's pain." I held out my hand to him. "Come. Let's go someplace where we can sit and talk. I'd like to get to know you better, Merrill – may I call you Merrill?"

He nodded.

"Perhaps we can…mean something to each other. I think that's what Derrick would have wanted."

He looked torn, but he nodded.

"There's a bar around the corner," I said. "We can find a quiet table." I gestured him towards the front of the theatre and he turned to go.

I steeled myself for what was to come.

"Derrick always liked a table near the back of a bar," Prentice said. "He liked to watch from the shadows as the people came and went."

As he spoke, I gripped the shaft of my walking stick in my left hand.

"Really?" I said. "As a human he liked to be in the centre of the room, leading the crowd in song."

With my right hand, I grabbed the head of my stick.

"He told me about that," Prentice said. "Said he lost the taste for music after he turned. Said it was the only thing about being human he missed. Not sure I believe that."

I swiftly drew the sword concealed in my walking stick. Prentice never even turned around. The sword – which I have taken the precaution of coating with silver – slid cleanly through his back into his heart.

The handsome young man collapsed in a puddle of goo. I stood for a moment, resheathed my sword and left the alley without a backwards glance.

It rained later, and one assumes the remains of Merrill Prentice are wending their way through the sewers of St. Louis to the Mississippi River.

With that, I have erased all traces of Derrick Pigeon from the earth, unless, of course, he has other progeny out there. But he will live on in my memory as he was before: beautiful, talented, vibrant – and human.

Despite emerging from that encounter victorious, when I returned to my suite I found myself feeling panicky and confined in my bedroom. I dragged my mattress to the outer room of my suite where it is more open and laid it on the floor. Even then, it took a swig of laudanum for me to finally fall asleep.

I had fitful dreams, the details of which I cannot recall.

This morning, I returned the mattress to my bedroom before the housekeeper came to clean, and after some tea and breakfast, I feel somewhat better. But I can't help but worry: will my life never be safe from these dreadful creatures?

I should be elated that I erased another vampire from the face of the earth. And yet he was once a man, like myself. He did not deserve what Derrick did to him, as Derrick did not deserve his fate. I believe that I released them both from an existence worse than death.

Then why am I still so disquieted? I suppose it's because my fears about encountering vampires in America proved to be well founded. And, it appears, I am famous among that crowd as well, though not for my lectures. I should have realised that they might seek me out.

TELEGRAM FROM ROBERT ROOSEVELT TO BRAM STOKER, 23RD OF SEPTEMBER 1882

=Dispatching bandits of the nocturnal nature. Trail gone cold. Need your special tracking skills and Irving's abilities. Could you take next train to Carson City?=

REPORT FROM AGENT CORA CHASE TO WHITE WORM SOCIETY

Archivist's note: The White Worm Society often secured employment for its operatives that would provide valuable intelligence or an opportunity to advance the Society's cause. Such was the case with Cora Chase, who was placed as an agent with the Pinkerton Detective Agency. (The income agents gained from this work could also be used to justify a lower stipend for their White Worm duties.)

Date: 23 September 1882
Subject: John King Fisher aka the Pale Horseman
I continue my cover as a Pinkerton agent in Salt Lake City and have been promoted to assistant detective. This will help me in my work for the White Worm Society as I will have better access to Pinkerton information and resources. I have already learned much that is both useful and troubling.

I am seeing an alarming uptick in vampiric activity in America. We were right to have our concerns. Reports of killings are coming in from all over the Nevada Territory.

My fellow Pinkertons and I have captured an outlaw by the name of Ben Thompson. He has related to me that Eagan Rayne is building a gang of vampires; for what purpose he did not know.

The most formidable of all is a vampire known as the Pale Horseman. This creature can seemingly be full strength in broad daylight and even rides a dead horse that has been reanimated.

Thompson tells us that in life the Pale Horseman was known as John King Fisher. He was one of the fastest guns in the West. A cruel and heartless man, he used his skill to kill dozens, if not hundreds, of people.

He and Thompson ran in the same circles.

Fisher grew up in Georgia and fought for the Confederacy in the

Civil War, at least until it became apparent the North was going to win. Then he deserted and ran off to make his fortune in the West, mainly in Arizona and Nevada.

In the early 1870s, Fisher made his name as a bandit when he started running with a gang of outlaws that raided ranches in Mexico. Fisher was known for his flamboyant style, which saw him wear brightly coloured clothes and carry twin ivory-handled pistols, as well as for his propensity for violence. He famously gunned down three members of his own gang in a dispute over money, and then killed seven Mexican *pistoleros* shortly after that, though nobody knows exactly why. In his most famous gunfight, Fisher is said to have taken on four Mexican cowboys single-handedly. After hitting one with a branding iron, he outdrew another and shot him. In his typical brutal style, he then shot two of the man's unarmed accomplices, went outside and killed the onlookers.

After being run out of Mexico, he headed back to his home in Nevada, where he continued his criminal ways. Eventually he went to work for Drumpf, taking out his business rivals and protecting his claims. Ben Thompson was also in Drumpf's employ during this period. He told us that Fisher quickly drew Drumpf's favour with his brutally effective tactics.

Then, about a year ago, he and Thompson found themselves ambushed in the desert outside of Carson City by friends of a saloon owner they had killed the night before. Thompson got away, but Fisher was shot twice in the back and once in the face and left for dead in the desert. Thompson was sure he had perished and waited for the killers to leave before going to bury his friend, who was already being picked at by crows and buzzards.

To his surprise, Fisher was still alive, though barely. Thompson took him to Drumpf, who called in a doctor and Rayne to tend to his wounds.

Thompson saw a woman give Fisher a drink of a thick, red liquid that quickly restored his health.

I believe this was the vampire, Carolyn le Fey. I know from briefing reports that Eagan Rayne had been in contact with her, offering her safe passage to America if she could bring him certain objects. I now believe she brought with her the last of the dragon's blood. The decanter of blood used in the Order of the Golden Dawn vampire ceremonies, as described by Mr. Wilde, was not found when the White Worm Society raided their headquarters.

I believe it was with this blood that Fisher was turned into a vampire. As you know, a vampire created by drinking dragon's blood is more powerful than one who is sired by another vampire as he is not forced to serve a vampire master. Any loyalty Fisher holds towards Rayne and Drumpf is of his own free will.

Thompson told us the Pale Horseman has sired others. I believe he is the single source of the current vampire plague in Nevada. It is possible that le Fey is also contributing to this, but Thompson said he never saw her again after that day so I suspect she has moved on.

Thompson himself left Drumpf's employ several months ago to resume his outlaw ways.

How the horse Fisher rides came to be risen from the dead or how he can be at full strength in the sun is still a mystery, although Rayne's blood magic must be involved somehow. Reanimating the dead, even a dead animal, requires some of the most powerful magic we know.

Thompson told us Rayne carries a gold scepter with a symbol carved into it and a glowing green stone on its top. I showed Thompson some Egyptian symbols, and he thought they may have matched what he saw. This very well may be the Osiris Scepter. This scepter has the power to raise the dead, although at a horrible cost: a life for a life. It could be a very dangerous object in the hands of a religious fanatic like Rayne.

—End Report—

LETTER FROM ELLEN TERRY TO LILLIE LANGTRY, 23RD OF SEPTEMBER 1882

My dearest Lillie,

I was delighted to receive your last letter! The Lyceum tour has concluded and I am happily heading back east and then will be on my way back home. I will stop in St. Louis to see you as I travel through, which will be the highlight of my journey.

Overall, I think the tour was successful on both professional and private fronts. Our performances were well received, and I met many fascinating people and saw some of America's bustling young cities as well as its remarkable natural beauty. The vast prairies are like nothing I've ever seen before, and the mountain ranges – whoever dared to cross them for the first time was truly courageous. I felt like a pioneer just travelling by train!

It was also a fulfilling experience to bring a touch of culture to some of the more rugged parts of the nation. I'm sure you've felt the same, Lillie, in your travels. Audiences are genuinely appreciative in a way they can't be in London's West End, where there are so many options available.

I had a mild flirtation with one of the young actors in our company. All right, two mild flirtations, with two of the young actors in our company. And perhaps with one or two of my most ardent fans along the way. And it's possible that several of these encounters may have progressed beyond the flirtation stage. It was a long tour; one must have something to do, especially when one is nursing a broken heart. I did try to keep things professional, but young actors are prone to overly romantic notions, as you know. I'm afraid some drama was stirred up, and not only on the stage. I put a stop to that as quickly as I could and kept myself mostly to myself from then on.

Speaking of my broken heart, it was kind of you to say that you think Bram still has feelings for me, but I'm afraid I must not go through that door again. He belongs to another, and I have accepted that. I think I did as well as could be expected in my interactions with the Stokers and we all kept a most civil relationship for the sake of the tour, though I doubt we will ever be friends.

If you think it was hard sharing close quarters with Florence, it was nothing compared to performing beside her. Her acting is atrocious now that she is no longer under my tutelage, and she dragged the whole troupe down. It is only her marriage to Bram and friendship with Henry Irving that has got her onto the stage with a company as prestigious as ours.

But the tour is behind us and hopefully when we return to our regular season in London she will be too busy running her quaint, middle-class household to tread the Lyceum boards.

The Stokers and Henry are staying behind in Salt Lake City to do some sightseeing, so I am free of them for the return trip.

This does amuse me, for I honestly cannot imagine Florence out on the trail. She had her reservations about going past the Mississippi River. Only the promise of an acting role from Henry got her to go into the Wild West in the first place.

God forbid she should develop a blister holding the reins of a horse. And I doubt one can ride over rocky terrain side-saddle.

In any event, I am happy to be going home to see my children. Edith and Edward are so big now you would hardly recognise them.

I must sign off and get this in the post. I will stop in St. Louis, most likely this Tuesday, and look forward to seeing you then.

Love,

Ellen

REPORT FROM WHITE WORM SOCIETY AGENT ANNABELL CHARLEMONT, ON ASSIGNMENT OBSERVING AND PROTECTING THE STOKER FAMILY

Date: 24 September 1882
    Subject: Bram Stoker and Henry Irving have left Salt Lake City
    The Lyceum tour has ended and the Stokers and Henry Irving
are taking some time now for a brief holiday. Their leisure time was
interrupted, however, by a telegram from Robert Roosevelt, after which
Bram Stoker and Henry Irving left to meet Roosevelt in Carson City.
    In my guise as the nanny, I stayed on in Salt Lake City with Mrs.
Stoker and Noel to await their return. Our operative Bill Morgan is
embedded with Roosevelt's riflemen and will be able to report on
their activities from there.
    Mrs. Stoker gave me the morning off today, and I took the
opportunity to meet with Agent Chase regarding the possibility that
Carolyn le Fey is here in Salt Lake City. I will keep Mrs. Stoker and
her son under close watch while the threat is being assessed.
    This afternoon there was an incident, not related to le Fey, in
which my cover was nearly exposed. Mrs. Stoker and I were taking
Noel for some fresh air in his pushchair. He was fussing at being
confined to the chair, and we decided to cut through an alley to an ice
cream shop. This proved to be a foolish move on my part as we found
ourselves accosted by some men who tried to rob us at knifepoint.
    My training kicked in and I took the two men down with a few
swift kicks and punches, to the astonishment of Mrs. Stoker.

"Wherever did you learn to defend yourself like that?" she asked as we waved down a policeman to take away the miscreants.

"My father was a military officer back in France. He taught me *savate*, the art of French foot fighting," I explained. "It has been quite useful on more than one occasion when I needed to keep my younger brothers in line or fend off the advances of unwanted suitors."

"During this past year I have felt quite confident that Noel is safe with you and now I see how right I was," she said. "What other secrets have I yet to uncover in you?"

"I cook excellent crepes," I said, hoping to steer the conversation back to more domestic matterss. It was left at that, but I cannot help but think she may suspect I am more than I seem to be.

—End Report—

LETTER FROM SAMUEL CLEMENS (MARK TWAIN) TO WALT WHITMAN, 24TH OF SEPTEMBER 1882

My dear Walt,

I had lunch with an acquaintance of yours today, Oscar Wilde. He struck me as an unusual young man. Amusing, yes, as all of his press coverage is quick to point out. But I sense more to him than that, and I suspect you do the same. There is a certain gravity to him – not melancholy, exactly, but close to it – that one would not suspect from his public persona. I was glad to see it; as someone who also on occasion earns a living by amusing the populace, I find that an essential part of any humorist's native equipment is a profound sympathy with the sorrows and sufferings of mankind.

I am in Missouri visiting relatives, and while I always find joy in the bosom of my family, a brief respite from such joy is also welcome. That is why, when I learned that Wilde was also in town, I set about to meet him through mutual connections. I had attended one of his lectures in New York City; entertaining stuff, though I confess I was baffled that he became such a sensation. People need their diversions, I suppose, and talking about Oscar Wilde is as good as any.

I invited him to lunch at the Lindell Hotel, a particularly ornate establishment in a European style that I thought would appeal to him. It was a sultry, sunny day and I was sitting in a shady spot on the verandah smoking a cigar when he arrived. I would have been hard-pressed to miss him; he was wearing a white linen suit with a boutonniere, cravat and derby hat all in lavender. I stood as the maitre'd directed him to my table, and I saw him notice that I was also dressed in white linen. I was amused to see that he seemed somewhat abashed at this, though I cared not at all.

We exchanged pleasantries and sipped cool drinks until we'd had a chance to peruse the menu and order our lunch. Once that business was settled, I asked, "What brings you to our humble continent, Mr. Wilde? I am surprised to see you here without a lecture tour."

He smiled, maybe a little uncomfortably, I thought. "I have found your continent to be anything but humble, Mr. Clemens. But to answer your question, I authored a play, which made its debut in New York City, and I came over to supervise its rehearsals. Once I was no longer needed in that capacity, I decided to do some traveling. There was so much I was unable to see before, with the hustle and bustle of the tour."

"Yes, I can see that your experiences would be quite different this time around. Are you enjoying Missouri?"

"Immensely. The weather is lovely, and the people are endlessly fascinating to me."

"How so?" I asked.

"Their preoccupation with the past, for one thing. Their 'golden age', which was, of course, built on the foundation of slavery and all its horrors. It's quite sad, really. Particularly the elderly, who have a melancholy tendency to date every event of importance in relation to the war. I once remarked to an older gentleman, 'How beautiful the moon is tonight.' He replied, 'Yes, but you should have seen it before the war.'"

I chuckled. "One of the reasons I live in the North now," I said.

We went on to discuss his work and mine while we ate, and I won't bore you with details of that, Walt, as I'm sure you've already had similar conversations with us both. We got on the subject of his lectures, particularly his thoughts on America.

"Is this trip changing your opinion about our country in any way?" I asked.

I could see him working out a diplomatic response.

"Well," he said, "it isn't, really. I find America and Americans just the same as when I was here before. It's refreshing, I suppose, to be treated as an ordinary tourist exactly as one was treated as a...." He trailed off.

"Celebrity?" I finished for him. He bowed his head, modestly.

"Yes, I suppose."

"Ah, but that's the thing with celebrity," I said. "You can't turn it off at will. You are still famous. You won't really know if you'd be treated the same until people have forgotten you."

He frowned.

"And how does it compare to England?" I asked.

"I'm not quite so famous there, yet."

"And do you think that would make a difference?" I asked.

He thought for a moment. "Yes, but not so much as you might suppose," he replied. "You must remember how deeply entrenched our class system is. Becoming famous would never put me on par with the true upper classes – the nobility. But I could definitely command better tables in restaurants, and invitations to all the best parties. And that is enough for a humble Dublin boy like myself."

(He's quite good at putting on a show of self-deprecation, isn't he? Though I'll admit to having a talent in that area myself.)

"Substitute wealth and power for nobility and I think it would be much the same here. Do you disagree?" I asked.

"Ah. Well, Americans are uniquely forthright people, I find. Big and friendly. Egalitarian, fair. Convinced that no one is better than anybody else. Honest when perhaps they should not be. They have not yet learned the art of the held tongue or the kindness of a good lie."

"You make us sound like children, Mr. Wilde."

"Yes, I suppose," he mused. "Oh, I mean no offense by it, Mr. Clemens. But you are a young country, with young ideals. You have not the weight of history that Great Britain has."

"Perhaps youth is not a bad thing if it means treating people with more fairness and friendliness," I said. "Maybe it will mean we will have fewer wars in our future, though I'll admit to being less than hopeful in that regard."

"It is a nice thought, nonetheless," he said. "But like it or not, Britain – all of Europe, for that matter – cannot escape our past. We have the legacies of monarchs bearing down upon us. And those who came before monarchs. Why, we have ancient monuments that predate history. Stonehenge, for example...."

For some reason his voice trailed off and he turned quite pale.

He took a sip of his wine to steady himself and I took up the mantle of conversation.

"Yes, I've been to Stonehenge. It is impressive. Fascinating in its mystery. And I've visited many of your castles, as well as ancient sites on the continent – the Colosseum, the Parthenon. One can picture scenes of triumph and despair there. It stirs the imagination."

"Yes," he said. "And that is my point. We of the 'Old World' have this history, these ancient memories, that shape our present in ways we don't even realize. They permeate our very essence. They haunt our dreams. They stalk our streets at night. If we are more guarded, perhaps that is the reason. We have our ghosts to contend with."

I gazed at him through a haze of cigar smoke. He still looked pallid and shaky.

"Your history goes back, what, a few hundred years?" he continued. "Your legends are modern ones – frontiersmen and outlaws and Wild West sheriffs. You fear nothing that you can't see or hear or kill if needed. In Ireland, we have banshees, leprechauns and mischievous pixies. Did you visit Hampton Court Palace when you were in London, Mr. Clemens? Did you know that the ghost of Katherine Howard, executed by her husband, King Henry VIII, roams its halls? And none of that even compares to other horrors, horrors you might think exist only in legend. Folklore often has a basis in fact, Mr. Clemens. I should know."

Yes, Walt, I would say this conversation had certainly taken a turn.

"How do you know?" I asked eagerly. "I am most curious to learn more."

He mopped his brow, took a deep breath and forced a chuckle. "I apologize, Mr. Clemens. I can get a bit over-emphatic. My mother is a student of the supernatural, you see. I have been raised on it."

"Is she really? I'd like to meet your mother someday," I replied. "But you're mistaken, Mr. Wilde, if you think that we have no such legends on our shores. You say our history only goes back a few hundred years, but you forget that the white man was not the first inhabitant of this land. I have read extensively on the subjects of indigenous history and folklore, from a number of our North American tribes. It is as vast and varied as any you would find in Europe. In the northern tribes of Michigan and Minnesota, for example, is the wendigo, a malevolent creature that feeds on human flesh. The Navajo have their skin-walkers, humans who use dark magic to possess or transform themselves into animals."

"My word," he said, stunned. "Mother really does need to visit America."

"Indeed, she does. These are some of the legends that permeate our land, Mr. Wilde, whether we white men know it or not. They go back, I daresay, at least as far in history as any European tale. How much of it is true? Who can say? But I would not for a minute say that it is all just fancy."

He was troubled, I could tell, and so I turned the conversation toward more innocuous subjects. We parted, with promises to meet again soon. I hope we will. It was a most invigorating discussion.

I leave for San Francisco later this week. It will be good to get out of this heat. The coldest winter I ever spent was a summer in San Francisco, but I suspect I've told you that before.

Do write back soon, if you are feeling up to it.

Sincerely,

Samuel

FROM THE JOURNAL OF BRAM STOKER, 25TH OF SEPTEMBER 1882

Monday 12:14 a.m.

Robert Roosevelt has sent word that he needs help in Carson City. Henry and I are on a train now making our way further west. Florence was reluctant to let me go, but I reminded her how Robert fought so hard to rescue Noel from the clutches of the Black Bishop. I feel we owe him what little help we can give.

I am not sure how well my sixth sense will work on a trail so cold since even by train it will be a day before we arrive, and apparently the incident was some days ago already. However, I am willing to give it a go. Irving, too, wishes to help put down this vampire outbreak.

As it happens, Henry was already planning to set out for Nevada later this week. He is in possession of the name of an Indian shaman who may lead him to an opening to the Realm. I have tried to convince him to abandon this quest, for I fear the Realm may actually be hell, but he feels it holds the cure to his vampirism and will not be dissuaded.

A search for the shaman will present significant peril for Henry. He has been warned that Nevada is mostly inhospitable desert, and very dangerous to cross by coach as it is a haven for displaced Indians and bandits on the run from the law. However, a coach is the best way he can travel to avoid the sun. By bundling up properly and wearing a wide hat and tinted glasses he can safely travel by horse, but, of course, this can be uncomfortably hot in the desert.

But our immediate task is quelling Robert's vampire bandits. Once we deal with that, Henry hopes to make enquiries in Carson City for a guide to take him into the wilderness.

Tuesday 10:15 a.m.

Our train was met by the Roosevelt boys: Robert and his nephew Theodore. Teddy, as his friends call him, is a boisterous young man. Although he is from New York City, he seems at home here in the West and dresses the part of cowboy and frontiersman. Robert tells me he is very handy with a rifle and has taken down both 'bears and bandits', and that he is quite a naturalist with an avid interest in zoology and other sciences.

Theodore currently is an assemblyman in the New York State government and has political aspirations like his uncle. I recall reading about him in the newspapers when we were in New York; apparently, he has done quite a bit to fight corruption in the government there.

The Roosevelts took us to a survey office where they are currently running their operations and filled us in on their work so far.

Robert and Teddy have been tasked by President Arthur to wipe out this current vampire scourge. Why nests have popped up here in the remote American West is a bit of a mystery; however, at least one vampire Robert put down was from England and it is feared many of the Black Bishop's followers fled to America to avoid the men sent by the Queen to hunt them down.

"Their behaviour is odd," Robert told me. "They seem to be making more vampires as they travel west. As soon as we burn down one nest, another pops up. This land is sparsely populated. Why they want to create more competition for food is a mystery."

I blanched a bit at the description of humans as 'food', but from a vampire's point of view, that is exactly what we are.

President Arthur has given the Roosevelts guns, silver bullets and men to help in the effort. Six skilled riflemen accompany them on their hunts, along with a mountain man tracker named 'Liver-Eating Johnson'. The man seems barely civilised, a feral creature dressed in buckskins and furs, with a long tangled beard and wild hair; however, he has been instrumental in sniffing out the vampires.

"I used to think the Cheyenne Dog Soldiers were the most vile creatures on earth until I ran into these bloodsuckers," he spat. "They're like fuckin' mosquitoes in human form. As soon as you swat one, another one bites you."

The riflemen were wearing U.S. Cavalry uniforms, as was Robert.

"The president has temporarily made Teddy and me army captains," Robert said. "And our small unit's mission is to discreetly put down the vampire threat. Any work you do with us, gentlemen, is of a covert nature and you are sworn to secrecy." Henry and I agreed, although I don't know who I would tell except for Florence.

Robert unfurled a map onto an empty desk. "We killed five in a barn here," he said, placing his finger on the map. "But two of them got away. Despite us attacking in the middle of the day, they managed to fight their way out with six-shooters. They crossed the river here and we lost them."

I told Robert that I doubted I could pick up their trail under these circumstances but would give it a try. We waited until dusk, so Henry could more easily join us. This necessitated telling our companions that Henry is a vampire, which didn't sit well with Johnson. He leapt to his feet, reaching for his rifle, but Robert immediately stepped between him and Irving.

"Out of my way, Roosevelt," Johnson growled. "I can't abide travelling with one o' them bloodsuckers."

Robert stayed where he was, replying, "I've worked with Henry before. He has killed more vampires than all of us put together, and I trust him with my life."

But Johnson wasn't ready to relent. "It's him or me," he said.

"Then I'll be sorry to see you go, Johnson," Robert said. "You've been a great help to the team, but at this point, we need Henry's skills more than we need yours."

Johnson stood for a moment, taking this in. He was still holding his gun, and I wondered whether he would attempt to get around Robert for a clear shot at Henry. I got to my feet, thinking I might be able to tackle him if he tried. But at that moment one of the riflemen – McGee is his name – stood up and placed himself shoulder-to-shoulder with Robert, further blocking Johnson's access to Henry. Teddy took up a post on the other side and one by one the other men arrayed themselves on Robert's side of the standoff.

Johnson sighed disgustedly, but laid his gun on the table and sat down. "Well, I reckon if you consorted with this fella before and lived to tell the tale, I may as well see what happens this time."

As the sun went down, we hit the trail on horseback. I took courage in our number, and particularly in the presence of the military men. Robert had told me that these were accomplished sharpshooters who had each been chosen for their skill, discipline and bravery. I could tell at once that they were all proficient horsemen, and as they rode alongside us in their dark blue uniforms, their bearing alert and their rifles at the ready, I felt confident that if we encountered our quarry the fighting would be left to the professionals.

We saddled up for a ride out into the desert. Henry's horse bucked at the sight of him, as horses are known to do around vampires. He looked into the creature's eyes, waved his hand and the animal calmed, allowing him to mount.

It had been a while since I had been on a horse and it took a few minutes for the animal and I to become comfortable with each other. It didn't help that the saddle was of a design I was not used to, but I was assured by Robert it was the latest in equestrian technology. There was a 'horn' up front which I admit was a nice enhancement over English saddles. It gives you something to hang on to while getting on and off the horse, as well as a place to tie a rope. A larger cantle cradles the lower back and allows you to ride at a full gallop without fear of falling out of the saddle.

We set off. We had a nearly full moon, but it was slow going in the dark and our quarry had a three-day head start on us.

We followed the river for a while and then stopped.

"It was here we lost them," Teddy said. He got off his horse, lit a lantern and went to the riverbank. "You can still see their footprints on the bank, but then the terrain is mostly rocks so we lost their tracks quickly."

I dismounted and inspected the footprints by the light of Teddy's lamp. "Extinguish the flame," I ordered. He did, and I concentrated and looked for the green glow that accompanies my supernatural vision.

To my surprise, it was bright and very visible in the darkness. I turned and looked into the rocky desert. A trail of green footprints led off into the distance. So very bright. I was astonished as I had never had such a strong vision before. A buzzing began in my ears. "These must be truly evil creatures," I said out loud, although I had not meant to.

"You are correct in that," Teddy said. "I was familiar with some of them in their human lives. Cactus Pete and Zip Ellsworth, they were pure evil before they were turned into vampires. They used to prey on wagon trains and had no compunction about killing women and children."

"We found a letter on one of the creatures we killed," Robert said. "It appears they were planning to join up with another gang for a job. If you can track them, Bram, it might lead us to another nest."

"I am certain they went that way." I pointed into the dark desert where I could see a line of footprints.

Vampires can move quite fast in the night and it seems they were a very long way ahead of us. Yet I could still see their trail, bright as day. The footprints became brighter as we went, giving us hope we could catch up.

At one point on our trail, we met up with another set of footprints. It was at a watering hole. There were at least three more vampires, maybe more. The footprints overlapped to the point I could no longer tell individual tracks from one another.

"They met up with six or seven people," Johnson said, examining the ground by lantern light. "At least four horses too."

There were footprints in the dirt that did not spark my supernatural vision. Clearly, the vampires had met up with another gang that was a mix of humans and vampires. A very odd crowd indeed. Vampires by themselves were bad enough, but it is never good when they mingle with humans. (With the exception of Henry, of course.) Whatever were they up to?

As the sun rose, we stopped to rest. We could see smoke off in the distance and were fairly certain it was our desperadoes. Robert sent a scout out for some reconnaissance, warning the young man not to get too close as the vampires could hear him a mile off.

"Let's get some sleep," Robert ordered. "We don't want a fight without being rested."

The men quickly set up tents and took to sleep. Our plan was to wait until high noon and then resume our hunt, hoping they were bedding down for the day.

I am exhausted but sleep will not come. I am worried about what we will soon face.

REPORT FROM AGENT CORA CHASE TO WHITE WORM SOCIETY

Date: 15 September 1882

Subject: Tracking Carolyn le Fey

I have got word from my sources that the preliminary reports from the home office are correct: Carolyn le Fey has established a nest in Salt Lake City. Whether she tracked the Stokers here is unknown, though it seems improbable that it is just a coincidence. I met with Agent Charlemont, embedded with the Stokers, so she knows to be watchful should le Fey try to attack them again.

I have been covertly following a woman I suspect is le Fey for more than a day.

I have interviewed prostitutes who have reported missing friends to the authorities only to have their claims dismissed; the local sheriff seems to think they have simply moved on to other brothels in other towns. Often these working girls have been seen talking to a nun who tries to rescue lost women.

A few nights ago, this nun was pointed out to me and I believe her to be Carolyn le Fey. Under the guise of a charity worker, she takes in wayward girls and, one supposes, continues her reign of depravity and death.

If this is le Fey, she has cleverly hidden herself in plain sight, posing as the 'mother superior' of her own convent on the outskirts of Salt Lake City. The townspeople I have spoken to thought the convent had been abandoned until they started seeing this new nun about town.

This identity would assure her a plentiful supply of victims. Many girls who are orphans or from broken or poverty-stricken homes make their way out west, hoping to find husbands or become waitresses at Harvey House restaurants at train stations.

Often these girls fall on hard times and become saloon girls or prostitutes. As bad as any of those fates are, it is better than becoming a meal for a vampire or, worse yet, one of le Fey's vampire slaves.

As a Pinkerton detective, I have an excuse to ask questions, and that is how I have learned what I know so far. However, I have no real authority to investigate her, let alone have her convent raided. I simply have no proof of what is going on behind those cloistered walls. Not yet, anyway.

Date: 22 September 1882
Subject: Carolyn le Fey

I am now certain that the nun is Carolyn le Fey. Today I followed her while she, in turn, appeared to be stalking a well-dressed woman in the marketplace. She watched the woman from afar as she shopped for boots.

When the woman was joined by Agent Charlemont with a child in a pushchair I knew this was Florence Stoker. I discreetly caught Agent Charlemont's attention and nodded in le Fey's direction to alert her to the danger.

Le Fey followed Mrs. Stoker so closely at times I thought she would actually pounce on her. However, if Mrs. Stoker looked in her direction, le Fey would turn to hide her face.

Le Fey eventually backed off when Mrs. Stoker, Agent Charlemont and the child were joined by another woman for lunch. I recognised her companion straightaway as Calamity Jane, having seen her perform in the Buffalo Bill Wild West show just a few days before.

I will try to bring in le Fey alive if possible, but will not hesitate to kill her should she attempt to abduct or attack Mrs. Stoker.

Date: 24 September 1882
Subject: Carolyn le Fey

I decided my best course of action was to pose as a desperate woman and let le Fey lure me into her trap.

I mingled with the crowd at the train station, dressed as a farmer's daughter in a flour-sack dress and carrying a single small satchel. I had a revolver with silver bullets strapped to my right ankle.

I wandered around aimlessly, looking forlornly about, hoping she would take the bait. I must have looked the part of a lost and helpless woman as I had to fend off more than a few lascivious men before le Fey showed up.

She came into the train station dressed head-to-toe in a black and white habit and tinted glasses. She was flanked by two similarly dressed girls who I guessed were also vampires. They all wore smiles that could be mistaken for benevolent, but I suspected that without the dark glasses one would see the malice in their eyes.

It didn't take her long to find me and strike up a conversation.

"You look lost, my dear," she said, putting a hand gently on my shoulder. "Can we direct you somewhere?"

I told her I was a mail-order bride there to meet my new farmer husband, only to be told he had died of the flu that very day. I had no home to go back to or even money for a ticket if I did.

"You poor thing! And you a stranger in these parts. We can put you up for the night in the convent." She took my arm in hers and started walking me out of the station. "I am Sister Victoria, the mother superior, and these are Sisters Abigail and Sarah."

"It is very nice to meet you," I said politely. "You are so kind to help me like this. What is the name of your order?"

"Our Lady of Perpetual Sorrow," le Fey said. "Don't let the sadness of the name frighten you. We are a happy order. We help lost women find their way back to the world, and nothing could bring us greater joy."

The convent was in great disrepair. Tending the gardens and performing upkeep on the buildings was apparently not a high priority for the good sisters.

We entered through a large iron gate, which she unlocked and relocked behind us. A long covered pathway took us behind the stone walls. My plan had been to pull my revolver and take her into custody as soon as I was sure she was le Fey. I thought there would be a courtyard, but I quickly realised I was being led into a building. A dimly lit building.

The last thing I wanted was to let her get me out of the sun, and here I was marching ever further into the darkness.

I could feel her grip on my arm strengthen as the sun left us. I thought it might already be too late to pull my gun.

It was.

In an instant, she turned from human to snarling beast. Her minions grabbed my arms as she laughed at my helplessness.

"Welcome to our happy home, my dear," she said with a sneer.

I was whisked deeper into the cavernous room, a great hall of stone and heavy wooden beams. From there we passed into a room off to the side, a chapel with a desecrated altar, a broken crucifix hung upside-down and smeared with blood. Christ's eyes were gouged out and a large phallus grotesquely drawn on his chest. The windows had been boarded over and torches on the walls provided the only illumination.

"Time to pray," she said, throwing me down in front of the altar. It was then I noticed other women tied to pews and pillars. Some were alive and squirming while others were long dead.

"Please, don't hurt me," I pleaded, trying to sound pitiful and frightened, which wasn't entirely untrue. I curled up into a foetal position as I discreetly reached under my dress for my gun.

She knelt down and gently stroked my hair. "But hurting you makes the blood taste sweeter."

She yanked me to my feet by my hair and tossed me up against the pulpit, but by then I had the gun in my hand.

She laughed. "I like a girl who can defend herself, but I'm afraid that won't do you much good."

"We'll see," I said. I fired into her but missed the heart as she twisted at the last second. Still, it was enough to make her fall to the floor. The other two lunged towards me, but two more shots sent them scattering into the shadows.

Le Fey lay writhing in pain on the ground, her flesh sizzling around her wound.

I looked into her surprised eyes. "Yes, silver bullets." I quickly drew silver handcuffs from my satchel, my gun never wavering from her. "Put these on if you don't want a bullet to the head."

She complied, and I bound her legs with a silver chain from my satchel. Then I set about freeing the women she had tied up.

As I was cutting the ropes that held one bedraggled young lady to a column, she yelled, "Behind you!" I turned to see 'Sister Abigail' leaping over a pew towards me, fangs bared. I grabbed my gun in the last second before she landed on top of me, knocking me to the ground. She held my arms down and loomed over me, about to go for my throat, but my legs were still free and I managed to wedge one under her and kick up, knocking her off me. I quickly scrambled up and shot her in the head. She dissolved into gore and several of the human survivors screamed.

But the attack had distracted me for too long. There was a rush of wind behind me and le Fey was gone! 'Sister Sarah' had grabbed her and whisked her away at vampire speed.

I ran out, knowing once they hit daylight they would slow down, but I saw no sign of them outside.

I went back into the convent to free and tend to the rest of the victims.

I have failed in my mission and le Fey is once again a fugitive. I'm gravely concerned about the potential consequences of this, and fully accept all responsibility. I've informed Agent Charlemont to redouble her vigilance over Mrs. Stoker and her son, although I am fairly certain le Fey will not stick around Salt Lake City for long. Among her possessions I found a telegram from Robert Roosevelt to Bram Stoker. How she got it I do not know, but she has learned where Mr. Stoker and Mr. Irving have gone and I feel that she will pursue them.

My plan now is to find Stoker and Irving before le Fey and her cohorts do.

—End Report—

FROM THE JOURNAL OF BRAM STOKER, 26TH OF SEPTEMBER 1882

3:10 p.m.

We made a horrible mistake not pursuing the vampires earlier in the day. The scout reported back that the smoke we saw at sunrise was not the gang setting up camp but a burning homestead. There was a massacre up ahead. We saddled up immediately and rode as fast as we could, in the hope of finding survivors. But we were too late.

It was a sight that will haunt me for the rest of my days. A family of cattle ranchers and their ranch hands, slaughtered and strewn about the grounds. Men, women and children drained of blood. Horses dead, ranch house on fire.

Robert fired his gun to drive off a pair of vultures that were scavenging the remains.

The fire had mostly burned itself out, but acrid smoke hung in the air, stinging my throat and eyes as I walked through the camp, heartsick at what I was seeing. Could we have prevented this?

In front of the burned-out house, I turned over the body of a young woman to check for signs of life. She had chestnut hair like Florence, and beneath her was the body of a young boy around Noel's age. She'd obviously been trying to shield him, but both of their throats were torn open, and I could see the green glow that told me a vampire had fed upon them. Probably two: one attacked the mother, and the other fed from the child while he was still in his mother's arms. I can only hope the vampires had mesmerised them before feeding so they did not die in terror.

Teddy approached. We did not speak, but I could see in his face the same grief and rage I felt. I know he is married and they are expecting their first child. Was he picturing his wife in the face of the woman, his future child in the crumpled body of the young boy?

One of the soldiers called to Teddy and nodded to the north. High on a hill were two Indians on horseback, looking down on us. One waved a white flag and started down the hill towards us.

"Dagnabit," Johnson said. "I say we put a bullet between his eyes and move on." He went to lift his rifle, but Robert stopped him.

"Let's hear what he has to say. He did wave a white flag."

Teddy added, "And there's only two of them."

"You'll usually find more, coming up right behind," Johnson said.

The brave, who I would learn was from the Ute tribe and named Shavano, spoke to Robert.

"We did not do this," he said in perfect English.

"We know," Robert said.

"They were monsters," Shavano said. "They slaughtered my hunting camp a few days ago. We have been tracking them since. We were eight men. Now my brother and I are all that is left."

"We are tracking them as well. You're welcome to join us," Robert said. "We will be stronger together." He called to one of his soldiers to bring over a spare rifle and handed it to Shavano. "This has special bullets of silver to kill them."

"What the hell are you doing?" Johnson yelled. "Don't give that savage a rifle!"

"This is their fight too," Robert said.

"They have made camp on a ridge not far from here," Shavano said. "Near a water tower by some train tracks. I think they are planning to rob a train."

"God help us," Teddy said. "Imagine how easily they could use their unholy powers to pull off a train robbery."

Shavano took his new rifle and rejoined his brother at the top of the hill.

"Teaming up with Indians and vampires," Johnson said. "Next thing you know we'll be joining up with wolves to attack cows."

7:15 p.m.

The sun is low in the sky and we are but a mile from the train robbers' camp. Henry tells us his acute vampire ears can hear them hooting and singing. It sounds like they are in a terrifyingly good mood.

Robert was looking at them through his spyglass. "Six humans for sure," he said.

"Five vampires, by my count," Henry said. His eyes could see even better than Robert's spyglass.

"What the hell is that?" Robert asked Henry. He pointed to someone on a horse who even at this distance looked odd to my eyes. I couldn't tell in the bright daylight whether there was a green glow about him, but I could see that he was very pale, like a vampire, though not bundled up to guard against the sun. He was talking to a young man on another horse. The young man was surveying the operations, so he seemed to be in charge.

"He's most definitely a vampire," Henry said. He turned his ear to listen better.

"The young man ordered him to 'Just destroy the sending equipment, no need to kill the telegraph operator.' I didn't hear the first part of his instructions."

The pale vampire rode off to the east at a fast gallop.

A Mexican *pistolero* rode up to the young man and was talking with him.

"The Mexican man is named Lobo," Henry informed us, straining to hear the conversation as the wind picked up. "He appears to be second in command in charge of the human bandits. He called the young man in charge 'Mr. Drumpf' and said everyone is in place."

"How the hell are we going to stop a gang that big? They outnumber us and they have more vampires," Teddy said to his uncle.

"They won't be expecting us to try to stop them," Robert said. "We have me, you, six riflemen, two Indians, Johnson and a vampire." He had not included me in that count and I don't blame him, as I did not know what help I could be. I am not trained for a gun battle.

One train has gone by but they let it pass. Teddy tells me another will be along in an hour.

Robert is consulting with his men and Shavano, planning their course of attack.

LETTER FROM ALEJO 'LOBO' LOPEZ TO LUZ LOPEZ, 26TH OF SEPTEMBER 1882

The letter below was translated from Spanish. Earlier in his life, Alejo Lopez was a literature professor at The Royal and Pontifical University of Mexico. He came to America in 1856 to make his fortune in the California Gold Rush, where his brother Luz Lopez had a claim. The claim was quickly mined out and Luz returned to Mexico while Alejo stayed in America to work a ranch he had bought with his share of the mining profits. After several years of drought, he abandoned his ranch and became a gun for hire, mostly working cattle drives. Luz Lopez became a wealthy land baron in Mexico and built a library to honour his brother. This letter and letters to follow are from Luz Lopez's archives, which were purchased by the White Worm Society in 1889.

Dear Luz,

I am happy to hear about your success. Someday I will return to Mexico. I was, in fact, on my way there when an unbelievable opportunity fell into my lap. I had been working for a mining company, providing security and recruiting men to protect the mine and its shipments to Carson City. I proved adept at this work, and so the owner, Drumpf, has hired me and my men to help him recover something, an artefact that is of great value to him. This will involve a train robbery, not the type of job I would normally undertake, as these things are rarely successful. However, the artefact onboard this train is, I believe, a book containing a map to El Dorado!

I know you think it to be a myth and that no city of gold actually exists outside of legends, but I believe now that it is real. Mr. Drumpf has a powerful *brujo* {*Archivist's note: Closest translation* is 'dark wizard'} working with him, who has described a land of vast riches. I have witnessed real magic and, God save my soul, encountered creatures of the occult. If such things can exist, why not a city of gold?

For you see, dear brother, I am travelling with a vampire. He, in turn, has created five more vampires to do his bidding. If my employers have the magic to create demons to walk among us, is it not also possible that they could know about the secret city of El Dorado?

Drumpf's son is supervising our mission, and I have heard him talking about 'the promised land' with the vampire we call 'the Pale Horseman'. He describes it as a new frontier, with untold riches waiting to be tapped. It is only the promise of seeing the City of Gold that keeps me and my men from fleeing in fear.

To see the Pale Horseman is to look upon evil itself. The dead one rides a dead horse brought back to life by the powerful magic of the *brujo*. He is as white as chalk, his flesh marked with sores and pustules he carried from his human days. His hair is thin and grey and looks as though it is made from cobwebs. His dead eyes are as pale as his skin and if you look directly at them, you can feel your very soul being dragged to hell. He wears a soldier's hat from the Confederacy, grey like his skin.

The horse he rides appears to be rotting, with large parts of its skin gone, revealing bones and muscles underneath. No flies bother it, for no living things dare go near. It is fiercely loyal to its master and will chomp and stomp at you if you get too near, but it never makes a sound. I have never seen it eat or drink, and I have only seen its rider drink the blood of men, women and children.

The Pale Horseman does not threaten me. There are times in our work when a human can be useful, and so we have achieved an uneasy trust between us. He sometimes, as a joke, I think, offers to turn me into a vampire, and I always laugh and decline. But I keep a supply of silver bullets, just in case, for I have been told that is one of the surest ways to kill a vampire.

The Pale Horseman wears a talisman that lets him walk by day with no ill effects. The minions he has created can also walk by day, but are weakened by the sun. They avoid it when they can and wear broad hats and shield themselves with blankets when they must go out by day.

The Pale Horsemen created these vampires to serve our cause. Three are gringos; two are from the Ute tribe. All are bound to obey the Pale Horseman as he is their sire.

The Pale Horseman was a gunslinger when he was alive and is the fastest and most accurate shot I have ever seen. When we came upon an Indian hunting party, he shot four of them in mere seconds and had two more under his spell before they hit the ground. It is these two who are now in our employ.

When I asked him why he didn't turn all six of them, he muttered that two was all we needed. However, I suspect that there is a limit to how many vampires he can control and he does not want to create more than he can handle.

This is fine with me as I do not care to have too many vampires about. Their violence sickens me. I have seen them kill at random with no remorse. We ran across a prospector on our way here. He was a young man with flaming red hair, and was singing to himself as he cooked his supper over a fire. One of the gringo vampires called to him and he turned around, but before he could even react the vampire was upon him. The man screamed as the vampire bit into him. The vampire was not even hungry. He drank a bit of blood and tossed the man into his own cooking fire.

My men and I fear that the vampires will at some point turn on us and may only be keeping us around to protect the ones that are weak in the daylight. Mr. Drumpf assures us that they will not and what we are doing is ultimately for the greater good. For you see, El Dorado is not just a city, but a whole world, the very land of Eden itself. Perhaps, when we get there, this world of violence and death will be over forever. For myself, I would be happy to find another claim to stake and mine enough gold to return to Mexico like you, my brother.

We wait for the train. The vampires with their speed and agility will make quick work of stopping it and retrieving the artefact, so I hope there will be little bloodshed and we can let the train go on its way.

The Pale Horseman has ridden down the line to destroy the

telegraph station in Mound House. Should the train not arrive on time, the operator in Mound House would be the first to alert the authorities. Taking out this telegraph office will buy us a good two hours before anyone knows a robbery has occurred.

I have to admit to feeling some excitement. I feel like I'll have one last taste of the adventure I sought as a young man when I came north.

Soon, I will visit El Dorado and return home with my pockets filled with gold and my head filled with stories.

Lobo

REPORT FROM THEODORE ROOSEVELT TO PRESIDENT CHESTER B. ARTHUR, 27TH OF SEPTEMBER 1882

Greetings, Mr. President,

It has been a day of tragedy and loss, but also of exhilarating victory. We failed to stop the brutal massacre of a party of settlers. But we did avenge them. And not only did we dispatch vampires, as is our main mission, we also stopped a bona fide train robbery.

We had tracked the varmints to a watering station near the V&T line. They had set up camp nearby and bided their time, waiting for their target, the midnight train out of Virginia City on its way to Carson City. Their gang was made up of both vampires and human gunslingers. It was a formidable force.

Their leader, from what we could tell at a distance, was a young greenhorn. No more than 22 years old, by my estimation, he seemed unfit to lead such an endeavor, yet there he was barking orders. What he was discussing with his men I could not hear, for we were very far away on a hilltop overlooking their camp. However, one of the people in our posse, an Englishman named Henry Irving, has excellent hearing and is, in fact, a vampire.

I realize that this goes against all reason and logic, teaming up with one of the Undead to take down more of his kind, but I assure you, Mr. President, this one was very much on our side and up to the task. His supernaturally enhanced senses provided much-needed intelligence. He told us the young man was called Mr. Drumpf by his bandits and was very much in charge. He was also able to identify at a distance which of our foes were vampires and which humans.

Along the way, we had also joined forces with two Ute men whose comrades had been murdered by the vampire gang.

When the sound of the train coming around the bend was heard around half past midnight, the bandits jumped into action.

As the train approached from the north, Drumpf ordered two vampires and three humans to one side of the track. There was a full moon that night. The vampires were easy to spot for they were running as fast as horses alongside the train! Two more men on horseback and three more vampires, along with Drumpf, remained on the side closest to us.

We had the element of surprise, but our success relied on precise timing. If we rushed down too soon, they would not be distracted by the robbery and would put up a full fight. Too late and we would all be trapped on one side of the train, unable to fight them on both fronts.

But here is where having our own vampire came in most handy. He was able to rush down at such a speed as to not be seen, and he was able to actually leap over the moving train to the other side. He assured us he could make quick work of newly created vampires as he is older and apparently swifter and more powerful. If only human strength and agility increased with age as they apparently do with vampires!

The rest of us rushed down the hill as the train sped by. The sound of the train drowned out our horses' hooves, and the bandits were most preoccupied with their task at hand. We came at them from the darkness and they were exposed by the interior lights of the train as it sped by.

They did not know what hit them.

Our silver bullets flew, hitting their targets. We took out two vampires straightaway, exploding them into guts before they could leap onto the train.

However, one vampire did make a leap between cars and busted down a door that was already being locked and barricaded by guards inside. They were no match for the vampire's strength! The door shattered into splinters and we could see him fighting his way through the guards; one was thrown out right through the window. Gunshots could be heard, but alas their bullets were not silver and the vampire put the guards down quickly.

We rode with all our might alongside the train. I took out one of the human horsemen and one of our men, Captain Chadwick, took out the other. We were not sure at this point what our vampire was doing on the other side of the train as we had lost sight of him.

The leader of the gang turned and rode off into the desert, abandoning his men in a most cowardly way.

The train suddenly braked. One of the vampires must have gotten to the engineer and forced him to halt the train. It stopped with such force that the caboose almost jumped the track.

We saw a vampire on top of the train making his way along to the front with Irving close behind him. Irving tackled the vampire and after a scuffle that involved a lot of snarling and hissing of the most animalistic kind, Irving emerged victorious.

The vampire who had taken out the engineer appeared at the top of the coal car to fight Irving. Unlike the scrawny one Irving had just dispatched, this was a large brute. Then a second vampire appeared, emerging from a puff of coal smoke behind Irving.

Robert took aim with his buffalo rifle and took out the one behind Irving, exploding him into a cloud of guts and gore.

The other one became frightened and turned tail to run, but it was too late as he took a bullet to the head from Captain Chadwick's gun.

We had won! The train and most of its occupants were safe.

It was indeed odd behavior from this gang. Firstly, men and vampires working together on a common cause, and secondly, they were robbing a train that had few valuables onboard. There was some gold and silver, but it was mainly carrying settlers and mail to Carson City.

The vampire has killed the engineer and damaged the boiler badly. Irving informed us that two of the humans on his side of the train managed to ride off, but one was killed by a bullet fired by one of the train guards.

We will guard the train until a repair crew can be sent to get it fully on its way again in the morning.

Theodore Roosevelt

FROM THE BOOK OF EAGAN RAYNE, 27TH OF SEPTEMBER 1882

Archivist's note: This was obtained from Rayne's personal collection. It appears he was writing a new New Testament of sorts, with himself as a prophet. It is mostly the incoherent rantings of a madman, but it does contain some interesting insights into Rayne's motives as well as his powers and the supernatural forces with which he was dabbling. How much is true and how much fantasy from a sick mind is unknown. This passage reads more like a confession than his other ramblings.

The path to our new Eden is a righteous one, but travelling it is an arduous journey fraught with peril and terrifying responsibility. I alone have been tasked by God to lead his people to the promised land. It is a duty that carries a great weight. Sometimes it suffocates me and I feel an almost irresistible desire to throw off this burden and settle into a peaceful life in the mundane world. Then I remember all those who would be denied the chance to live in paradise were I to give in to my weakness, and I am ashamed. I flagellate myself with chains on my bare back and let the pain cleanse me.

I must be purified if I am to continue to wield this black magic. The power to raise the dead has been bestowed upon me and though I know I use this power for good, I must guard against its potential to corrupt my soul. Even as I create creatures of the night to do his bidding, I must keep my heart turned towards the light.

But I fear the more I use the power, the darker my heart gets. I pray for God to show me the way, and yet he often does not.

He sent me the Pale Horseman, as prophesied in a dream I had, to serve our holy cause. The Pale Horseman was wicked in life, and most would say he is even more wicked in his undead state, for he has taken many lives. Yet, are they not mostly sinners and red men who have rejected God? Surely God is directing the Pale Horseman to take only those who do not serve his holy purpose.

The price I pay to use the magic is sometimes too much to bear. Sometimes I must decide who lives and who dies. It is a humbling responsibility that has been thrust upon me, and I strive to use it wisely. When God first commanded me to kill my parents, I hesitated. I shall never hesitate again when his hand guides me.

The first creature I successfully raised from the dead was the Pale Horseman's steed. I felt God's power flow through me like lightning that day! Another horse's life was sacrificed to balance the scales, but its essence now imbues and strengthens that magnificent animal. Surely I created a better horse than either animal was on its own. Was that not worth the life of a horse?

But would it be the same with a human? Thankfully, I did not need to take a life to raise the Pale Horseman from death, for I had the blood of the dragon. But a time may come when Mr. Drumpf asks me to return a man to life like I did the horse. Who would I sacrifice to do so? We are created in God's image. Can our essence be traded freely in the same way as a horse's can? These are the thoughts that plague me.

If only dark thoughts were the only things that haunted me. Using this black magic has attracted demons to me. I see them watching from the shadows upon the hills and mountains, tall dark figures whose features I cannot make out. Others see them as well so I know they are real. Whenever I see them, I can't help but feel a great foreboding, and I know it is me they seek. They do not like me doing God's work.

The Indians call them 'the Dark Watchers' and say they first started appearing around the time the Spanish settlers began moving into the area. Many have seen them, watching from the cliffs. The Spanish called them 'los Vigilantes Oscuros'. Some natives say these demons come down into the canyons to kill those who turn to the white man's God.

As of late, they grow stronger. I fear they are drawn to black magic like flies to sickly sweet molasses.

They make no move towards me, no gesture that could be considered threatening, but they whisper to me to stop what I am doing. They call my name on the wind. They trespass in my dreams and tell me I am not worthy, that I should abandon my cause, that I should kill myself. It is getting harder and harder to resist them. I know now they will block our way into the holy land, or try to.

But there is hope. I have found references to similar creatures in the ancient texts, as well as a way to keep them at bay. I can perform a ceremony to drive them away, though it is clear from the texts the spell is temporary. Still, even a brief reprieve will help me clear my head and focus my thoughts on the path ahead.

I will have the Pale Horseman gather what I need for the ceremony, as soon as he is done with his current mission.

LETTER FROM WILLIAM DRUMPF TO JOHN D. ROCKEFELLER, 27TH OF SEPTEMBER 1882

Archivist's note: Though Rockefeller will not play any further role in Drumpf's scheme, it is interesting to note that when Teddy Roosevelt became president, one of his priorities was breaking up monopolies, including Rockefeller's Standard Oil. One wonders whether he was aware of the Drumpf-Rockefeller connection.

Dear J.D.,

I have been reflecting recently upon my long career and the factors that contributed to my success. I must say that you, J.D., have been one of those factors. Your friendship and tutelage in all things business have helped make me the man I am today.

I would like to show my gratitude by offering you an opportunity to take part in my next venture, which promises to be the most exciting and lucrative yet. As my most pious friend, I wanted you to be the first to know we are very close to finding our way to a new world, a world that might possibly be Eden itself.

I know how that sounds, J.D. But as I write to you, we are close to gaining the knowledge that will lead us to the new New World. I have told you of my prophet, Eagan Rayne. While I normally wouldn't hold with someone calling himself a prophet, he has proven himself to be knowledgeable on the matter at hand and has demonstrated other abilities, which I will further describe below. He tells me this new land may be as big as the West, if not bigger.

Imagine, an unlimited supply of virgin timber, untapped oil wells and farm fields as big as states! Why, we might find new minerals, miraculous vegetation, animals beyond anything we've seen before, any of which might have properties that we cannot yet imagine.

And it can all be ours.

In my quest to find this land, I have discovered something that puts all other natural resources to shame. We have long known of its existence through folklore and ancient writings, including the Bible itself. I am talking about magic.

I have in my possession a vampire, a supernatural creature with incredible strength, swiftness of foot and a life free of disease and death. What's more, he can, in turn, make more such creatures that then become his willing slaves. Imagine, workers whose very nature compels them to do as they are told! Workers that only require a meal of blood once or twice a week. Workers that never tire and demand no wages.

As amazing as this is, it is only a drop in the bucket of what magic can do. If we can harness it, which I believe we can, it could usher in a new age of untapped wealth and power.

Eagan Rayne is a man who can wield such power. And I am a man who can wield Eagan Rayne.

With all magic, there is a price to pay, but it is a pittance compared to the wonders it can bring and the good it can do. Rayne claims magic is but another form of energy that has been given to us by God. Just as we have learned to harness lightning to power machines, we can harness magic's energy. Magical talismans, incantations and rituals are the coal, oil and kerosene of the supernatural world.

Rayne gained his control of magic from years of study in Egypt and training from necromancers aligned with the Order of the Golden Dawn. He wields this power with a magical stone he says came from the Garden of Eden itself. More importantly, he says the garden still exists and he can gain entrance to it.

Think of it, J.D., seeing the wonders of the first creation itself. A land where all magical things come from; a magic that was lost to us long ago when Eve's sin expelled us from the garden.

Rayne tells me if we can find an entrance to this world, we will have a virgin land to make our own and, in turn, it will give us power to take full control of this one. There is magic there that can vanquish entire armies, magic that can cure all sickness and give one power over death itself.

Rayne, though a bit of a religious fanatic, is totally devoted to me.

He also needs my wealth to search for religious artifacts that will point the way to the new New World.

It is unknown as of now if there will be natives there that will give us trouble. We will need to build an army to protect our people and tame any savages we find, turning them to the Christian faith, if possible. I am amassing armaments and hope you will contribute to our cause.

It will take industrious men like you and me to mold this world. I hope you will decide to join us on our journey going forward. It promises to be the most ambitious project ever undertaken by mankind.

I know you are distracted at the moment with union uprisings, but when you get things under control there, I ask you to consider coming out West and joining me on this grand adventure.

Sincerely,

William Drumpf

FROM THE JOURNAL OF BRAM STOKER, 27TH OF SEPTEMBER 1882

7:15 a.m.

We have successfully stopped the train robbery and killed most of the vampires. Although the train's boiler is damaged, most onboard are safe. The vampire bandits killed four postal guards but were not able to get away with what they came for, which, we have come to learn, is a curious artifact.

Once Robert and his men (with the help of Henry and the Indians) had dispatched the villains, we went through the train checking on the passengers. We quickly ascertained that the robbers had not taken anything from them and had not even stopped in the passenger cars. Clearly, they were there for the train's cargo.

Henry and I made our way to the mail car and began to search. Hidden among the mail pouches we found a strongbox, about the size of a small suitcase. Henry easily broke off the padlock and revealed its contents: an ornate golden box. He lifted its lid and was quite surprised and pleased at what he found.

"It's a copy of the Doyle Vellum Manuscript," he said. He had owned one previously, but the Black Bishop had stolen it to learn how to open the gate to the Realm. That book is now in the hands of the White Worm Society, who deemed it too dangerous to be out of their custody.

"I have long regretted the loss of my copy of this book. However, it troubles me greatly that this is what they were after," he said. "The Black Bishop nearly destroyed the world by opening the gate at Stonehenge."

I would have liked to hand the book over to the Roosevelts, but out of loyalty to Henry agreed to keep it secret, for they would surely report it to the president and he, in turn, would notify the White Worm Society. Henry tucked it under his coat and returned to the passenger car. As it was daylight now, he was grateful to have a shady place to rest.

Robert and Teddy are seeing to the repair of the train. There is a telegraph machine onboard and the operator has scurried up one of the telegraph poles that run alongside the train track and hooked up the machine to call for help. Apparently the railroad will dispatch another engineer and repair crew and return the train to working order. In mere hours we will be able to return to Carson City, where we will catch a train back to Salt Lake City.

12:17 p.m.
Terror on the tracks!

I have done my share of killing vampires but have not killed a man until today. It troubles me greatly. Despite the fact the man was a criminal and is responsible for the deaths of many in our group, I nevertheless feel the weight of his death on my heart.

After Henry and I retrieved the artefact, I exited the car to join the Roosevelts near the caboose.

Two riders approached from the east, their horses moving fast and kicking up a cloud of dust.

As they got closer to us they slowed down and stopped at what I suppose was out of shooting range. It was Drumpf, the leader of the gang, who had fled as we foiled the robbery!

I had only seen him at a distance, or when he'd turned and galloped away. At closer range I could see he was younger than I'd thought, perhaps in his early twenties or even younger. I wondered how one so young came to be in command of a band of criminals and vampires.

He fired his gun into the air, I assume to ensure he had our attention.

"We will take what we came for," Drumpf said. He was chewing tobacco and spat on the ground.

Alongside him was another rider. Even without the green glow around him, I would have been able to see he was a vampire, with his pallid face and the fangs he made no attempt to hide. Yet he was out in broad daylight, with only the scant shade provided by his Confederate hat. This was the vampire who had ridden off before the robbery, on Drumpf's orders.

His skin was the palest I have ever seen, like it had been bleached by the sun itself. His cheeks were dry and marked by smallpox. He wore a long, faded black coat that showed signs of decay. Over his chest was a vest made of what looked like small bones. I had seen similar chest armour worn by Indian warriors in the Wild West show. Around his neck, he wore an amulet that also looked to be in the style of one of the western Indian tribes. It resembled a tiny birdcage made of copper, and inside it was a green stone. The stone gave off a small, faint, pulsing glow, so I could tell it was supernatural in nature.

But it was his mount to which my eyes were continually drawn. He was riding the reanimated corpse of a horse. The beast's flesh had rotted or been torn away in spots, exposing parts of its ribcage and hip bone. What hide that remained was a dappled grey. Though Drumpf's horse twitched its tail and ears to shoo away flies, this creature stayed perfectly still, as if it could not even feel, or was not bothered by, biting insects. How such an abomination was created I could not fathom.

Robert and Teddy drew their guns. "Just stay where you are," Robert ordered.

"We will not repeat ourselves," said Drumpf. "Hand over the book."

Teddy and Robert glanced at each other. Of course, they did not know about the book.

Henry came to the window of the train, but it being midday he could do little to help us.

By then Robert's soldiers had come to his side with their guns drawn. The vampire rider urged his horse forward slowly.

"Back, I said," Robert yelled, but it was too late, for the vampire was now within shooting range.

He fired so quickly I never saw the gun come out of his holster! All six of the soldiers were shot through the head and fell dead almost in unison!

Before Robert and Teddy could react, the gun was trained in their direction, the vampire regarding them coolly.

"Surely that convinced you to just give us the book," Drumpf yelled. He had a big stupid grin on his face, elated that we were obviously up against the ropes.

"Bram," Henry shouted. He took the book out of his coat. I went to the window, and he handed me the book, but under it was a small derringer pistol. I fumbled with the book awkwardly, palming the derringer in my right hand as I grabbed it through the window.

I walked over to the vampire on shaky legs, for I knew once they had the book there was nothing stopping them from killing us. I only had one shot with the pistol against a vampire that had the fastest of reflexes.

I raised the book up to hand it to him. Our fingers touched as he took it, and in a flash, I saw a vision of his past: a man in robes giving him a drink of dragon's blood from a goblet and hanging the amulet around his neck. Later, a ritual where his horse was raised from the dead…all this in only the second our fingers touched. He too felt and saw something, and yanked the book from my hand with a startled look in his dead eyes.

"What in tarnation are you, Stoker?" he said, his voice as dry and raspy as a pump that hasn't been used in years. He knew my name! What other information had he pulled from my brain? Florence? Noel?

I momentarily forgot about the gun in my right hand but felt its heft once more. Before I could bring it up to fire, a shot rang out from the train car. Henry had a rifle and had fired on the vampire, hitting him in the cheekbone. He was flung back from the force, then lurched forward, grabbing the horse around the neck to keep from falling.

I pulled up my gun and fired, but the vampire's horse had sped off at a full gallop and I hit Drumpf in the head instead, killing him instantly.

The vampire rider was a way off when I saw him rise up and regain control of his horse. He stopped for a moment to curse us, I remember not what he said, then he turned the horse to the south and rode off.

The book was lying at my feet.

I scooped up the book and then had to confess to Robert and Teddy that we had found it. I also explained the danger of the book in the wrong hands.

"Damn it, Stoker, we can't have secrets among ourselves," Robert said, and rightly so.

He agreed to let us hang on to it, as he wasn't sure it was any safer in the hands of the government or the White Worms.

"Maybe we should burn the damn thing," Robert said. "Look at all the death it has caused thus far."

He left it at that and I tucked the book away inside my coat.

3:10 p.m.

We have wrapped up the bodies of Drumpf and our dead soldiers and they will be brought back to Carson City by train.

I hope that we have put down the vampire threat, but fear that since one has got away it may not be over. But I will let the Roosevelt boys handle it from here. Henry and I will take the train on to Carson City, where we can catch a train back to Salt Lake City.

TELEGRAM FROM BRAM STOKER TO FLORENCE STOKER, 28TH OF SEPTEMBER 1882

=We have concluded our mission. Waiting for repair of train. Will return to Salt Lake City within a day or two=

LETTER FROM EAGAN RAYNE TO WILLIAM DRUMPF, 28TH OF SEPTEMBER 1882

Dear Mr. Drumpf,

It is with a heavy heart that I must share with you some terrible news passed on to me by the Pale Horseman. Please call on your faith and God's strength, for your son, Tom, has been killed.

You may receive some comfort from knowing that he died bravely, trying to retrieve the holy book. During the mission, he was killed in the most cowardly way by the leader of a gang of outlaws led by an Irishman known as 'Bram Stoker'.

He is a large, ginger-haired brute, and his gang includes two Easterners, some Ute savages, a grizzled old mountain man and an older Englishman who the Pale Horseman believes to be a vampire. He also had the aid of several men in U.S. Army uniforms, who must surely have been deserters to be in such nefarious company. They, at least, will no longer be a problem, for they got what was coming to them through the swift marksmanship of the Pale Horseman.

I have enclosed a drawing of the dastardly villain and have given a copy to your man, Sheriff Calhoun, who is gathering a posse to hunt down the murderer.

Wanted posters are being printed and distributed around Carson City and nearby railway stations. We will catch him, I promise you, and he will receive the justice he so richly deserves.

The killer and his gang have the book, but with the Pale Horseman, Lopez and Calhoun's posse on the hunt, not to mention my magic, we will surely retrieve it in short order. Tom will not have died in vain. He is a martyr to our cause and will be known from this day forward as a saint who helped lead our people to the promised land.

My prayers are with you and Mrs. Drumpf during this difficult time.
Your humble servant,
E.R.

FROM THE JOURNAL OF WILLIAM DRUMPF, 28TH OF SEPTEMBER 1882

My heart seethes with anger. I am ashamed that I cannot contain it, but turning the other cheek has never been in my nature. My son has been murdered. He was to be my legacy and carry on the Drumpf name, in this world or the new one. Now he has been taken from me.

I have assured the prophet that my determination and faith have never been stronger. Yet I feel my rage blinding me to our mission.

How can I fulfill my destiny if I am stricken with such sorrow and anger?

I will kill this bastard of an Irishman who murdered my son and retrieve the book that will lead us to the new frontier. If he has any loved ones, I will take him from them, as he took my Tom.

Once I have avenged my son, nothing will distract me from my goal. We will make it to the promised land and its riches will be mine.

This will not return my son to me, but when I see him again in heaven he will know he did not die in vain.

But I fear further tragedy to come. With her only son dead, my dear Edina has been made sicker with grief. I fear she may not live long enough to see the promised land. She continues to cough up blood, and our relocation to Phoenix has done little to cure her consumption.

We head back to Carson City now by train. I would not put her through the strain of a journey, but we must return to bury our son. She is resting comfortably in her private car and is treated around the clock by the best physicians I could buy.

I must steel myself for what lies ahead. The road will not be easy, but nor was it easy to conquer the American frontier. Nothing will stop me from making the new world mine.

FROM THE JOURNAL OF BRAM STOKER, 29TH OF SEPTEMBER 1882

6:10 p.m.

The train has been repaired and Henry and I are on our way back to Carson City, where we can catch a train to Salt Lake City. I am eager to return to Florence and Noel. It is a very slow-moving train, but I am saddle-sore and thankful to have a cushioned seat for our way back.

Henry is grateful to be out of the sun. We are currently passing through a pine forest and gaining elevation to cooler climes.

Henry was able to slake his thirst on one of the freshly dead human bandits we killed, so he is at full strength. (Honestly, what an extraordinary sentence to write about one's employer!) He is frantically trying to decipher the book from the Realm, as it is written in some unrecognisable language. It contains pictures of unusual animals, strange flora and – most importantly – maps. However, none of the maps display any familiar continents or landmarks. If it is a map from inside the other Realm it may be of little use to him.

"Still," Henry said, "someone wanted it badly enough to rob a train for it, so it must be of some importance."

He then told me that Arthur Conan Doyle had actually travelled into the Realm at one point on one of his expeditions and brought back a similar book. I was astonished to hear this, as he is a mutual acquaintance and Henry had never mentioned this before.

"Oh, yes," Henry said. "He never wants to talk about it. I have always had the impression that something horrible happened to him there."

"I see," I said. "But can't he show you the entrance he used?"

"I'm afraid not. He found it quite by accident when he was exploring a cave in the South of France. He was never able to find the entrance again. His theory is that they move or are only open at certain times, something we know to be true about the entrance at Stonehenge."

"But he obviously found his way out," I said.

"Indeed, but not where he went in. He came out here in America, someplace near Cleveland, Ohio. And he swore he only travelled a few miles inside the Realm. He found the book in an old abandoned temple of some kind. The builders were long gone. He did not run into any humans in the short time he was in there, nor any sufficiently intelligent creature that could have built the temple."

I imagine it would be nice to cross an entire ocean in only a few miles, and said as much.

"Yes, I suppose it could be good for commerce and the like," Henry said. "But Doyle said the place is full of monsters and he barely escaped with his life."

"That is reason enough for you not to go in there," I said.

He smiled sadly. "You sometimes forget, Bram, that I too am a monster."

8:17 p.m.

The train has stopped in a small town named Mound House to take on coal and water and let passengers off. We were told it was an hour-long stop so we got out to stretch our legs. A most shocking sight awaited us: a poster on the station wall with my likeness on it!

It was a wanted poster, the kind mentioned in the dime novels. *Wanted: Bram Stoker, leader of the Irish Fancy Pants Gang. $200 reward. Wanted alive.*

I was stunned.

"But he was a bandit," I protested. "Why is there a price on *my* head?"

"I'm sure it is just a misunderstanding," Henry said. "At least you can take some comfort in the fact that they want to bring you in alive."

I ripped the poster down. "Be that as it may, we should probably clear this up before we get to Carson City. Let's find the telegraph office and send a message to the Roosevelts."

Having a price on my head has made me feel as though all eyes are upon me, and I did my best to lurk behind Henry as we made our way through the town, to keep my face from view.

When we reached the telegraph office, a sign on the door said, *Closed, Open 8 a.m.*, although there was a lit lamp and someone moving around inside. I peered through the glass, hoping to catch the telegraph operator's attention, but withdrew quickly when I saw another wanted poster on the wall.

"Damn it!" I exclaimed, ducking back into the shadow of night.

Henry looked in and saw the poster. "We should return to the train and get you out of sight."

I turned up my collar and kept my head down as we walked. Men – mostly cowboys and gamblers, by their appearance – were going in and out of saloons and boarding houses and I did my best not to make eye contact, hoping that the darkness would protect my anonymity.

But luck would not have it. Someone must have seen me and reported me to the law, because before we could reach the railway station a sheriff stepped out in front of us with gun drawn.

"Well, well, well," he said. "Looks like I'll get to do some sheriffing today."

Before I could even put my hands up, Henry quietly said, "The man you are looking for is heading north out of town." Henry was staring the man directly in the eyes, working his 'glamour' as he calls it. The sheriff instantly seemed bewildered.

"Oh, sorry. The man I am looking for is heading north out of town."

"Perhaps you should get a drink," Henry continued.

"I need a drink," the sheriff said. With that, he turned and walked into a saloon. We moved on, and Henry guided me into an alley where we would be less conspicuous.

"People from the train will have seen the posters by now," he said. "I cannot glamour all of them. Maybe we should scram, as the Americans say." He bent over a bit and pointed to his back.

I knew instantly what he was suggesting, and stared at him, appalled. It is humiliating for a grown man to ride on another man's back. However, under the circumstances, it would have been foolish to turn down the offer. I climbed on and we sped off at vampire speed into the wilderness.

Now we are spending the night under the stars near a stream, far from civilisation. We have built a fire that I am sitting by as I write this. Henry was nice enough to catch me a rabbit for dinner, and fortunately I had taken a knife with me on our mission with the Roosevelts so I was able to skin and dress it. Our hope is that we – or at least Henry – can get to a telegraph tomorrow and get a message out. I am certain he's right that this is some sort of misunderstanding. Something the Roosevelts with their connections can easily clear up.

Meanwhile, I look up at the stars. I have never seen so many, so bright. It makes one think of God and his expansive creation. I understand now the appeal of the frontier and how so many are compelled to risk life and limb to settle the wild spaces.

It is quiet here, only the occasional sounds of howling coyotes to break the silence and nothing to do but think. And what I am thinking about now is how much I love Florence and Noel. I must clear my name and return to them as soon as I can.

LETTER FROM CALAMITY JANE TO CHARLIE UTTER, 29TH OF SEPTEMBER 1882

Archivist's note: Original spelling retained.

Dear Charlie,

I write to you this letter and hope you are well. I am in Salt Lake with Bill's Wild West show. I make five dollars a week and get three square meals a day and all the liquor I dare drink. For that I do some ropin, trick ridin and break up the occasional fight.

As you can see my writtin has improved greatly. Chief Watum of the show is helping me with this. He is not a real Indian. His folks are from Italy and Bill reckons he looks Indian enough to play his part. He was a schoolteacher back in New York and teaches me and any children whose parents are in the show.

You meet all sorts travelin with Bill. I have made many new friends. This week I met a bunch of actors from England, though I did not get to see the play they was putting on because we was busy with our own show.

The troop manager's wife, Mrs. Stoker, has taken a shine to me and I am showing her the rough and tumble sights of the frontier.

She is shocked by my tales of Deadwood and Tombstone. Tellin my tales, I sometimes wonder how I have survived it all myself.

I often times wake up in a cold sweat from nightmares of the smallpox camp where I tended the sick. So many dyin, so many dead. Funny how I have shot men dead and have never seen their faces disturb my sleep. But those poor folk who died from the pox are always with me.

The city at Salt Lake is much more civilized today although mighty wild to Mrs. Stoker's eyes. There are very few saloons here so not so many men sleeping it off in the streets.

The Mormons are pullin down the shacks and runnin the criminal types out of town. Tis like that every town you go to now out here. First come the churches, then the schools, then the dress shops and opera houses. I reckon taming the West is why we all came out here in the first place, but there is hardly any room anymore for cattle or cowpokes to roam, not to mention a disreputable old cuss like myself.

I had to take Mrs. Stoker to the outskirts far from the lake to show her the genuwine frontier. I am surprised she wanted to see it at all as she is so refined, but she said she wanted to get a look at the real West and the people that live there.

I made her change her beautiful dress for britches and boots as we would be most likely walking through mud and maybe have to make a run for it should trouble break out.

In this shantytown it is more like it once was. There are saloons and gambling, ladies of the evening pulling men off the streets. Smells like the Old West too. Strange that I miss the smell of horseshit and sweaty cowpokes.

It was a thrill for her, seein it all, and I was glad I could show it to her. I did have to pull my gun a few times to wave off men who came sniffin round her. She was surely a diamond in a bin of coal that day.

I will stay on with the Wild West show until it turns back east. Then I have my heart set on visiting you in Deadwood. I suspect that will be sometime in the late fall.

Yours truly,

Jane

FROM THE JOURNAL OF WILLIAM DRUMPF, 30TH OF SEPTEMBER 1882

Death and madness!

What good is having a prophet who can wield black magic if he can't even keep my only son alive? Or return him to me after death? Had I not been so deep in grief, I might have said no to the idea of bringing Tom back from the dead. It seemed too good to be true that Rayne had this power over death, but I had seen him raise a horse from the dead. Was it any more difficult to believe he could do it with a human?

But I was skeptical it could be done and said as much to Rayne. "He was shot in the head. Will your magic fix that when it brings him back?"

"I can make no promises. God will do what he will."

Yes, I suppose it is ever so.

Edina was vehemently against it. "You will be dragging him out of heaven," she cried. I dared not say that I might be dragging him out of hell since he died committing a crime.

"He will enter there again," I told her. "I need him by my side as we rediscover the promised land. God owes me that much."

Rayne took us and Tom's body to a high hill in the middle of the night. I forbade Edina to come to witness such a thing, but she said she wanted to be there for Tom if he returned, and for me should it fail. She did not want me to go through it alone, and she assured me she was feeling strong enough to climb the hill. We walked together slowly, her arm in mine, and did not speak, each thinking our own thoughts about our beloved son who would soon, God willing, be in our embrace once more.

With us was our sacrifice, a criminal plucked from the streets of Carson City by the Pale Horseman. Just by looking at him I could see he was a hot-tempered drunk, probably a robber and a rapist. The good people of Carson City should thank us for taking him off their hands.

Torches were set along the path and all around the circle where the ceremony would take place. A slab of marble had been brought up the hill earlier, and the men who were bearing Tom's body laid him gently upon it. The bullet hole in his head had been cleaned and bandaged and he'd been washed and dressed in clean clothes – his best suit, gray linen, finely tailored during a trip back east last year. His face looked so peaceful.

The sacrifice was brought forward, bound and gagged. He had been bathed and shaved and dressed in a white robe. He grunted and screamed, futilely, behind his gag, and struggled in the grip of two vampires. They were seemingly unbothered by his violent thrashing about and there was no danger he would escape their grasp. They forced him to his knees before Rayne, who was standing still as an oak tree, his eyes closed. He appeared to be in silent prayer or meditation.

When all were in position, Rayne opened his eyes. He pointed his staff to the sky and recited ancient, unknown words. The clouds directly above him parted and revealed the moon.

He turned his attention to the criminal before him. The man's eyes grew wide, and he struggled some more, but the vampires' grip did not falter.

Rayne knelt and picked up a blade at his feet. The sacrifice stopped his struggle, but I could see a wetness spread on his white robes as he pissed himself in fear.

Rayne's voice boomed out with one last incantation, then he raised his hand, the one holding the knife. With one swift, sure motion, he brought his arm down, slitting the man's throat.

As the man slumped, bleeding, to the dirt, Rayne slammed the base of his staff into the blood-soaked ground with great force and shouted into the sky. It was not his voice that poured forth, but an unearthly cacophony that sounded like a choir of demons speaking in unison!

Lightning shot from the tip of his staff into Tom's body, and it jerked and flopped around on the marble slab. This continued for several seconds, then the lightning stopped. Rayne, looking spent, fell to his knees.

Edina and I just stood there in horror and strangely hopeful anticipation. She gripped my arm with a strength that I could scarcely believe she possessed after her long illness.

The silence dragged on for what seemed like minutes but was probably only a few seconds. Then a deep groan came from Tom's mouth! His joints cracked; his tendons tightened in one great seizure. He writhed around on the table in what looked like horrible pain.

Tears streamed down Edina's face as she watched our son come back to life.

Then he became still and silent for a moment before taking a giant gasp of air. His eyes sprang open, and he sat up!

"Tom!" Edina cried with joy.

She tried to run toward him but I restrained her.

"Edina, wait!"

But her motherly concern could not be held back. Even with her body stricken with consumption, she found the strength to wrench herself from my grasp and ran to him.

Tom groaned and moaned and then tried to speak. All that came out were the sounds of a feral animal.

She flung herself onto the slab next to him and pulled him to her, hugging him to her bosom, sobbing and apologizing to him for what we – what I – had put him through.

Meanwhile, I was frozen where I stood, staring at the scene before me. This is what I had hoped for, but my joy was tempered by the feeling that it was wrong somehow. The glimpses I'd had of Tom's eyes were disquieting.

Tom's arms tightened around his mother. At first this looked like an expression of love, but then, to my horror, I saw that he was trying to crush her and his mouth grew wide as if to bite her! Rayne, who had regained his senses, lunged forward quickly and grabbed and restrained Tom before he could sink his teeth into Edina's shoulder. She fell back in terror and ran to me, and I caught her.

Tom snarled and snapped at Rayne, who was doing his best to hold him down. But Rayne, still weakened by the effort of the magic he had performed, was no match for Tom, who pushed him away and leapt off the table.

Rayne raised his scepter to perform some sort of magic to restrain Tom, but Tom attacked him before he could, clawing at Rayne's face with his hands, tearing deep scratches along his cheeks.

Gently releasing Edina from my arms, I pulled my pistol and shouted, "Tom!"

He stopped his attack on Rayne and turned towards me. For a moment there was a recognition in his eyes. He tried to speak and became frustrated when the words would not come. But then he gargled out, "Fa...Fa...Father."

He smiled. Not a smile of joy, but a manic grin. Drool came out of his mouth and he stumbled toward me. "Father...Father...Father," he said as he lurched ever closer. I had a momentary flash of memory, a tiny child taking his first steps toward my outstretched arms.

"Stay where you are, Tom," I said, holding my pistol up. "You have been through a great ordeal and you aren't yet yourself."

"Myself," he said. "Myself, myself. Not you!" He lunged at me and I had no choice but to fire my gun. It knocked him back, and he fell to the ground, but quickly got back up to continue the attack.

I fired again, but he kept coming. "Come...to...hell with me... Father!"

My gun was empty of bullets.

"Tom! No!" Edina yelled. He stopped his advance for a moment. He looked at her, confused, as if he was trying to access a deep memory but it would not come.

Then he lunged toward her.

I have always been decisive in my actions and in that moment I knew there was only one thing to do. Tom was never going to be himself again.

I took my gun by the barrel and smashed the butt into my son's head again and again. His skull split open and his brains spilt out before us. He dropped to the ground, twitched one last time and lay motionless, once again one of the still, silent dead.

Rayne scurried up to me, groveling. "I thought it would work. I didn't know he would come back wrong! I didn't know! I'm sorry."

"Clean up your mess," I ordered. I collected Edina, who was

trembling and staring at Tom's lifeless body. Witnessing our son come back as a ravening beast was almost too much for me; I can only imagine the effect it had on a woman of Edina's delicate sensibilities, and when she is so ill at that. She sobbed as I took her in my arms.

"We created an abomination," she said, her voice muffled against my coat. "Do you think God will forgive us for our hubris?"

"I am sure he will," I said, leading her down the hill. "All will be forgiven in the promised land."

The photograph of Tom that I carry with me is up on my desk as I write this, but I find I can hardly bear to look at it now and I have laid it facedown. My son, who I ruined. Can he pass the gates of heaven after what he became – what Rayne made him at my behest? I will not know until I get there myself.

TELEGRAM TO OSCAR WILDE FROM FLORENCE STOKER, 1ST OF OCTOBER 1882

=I need your help. Bram and Henry went west to help Roosevelt. Have not returned. Silly to worry but need a friend by my side. Can you come to Salt Lake City?=

FROM THE JOURNAL OF BRAM STOKER, 1ST OF OCTOBER 1882

1:15 p.m.

A horrible turn of events.

We are now both wanted men and have been forced to go on the run! Henry returned to Mound House yesterday morning to send a telegram, only to find a second wanted poster with his likeness on it plastered all over town. There were too many people around to glamour so he was unable to send the message.

I was unsure what our next steps should be. Henry can carry me at great speed, but only for short distances, certainly not all the way back to Salt Lake City. Should we try to walk to Carson City and attempt to sneak onboard a train back to Salt Lake? Henry had snatched a map off the wall of the telegraph office and we have been studying it to decide our best course of action in these unfamiliar circumstances.

We have concluded that our best option is to try to jump a freight train. There is a water stop marked on the map not too far from here and we will try to get on the train there. We aren't sure when a train will be by, or where it will take us, as the tracks branch off in several directions, but getting far away from the area seems like a good idea and our only option.

"You're going to need some water," Henry said. I did not hazard to ask him if he would need water as well, or blood, but both were a concern out in the middle of nowhere. As the water at the water station would most likely not be potable, we consulted our map.

"There is a river here," he said, pointing. "We will get water there then be on our way to the train tracks. We will follow them until the water stop or anywhere the train slows down enough to jump it. I suppose I could carry you on my back and we could jump onboard even if it were going at a decent speed."

It was more of a plan than I had, and we started our journey over rocky terrain.

At some point, we heard a rattling sound. It sent a primal fear into my heart, even though I had never heard the sound before. It was a snake! It rose up from its coiled position and bit Henry in the back of his calf.

He shook it off, and it slithered away.

"Can vampires be killed by snake venom?" I asked.

"Not sure. I guess we will find out. It doesn't hurt so I think that is a good sign."

I then wondered if a vampire snake was now slithering through the underbrush. Henry displayed no ill effects, and we moved on. It reminded me of what a dangerous land we were travelling through. Had that snake bitten me I would be dead by now.

"There are voices and the sound of work ahead," Henry cautioned. We climbed a nearby hill and down in a gully we saw men working at the opening of a mine. Timbers were holding up the entryway and men pushed out wheelbarrows of dirt. These were Chinamen, by the looks of them. Two white men on horseback were supervising the work.

It was then I noticed the men were walking in small steps. Their feet were secured in manacles with only about two feet of chain between them. They shuffled along, emptying dirt onto piles.

"This is barbaric!" I whispered. Henry nodded.

One of the white men on horseback had a whip he was using to threaten the Chinamen as he shouted abuse.

"I've seen faster tortoises! Get moving or get whipped!"

The miners looked up at him in anger but returned to their duties.

"We should do something," Henry said.

"We are hardly in the position to do anything," I pointed out. "There are two armed men, we have no weapons but a knife, and you are powerless in the daytime."

I was kicking myself for not taking the pistol Robert had offered me when we left. I had felt the threat was over and I was still shaken from just having killed a man. The last thing I wanted was that killing gun strapped to my side.

"They have food, water and horses," Henry said. "We are already on the run from the law. What's a little larceny?"

One of the men got off his horse and walked to the base of the hill, where he started relieving himself on the trunk of a tree. His friend continued on his way and started taking shots with his rifle at a rabbit that was running by.

We moved back to be out of sight, but unfortunately, that sent a stone rolling down the hill.

"Who's there?" the man at the bottom of the hill shouted.

We scurried behind some boulders as he came to the top of the hill with his pistol drawn. "I know you're behind those rocks. Come out with your hands up!"

I picked up a rock to arm myself.

Henry went around one side of the boulders with his hands up and sent me around the other side.

"What are you doing spying on us?" the man yelled at Henry. Then he laughed. "Why, ain't you dressed like a fancy gentleman."

"I am but a lost traveller," Henry said. The gunman apparently didn't know there were two of us, and I remained hidden with my rock at the ready.

"Lost claim jumper is more like it," the man said.

"Would an unarmed man be trying to take your gold?" Henry asked. I could tell he was trying to use his vampire glamour to bend the man's will but it wasn't working, probably due to the dark glasses he was wearing to be out in the sun.

"If'n you are without a gun it don't mean you ain't a scout sent to check us out," the man replied.

"I don't want any trouble," Henry said. "I will just be on my way."

"Oh, you will be on your way, all right," the man said with a cruel laugh. "You is on your way to meet your maker."

Those words sent a chill down my spine and I came rushing out from my hiding spot and threw my rock with great force at our assailant. The rock only grazed his shoulder; rather than eliminating the threat, I had only alerted him to my position.

In his surprise, he swung his handgun towards me and fired off a quick shot. The bullet ricocheted off the boulder just inches from my head. I threw my hands up and put my head down, waiting for the second bullet.

"Please, we just want to go in peace!" I shouted.

"Well, shit," he said.

I slowly looked up to see the ricocheted bullet had struck him in the chest. He was looking down at the blood soaking his shirt. He had a bewildered look on his face. "Don't even hurt."

I just stood there waiting to see if he was going to fire again. He dropped his gun and tried to stop the bleeding with both his hands. "It's bad, ain't it?" He dropped to his knees and looked up at me with eyes pleading for me to help him. He took off the kerchief around his neck and pressed that to the wound in a futile attempt to stop the gushing blood. He fell to the ground, gurgling his last breath.

His friend, who I had forgotten about, came roaring up the hill on his horse. I dived for the dead man's gun, grabbed it and fired it up at the approaching horseman.

My bullet went wide and missed the man, but his horse bucked wildly, throwing him off. The man fell, striking his head hard on a rock, and became the third man whose death I had caused in two days.

We went down to the workers and freed them.

It seems the men who enslaved them were digging for gold. The mine was tapped out weeks ago, yet they wanted the men they hired to keep digging. When the men refused they were forced to continue at gunpoint.

The men have left and taken the horses as we won't need them to jump the train.

We are in the mine owner's tent. When the sun sets, Henry will help me bury the bodies. I know I did not set out to kill these men, but I feel responsible nonetheless. I am happy we were able to free the Chinamen, but wish it could have been done without racking up two more deaths on this already bloody trip.

I found a letter one of the dead miners had started to a wife or sweetheart back home and wondered if she would ever learn that her man was dead. If we get out of this I will alert the authorities to look for the bodies. But first we have to clear our names.

I had a nice meal of beans and tinned peaches, and filled several canteens with water from the stream. Henry fed on the dead men.

We found one of the miners' logbooks, which says a train stops at the water stop on Thursdays and brings supplies to the miners. We will wait here until Thursday morning and jump that train.

TELEGRAM FROM OSCAR WILDE, ST. LOUIS, TO FLORENCE STOKER, SALT LAKE CITY, 1ST OF OCTOBER 1882

=On my way. Will arrive tomorrow. Sure it is nothing but better I am there if it isn't. Put on the tea and give Noel a kiss from Uncle Oscar=

FROM THE DIARY OF OSCAR WILDE, 3RD OF OCTOBER 1882

Dear yours truly

I have arrived in the Great Salt Lake City to a very distraught Florrie. She is beside herself, as Stoker and Irving have gone off to help the Roosevelts and have not returned. I cannot blame her for worrying; hunting vampires is a very risky hobby for a family man.

Little Noel was quite happy to see his Uncle Oscar, however. He's an exceptionally bright child – he must get it from his mother. He has taken to wearing a child-size Stetson hat and referring to everyone as 'pardner'. It is an utterly adorable habit that I do hope he tires of soon.

Florence had telegraphed Robert in Carson City and the reply came this morning. He says that Bram and Henry went ahead of them and he had assumed they'd caught the train to Salt Lake City days ago. Upon receiving Florence's telegram, he enquired at the railway station and found they had not returned to Carson City as was planned. They have vanished!

The authorities have been of little help and I find I must take matters into my own hands. It has become tiring saving Stoker's life so many times, but for the sake of Florrie and Noel, I must do it at least once more.

My plan is to go to Carson City by train and start the search there. Florrie insists on coming along and there is little I can do to dissuade her. She will leave Noel in Salt Lake City with the nanny while we undertake the search.

Though the Roosevelts are also searching, I have decided the best course of action is to hire our own tracker; after all, two heads are better than one. Florence has become fast friends with a woman, named 'Calamity Jane' of all things, who has a great deal of experience in the West. She has offered to make introductions to the 'best tracker in these here parts'.

The friendship between Florence and Jane is reminiscent of my friendship with Stoker, in that they could not be more different from one another. Florrie is elegant, refined and beautiful. (She is the 'me' in this regard.) She manages to dress and act the part of a lady even in the wilds of America. It should not surprise me in the slightest if, on some dusty trail in the days ahead, she opens her bag at half past three on the dot to pull out a silver teapot.

In contrast, Calamity Jane earns her name, as she is a disaster from head to toe. (In this, she is the epitome of Stoker.) She dresses as a man and has taken only the bad mannerisms from the masculine sex. Her hair is a tangled mess despite its short length. She wears buckskins that most likely did not flatter the animal when it was alive. When tobacco juice isn't coming out of her mouth, a string of obscenities is.

The fact that Florence has taken her under her wing is admirable, but a lost cause, I am afraid. In fact, at times I think Calamity is under the impression it is she who is taking Florence under *her* wing. Perhaps she is. The West can be a dangerous place and, say what I will about Calamity, she knows how to survive in a world like this.

In any event, it was kind of the Calamity to help us secure a proper scout.

She took us to a seedier part of town (which I did not think could exist, but there we were). After trotting around pig troughs and horse stables, we were led into a small squalid saloon, more of a shack, really. It had no door, so it was thick with flies and miscreants. The smell of horse manure from the street outside gave way to the odour of sweat, cheap whiskey and tobacco smoke as we moved further into the room.

I stayed close to Florence for her protection.

I followed Jane's eye to a table in the centre of the room, around which Negroes and Chinamen were playing cards. A well-dressed, handsome Negro was apparently winning, as he had all the poker chips in front of him. He was leaning back in his chair, his fancy cowboy boots on the table, his cards close to his vest. He was certainly a diamond in the rough. The other players were unwashed stable workers and labourers. This man was dressed as a proper cowboy and obviously had taken a bath recently. He had a thick, well-groomed moustache, a white cowboy hat with a silver band, and a turquoise bolo tie. He looked towards us and smiled.

"Well, if it ain't Calamity Jane herself," he said, taking his feet off the table and returning to an upright position. "I heard you were in town. What brings you to these parts?"

"Buffalo Bill has been dragging me all over the West," she said, then spat her wad of tobacco into the spittoon in the corner with impressive accuracy. She wiped the last of the tobacco juice off of her lip with her sleeve, then added, "You up for some tracking work, Bass?"

"Depends," he said. He put his cards down and they must have been good, for the others, grumbling, tossed their cards on the table. He gestured, and they got up and walked away as he pulled the remaining chips towards him.

"On what?" Jane asked.

"On who's offering the work and what needs tracking," he said, eyeing me and Florrie. I stepped forward.

"I am Oscar Wilde," I said. "Perhaps you have heard of me."

"I have," he said, to my relief. "I'm Bass Reeves." He stood to shake my hand. "This is the first time I have shaken the hand of a bona fide famous person."

I searched my memory. Was this the first time I had shaken the hand of a Negro? I had a Negro valet on my last tour of America, but I can't remember ever shaking his hand. I must have, certainly? I should feel ashamed of myself if I hadn't.

"I am pleased that you consider me famous and not merely notorious," I said. "And this is Florence Stoker."

He tipped his hat to Florrie. "Ma'am."

"We are in need of a tracker to find my missing husband and his employer," Florence said.

"Missing as in 'has run off', or missing as in properly lost?" he asked.

"Lost, surely," I said. I glanced over to Florrie to make sure.

"Yes, lost," she said, with more than a little irritation in her voice, directed at me. "They were part of a posse hunting down some outlaws, which they successfully did. They boarded a train on Thursday and did not get off at the end."

"Any reason you know of why they would jump off the train?"

"No. None that we know of," Florrie said.

"They got off somewhere between Virginia City and Carson City," Jane added. "Shouldn't be too hard to pick up the trail."

"Rough area, that," Bass said. "I charge ten dollars a day plus expenses. Eleven dollars a day if you tag along."

Florence turned to Jane. "Is that a fair price?" she asked coolly. She has become quite business-savvy in her travels in America, I must say!

"'Tis," Jane said. "Bass here was a United States Marshal. He is the best tracker I know, next to an Indian, and he comes with one of those." She pointed to the corner where an Indian woman was seated. She was so still and quiet I had not noticed her before, but I could see that she was watching us closely.

"My woman, Shada," Bass said. "She knows those parts pretty well and speaks more native languages than I do." He waved to her, and she came over to introduce herself.

She was tall and slim, with dark hair that hung down in twin braids. She was dressed in buckskins and adorned with a bead bracelet and matching bead necklaces that draped down her body and made a pleasing rattling sound as she walked over to us.

She looked me over and from my manner of dress must have assumed I was a diplomat, so she spoke to me in French. "It is very nice to meet you."

I responded in French and told her I thought she was very lovely, which made her blush. I then switched back to English.

"So how do these things work?" I asked Bass.

"I reckon we take the train to Virginia City, rent some horses and retrace their steps," he said.

I feel we are in very good hands and grow optimistic we will find Bram and Henry. I just hope they'll be alive and well when we do. Well, I suppose the best we can hope for is to find Bram alive, as Henry is one of the Undead.

So, dear diary, we are off to Virginia City.

FROM THE JOURNAL OF BRAM STOKER, 4TH OF OCTOBER 1882

12:14 p.m.

We were packing up the last of the miners' supplies this morning in preparation for jumping the freight train when, to our surprise, Liver-Eating Johnson found us in the gold miners' camp. I for one must commend the man's tracking skills.

"If I found you, the Pinkertons surely will," he said. "You ain't exactly making it hard."

He told us the Roosevelts are aware of the price on our heads and sent him to find us. They are going to see the territorial governor to secure us a pardon. Until then we are to stay with Johnson and he will smuggle us back into Utah.

It appears the man leading the train robbery – the human – was the son of a powerful mining baron named Drumpf. And furthermore, this Drumpf owns the law in the Nevada Territory, so going to the authorities is not an option. Apparently the only people more powerful in Nevada are the railroad tycoons. That would explain his need to rob the train.

What Drumpf wants with the book I do not know, but it cannot be good. I wish we had never found it, though for Henry's sake I suppose I should be glad. At least the White Worms aren't here in America to take it away from him this time.

We told Johnson of our plan to jump the train that would be by shortly.

"That train will just take you deeper into Nevada," he warned. "We have to get you out of the territory. The best place to go is Utah since Brigham Young has no love for Drumpf and won't let Drumpf send his private army in there to get you."

Johnson has taken us to a hunting cabin of his and it is quite well hidden in the hills. Tomorrow he will take us on the back trails to Salt Lake City. He assures us we will not run into trouble or the authorities on the way.

The cabin is small and poorly constructed. The wind blows right through several gaps in the walls. But it has a bunk and a stove for heat and cooking. Johnson brought some supplies – beans and carrots and a rabbit he shot along the way – so I will have something to eat. Henry says he will catch a squirrel or other small animal tonight, and that will suffice for him. He says the blood of an animal will quench his thirst but not his hunger. (I suppose it is for the good that he is more open with me about his ways, but confess that there are times when I do not need all the detail he provides.)

In our little hideaway, I have finally learned how Mr. Johnson (whose given name, I've learned, is Jeremiah) came to have such a colourful nickname.

He told us that in 1847, his wife, a member of the Flathead American Indian tribe, was killed by a young Crow brave and his fellow hunters. In his grief and rage, Johnson embarked on a vendetta against the Crow tribe. He claims to have killed and scalped more than three hundred Crow Indians and then devoured their livers. I doubt he could have really killed that many single-handedly, but then again to do that even once is appalling.

His selective cannibalism was not without reason, at least the reason of a madman.

Removing the liver is apparently an insult to the Crow because they believe that organ to be vital if one is to go on to the afterlife. As his reputation and collection of scalps and livers grew, Johnson became an object of fear among the Crow and other tribes of the area.

Eventually he realised that his actions were not bringing him peace. He searched his heart and finally stopped his mission of vengeance. He made peace with the Crow and his personal vendetta against them finally ended after twenty five years. He refers to them now as 'his brothers'. How they managed to forgive him I do not know. Perhaps, deep down, many of us know the pain of loss and understand the rage it can bring.

"Hate drove me insane," Johnson said. "Some say it may have turned me into a wendigo. I was a monster, all right." A tear actually came to his eye as he became lost in reverie. "It's a terrible thing to kill a man and not feel remorse. As awful as it feels, living with this regret and shame for what I did, it's better than feeling nothing, like I did before."

I was beginning to know what he meant. The longer I live with the killing of Drumpf's son, the further away the memory of it feels. It now seems like it was just something that happened and I feel my remorse slipping away. I know he was the instigator in his own death, but I still pulled the trigger. Not feeling bad about it makes me feel worse.

I pray when my time comes, God will understand and grant me mercy.

REPORT FROM AGENT ANNABELL CHARLEMONT

Date: 4 October 1882
Subject: Mrs. Stoker has left Salt Lake City

Mr. Stoker has failed to return from his mission to help the Roosevelts, and Mrs. Stoker has grown increasingly uneasy. She left Salt Lake City today with Oscar Wilde, Martha (Calamity) Jane Canary and trackers they hired to find them.

My attempts to dissuade Mrs. Stoker from undertaking this mission have failed. She is quite stubborn.

I have informed the North American office about these new events. Agent Chase has already left to track down Mr. Stoker and Mr. Irving. We know le Fey was aware of Mr. Stoker's destination, and I fear foul play. It may also be some other, previously unknown supernatural threat. It is also possible, of course, that they fell prey to some more mundane threat; the West is a dangerous place, after all.

In any case, I am certain that Agent Chase will get to the bottom of it. My sole duty now is to protect Noel and hope that the Stokers return safely.

—End Report—

TELEGRAM FROM ROBERT ROOSEVELT, CARSON CITY, TO FLORENCE STOKER, SALT LAKE CITY, 5TH OF OCTOBER 1882

=Bad news. Bram missing and wanted by the law. All a misunderstanding. On my way to governor to clear things up. This will delay our search for Bram. Do not worry=

Archivist's note: This telegram arrived after Florence Stoker had left Salt Lake City. Agent Charlemont was unable to reach her to relay the news.

FROM THE DIARY OF OSCAR WILDE, 5TH OF OCTOBER 1882

Dear yours truly,

We are in Virginia City and with still no word from Stoker and Irving we are going to 'hit the trail', as the cowboys say, and search for them. Noel did not appreciate being left behind with his nanny in Salt Lake City, and dear Florence was quite tearful at their parting but is determined to present a brave face and do all she can to find her husband and Henry.

We spent the night at a small hotel where we had a surprisingly tasty supper before retiring to rest up for the next leg of our journey.

This morning I met everyone at the livery stable where we were to secure horses. I was appalled to see my beautiful Florrie dressed by Calamity Jane!

She is actually wearing trousers! It is quite shocking to see the shape of her legs. She is also clad in a blue gingham shirt, which she does wear beautifully, but I am not sure if she is even wearing a corset and, of course, I am too polite to ask. Her cowboy boots are a necessity, I suppose, but an awful brown colour with no embellishments or embroidery. Why, Mr. Reeves's boots are more stylish. At least her cowboy hat matches her shirt, being white with a cornflower blue band.

"Well, look at the dandy fancy pants," Calamity said, eyeing me up and down.

I was wearing my white suit and Stetson, with a pink carnation and white leather riding boots. The last time I was this far west I found this to be an ideal outfit for being out in the sun, if that is what one must do.

"Being in the wilderness is no reason to dress like a savage," I told her. She just grunted and spat some tobacco juice in my direction, which fortunately missed its target.

She sniffed the air. "What is that smell?"

How she could smell anything over the manure was beyond me, but I informed her, "It is Acqua Classica cologne."

She gave me another sniff. "You smell like a piano player in a whorehouse."

She had no idea how close she was to the truth, as Derrick had held that position at one time (before I knew him) and this was his favourite cologne.

"And you smell like that piano player's socks," I countered with a wrinkling of my nose.

"I didn't say it was a bad smell, did I?" she said. "Just a bit too sweet for riding a sweaty horse is all. It's kind of nice, like a campfire of balsa wood. Might keep the flies away, I suppose. Away from me, I mean, as they'll all be swarming around you."

She patted my horse's side. I was to be riding a sturdy grey mare.

"You have over-packed this horse," she said. "It might buck you."

I, in fact, had packed very lightly. Only three suits, pyjamas, socks and undergarments. Two pairs of riding gloves, a wool hat should it get cold and six handkerchiefs. This wasn't my first rodeo, as the cowboys would say. I knew we were heading into the wilderness.

Shada was already on her horse, riding bareback. She was wearing a full-skirted buckskin dress quite nicely adorned with colourful beads and stitching. I was pleased to see that one does not have to wear store-bought clothes to look aesthetically pleasing and told her as much.

She thanked me and said, "You will blind the sun in that suit." I took this to be a compliment, although looking back on it I am not so sure.

With our horses rented, we trotted over to the mercantile to buy supplies, filled our canteens at the public pump, and were on our way.

Horses and I have always got along. You can tell them anything and they seldom judge you. I do so enjoy riding, and as we started down the trail I wondered why I don't do it more often.

Our first stop was to be the sleepy little village of Gold Hill, the first place Stoker and Irving could have got off the train. That is, if they weren't thrown off the train. I don't know why they would be, but with Stoker anything is possible.

We followed a trail along the railroad tracks. The surrounding countryside is dreadfully drab. In this country of spectacular vistas and natural beauty, leave it to Bram to get lost in the most boring place imaginable. Nothing but scrub brush and dirt as far as the eye can see. We are at a high elevation so the air is thin but cooler than one would expect for this time of year.

I am told we will see few Indians in the area, but will see plenty of coyotes and wild mustangs.

Of course, all I saw starting out was the rear ends of three horses ahead of me. Calamity was bringing up the rear and was quite drunk, having already consumed half a bottle of whiskey.

She was singing Western ditties. Her voice was as rough as the rest of her, but at least she was keeping the buzzards away.

"Come all you pretty girls, to you these lines I'll write,
We are going to the range in which we take delight;
We are going on the range as we poor hunters do,
And the tender-footed fellows can stay at home with you.
It's all of the day long as we go tramping round,
In search of the buffalo that we may shoot him down;
Our guns upon our shoulders, our belts of 40 rounds,
We send them up Salt River to some happy hunting grounds.
Our neighbours are the Cheyennes, the 'Rapahoes, and Sioux,
Their mode of navigation is a buffalo-hide canoe.
And when they come upon you they take you unaware,
And such a peculiar way they have of raising hunter's hair!"

Her singing was suddenly interrupted by a gunshot, which startled us all and our horses.

We turned to see she had a rifle in her hands. "Lunch!" she yelled. She jumped off her horse to retrieve a skinny hare in the brush. She examined the emaciated rodent. "This here is good eatin'."

"A little warning next time, Jane," Bass said.

"Oh, right. Sorry." She looped a rope around the dead animal and hung it from her saddlebag, then remounted her horse with a gracefulness I had not expected from her, especially in her inebriated state.

Bass looked off into the distance. "Gold Hill is just up ahead. Stay alert, the town is a tad bit rough. Let me do the talking. I don't expect to run into any trouble, but the locals don't take to strangers." I swear he looked at me as he said this, and I took some offence.

We trotted into town, which was only a single street lined with saloons and shops.

We stopped and dismounted. Bass made sure his marshal badge was visible and went into the small railway station to talk to the station agent while the rest of us watered the horses in a trough just outside. The sun was getting higher, and we were getting hotter. I fanned myself with my hat.

A gang of dusty miners and cowboys were glancing at us and muttering among themselves. After a moment, they made their way towards us. Not knowing their intent, I stepped in front of Florrie to offer my protection. Jane was also at the ready, her hand inching closer to the pistol in her holster.

They surrounded us.

"Hey, fancy boy," one of them said to me. "Aren't you that Oscar Wilde fella?"

Even out here I am recognised! Had I visited this place before? I did not think so.

I stood a bit taller. "Why, yes, I am."

"I like your chewing tobacco," he said, pulling a pouch from his pocket and holding it up. To my astonishment and horror, it had my likeness on it! A crude caricature, to be sure, but most definitely me, in a top hat and tails, standing before a rapt audience. (Well, at least they got that part right.)

More people started to join the crowd, as I suppose my presence was the most interesting thing to happen there in some time.

"My wife uses your bosom cream," another man shouted from the back. "It don't do shit!" The crowd laughed and, to my consternation, so did Jane. Even Florrie was smiling. Shada, however, was becoming uneasy at the gathering throng and had the good sense to hide behind the horses.

A woman pushed her way through the crowd, a shopkeeper by the looks of her, and pushed a small book into my hand. Why, it was my book of poems!

"Could you sign this for me, Mr. Wilde?" She handed me a pencil.

"Why certainly, I should be delighted. To whom should I make it out, my dear?"

"Etta Mae," she said, blushing.

Despite the crude advertisement – for which I was not even being paid – I was elated to see my fame had permeated into the deepest backwater of America, as had been my intent. All the interviews, the lectures and distribution of my photos had paid off more than I could have ever expected.

Others came up with things for me to sign – the tobacco pouch was the most common object offered.

Bass came out of the train depot office and I could see he was concerned about the mob. He put his hand on his revolver, but did not draw when he saw I had taken charge of the situation with my wit and charm.

"Would you like me to sign your wife's bosom?" I shouted to the man at the back. The crowd found this very amusing.

Unfortunately, I could not hold everyone's attention.

"Hey, boy!" a particularly grimy miner called to Mr. Reeves. "You that marshal from Arkansas? I can't believe they let one of your kind wear a badge."

Reeves kept his hand on his six-shooter. "The name is *Mr.* Reeves," he said, his voice unwavering. The gun remained in its holster, but the look he gave the miscreant clearly said he would use it if necessary.

"Meant no offence," the man said, turning his stare to his boots.

A loud steam whistle went off in the distance, calling the miners back to work, and the crowd thinned and then completely dissipated as the thrill of meeting me came to an end.

"Station agent says they got off here to buy some food and then got back on the train," Reeves said. "Looks like we are going on to the next stop in Mound House."

So it was back on our horses. I must admit, the thrill of the trail was already starting to wear thin as I was beginning to feel a bit saddle-sore.

As we rode on to our next stop, we passed through a most shocking landscape. The land was even more barren here. Everything was dead, the green scrub brush now white, the air eerily free of bird or insect.

Bass stopped. "Put a handkerchief over your mouths," he ordered. He poured water on his and wrung it out. Then he tied it bandit-style across his face. We all did the same.

"Comstock Merger Mill," Bass said, pointing to a group of sprawling buildings in the distance. "They use cyanide to process silver and gold. It poisons the land. Best to get out of the area as fast as we can. But not too fast, as to kick up as little dust as possible."

He gave his horse a little tap of his heels and set a cantering pace, and we rode steadily across the barren land. I rode up next to him and asked, "Will the horses be all right?"

"If we don't linger too long," he said. "We'll be out of here soon enough, and they're hardier than we are."

He was right; we soon passed out of the dead landscape and into the one that was merely bleak.

Now, with the poisoned earth far behind us and the sun setting, we have made camp.

We built a fire and Jane roasted her hare, while the rest of us cooked beans and bacon and opened tins of peaches.

A canopy of stars shines above us and once again my thoughts turn to our missing comrades. And cabernet. Yes, a nice bottle of cabernet would improve the evening immeasurably.

FROM THE JOURNAL OF FLORENCE STOKER, 5TH OF OCTOBER 1882

My fret about Bram is eased some now that our search is underway. At least I am doing something. Oscar and I have assembled an excellent search party, including a former U.S. Marshal named Bass Reeves and his Indian wife, Shada – a skilled tracker in her own right. Calamity Jane rounds out the group, which gives me great comfort as she certainly knows her way around 'these here parts', as she would say.

We know that Bram and Henry were alive and well as of four days ago, and on the train leaving Gold Hill. This gives me hope, though where they have gone after that is a mystery. Perhaps on one of Henry's side trips to talk to a shaman or investigate a possible entrance to the Realm, but it is difficult for me to believe that Bram would have gone along on such a journey. And if he did, he would have cabled to tell me where they were going and that they would be longer than anticipated, especially now that telegraph stations are so readily available.

We are bedding down for the night near a tranquil river. It is a clear, cool night and the stars are amazingly bright. Such an open sky here. I can hear coyotes calling to each other in the distance, a sad and lonely song. I would find it all a glorious adventure were we here under happier circumstances.

Now that I am here in the actual wilderness, I feel foolish that I feared travelling west of the Mississippi. Even our most remote tour stops were all more civilised than I was led to believe. I know now that Indian attacks are a thing of the past and were a rare event even in older times.

A herd of wild mustangs is nearby, on the other side of the river. We watched fifteen horses with brown and white coats feeding on tumbleweed and grass among the rocks. "They usually spook so close to people," Mr. Reeves said. "You must have a calming effect on them, Mrs. Stoker."

Shada waded across the river and was able to get close enough to one to offer it an apple, which it gratefully accepted.

"Don't rile them up, Shada," Mr. Reeves warned. "We don't want a stampede to ruin our lovely picnic spot."

When we built a fire, the mustangs moved further away, but still remained close enough that we could see them nuzzling and playing with one another. Such magnificent creatures.

After a few complaints from her fellow travellers, Jane agreed to take a bath and wash her clothes. "I bathe enough when I'm doing the Wild West show. Buffalo Bill makes me do it once a week," was one of her more colourful excuses for neglecting her hygiene. Thank goodness she acquiesced, as we are sharing a tent.

When she returned from her bathing spot downstream, Oscar commented that she is actually attractive with a layer of dirt taken off her. "Why, Jane," he said, "you have blonde hair. I honestly did not realise until you washed it." In response, she just spat tobacco juice in his general direction.

I lent her a nightshirt as her clothes are drying by the fire. "No need to fuss over me," she protested, as I brushed the tangles out of her short hair.

"It will just take a minute, no trouble at all," I said. When I finished, she ran her hands through her hair.

"Dang, you are as good as one of them fancy barbers in Deadwood."

Oscar was in his tent writing in his journal and Bass and Shada had bedrolls unfurled by the fire.

They are so affectionate and attentive with one another; it makes me envious. I wish Bram and I could be that way again.

I asked them how they met.

"I had given up my marshalling days and settled down on a farm in Arkansas. Then my wife run off so I sold the farm and became a peace officer in the Indian territory in Oklahoma. There was a band of Apache horse thieves that was terrorising the area. When we caught up with them I discovered they had kidnapped a passel of women from the Salish Flathead Tribe. Shada was one of them."

She hugged his arm and rested her head on his shoulder. "My hero," she cooed.

She told me her people are from Oregon and don't much like the desert we were travelling through. Her tribe was once very large, but they had been mostly wiped out by the U.S. Cavalry to make way for settlers. Only small groups remained, scattered throughout the West.

"I don't know where my family is," she said. "Someday I will find them again."

I found this unspeakably sad. I do not see my family often, but I know where they are and we write many letters back and forth. To not know where they are and be essentially alone in this vast, strange, wild land would terrify me. I was glad that Shada had Bass to rely on and be her family now.

I was also surprised to learn Bass had once been a slave. I don't know why it surprised me so much, except he doesn't strike me as a man who carries that horrible past with him.

"Back in Arkansas, I was the personal valet to Colonel George R. Reeves during the War. One night he was really drunk and angry the war was not going well. In a fit of rage directed at me and all my kind he took a riding crop to me like I was a horse."

I gasped.

"I'd been beaten before, of course." (How matter-of-factly he said it!) "I was the same age as Colonel Reeves's son, and when we were children he'd blame me for anything that might get him in trouble. I took many a whupping that was rightly his. Even as an adult, it wasn't unusual to be punished for no other reason than that Reeves wanted to be sure I knew my place. I finally couldn't take any more of it. I tore that riding crop right out of the colonel's hand and beat the tar out of him. Years of rage just flowed out of me through my arm and into that crop. I can't say I feel sorry about it either. The best part was the look in the colonel's eyes. He just couldn't believe it was happening. He was not a man accustomed to being stood up to, especially by a slave."

He paused for a moment, and I realised I was holding my breath and my hand was clapped over my mouth in shock as I listened to his story. I hoped he didn't think I was appalled at *his* actions. "Well," I said, "I am certainly glad you were able to provide him with that new experience. It must have been dangerous, though. If you'd been caught they would have killed you, wouldn't they?"

"Oh yes," he said. "Slowly and painfully. The moment I'd struck the last blow I ran for my life. I fled north to the Indian Territory, and the Cherokee took me in as one of their own. I've had my ups and downs since then, but at least I'm a free man."

He changed the subject then, asking about me and Bram, and I told them how we had met.

"So you was betrothed to Mr. Wilde and Mr. Stoker stole you away?" Jane asked. "I have to meet this man!"

"He hardly stole me," I protested. "I had a say in the matter."

"And yet Mr. Wilde still helps you," Shada said. "He is a good man."

"Yes, a very good friend," I said. I could see his silhouette cast on the tent by the kerosene lamp as he briskly wrote in his journal. I thought about how people often underestimate Oscar. Perhaps I myself am guilty of taking him for granted.

We said our goodnights and settled down in our tent. I snuffed out the lamp.

"Miss Florrie," Jane said, "I'm sorry your man done run off. If I was him, nothing would keep me from your side."

"He did not run off," I said, more than a little tersely. I was beginning to wonder myself if he had.

"I meant no offence," she said. "I just meant I think you are a kind and beautiful woman is all."

"Thank you," I said. "I like you too, Jane."

"Goodnight," she said. "I apologise now should I fart in my sleep."

"Apology accepted."

FROM THE JOURNAL OF BRAM STOKER, 5TH OF OCTOBER 1882

6:00 a.m.

Johnson left at sunrise to hunt. I have spent the time studying his maps, in anticipation of the journey ahead of us back to Salt Lake City. It is a long distance, but Johnson says we only need to get over the Utah border to be safe from Drumpf's detectives. Once there, we can resume travel by stagecoach and train.

Henry is asleep. Learning how my employer sleeps is certainly not the worst aspect of our current predicament, but it is on the list, for it is a disturbing sight. He lies flat on the hard floor, no pillow under his head. By all appearances, he looks dead. You see no rising and falling of his chest. He is very still with his hands crossed over his heart. Had you come across a corpse that looks like this, you would think rigor mortis had set in. When he is in this state, his skin becomes even paler and translucent. You can see blue veins prominently under his waxy skin.

At home, he prefers to sleep in a box of damp dirt. He cannot explain why, but he is compelled to do so. He told me this as we were preparing for the tour. He was glad to have a theatre manager who knew his secret so that I could arrange to have his box discreetly shipped with the rest of our equipment and supplies, and he could sleep comfortably with a minimum of fuss or questions.

Now that we're on the run, of course, he must make do. The arid dirt here offers him little comfort, and he prefers to sleep on the hard wood of the floor.

He has told me that he does not dream and is always aware of what goes on around him as if he is watching from afar.

5:15 p.m.

(At least I think that's the time; I have forgotten to wind my pocket watch.)

We are out of the frying pan and into the fire now. We have been captured by Pinkerton agents.

It was high noon and Henry was asleep when there was a light knock on the cabin door. So light I did not think to be startled by it.

I peered out through the window (which was covered with newspapers) and saw a tall, auburn-haired woman standing there. She was dressed in a fashionable suit, practical yet still feminine. She must have seen my eye peeping through the tear in the newspaper as she smiled and waved to me.

Again, no fear in my heart. It was just an odd sight to see a refined woman standing at the door of a cabin in the middle of nowhere.

I opened the door, assuming her to be an acquaintance of Johnson's, perhaps a neighbour from a nearby homestead.

"Mr. Stoker, I presume," she said, in a friendly tone.

"Yes, h-how...may I help you?" I stammered.

"My name is Cora Chase. I'm afraid I am here to arrest you on behalf of the Governor of the Nevada Territory."

Henry had awoken and come to the door.

"Ah, and this must be Mr. Henry Irving," she said. "He too is under arrest." She pulled back the lapel of her jacket to reveal a badge. "I am a Pinkerton detective and this cabin is surrounded by six armed agents."

We just stood there, dumbfounded.

"I thought it best to give you a chance to come along peacefully," she said, producing two sets of handcuffs from her pockets. "If you would be so kind as to hold out your wrists."

We did not immediately comply. I was still processing the situation and Henry was no doubt thinking we could rush and subdue her.

Before we could act she said, "No sudden moves, please. We do not wish to kill you." She then shouted, "Let them know we mean business, boys."

Pistol shots were fired into the air all around us.

In the broad daylight, there was little Henry could do to get us out of this predicament, but he did try.

"You *shall* let us go," he commanded, staring deeply into her eyes.

"Not my job," she said, grabbing Henry's wrists and closing the handcuffs around them. "That is up to a judge in Carson City."

"Doesn't work on everybody," Henry mumbled to me, as she handcuffed me as well.

After a search of the cabin and our satchels, they kindly let us gather our things as best we could with our hands chained.

"How ever did you find us?" I finally had to ask.

"Johnson turned you in for the reward," she said.

I felt immediately foolish for trusting a cannibal with our lives. He was not with the Roosevelts out of any sense of duty to protect the world from vampires, but merely for his own mercenary ends. Was it any wonder that once his payday with them was coming to an end that he would immediately find alternative employment?

They marched us about a mile down a trail to where a stagecoach was waiting.

Once inside, she sat in the seat across from us. Two agents were up top and more ahead and behind the coach on horseback.

"You are very lucky we found you first," she said. "If Drumpf's men had found you, I'm sure they would have brought you straight to him, and it is unlikely you would have emerged from that encounter alive."

"The men we killed were robbing a train—"

She held up her hand to silence me. "If that is the case, it will all be worked out in Carson City. I assure you, Mr. Stoker, the president himself is interested in ensuring that justice is done in this matter. We just need to do things by the book and try not to ruffle the feathers of the richest man in the West."

My hopes were raised slightly by these words. Maybe our day in court could straighten it all out.

"We might as well get comfortable. It is a long way back to Carson City."

"If this is a federal matter," said Henry, "could you not instead bring us to Salt Lake City, outside of Drumpf's sphere of influence?" I could tell he was again trying to use his vampire powers to influence her.

She merely smiled and pulled out a novel, *The Merry Adventures of Robin Hood*, and started to read it.

I asked if I could have my hands free to write in my journal. She agreed to keep me cuffed to the stagecoach door with one hand while freeing the other to write. And here we are.

FROM THE DIARY OF OSCAR WILDE, 6TH OF OCTOBER 1882

I am never free of monsters, dear diary, and tonight I once again might be dead were it not for Florrie's quick thinking.

I had awakened in the middle of the night from a troubling dream I could not recall. The feeling of unease from the dream was difficult to shake off, and the confines of my tent were too much for me to bear. I quickly exited into the fresh air and wide-open space of the night.

Needing to relieve myself, I looked for an appropriate place to do so. I went quite a way downstream from the camp and found a nice, private boulder where I was happily answering nature's call when I heard hushed voices.

Though it was very dark, I could see two silhouettes on the riverbank. Straightaway I recognised Florrie and momentarily thought the other to be Calamity, but the silhouette was too tall.

"Don't hurt the others," I heard Florrie say, and my heart started to race as the other figure moved into a beam of moonlight and I saw it was le Fey!

She was dressed in Western riding garb and a long flowing cloak that flapped gently in the breeze.

I didn't have my gun on me, being only in my silk pyjamas, and feared any movement back towards my tent would alert le Fey to my presence. I just froze, standing there with pyjama bottoms around my ankles.

"It is only you that I want," le Fey said, stroking Florrie's hair. "Take off that silver cross you are wearing, look into my eyes and become mine and I will let the others live."

I knew there was no time to waste. I hoisted up my trousers, grabbed a rock from the ground and charged towards the riverbank to save Florrie!

I am ashamed to say, in my haste I had not tied my pyjamas properly and they came down, tripping me and sending my rock flying.

A startled le Fey hissed at me and put Florrie in front of herself as a shield against my failed attack.

"Run, Oscar," Florrie pleaded. She said it quietly, I suspect not wanting to wake the others. I was flat on my face and in no position to run. I staggered to my feet and pulled up and secured my pyjamas.

Then I noticed there was a second woman in the shadows; she was almost invisible as she was wearing a black nun's habit. She came to le Fey's side, baring her fangs.

"I should kill you for shooting me, Wilde," le Fey said. "However, I saw your play's opening night in New York, and I enjoyed it very much. I think I will let you live to write another day." (Was I wrong to feel pride in that moment?)

Our horses were nearby and I could hear they were becoming agitated; Florrie seemed to notice too. "Oscar, please, don't wake the others." The others were sleeping far enough away they might not hear us, but should the horses start bucking and whinnying at the presence of vampires, they just might hear that.

Florrie then, in one quick motion, yanked the silver cross from around her neck and pressed it onto le Fey's hand. Le Fey let go in pain and Florrie ran into the river.

The two vampires made a move towards her and then stopped. They seemed to be afraid of the water. Was there silver in it? During our fight against the Black Bishop, our vampire expert, Dr. Hesselius, told us vampires can't cross running water, but surely that couldn't be true. How would they get anywhere?

I took that moment to run into the water as well, just as Florrie had made her way to the other bank and I lost her in the darkness.

The vampires were very agitated, hissing and growling, revealing their true animal natures. Then le Fey took a few steps back and leapt high into the air and over the river to the other side. The other vampire did the same.

I saw Florrie emerge from the shadows. She was running towards the wild mustang herd, causing them to disperse. The vampires again stopped. The horses had let Florrie pass but now were regrouping and blocking the vampires' path.

The vampires froze, seemingly as afraid of the horses as the horses were of them.

In a burst, the horses charged and swarmed the vampires!

I just stood there, up to my waist in the cold water, not believing what I was seeing. The mustangs were ferociously rising up, pummelling the vampires into the ground, kicking and stomping them in a cloud of dust and fury! After a few minutes, the horses ran off away from me and the river, leaving the vampires crumpled and broken on the ground.

I finished wading across the river to the other side as Florrie came out of the dust and up to the crumpled bodies with a sturdy stick in her hand. The vampires were both alive and starting to heal and pick themselves up. (You have to admit, vampires are a very hardy kind of monster.)

"I have had enough of you and your kind," Florrie said as she staked le Fey's companion in the back, who exploded in the gory fashion the young ones are known to do.

Le Fey was struggling to get to her knees. Florrie pushed the stake towards her and le Fey caught it with one hand. Her other arm was still healing and hung limply at her side.

"Please don't," she pleaded with Florrie. "I can give you so much."

"You have nothing I want," Florrie said.

The vampire must have still been weakened by the horse attack. Florrie mustered all her strength and the stake continued its journey into le Fey's heart. I heard her body explode with that all too familiar splooshing sound the younger vampires make when staked through the chest.

Florrie calmly walked into the river and washed off the blood. It wasn't until she got closer that I could see she was trembling, and not just because of her wet skin and the cold night air.

The others had awakened in all the commotion and were running towards us.

"What's going on?" Calamity yelled.

"Mustangs stampeded," Florrie said.

"Are you two okay?" Mr. Reeves asked, helping Florrie out of the water.

"Yes," I said. "Just shaken."

I assumed that since Florrie had dealt with the vampires, there was no need to worry the others by telling them about it.

We dried ourselves by the fire, then said our goodnights to the others.

"I have no idea how she called me out to her," Florrie said as I walked her to her tent. "I just found myself standing before her."

"They have ways of getting into your head after they bite you," I told her.

I then confided in Florrie that after the night's terror I would be sleeping outside the tent as my claustrophobia was in full swing. I confessed all about my fear of tight spaces.

"After I almost died giving birth to Noel you know how melancholy I was. I think such things imprint on us and change us."

I enquired if she would have trouble sleeping after the night's trauma.

"I am going to sleep like a baby," she said in a surprisingly cheerful tone. She gave me a kiss on the cheek and entered her tent. It seems we can add another Stoker to the monster-killing business.

LETTER FROM ALEJO 'LOBO' LOPEZ TO LUZ LOPEZ, 6TH OF OCTOBER 1882

Dear Luz,

Today I witnessed first-hand the power that the Prophet Rayne possesses. As of late, he has confided in me that he and Mr. Drumpf are being tormented by creatures he calls 'the Dark Watchers'.

Tribes in this region talk of these creatures, but I had believed them to be only myths. When Rayne said he needed to banish them from the earth and that he'd found a way to do so, I thought it was a waste of time to bow to such superstition.

Shortly before sunset today he brought a select few of us to a large open field to witness a ceremony. Scrubby patches of grass dotted the ground and a large hare scampered away, startled at our approach. I know from my travels in the area that the Walapi tribe used this field to cremate their dead, and at the centre of the field was a large, scorched rock.

Rayne was dressed in his priestly robes and carried his golden sceptre that is adorned with a green jewel on its top.

The Prophet climbed to the top of the scorched rock, and suddenly my scepticism fell away as Dark Watchers appeared all around us! A dark shadow circled us like a cloud of smoke. From inside the smoke, we could make out the silhouettes of dark, featureless men, their eyes glowing red. The harder you looked at them, the less you could see them.

They talked in hushed whispers and we could not make out what they were saying. I had a terrible fear that they would attack us at any moment and only Rayne's magic kept them at bay. He waved his sceptre and shouted words in a language I could not understand.

A young gringo, a horse thief named Simon who the Pale Horseman had captured just for this purpose, was dragged forward to the rock by two of Drumpf's men. His hands were bound and he had been dressed in a long white robe. Rayne climbed down from his perch and pushed Simon to his knees before him. Rayne placed his hand on the gringo's shoulder and spoke to him in a voice too quiet for me to hear. He pulled the young man to his feet.

Rayne produced a curved knife from under his robe.

He held the knife aloft in his right hand and the sceptre in his left. He closed his eyes and chanted words in that unfamiliar language. Simon, panicking now, struggled, but was held firmly in place by Drumpf's men. This went on for no more than a minute.

Rayne stopped speaking, drew a long breath and opened his eyes. He turned his head from side to side, taking in the Dark Watchers still circling around us. Their whispers grew more intense.

Then Rayne turned to Simon and, with one more whispered word, stabbed him under the chin with a hard thrust. He drew the blade all the way down to the man's genitals in one swift motion. His magic must be powerful indeed, for he had the strength to slice through bone as he dragged the knife through the man's chest. From where I stood I could hear ribs cracking with a muffled, wet snap and the rush of gurgling air as a lung was punctured.

Simon's eyes were wide and his mouth was gasping soundlessly. He remained standing for a moment as his entrails spilt out and the gathered witnesses gasped.

The young man collapsed to the ground still alive and writhing, but in mere moments he grew still. Then a blinding white light emanated from his body and shot into the stone at the top of the Prophet's sceptre! Rayne appeared to be bracing himself, as though he were being buffeted by a strong wind, though I could feel not so much as a breeze on the hot desert air.

When the light had all been absorbed by the green stone, Rayne lifted the sceptre and slammed its bottom point into the ground. A circle of white light exploded, shooting out like ripples in a pond and passing through us. When the wave reached the Dark Watchers, they disappeared in a puff of smoke. I could still hear the echoes of their whispers for a moment as the smoke dissipated, then there was silence.

We stood for a moment, then bowed down before Rayne. I had tears in my eyes as he walked through the crowd, touching us each upon the shoulder as he passed, and made his solitary way back to his quarters.

Luz, when the light passed through me, I felt a joy I did not know was possible. I know now that Rayne is a true disciple of God and he has the power to rid the world of darkness. But at what cost? Simon could not have been more than twenty five years old – is that an acceptable price to banish the Dark Watchers?

I have much to ponder, my brother.

Lobo

FROM THE DIARY OF OSCAR WILDE, 6TH OF OCTOBER 1882

In the West they say there is nothing lower than a horse thief. I can now attest to that from personal experience.

We were having breakfast before hitting the trail. Florrie had possessed the good sense to bring along some quite good tea, and though we had no eggs we at least had bacon. As I was taking my last sip, we were confronted by bandits!

Three men dressed in black with bandanas tied around their faces emerged suddenly from a nearby stand of trees, their guns drawn.

Mr. Reeves and Calamity Jane instinctively reached for their sidearms.

"I would not move if I was you," one of the miscreants said, with his gun pointed at the back of Florrie's head.

Reeves and Calamity put their hands down slowly to their sides.

"We're just here for the horses," another one said, untying my mount from a tree. "No one has to get themselves hurt."

The one standing behind Florrie, a lean and grizzled sort with sharp, cruel eyes, ran his free hand through her hair. "Well, maybe the horses ain't the only things we is here for."

I could see the look of terror in Florrie's eyes. My heart was pounding so I knew hers must be too. The sight of that smelly man touching her was almost too much to bear.

"Now, we might have some trouble if you're thinking of taking anything else," Reeves said calmly. "Just take the horses and go, and we can all part ways friendly like."

The bandit leaned in close to Florrie's ear and said, "Tell your boy to shut his mouth."

"I ain't nobody's boy and I think a few horses is a good day's work, don't you? I'm pretty handy with a gun, and so is my friend

Calamity Jane here," he said, with a slight tilt of his head in her direction. "Why take a chance that one of us can outdraw you?"

"You'se Calamity Jane?" the one untying the horses asked, with some fascination in his voice.

"What other woman do you know who is as ugly?" Calamity said. "And is so very fast on the draw."

The third man must have been in charge. "Come on," he barked, and the man behind Florrie gave her hair a quick, vicious tug, then backed away.

"It was nice doin' business with ya," he said.

They led the horses away and Jane stood up and drew her gun. Reeves shook his head 'no', and she re-holstered it.

"We don't know if they got more men waiting out of sight. It's not worth dying over some horses that ain't even ours."

I went over to Florence and put my arm around her shoulders, but she shrugged me off. "I'm fine," she said, but when she reached up to repin her hair, I could see that her hands were trembling.

"Let's pack up our things," said Shada. "The trip will take longer now that we're on foot. No sense putting it off."

We all started gathering our belongings. I could see that it helped Florence to have something practical to do.

"Those bastards stole my rifle and a half a bottle of whiskey!" Calamity clamoured. "That's what I get for packing up early."

Thank goodness most of my clothes were in my tent. The lowlifes managed to get only one of my suits and a book of poetry by yours truly. I hope they read it and it can bring them some culture, perhaps inspire them to stop their thieving ways.

Unfortunately, without horses, I was forced to leave some of my things behind. I decided I could live without pyjamas and most of my extra handkerchiefs, socks and pants. I stuffed my remaining suit, the wool hat and two handkerchiefs – and you, of course, dear diary – into a saddlebag, which I slung over my shoulder. Shada tied a frying pan to one of the saddlebag's straps, as of course, we must all take some of our communal equipment if we wish to eat and drink at our next stop. The pan bounces behind me as we walk, and I am certain to have a large bruise on my backside.

So, now we are forced to walk across the desert all the way to our next stop. We have stopped for a brief rest. Reeves tells us it is still a good 10 miles to our destination! Oh, the things Stoker puts me through. I suspect we will find him in Mound House taking a bath and sipping a whiskey, totally unaware of the trouble and worry he has put upon us.

Still, stiff upper lip and all that. Luckily I retained my parasol to protect myself from the sun, and I have my cowboy boots, which will keep rattlesnakes from biting me on the ankle. Break time is over. Off we go!

FROM THE JOURNAL OF FLORENCE STOKER, 6TH OF OCTOBER 1882

My feet are throbbing. We are forced to continue our journey to Silver City on foot this morning as our horses were stolen at gunpoint. I should not complain, I suppose. I had made up my mind to experience the real Wild West, and I am certainly doing so.

I must admit that I am still full of confidence and bravado after killing le Fey and her minion. I feel closer to Bram somehow. The whole ordeal was both terrifying and exhilarating. More importantly, I feel as though I can take care of myself, and Noel, whenever I get back to him.

I'm afraid Oscar is still shaken from the attack last night and a second attack by bandits did not put him in a better mood. Not to mention, I wonder if he is capable of walking the rest of the way. He has put on a few pounds as of late and he is hardly dressed for a hike, especially in this hot desert with very little shade.

We stopped for a moment because Oscar's boot became stuck between two rocks. Shada and Jane were assisting in freeing his foot.

"I'm sorry this happened, ma'am," Mr. Reeves said to me.

"It certainly isn't your fault, Mr. Reeves," I said.

"I feel like it was. In the old days, I could have dropped them boys. I'm losing my nerve in my old age."

He didn't appear to me to be older than thirty five, and I said so.

"You are kind, but I am older than that. Bringing in criminals is hard on a man. I am grateful to be doing a simple search and rescue."

"It hardly feels simple to me," I said. "It is my fault we are on this search and rescue. In fact, I feel like the responsibility for everything that happens on this journey lies with me. I will feel very foolish indeed if Bram and Henry are safe and I just missed their telegram saying they're going off on a side trip before returning to Salt Lake City."

"I think you are right to be worried, ma'am. Nothing about this feels right somehow."

Oscar's boot was now free, and we resumed our march.

"I feel like I took this job under false pretences," Mr. Reeves said to me quietly, as we walked along.

"Oh?"

"Truth is, I had given up being a marshal because I nearly died doing it. The last criminal I brought in got the drop on me. He filled me with six shots of lead and left me for dead."

"Oh, heavens," I exclaimed.

"As you can see I recovered," he said. "But I ain't the gunslinger I once was. A thing like that makes a man lose his nerve. These days fear keeps my gun in my holster a little too long, and that can make me a liability. I hope a time doesn't come when you need my gun and I'm slow to pull it. Like this morning."

"Well, I for one am glad it didn't turn into a shootout," I said. "We could have all been killed! Horses can be replaced. No, Mr. Reeves. It was not nerves that stayed your hand this morning. It was logic."

I write this as we have stopped to rest in the shade of a water tower. If we can acquire horses in Silver City, we should be in Mound House within the next few hours. According to the Roosevelts it was the last place Bram and Henry were seen. This is just a little setback and nothing we can't overcome.

FROM THE DIARY OF OSCAR WILDE, 6TH OF OCTOBER 1882

I don't believe it! We trudge into Silver City, hot and exhausted, and what is the first thing we see? A wanted poster with Bram's ursine face on it!

He and Irving are apparently wanted for murder, of all things. It must be why they have disappeared into the wilderness: they have a price on their heads.

I know I should expect these things from Stoker, but not even my fruitful imagination could have guessed at this.

"Oh dear," was all Florence could manage to say after seeing her beloved's visage with a bounty upon it.

Mr. Reeves took the poster down. "They could be anywhere by now," he said. "I'll go have a talk with the sheriff. I'll flash my marshal's badge, see what he knows. Why don't you all get some lunch at the hotel and I will meet you there shortly."

"Well, now at least we know why they haven't contacted me," Florrie said.

Silver City is a small community, but reasonably bustling. Its main thoroughfare is short and dusty, with several businesses lining it: a general mercantile, a post office and a hotel, as well as less savoury establishments; I saw several rough-looking saloons and at least two brothels. At the end of the street, I could see the railway station where Bram and Henry must have disembarked from their train, never to return. (Goodness, that does sound final, diary. I do not mean it like that.)

Shada, Calamity, Florrie and I went to the hotel, which really was more of a saloon with rooms upstairs, for a bite to eat. There were no tablecloths, the decor was non-existent, and the menu limited, but it was clean (mostly) and I could sit on a chair rather than a rock, and at the moment that was enough for me.

The food was uninspired but serviceable. I had the roast chicken and potatoes, with a bland and lumpy gravy. While Shada, Calamity and I ate, Florrie picked at her food. Finally, she dropped her fork to her plate with an exasperated sigh. "I just don't understand," she said. "What could possibly have happened? Bram would never kill anyone."

"Unless it was a…. You know," I said, my voice low. I didn't want to say the word *vampire* in front of the others. But my diffidence only piqued their interest.

"A what?" asked Shada quietly. Florrie and I stayed silent.

"Mrs. Stoker, withholding information will only make it more difficult for us to help you," Shada continued. "If your husband has enemies, that is crucial for us to know."

Florrie and I looked at each other and wordlessly came to the same conclusion. She nodded to me, then said, "All right, we do have something more to share. But we may as well wait so Mr. Reeves can hear it at the same time."

With fortuitous timing, Reeves entered at that very moment. The barman, who had already been casting dark glances at Shada, seemed about to object to having a Negro in the saloon, but Reeves casually adjusted the lapel of his coat to reveal his marshal's badge, and the barman backed down. Reeves joined us at our table.

Several other patrons started to make a fuss, but the barman shook his head at them. Most just sat there, seething and glancing dark looks our way, but one got up and made a show of leaving in disgust. This was fine with me, as he was wearing the most awful shade of mustard yellow, and it was quite putting me off my meal.

Shada had already ordered Reeves some food, and as he started to eat he told us, "Well, here's the story. Apparently, your husband shot and killed a man named Tom Drumpf. There's a witness says he did it in cold blood."

"That's impossible," Florence cried in dismay. "Bram would never do such a thing. If he killed someone it was in self-defence, or in defence of someone else."

"Might be," Reeves said. "I don't know the man, nor do I know the witness, so I can't offer an opinion. What I do know is that he deserves a chance to prove his innocence, same as anyone else accused of a crime. I also know that we'd better find him before Drumpf's father does – he's a big-time mine operator 'round these parts. If he gets to your husband first, I wouldn't count on him living long enough to stand before a judge and jury."

Florrie went pale. "Then we haven't a moment to lose," she said, starting to rise. Shada put a hand on her arm, gently coaxing her back into her seat.

"There was something you were going to tell us, Mrs. Stoker," she said.

Bass looked up from his plate sharply, and Florence hesitated for a moment before saying, "Yes. Yes, of course. Though I fear you will think us mad."

"Nah," Calamity interjected. "Whatever you got to say, I can guaran-damn-tee you I've heard something crazier. Hell, I've probably *done* something crazier."

"When Bram and Henry left Salt Lake City, they were on the trail of something…not quite human," I said, my voice low.

"Enough beating around the bush, Mr. Wilde," said Reeves. "Whatever trouble these men are in, it's time to speak about it plainly."

I sighed. "Speaking plainly is such a bore," I said. "But all right. They were hunting vampires."

Shada and Bass stared at me and Jane gave a short, sharp laugh of disbelief. (There's something to add to my list of accomplishments, diary: I shocked Calamity Jane.)

"Vampires? Bite-you-in-the-neck, suck-your-blood vampires?" she asked.

"Is there another kind?" I enquired. (I thought of telling her we had been visited by two the night before, but that is Florrie's story to tell if she so chooses.)

"Mr. Wilde, if this is some kind of joke—" Reeves began.

"I can assure you it's not," Florrie interjected. "We have encountered such creatures before. Oscar, Bram and some others battled them in England several years ago. My closest friend was…. Well, she was turned into a vampire. She almost turned me." She blushed then, which I found curious.

"Robert Roosevelt was one of our compatriots in that cause," I said. "He knew Henry and Bram were nearby and asked for their help in destroying a gang of vampires that was causing trouble in the area. That is what they were doing. If Bram killed this Drumpf, he must have been a vampire. There is no other rational explanation."

Reeves sat back in his chair, looking first at me then at Florence. Finally, he shook his head. "I heard rumours of these things. Down in New Mexico, they call them 'Dust Devils'. In Kansas, the Pawnee call them 'Mosquito Men'. I thought they were just campfire stories." He looked at Shada. "Have you ever heard of such a thing?" he asked.

She nodded slowly. "Yes, there are legends of such creatures. I have never seen one, nor do I know anyone who has."

"I knew I should have charged you folks more," he muttered.

"Mr. Reeves, I know this sounds insane," Florence said. "But I swear to you it's true. And in any case, this does not fundamentally change the task at hand. Help us find Bram and Henry, hear their tale for yourself. Then you can decide what to believe."

"With all due respect, Mrs. Stoker, this does change the task at hand. It changes it a great deal. You hired me to find your missing husband. Now, in order to do so, I'm competing with the law, Drumpf's hired guns and, if your story is to be believed, a gang of vampires. That is not what I signed up for."

Florrie's face fell. "Of course, you're right, Mr. Reeves. I apologise. And I am willing to pay more to keep you on the case."

Shada looked at her husband. "They need our help, Bass," she said quietly.

He sighed heavily. "Yeah, I know. All right, Mrs. Stoker. Our agreed-upon rate is still in effect. But if there's anything else you haven't told me—"

"There isn't," Florrie rushed to say. "Thank you, Mr. Reeves. I am in your debt."

"What about you, Jane?" I asked. "Are you still on the team?"

"Hell yeah!" she exclaimed. "I ain't never seen a vampire before. This should be fun!"

FROM THE JOURNAL OF BRAM STOKER, 6TH OF OCTOBER 1882

1:10 a.m.

What a thrilling evening it has been! To think earlier today, I was in deepest despair on my way to heaven knows what fate in Carson City.

Miss Chase refused to talk to us in the stagecoach for most of the trip, her nose buried in her Robin Hood book. Finally, I could stand it no more.

"You have to believe me, Miss Chase," I pleaded again. "The man I killed was leading a train robbery and was trying to kill me."

She put her book down. "Then it should be easy to clear this all up, Mr. Stoker. You will have your day in court."

"In a court owned by William Drumpf," Henry pointed out. "You have to see we are being railroaded here."

She swapped out her book for the Vellum Manuscript. "There is quite a bit of fuss over this book," she said, flipping through its pages and looking at the incomprehensible text and unusual drawings. "Brigham Young wants it. Drumpf will rob a train to get it. Yes, it must be a very special tome indeed."

"It is a dangerous book, in the wrong hands," I said. "If you deliver us to Drumpf, we are as good as dead, and he will have the book, which would prove calamitous."

"Yes, but as of now I have the book," Miss Chase said. She lowered her voice. "And I don't intend to hand it or you over to Drumpf." She pulled the window shade back a bit and peered outside at the rocky landscape. "It will be dark soon, then we can make our move."

To my surprise, she uncuffed me.

"Our move? So you aren't working for Drumpf?" I asked.

"I am not. Nor am I a Pinkerton agent, at least not entirely. In reality, I am an operative for the White Worm Society. I believe you are familiar with our work."

She unlocked Henry's cuffs, and he rubbed his wrists in relief.

I have never in my life been so happy to hear the words *White Worm Society*. Normally they are an irritation at best, as they occasionally badger me to hunt vampires in their service. I was aware I was under their surveillance but had no idea their reach extended this far.

"It is my understanding that when it is dark, Mr. Irving will be at full strength," she said. Henry's eyes widened at this and she added, "Yes, I am well aware of your nature, Mr. Irving."

"What's our next move?" I asked.

"You will overpower me and escape. I suppose I must let you keep the book for the time being so it doesn't fall into the hands of Drumpf," she said. "Your wife and Oscar Wilde are currently on the trail looking for you. They should be at Mound House by now, or even on to Carson City."

I was very surprised by this revelation, although knowing Florence I should not have been. When we failed to return, of course she would take action to find us.

"The Roosevelts have cleared your names on the federal level, but I'm afraid Drumpf has a tight rein on the Nevada Territory. He owns the governor and most of the lawmen. That is why it is imperative we get you out of Nevada. Your best bet is to get north of Carson City, then head west to Lake Tahoe and cross over into California. We will get word to Mrs. Stoker and Mr. Wilde to do the same."

I was suddenly in fear that Drumpf would try to capture Florence to use as leverage against us. Could he send men to Salt Lake to snatch Noel? I voiced my fears to Miss Chase.

"Your son is quite safe, I assure you," she said. "We have him under constant surveillance by an agent specially trained in the martial arts and combat against foes both human and supernatural. Now, I will try to rendezvous with you at Lake Tahoe and make sure you get safe passage across."

Our planning was interrupted by an arrow shattering the window! It embedded itself in the opposite wall with a loud *thunk*. We sank down into our seats in anticipation of more arrows to come.

The men up top started to fire their rifles and Miss Chase pulled out her revolver.

I carefully lifted the blinds to take a look out the back window. The Pinkertons who had been riding behind us were nowhere to be seen. Gaining on us fast were vampires, running as swiftly as horses! Three vampire cowboys and three vampire Indians. To my eyes, they shone brightly of the supernatural, and the glow streamed out behind them as they sped along.

"Damn it," Miss Chase exclaimed. "I think my cover has been blown! Drumpf has spies everywhere. I'm not sure I can even trust my fellow Pinkertons."

Drumpf somehow knew this stagecoach was not going to bring us to him and sent his lackeys to make sure we were delivered into his clutches. I couldn't help but think that Liver-Eating Johnson had sold us out a second time.

The lead vampires were nearly upon us now, and with a great burst of speed three of them were on top of the stagecoach. We could hear the Pinkertons firing at them, but they must have had ordinary bullets, for the shots did little to stop their assailants. The humans were tossed off with ease. With no driver, the horses sped up in a panic and the stage was wildly shaking from side to side, so violently one of the vampires was tossed off the roof.

Miss Chase fired blindly into the ceiling. She surely had silver bullets in her gun because we could hear the scream of a vampire being hit. The remaining vampire leapt off the roof to join his comrades, who were now running alongside the stagecoach, easily keeping up with the speed of the horses.

Miss Chase retrieved guns she had hidden under the seat and tossed them to us.

"These have silver bullets!"

We fired out both sides of the coach; miraculously at least a few of our bullets found their marks. We apparently missed their hearts and heads because they still were on their feet, but we did manage to make them retreat to avoid our bullets.

The coach was off-trail now, bouncing uncontrollably as the wheels clattered over rocks and boulders. Pieces of the coach were breaking apart; the wheels surely would not last much longer.

"Henry," I yelled. "Get up top and get control of those horses!"

With his superior strength and agility I'd thought he would climb out, but instead he disappeared into a puff of smoke and was instantly on top of the coach. I had no idea his apparition could work while in motion, but it had.

"Remarkable!" Miss Chase exclaimed.

Henry grabbed the reins and did his best to get the horses under control, while Miss Chase and I fired at our pursuers.

Henry got us back on the trail and our ride smoothed out enough for us to take better aim. Miss Chase was an astonishingly accurate shooter and took out one of the cowboy vampires with a shot to the head. At his accelerated speed he exploded into a cloud of red mist.

I took out one of the Indian vampires on my side of the coach with a lucky shot to the chest.

That left us only three to deal with. They must have been told to take us alive because the Indians were no longer shooting arrows at us and the cowboy's six-shooters were back in his holsters.

The cowboy and one of the Indians grabbed hold of the carriage door and ripped it off its hinges. A very stupid move on their part as it gave us clearer shots of their chests and heads.

Miss Chase shot the cowboy straight through the eye and he exploded. The resulting cloud of red momentarily blinded us all, and when it cleared a second later the other vampire had his hands around my throat. I grabbed his wrists and tried to free myself but he was much too strong.

I heard Miss Chase's gun clicking, the unlucky sound of an empty gun barrel.

Although I should have been in a full panic, a sudden calm swept over me. It was as if the demon inside me was taking over and I let go of the vampire's wrists, reached my hands up to his face and shoved my thumbs into his eye sockets. Still, he did not release me. I felt a strength that was not entirely my own well up inside me, and pressed my thumbs deeply into his eyes. I felt them pop like grapes. With one final push of strength, I squeezed and his head exploded into a mass of gore in my hands. What was left of his body slid out of the carriage to the moving ground below, where it burst into goo.

Miss Chase was staring at me with a look of equal horror and admiration. "Well done, Mr. Stoker!"

I was horrified myself, but there was no time to think about that. The carriage lurched violently. One of the wheels had finally broken completely. Henry was forced to bring the horses up sharply to a stop to avoid overturning the carriage altogether.

The last vampire was coming up fast as Miss Chase and I emerged from the carriage. Henry sprang down from the driver's seat to intercept him, but the vampire dodged around him in a blur and made a grab for Miss Chase. She ducked out of his grasp, swinging a stake that she must have had concealed on her person. But she was at the wrong angle for a fatal attack and managed only to pierce his side.

As he turned again, I saw a piece of the broken stagecoach wheel on the ground. I grabbed it and swung with all my might at the approaching vampire. The jagged end of a broken spoke caught him squarely in the chest and once more I found myself splattered with vampire remains. I dropped the wheel and leaned against the stagecoach to catch my breath.

When I had recovered, we unhitched the horses and rode them bareback to a nearby stream, where we let them drink. They had done an admirable job of outrunning the vampires and deserved a well-earned rest.

I walked downstream a bit and washed the vampire gore off my hands and clothes as best I could in the cold water.

"I guess we bed down for the night here," Miss Chase said. "Mr. Irving, if you will take the first watch."

"Certainly," he said, keeping his vampire ears to the wind. "There are no vampires nearby," he assured us. Though I did not say so in front of Miss Chase, I could confirm this, for I could see for quite a long way and did not detect a green glow anywhere on the dark horizon.

"Most likely Drumpf will send reinforcements when he realises they have failed," Miss Chase said. "We shouldn't rest long. In the morning I'll ride into Mound House and telegraph for reinforcements of our own from the White Worm Society. Then we can set off for Lake Tahoe."

We built a campfire and as we sat around its warmth, she explained to us that the Worms are, in fact, a worldwide organisation, although they had only recently opened a branch in America. She was originally working for the Canadian office in Winnipeg when she was transferred.

"We had a horrible lake monster problem up there," she said.

Talks with the U.S. president and White Worms are underway, but until agreements could be reached they remain a clandestine operation in the States. Well, even more clandestine than they are in Britain.

"We have an agreement with Mr. Pinkerton, but theirs is a mercenary operation so we dare not let them in on too much of the Society's workings. A wise decision, as now I suspect that some Pinkertons are in Drumpf's employ."

As I finish writing this on my turn at the watch, the horses are feeding on some scrub brush. Henry has gone back to feed off a freshly dead Pinkerton agent, as he will need all his strength.

LETTER FROM BASS REEVES TO ROBERT REEVES, 6TH OF OCTOBER 1882

Dear Bobby,

I am no longer in Salt Lake City but am on the trail in Nevada. A woman, Mrs. Stoker, has hired me to help find her missing husband.

I have been thinking lately about returning home. That is if I can talk Shada into coming with me. I very much want to see you and your brothers and sisters again.

I almost lost my life today in a gunfight and that sets a man thinking about things like home and settling down.

Mrs. Stoker and a friend of hers who you may have heard of, Oscar Wilde, insisted upon joining the expedition, which is not how I would have preferred to work it, but she has proven less cumbersome than I would have expected. (Wilde is a different story, though he could be worse.) Calamity Jane has also tagged along, but she is useful in a pinch.

Our search party had stopped to water our horses and ourselves in Mound House. It is a true shithole of a place with not much of anything to recommend it. And like most towns in that circumstance, it was a good place to find trouble.

Shada and Mrs. Stoker were getting supplies. Wilde and I decided to have a drink at what passes for a saloon. Jane had already gone ahead to do so.

That's when I ran into the Colorado Kid. He saw me first, and stepped off the boardwalk onto the muddy street and into my line of sight.

Ever since he nearly killed me in Oklahoma, I have spells of nerves. This sometimes happens after a nightmare where I relive taking six bullets in me. Sometimes just seeing something that reminds me of the fight can set it off.

There was a woman wearing a cornflower-blue dress that day as I lay in the gutter oozing life. One time, years later, I saw the same color dress and my heart started to race so fast it brought me to my knees.

So you can imagine how I felt when the man who nearly killed me was standing at the end of the street grinning at me. I had trouble catching my breath. My arm was frozen to my side and unable to grab my gun. My heart was galloping in my chest and I nearly couldn't stop myself from running off in the other direction.

Luckily for me, Calamity Jane had seen trouble brewing and come out of the saloon. She pulled her gun on him forthwith.

"Don't you even think about it, you scurvy jackass," she said from behind him. "I know what you done, and I would not lose a minute's sleep about shooting you in the back."

He grinned even broader. "Hey, Reeves!" he shouted. "You always let a woman do your fighting for you?" He looked over his shoulder at Jane for a second. "At least I think it's a woman."

I just stood there, unable to respond. I thought I might faint and a great shame welled up in me. I knew he was quite capable of shooting Jane then turning on me. *Bass,* I said to myself, *pull it together or you're going to die right here and take Jane with you.*

The sun was to his back, so he had the advantage there.

He took the fighting position, so I knew this was happening. I gestured for Wilde to move off, then widened my stance and braced myself on shaky legs. I thought for sure they were going to buckle.

"Well, ain't this a pleasant surprise," he yelled. "I thought I left you for dead in Oklahoma. Now I get to kill you all over again!"

"You was lucky is all," I yelled back. "Make your move if you want me to return the six bullets you gave me."

He laughed and his hand hovered lightly over his gun in its holster. Mine was already on the grip, so I had the advantage there.

It was then I knew I needed to get into his head like he had gotten into mine.

"You know how I knew you were hiding out in that barn?" I yelled, working hard to keep my voice steady. "Your woman told me. She wanted me to kill you 'cause you gave her quite a beating."

"Liar!" He lurched forward a bit trying to make me go for my gun. I didn't. I'd like to say I just didn't fall for his trick, but partly it was because I was still shaking so bad.

"Yeah, she told me where you was when me and her were lying on her big feather bed."

"She'd've never done nothing like that to me! Specially not with the likes of you."

"I always thought it was a pretty cowardly thing to do, beating a woman. She thought so too."

"Fuck you!" he screamed.

"Didn't you never wonder why she wasn't there when you got home? She was so happy to be with a real man, she knew she couldn't settle for you no more."

His head was full of angry thoughts, and his mouth was busy cursing me. That slowed him enough. He had his gun out but didn't have time to aim, much less shoot.

My bullet went right through his wrist, knocking the gun out of his hand. He dropped to the ground, clutching his wound as it gushed blood. Jane ran up and kicked the gun away.

Then she and Wilde both ran up to me. "Damn, Bass. I've never seen anything like that," Jane said. "Shot the gun right out of his hand!"

"Yeah, wasn't that great. I was aiming for his chest," I confessed.

Wilde clapped me on the shoulder and said, "Be that as it may, Mr. Reeves, you have bested the villain and live to fight another day. I for one am happy that you are on our side."

I picked up the Colorado Kid's gun in case he got any ideas. His buddies ran out of the saloon to help him to the doctor's office. I really wanted to finish him off, but I knew it meant fighting off his friends and explaining the killing to the sheriff. I didn't have neither time nor the inclination for that, and besides, the Colorado Kid's days with a gun are over as I am pretty sure he will lose the hand.

We proceeded to the saloon to have that drink. My hand only shook a little as I raised the whiskey to my lips. Then we collected the others and headed back out on the trail.

Son, I am praying to God that was my last gunfight. I am sincerely hoping to be heading east soon.

Your loving father

LETTER FROM WILLIAM DRUMPF TO SHERIFF RORY CALHOUN, 6TH OF OCTOBER 1882

Dear Sheriff Calhoun,

I am not a happy man at the moment. I put you in office and I could easily take you out.

How hard can it be to find two foreigners with their pictures plastered throughout Nevada?

I have word that Pinkerton agents are now involved, sent by that fool in the White House. I had to send my own men to intercept them and lost several of them in the process!

Luckily, Stoker and Irving are now on the run again and we have a chance to grab them before the Pinkertons do and before they make it out of Nevada territory.

These two are not bandits. They are not gunslingers. They are not even Westerners. They are a couple of greenhorns stumbling around in the desert! Find them and find them NOW!

I am authorizing you to hire as many deputies as you need and will send you the funds required up to $10,000. We will up the bounty to $500 for anyone who can bring them in ALIVE.

I want to hang Stoker myself, and I want that book he is carrying delivered into my hands. Anything less will be failure on your part and I am not one who looks kindly on failure.

Sincerely, ·

William Drumpf

RECRUITMENT POSTER, 7TH OF OCTOBER 1882

To Horse! To Horse!
  Join our Posse for $50 cash!
  Wanted, men good with guns and riding for our most righteous posse.
  $50 plus food and drink. Guns and horses provided. See sheriffs in Carson City or in Silver City to sign up.
  $500 bounty to the first man who brings in Abraham Stoker and Henry Irving alive.

FROM THE DIARY OF OSCAR WILDE, 7TH OF OCTOBER 1882

Dear yours truly,

Once again, I have rescued Stoker. You'd think it would grow tiresome and you would be right.

Earlier in Mound House we made a new acquaintance, a handsome woman named Cora Chase. Surprisingly, she is one of those White Worm Society members posing as something called a 'Pinkerton'. I didn't quite understand all that she was telling me about that, but she knew the whereabouts of Stoker and Irving.

"This is quite a stroke of luck, finding you here," she said. "Come with me. We'll pick up Mr. Stoker and Mr. Irving and continue on together."

Florence and I looked at each other warily. By this time, Reeves, Shada and Jane had joined us, and they were watching our reactions closely.

"If you'd allow us a moment to confer," I said. Miss Chase looked momentarily taken aback, but nodded and removed herself from earshot.

"Who the hell is this woman?" said Jane.

"And how did she find us?" asked Shada.

"And why should we trust her?" Reeves asked.

I gave them a cursory description of the White Worm Society, then said, "It is strange to find them here, but I think we can trust her. The Worms are secretive and meddling, but they are not the worst secret society I have ever been in contact with."

Florence agreed, and the others put up no argument, though I heard Reeves quietly tell Jane to be on her guard, and I noticed that he also has been keeping a close eye on Miss Chase.

As Stoker and Irving are wanted fugitives, it was not safe to meet them in town, so we acquired horses and supplies in Mound House and collected our wayward friends in the desert outside town. (I must remember to send Stoker a bill for my expenses as I am funding this expedition entirely out of my own pocket.)

After the Stokers' rather maudlin reunion, we introduced Bram and Henry to the rest of our search party.

"You did worry Miss Florrie," Calamity scolded. "She thought you had run off."

"I did *not* think that," Florrie protested.

I later overheard Shada say to Florence, "I can see now why you chose as you did." I believe I've been insulted, diary.

Miss Chase took us to a ranch called Indian Hills. The ranch is what Miss Chase called a 'hideout'. Our horses are stabled and we are quartered in accommodations that could charitably be described as 'rustic'. She warned us to check bedding and dark corners of the rooms for scorpions and black widow spiders. Still, it is nice to get out of the sun and rest.

Miss Chase has assured us we are safely hidden here, and in the morning she will lead us down a secluded trail to Lake Tahoe, where we can cross into California.

I can tell that Florrie took an immediate dislike to Miss Chase. She is quite beautiful in a stylish schoolmistress way, but I don't think it is jealousy on Florrie's part. Miss Chase has this air about her where she seems to think she is in charge. I suppose she is; after all, she did free Stoker and Irving, and she is the only one offering any suggestions for what to do next. Still, it is most troubling putting yourself under the care of someone you don't know at all.

More beans and bacon for dinner, along with what Americans call biscuits but are actually overly dry scones. At least we had some of Jane's whiskey and cold well water to wash it all down.

Over dinner by a roaring fire, Bram and Irving regaled us with tales of their exciting journey, which began with tracking vampires and ended with a train robbery, which they stopped in a most heroic way. How much is fabricated by Stoker is unknown, but most of it must be true or he wouldn't be on the run now.

Apparently, a mining tycoon named Drumpf is out to get Bram for killing his train-robbing son. It all sounds very Shakespearian.

They showed us what the robbers were after: a strange book. It is printed on vellum (most likely calf or lambskin, but could be human skin, knowing these vampire types). It contains drawings of unusual animals, strange plants and maps of unknown countries. I know several languages but I did not recognise it or its alphabet.

Shada was of more use than I. "I recognise the writing but I can't translate it," she said. "I have seen writing like it in a Yahi village."

"Yahi!" Calamity exclaimed. "I heard those people were wiped out years ago."

"No, they went into hiding," Shada explained. "Their shaman uses powerful magic to hide their village. They cannot be seen if they do not wish you to see them."

"Poppycock!" Jane said, with a wave of her hand. "A myth at best."

"I wouldn't be so sure, Jane," said Florrie. "I have seen many strange things in the last few years, things I would have dismissed as fairy tales if I hadn't witnessed them myself."

"Do you know how to find this hidden village?" Irving asked.

She said she did. Furthermore, it is nearby and only a short detour on our trail to Lake Tahoe.

"It might be worth a stop," Bram said, to my great surprise. This life of adventure must be growing on him.

Miss Chase seemed concerned for a moment, then said, "Yes, if there is someone who can translate this book I would like to meet them." Again she was dictating what we would do as a group and not sounding at all democratic as the Americans are so fond of being known as.

"We can take you as far as the village, Mrs. Stoker," Mr. Reeves said. "Then we'll be turning back as our mission to find your husband is completed."

"That is very kind of you," Florrie said. "We will compensate you for your extra time."

With our business concluded, we retired for the night. I was not up for yet another adventure, but here we are about to meet with the natives and smuggle Bram and Irving into California. How ever do I get myself into these things?

As I prepared to settle in, there was a knock on what passed for a bedroom door. There were big gaps in the slats and I could see Calamity standing there.

"Enter," I called. She did, and was carrying half a bottle of whiskey and two tin cups.

"The others are going to bed and don't want to finish the bottle, which I am told is bad luck."

"I could use a nightcap," I admitted, and offered her a seat on the only piece of furniture in the room aside from the bed, a rocking chair that had long stopped rocking and was slanted ever so slightly to the left. As Calamity was slanting slightly to the right, I thought they might balance each other out.

"I get the feeling I have been a thorn in your side this whole trip. I did not mean to be," she said, pouring me a cup.

"Perhaps, but you have grown on me like mould on a plum," I said, raising my cup for a toast.

We clinked tin and drank. I then said, "American whiskey, I am told, is made by using strychnine. Is that true?"

"Nah, not for a lot of years now," she said. "You see, the Chinese had a different method, using that sugarcane of theirs, so it doesn't rot your gut like it used to."

She splashed more of the potent liquid into my cup.

"Hear, hear to the Chinamen," I said.

"Hear, hear," she said, her voice echoing into the tin cup. "I also very much like their way of cooking pigs."

I had to agree, and then we found ourselves talking about one of my favourite subjects, food.

"What's the best thing you ever ate?" she asked.

"So hard to pick one dish. I've eaten in Paris, Rome and Vienna. They all had their specialities that were exquisite. I think quite fondly of the *chateaubriand* I had at a restaurant on the Champs-Élysées, and a heavenly walnut torte they serve at my favourite hotel in Vienna."

"You sure do talk all fancy," she said. I did not take it as an insult and I do not think she meant it as such, as I find so many people do. "I had a steak once in Kansas City that melted in my mouth like butter. I had moose in Pig's Eye, and I did not care for that. Too greasy, like bear. I guess my favourite eating would be my mama's biscuits and gravy, which I have not had since I was a little girl. I would give anything to taste those again."

I thought about my own mother, who had never cooked anything in her life but knew how to hire good cooks. At that moment I missed her and hope to see her again soon.

"I suppose the best meal I have ever eaten was at the bottom of a mine," I said. "I was on my lecture tour in Leadville, Colorado, and was invited by the miners to go down and share a dinner with them. They, of course, thought I would never do it, but I did. They lowered me down in a bucket and it took a full fifteen minutes to descend."

"You're braver than I thought," Calamity said, raising her cup to me. "You wouldn't get me into a hole that deep. I don't like going underground like a rabbit."

"At the bottom, I am told, the plan was to get me drunk and leave me alone in the dark, but I quickly won them over with humorous stories and proceeded to drink them under the table. I had a delicious dinner of Cornish pasties with redeye gravy served on a dirty tin plate. Washed it down with strong cider. At the end of the evening, I had to run the winch to hoist them all out in the bucket as I was the only one left standing."

We finished the bottle, and she made her way drunkenly to her bed.

I lay on the bed in the tiny room and realised that before this journey I would have been bothered by the confinement of it. I was not now. Maybe it was the alcohol or maybe it was the sound of the crickets outside. It seems wherever you are in America you feel like you are in the wide-open outdoors.

Until the morrow, dear diary.

TELEGRAM FROM ALEJO 'LOBO' LOPEZ TO WILLIAM DRUMPF, 7TH OF OCTOBER 1882

=Tracked Stoker. He is near Mound House. Think they are making run for California. Lake Tahoe most likely route. Send posse to Mound House=

LETTER FROM ALEJO 'LOBO' LOPEZ TO LUZ LOPEZ, 7TH OF OCTOBER 1882

Dear Luz,

As I write this, I am eating beans and jerky. The one I ride with is off draining the blood of an old prospector. Yes, I again ride with the monster, the Pale Horseman.

Drumpf has sent us on a quest to find the man who killed his son and stole the holy book.

The Pale Horseman prefers to ride with a human, I know not why. Perhaps I am food should it become scarce. Or, maybe it is because a human can approach other humans without terrifying them. Even if one does not know the Pale Horseman is a vampire, he still exudes an air of menace. Partly it is his sneer and swagger, qualities that I'm sure served him well in his previous life as an outlaw. But even when he is standing still, doing nothing, humans sense something about him that makes them want to move away from him as quickly as possible.

I have gotten used to it, but I still am happy that we take our meals separately.

This morning we set out on our horses. "Let's go, Lobo," he said to me in a husky voice as dry as desert sand. He does not breathe except to speak and there are times a puff of dust will come out when he does.

We rode for a good part of the morning. Despite his ability to ride in the daylight, he does not like the strong sun of noon and seeks the shadows. This siesta is the only time I can rest and eat, for we ride day and night. I know I slow him down and see the irritation in his eyes, but my horse needs water and rest even if his does not.

We had heard reports that the two men were spotted in Mound House and it is there we started our search. He occasionally jumps off his horse, picks up sand from the ground and sniffs it. "They went this way," he tells me. Once he noticed a scorpion on the ground, and he picked it up and held it in his open palm. It stung his wrist several times, and he just smiled. "I used to be able to feel that," he said. "Now I don't feel anything." He crushed it and threw it to the ground.

He has had his fill of the prospector and just tossed him into the brush.

"We are close," he told me. "I catch their scent in the wind now. Not more than ten miles. We will ride again at three." He then found a shady spot, lay down and covered himself with sand from head to toe like a lizard escaping the noonday sun.

I often wonder if he will try to eat me. And, if he does, will ripping off that amulet he wears rob him of his powers against the sun? I feel under my shirt for my silver cross and wonder if it would be enough protection.

I too must get what sleep I can now. For soon we will catch up with our quarry.

Lobo

FROM THE JOURNAL OF BRAM STOKER, 8TH OF OCTOBER 1882

4:00 p.m.

We have arrived at the Yahi village and it is a wondrous sight to behold. It is like we have stumbled upon Shangri-La itself – a large pasture along a babbling stream nestled in a valley between two mountains. Getting here is a strange story in itself.

From our hideout at the Indian Hills ranch, Shada led our riding party down a particularly difficult trail for the horses. It was a very narrow passage between large boulders, and the ground was rocky. Shada promised us the trail would become less rocky as we went, and it did, opening up into meadowlands flanked by pine trees.

"We now must get lost," she said.

"I nearly always am," Oscar said.

"Whatever do you mean, Shada?" Florence asked.

"It is how the magic works," Shada said. She picked up the pace a bit on her horse and we all followed suit. "To find the village, you must be lost."

"That sounds like a whole lot of mumbo jumbo," Jane grumbled.

Mr. Reeves laughed, then said, "I learned a long time ago not to question her ways."

Miss Chase remained quiet, seemingly content to let Shada lead the way. I suppose as a White Worm operative she is accustomed to dealing with the mysterious. I hoped it wasn't a mistake leading her here. The Worms do have a way of making pests of themselves when they learn someone has a supernatural talent.

Getting lost was not difficult. A fog had moved in as thick as any I had seen in London.

"I like this weather," Henry said, taking off his scarf and cape.

Soon we could only see a few feet in front of us and had to trust the horses to find their way.

We randomly went down trails that the horses chose. It became eerily quiet and only the slow clop of hooves broke the silence.

From time to time Shada would stop suddenly and we would all do the same. She would raise her right palm into the air as if she were testing a wind we could not feel. "We must get more lost," she would command, and off we would go again.

The fog was getting so thick I could no longer see the others behind me or Shada in front of me. The next time she stopped our horses gently collided.

"Here," she said. "I think we are the most lost here."

The fog started to clear and suddenly I could see a man – a member of the Yahi tribe, I presumed – standing on the trail in front of us. He was wearing buckskins and carrying no weapons. He wore no headdress or face paint as the Indians in the Wild West show had done.

He spoke to Shada in what I took to be his language and they conversed briefly.

He then came up to each of us, inspecting us.

A second person came out of the fog: another man carrying a woven basket.

"No weapons can come into the village," he said.

We complied and put our guns into the basket.

"All of them," he said to Jane. She grumbled and pulled a derringer and knife from her boot. She deposited them into the basket.

With our weapons secured, the first man waved his hand. The fog instantly vanished, and we were surprised to find ourselves smack bang in the middle of the village, under a clear blue sky! It was a vibrant, busy village with children playing, people working and cooking fires burning. There were dozens and dozens of earthen wigwams surrounding us; how we had not run into them in the fog I do not know.

Curious children swarmed around us, smiling and laughing. It at once lightened my heart and made me miss Noel fiercely.

As we looked around, Shada's eyes lit on a woman tending a fire. The woman looked up and saw Shada and smiled broadly. They ran to each other and embraced. I could not understand what they were saying to each other, but our new guide said, "We are not only Yahi here in the village. People from many tribes have found their way here and have been taken in for protection, either from the white man or from other tribes."

There are Negroes here as well, and Mr. Reeves talked with them. Many have been here since before the American Civil War started and did not know it was over and they are free.

"We are already free here," one woman told him. "There is nothing out there for us any more."

Adults came to help us dismount and then tended to our horses. Florence, Jane and Miss Chase were led away by village women. Miss Chase protested, but Shada said something to her in a low voice and she relented.

We men were taken to a large structure built of sticks and covered in animal hide with a roof of thatched grass. It appeared to be the village meeting hall, similar to structures I have read about in stories of the Vikings.

Inside, a large bonfire was burning at the centre, its smoke billowing up through a hole in the roof. Men, who I suspected were the chief and his elders, sat around the fire cross-legged on the floor. They motioned to us to sit down, and we did.

The chief spoke to us in English. "We have been expecting you. Our medicine man saw in the smoke that you would come. I am the chosen leader, Ishi."

A man stood up. His buckskins were adorned with turquoise jewellery. He had a staff made from wood that had a green stone on top. I saw it gave off that same green glow I had seen in the vampire gunslinger's amulet.

"This is our shaman, Dacala."

Shada later told me it was a great honour to hear their names, for Yahi believe letting others know your name could give them power over you.

"He follows you," Dacala said. It sounded more like an accusation than information. "The dead one who rides a dead horse." He pointed his staff into the fire and to my amazement, we could see an image of the gunslinger in the flames. He was riding his horse and being followed by another man, also on horseback, who appeared to be a Mexican *vaquero*.

"What in tarnation is that?" Reeves said.

"A most powerful vampire," Henry said.

"Yes," I said. "An especially nasty one who has all his powers even in the day."

"Can he find this place?" Oscar asked the shaman.

"I do not think so," Dacala said. However, there was a worried look in his eyes.

"You may stay here until he passes," Chief Ishi graciously offered.

We all thanked them, and Henry pulled out the book. "We came to see if you could read this." He handed it to the shaman, who took it and flipped through its pages.

"I can read some of the writing, and I recognise the pictures. These are creatures from the other place. And this is a map to the entrance near the southern coast of the big ocean. I have been there."

Henry excitedly sprang to his feet, much too fast. In his zeal he gave away that he is not human, startling the others. "Where is it? Where is the opening?"

Henry was next to Dacala now and his attention was fully on the book. He did not see Reeves and the tribal elders staring at him in disbelief.

"Henry," I quietly said.

"What, Bram—?" He noticed. "Ah, yes. As you can see, I am not fully human."

Sensing trouble, Reeves went for his gun then remembered it had been confiscated. The chief and elders rose into a defensive position. Dacala, however, remained calm and made no attempt to move away from Henry.

I jumped to my feet. "I assure you, Henry is not one of these blood-sucking monsters!"

The shaman raised his hand and said something to his fellow villagers in their language.

"It is true," Dacala said directly to Reeves, who was also standing in a fighting posture. "I foresaw his coming in my dreams. He is on the side of light and has sent many of these creatures back to the dark place." He turned to Henry and said, "I will show you where this place is on the white man's map. And I will tell you how to enter the other place. But there is something we need from you in trade."

He led us out of the meeting hall and to a dwelling at the edge of the village. Inside there were six children and three adults lying on blankets on the floor. They were sick and we could see it was smallpox.

Henry rolled up his sleeve. "Yes, I can help them."

Henry gave some of his blood to the sick and they immediately started to rally.

Reeves and I left the tent. "He's not turning them into…?"

"Heavens, no," I said. "Receiving Henry's vampire blood without draining their blood first will not turn them."

Dacala joined us. I saw Florence, Jane, and Miss Chase circled by village women. They were now dressed in buckskins like the Yahi women.

Dacala quietly said to me, "I do not trust the tall woman," indicating Miss Chase. "The fire was not clear about her intentions, so we chose to separate her from your group."

"She has been most helpful to us and has saved my life," I said. "But she was sent by a group that collects information on magic, and they sometimes lie and steal to get what they want. It is best to keep information about your magic secret from her, I think." He nodded.

As a thanks for Henry saving his people, the chief invited us to stay the night, and we accepted. We hope that the vampire hunting us will be far past this place by morning.

REPORT FROM AGENT CORA CHASE TO WHITE WORM SOCIETY

Date: 8 October 1882
Subject: Yahi Village
On the way to getting the Stokers and Mr. Irving out of Nevada, we decided to make a small detour to the hidden Yahi village, of which I have heard rumours before.

All these rumours turned out to be true. It is hidden by magic and is a sanctuary for displaced natives and others on the run from white men and their guns. One must 'get lost' to find the place and even then they find you and decide if you are worthy to enter.

I am eager to speak with their shaman. He must be wielding powerful magic indeed to hide a village of this size. However, I was whisked off with the other women, which appears to be their custom. How predictable.

Fortunately, I have often found that – despite the best efforts of the men – women generally know as much as, if not more than, the menfolk. And, if all else fails, Stoker will surely tell me everything I wish to know; he is a man not well suited to subterfuge.

We were led to the stream to wash off the dust of the trail and given food and water. They washed our clothes and loaned us traditional buckskin dresses to wear, which are quite comfortable.

Our Salish guide, Shada, has found others from her tribe here and asked them about the shaman.

Like Rayne, he possesses a green stone that seems to be the source of his magic. With it, he can hide the village in mist, and 'see great distances in the fire'. He can also predict future events when he enters a dream state while using mind-altering herbs.

I would like to retrieve the magic stone for study, but I'm afraid I won't get close enough to the shaman for the opportunity. And no doubt the community would object to my taking it.

Perhaps I will get my hands on Rayne's stone one day.

Mr. Stoker told me the shaman recognised the writing in the Vellum Manuscript as being from 'the other place', but could not translate it. However, he was able to decipher some of the maps and has drawn Irving a map to one of the openings into the Realm. I will try to steal it when I get the chance, or at the very least make a copy of it.

I am afraid we are stuck here in this hidden village for the moment as the Pale Horseman is close on our heels. So says the shaman, and I am inclined to believe him.

I have enclosed a map to the Yahi village, or at least the last known location before we became purposely lost. This would be useful magic to study, and I recommend sending researchers from the Magical Geography Division at the earliest convenience.

—End Report—

FROM THE DIARY OF OSCAR WILDE, 8TH OF OCTOBER 1882

Dear yours truly,

We are in an idyllic Indian village in literally nowhere, meaning it cannot be found on any map or by any white man. I am grateful to be off that horse and to have a full belly and a place to lay my head. I had a wonderful meal of what I was told was elk, squash and blueberries.

Tomorrow we should be safely in California and I plan to take the next train as far east as I can go. Stoker must be sure his name is cleared before embarking back through territory in which Drumpf holds sway, so he and Florrie will likely stay until that is accomplished. Irving has his heart set on finding the entrance to the Realm and though I cannot imagine why, I wish him all the luck. No more adventures for me, at least for the time being. I've been dragged along by the Stokers long enough. I must return to my life and try to salvage what I can of my fame. I think I will try my hand at another play, perhaps something light and witty this time.

I was given a very nice wigwam. It appeared to be a conglomeration of different native styles. It was dome-shaped, made of a combination of animal skins and wood, and roofed with grass. Two fist-sized holes in the roof allowed smoke out and fresh air in at the same time, keeping the room at a nice, even temperature.

Our hosts provided me with plenty of blankets and I was nice and cosy by the light of my lantern. It is surprising how comfortable buffalo hides can be as a mattress, and I was very much looking forward to going fully comatose when I heard a rap on my wigwam. (I had no idea one could rap on a wigwam, but there you are.)

Without a word of invitation, a handsome Indian man entered my chambers. He was not much younger than I, and tall and lanky, yet muscular. I could tell he was muscular because he was shirtless.

He wore only tight-fitting buckskin trousers, nicely accented with fringes and beadwork. The trousers were similar to what I had seen the women wearing, but not any of the men, who went about with very drab britches.

"I am sorry to bother you," he said.

He had, but I thought it best to be a gracious guest so did not say so. "Not at all. What can I do for you?" At first, I wondered if my fame had somehow found this village when nothing else could. I was ready to sign a beaver pelt or something. I pushed that thought out of my mind as preposterous, if only slightly.

He tried to speak to me in English but was having trouble finding the words. Then, to my surprise, he started talking to me in French, which fortunately he could speak quite well. As you know, diary, I am quite fluent in French too.

So, we continued to speak *a français*.

He told me that, like many in the village, he was displaced from his people and had been taken into this hidden tribe. He is an Ojibwe from the shores of Lake Superior, which they call *gitchi-gami*. He told me his name is Maa'ingan, which means *wolf* in his language. He had come west with French fur traders and parted ways with them when they returned to Canada.

"I see you are two-spirits like I am," he said. We were sitting down across from each other, so we could be eye to eye.

"I do not understand," I said.

"You are both man and woman," he said.

I should have been offended, but these are primitive people after all, and at once I understood what he was getting at.

"No. Perhaps my manner of dress confuses you. I am sure you are accustomed to seeing white men wearing only the most drab clothing. I assure you, in my country, these are fashionable men's clothes. I am what is known as an aesthete, a man of exceptional tastes and a lover of beauty."

"I am too an...aesthete," he said, smiling a shy grin of pearly white teeth. He pointed to his chest and added. "Two-spirits."

"I can assure you I am all man. No woman," I said firmly.

"I like all man," he said, moving closer to me.

I was dumbfounded. I have been in situations like this before (and have to admit I am usually the instigator), but I was not expecting someone to be making overtures to Oscar Wilde in the Wild West.

But when in Rome, dear diary, you do as the Romans do.

As we melted into the buffalo pelts, my mind went to tales of ancient lands and swarthy men in Bedouin tents. A primal force surged up inside me and pushed out all rational thought and every vestige of civilisation.

He is dozing now, and I am musing upon the strange twists of fate that have led me to this mysterious and magical village. I know I will never forget the time I've spent here, and hope that you, future Oscar, are smiling as you read these words, as I am smiling while writing them.

I suppose by conventional wisdom this puts yet another black mark on the devil's side in the ledger of my life. Fortunately, I am not conventional. But in any event, I will make up all these indiscretions to Constance when I return to England and devote myself to a more domestic life. That is my goal, I have decided, but following Stoker around does make it difficult.

FROM THE JOURNAL OF FLORENCE STOKER, 8TH OF OCTOBER 1882

We are bedded down for the night as guests in a mysterious Yahi village. It is such a wonderful place, so tranquil and pastoral, with wigwams winding through rolling grassy hills along the banks of a mountain stream. At the same time, it is quite thrilling. How many Englishwomen have crossed the threshold into a hidden Indian colony? Surely not Ellen Terry!

Poplar and birch trees dot the landscape as cattle and sheep graze and children kick balls and fly kites. I wonder if the American Indians have always had kites or if they got them from the Chinese. I have seen some Orientals in the village. Apparently, they had been working in horrific conditions on the railroads and escaped, whereupon they were fortunately taken in by the Yahi.

Now Bram and I are nestled on buffalo pelts in our own wigwam, as crickets chirp outside. It gets very cool at night here and as I write this we are snuggled up by a fire that is burning in the middle of our room. How the room doesn't fill with smoke, I do not know, but it quickly finds its way out of a hole in the ceiling.

"I am so sorry I have put you through all this," Bram said.

"You need not be. It has been a grand adventure for me and Oscar."

"Oscar is never going to let me forget this rescue of me, is he?" Bram sighed.

"I think not," I said. "I wish you would be nicer to Oscar," I added. "He is more of a friend to you than you know. I have never heard him say a bad word about you."

"Never?" Bram asked incredulously.

"Well, maybe a few, but always in jest. Even the times I was directly complaining about you."

"I know. He just makes it so hard sometimes," he said, throwing another small log on the fire and poking at it with a stick. Men very much like to mess about with fire. I think it brings out the caveman in them.

"I often think Oscar could be a great artist if he would just get out of his own way," I said.

"Aye, but that applies to most men," Bram said.

There was a great lull in our conversation as we both sat with our thoughts. I finally broke the silence. "Jane was thinking this would be a good place to settle down in her old age, but then she found out there is no alcohol allowed here."

"It is a charming village, and I myself gave a thought to staying hidden in here," Bram said. "We could send for Noel, build a little cabin and live our lives free of responsibilities and monsters."

"What of your meeting with the shaman?" I asked. They had been gone most of the afternoon and I was truly curious.

"Henry has his map. The shaman could only translate a few phrases in the book but he was able to identify some locations on the maps. One details an opening to the Realm, and he knows the place well. He said there is an old Spanish mission near the opening. There were monks at the mission who at one time regularly went into the Realm. If they are still there, they might be able to read the book."

"So Henry will be going then?"

"I think so. I'm not sure what he will find in there. It could be the very pit of hell itself."

I agreed and said, "On the other hand, if he can find a cure for his vampirism, perhaps he can cure all vampires. Then we can be rid of them once and for all. Maybe that is his destiny."

He looked at me, amazed. "You do think big sometimes, my dear. I certainly hope you are right. But I am not risking my life or yours on it. If he goes in there, he can do it without me."

FROM THE DIARY OF OSCAR WILDE, 9TH OF OCTOBER 1882

Maa'ingan woke up shortly after I finished my last entry. Through the course of the evening, he and I talked about many things. It was nice to have someone I could confide in and he, in turn, found it liberating to talk to another outsider. Despite his being of the same race, he is a foreigner in this village. He misses the forests and the stony shores of the big lake, which he was happy to hear was indeed the largest body of fresh water in the world yet discovered.

I found myself telling him so many of my secrets, probably because I knew he would never have the chance to tell anyone I knew. I told him of my brushes with the supernatural, and my loss of Derrick at the hands of the Black Bishop and his minions. I confessed my jealousy of Stoker and how I wished I was the one who possessed a second sight into the other world. (I suppose this technically counts as telling Stoker's secret, but as it was in service of confiding mine I do not feel overly guilty about it.)

He then told me he knew a way I could experience such visions, a way to lift the veil off this world and see into the next.

He brought me a gourd and in it was a thick, yellow liquid he poured onto a wooden spoon. It glowed in the light from the lantern, dancing as if it were smoke. I have drunk absinthe and smoked opium, so I was no stranger to mind-altering substances, but he assured me this was life-changing and perfectly safe.

I really don't know what came over me. I simply took the spoonful and swallowed it without any fear or hesitation. It was almost as if it commanded me to drink it and I could not say no.

It was viscous and bitter, and I winced as the taste hit my tongue.

At first, I felt nothing, but then I found myself vomiting violently into a clay jar he held out for me. Normally that sort of thing is unpleasant, but this time I felt as though I were purging myself of all doubt and sin.

I fell back, nestled among the soft fur of the buffalo skins, then sank into them deeper and deeper, the real world falling away. For a moment I thought myself to be Alice falling into Wonderland. As I fell, flowers grew up all around me then exploded and showered me with fragrant petals of pink and purple, yellow and blue. Beautiful birdsong surrounded me. I felt a joy I had never experienced before. I laughed but heard the laugh of myself as a child.

I landed with a soft thud onto a giant sunflower. I sat up and looked around and saw nothing but twinkling stars. I could see a comet in the distance speeding towards me. Just as I thought it would hit me, it veered off to the left, and I found myself in the cloud of the comet's tail, a cloud made of sparkling stardust. When the cloud cleared, I was standing in a field. It was very familiar. I turned to see Stonehenge in the distance. A plump woman stood at the centre of the stone circle and waved me over.

As I got closer, I could see it was Mother!

I ran to her, and she wrapped me in a warm embrace. "It has been months since I've seen you," I said. I have never felt so loved and so at peace.

But then she broke from our hug and put me at arm's length. "I am so disappointed in you, Oscar," she said.

"Whatever for?" I asked, finding that I had broken into tears.

"You know, Oscar, you always know. Yet you continue to break your mother's heart." With that she turned and walked out of the circle, quickly disappearing into the distance.

"Do you even love me, Oscar?" another voice said from behind me. I wheeled around to see Constance there. She had Willie on a leash. He wasn't in his werewolf form but on a leash nonetheless.

"He doesn't love me," Willie said. "That much I can tell you. He only loves himself."

"I am greatly fond of you," I told Constance. "And, Willie, you are my brother. Of course I love you."

"You only love beautiful things," Constance spat. "And you *don't* find me beautiful. Your aestheticism is a velvet cloak you hide behind. Why do you get to decide what is beautiful and what is not, you ugly, ugly man!"

Another voice called from behind me. "If he busies himself with looking at the wallpaper, he doesn't have to look in the mirror!" I wheeled around to see Derrick slowly walking towards me. He bared his teeth and I could see his vampire fangs.

My father was with him.

Normally, I enjoy being the centre of attention but this was getting to be too much. I ran out of the circle of stones, trying to escape my tormentors.

I found myself in my childhood home and I ran upstairs to my bedroom. It offered me a bit of comfort to be surrounded by nostalgia and my books. I marvelled at how real it all looked, how solid it felt, yet I knew this was a drug-induced dream.

My bedroom door burst open and my father was there with the strap. "You reprobate!" he screamed. "Come here and take your beating!"

I cowered like a child momentarily but remembered I had fought demons worse than this. I stood and faced him.

"You have no power over me, old man!" I yelled. I could feel my confidence bursting forth. "You were more of a reprobate than I could be in two lifetimes. Raping women. Beating children. The great Sir William Wilde, indeed. I'm embarrassed to be your son."

He shrank before me, becoming the size of a mouse. I stomped on him with my heel, squishing him into non-existence. I went downstairs to find my sisters, Emily and Mary, sitting in the parlour. The horrible memory of their death in a fire was pushed out of my mind and I rejoiced to see them alive. I wrapped them both in an embrace and kissed their cheeks, weeping with joy.

"Oh, Oscar," Mary cried. "Thank you so much for driving Father away."

"We can rest in peace now," Emily said, smiling.

They disappeared from my arms in a puff of white smoke.

Derrick was by the fireplace, admiring his portrait that hung above the mantle, the one that Frank Miles had painted. The man in the painting was still the most beautiful I have ever seen. The man staring at it looked much the same, only colder.

He turned to look at me. There was so much disdain in his eyes. "Oh, Oscar, why did you reject me? We could have been together forever."

His mouth opened, and he bared his fangs. He came towards me and I was frozen in place. I could not move even though I wanted to run.

He embraced me and sank his fangs into my neck. I waited for the sweet release of death. For all my suffering to be over. Then suddenly he screamed and disappeared in an explosion of black smoke.

Stoker was standing there with the stake he had moments before plunged into Derrick's back.

"Thank you, Bram!" I cried.

He looked confused for a moment and dropped the stake. "What the hell are you doing in my dream, Oscar? Can I get no respite from you even in sleep?"

Bram walked out of the room and I was once again alone.

A wolf trotted in. I knew at once he was friendly. I thought perhaps it was Willie, but quickly realised it was my brave Maa'ingan coming to lead me out of this nightmare. I followed him outside, which was now a sweeping American landscape. We walked in a beautiful meadow lined with sunflowers, surrounded by majestic mountains against an azure sky.

I gasped awake, finding myself once again in my wigwam with Maa'ingan asleep next to me. I felt such relief and ecstasy. I lay there listening to crickets outside and fell into a deep, natural sleep.

I awoke before dawn, fully rested and revitalised. I was nicely snuggled up deep under the covers. Previously I would have thrown off blankets as tight as these due to my fear of constriction. Could this elixir have some sort of restorative powers against my claustrophobia?

Maa'ingan awoke and left to perform whatever duties he has as a member of this village. I was glad I had some time before the others awaken to record last night's visions while they are still fresh in my mind. They certainly gave me a lot to think about.

LETTER FROM HENRY IRVING TO BRAM STOKER, 9TH OF OCTOBER 1882

Dear Bram,

By the time you read this, I will be gone.

I am sorry to leave without a word, but I finally have my chance to enter the Realm and I must do so. I have the book with me, which I know upsets Miss Chase and the White Worms. I am certain it is safer with me than with them, and I might need it once inside the Realm. Besides, I am hoping that the Spanish monks in the mission near the opening might have the key to translating the text.

I know you feel that it is foolish of me to seek entrance to the Realm. However, there is something I have not told you about my affliction and why I must find a cure. Each year that passes it becomes harder for me to fight the demon within. As my humanity becomes weaker I no longer find pleasure in worldly things – in listening to music, or walks in the garden, or in any of the human pursuits that you and others take for granted. I sometimes find myself daydreaming about draining the life from a human. These urges appal and frighten me, and I have so far managed to resist them, but I am not confident in my ability to always do so.

I am afraid the demon will consume me completely one day. I hope I would have the strength to kill myself if I felt this was going to happen, but if that were true, why would I not do so now?

So you see it is very important that I try to get this thing out of me and return to being fully human. If I die in the process, at least my soul will be worthy of going to heaven.

Whether I succeed or not, I will endeavour to return to England. Until I do, you are fully in charge of the theatre and the acting company. I have left instructions with my solicitor on these matters that you are to inherit the theatre should I not return.

I know you will be in good hands with Mr. Reeves; he will see you safely to California.

Sincerely, your friend,

Henry Irving

FROM THE JOURNAL OF BRAM STOKER, 9TH OF OCTOBER 1882

6:00 a.m.

After days on the trail, evading enemies and fearing for my life, I finally reached a place where I thought I could spend the night safely, and yet my sleep is troubled.

Oscar invaded my dreams, and I found myself once again saving him from a vampire. It was so vivid, and yet I knew it was a dream and even commented on it. I awoke with a start and could not get back to sleep.

I got up and left the wigwam, hoping a walk in the cool night air might help me get back to sleep, but it has just given me something else to worry about. As I walked I saw the shaman standing by the fire, as though anticipating my arrival.

He told me the Pale Horseman – as the shaman has learned through his mysterious ways is what the vampire who pursues us calls himself – has not moved on past the hidden village. He is circling us as if he is aware we are here and is looking for a way in.

I have decided it is best to lead him away from the village. I have not discussed this with the others as Florence would forbid me to go, or worse yet, insist on coming with me. I was packing my horse with supplies when I was interrupted by Oscar carrying a lantern.

"Going for a sunrise ride?" he asked.

"It isn't safe for any of you, or for our hosts if I stay here. It is only me he wants." I told him Henry had left and taken the book with him, so at least that was safe from the Pale Horseman.

"He will kill you," Oscar said. "It is best to stay here and wait until the vampire tires and leaves."

"He doesn't tire, and he isn't leaving," I said, securing the last of my supplies into saddlebags and wondering if I would live to use any of them.

Oscar hoisted a saddle onto his horse.

"You aren't coming with me, Oscar."

"I am. It is the only way Florrie will be all right with it. I will tell Mr. Reeves to keep her here for a day, then head to Lake Tahoe tomorrow. We can meet up with them there."

"If we make it that far," I muttered.

Oscar ignored my pessimism. "The shaman can tell us when the vampire bounty hunter is near the east side of the village and we can make a run for it in the opposite direction." He put down his lantern and pulled out a map, unfolded it and placed it on the ground in the light. "With luck, we'll make a clean getaway. But if they do follow us, I thought this might be a good place for us to hide," he said.

It was a hand-drawn map. He said he had got it from someone he referred to as his 'wolf' friend. Leave it to Oscar to make friends wherever he goes. There was an X where he had written *mining camp*. He seemed very pleased with himself. "It is a silver mining camp. We can hide inside the mine and he won't be able to find us. If he does, the silver will keep the vampire from entering. We would only have to deal with his human companion and there are two of us."

"Even if we manage to overpower his companion, we'll be trapped in the mine!"

He shrugged. "I still think he won't be able to detect us encased in silver. In any case, it is a last resort. Escaping them entirely is still my first choice."

"How far?"

"Not too far as the crow flies, but we do have to get down into this valley by the river. No more than four or five miles, a quick trip by horse if you have a map of the trail, which we do."

It was actually a good plan. I really hadn't thought about how I would outrun the Pale Horseman, but maybe we didn't have to. Maybe Oscar is right and they will pass right by us.

As we finished readying our horses, he said, "Er, Bram, did you dream last night? I know it is an odd question."

I was taken aback. "Yes, as a matter of fact, I did. Why?"

"Did you save me from vampire Derrick?"

A shiver ran up my spine. "Yes. And I even asked you why you were in my dream."

He produced a small gourd from his pocket. "My friend gave me a sip of this concoction to help me see beyond the veil. I think I understand your concerns about using your visions now. Parts of the experience were…unpleasant."

We agreed it was a strange night and left it at that. However, I can't help but think we were getting pulled ever deeper into the supernatural once more.

"Once one gets used to the visions this stuff really is good for the nerves," Oscar said. "I highly recommend it for a good night's sleep."

"You will need these," a voice said from behind us, startling me. It was Dacala the shaman, holding out two six-shooters and ammunition. We thanked him and he disappeared into the darkness from which he came.

"Miss Chase has supplied us with these guns and silver bullets," I said, opening the cylinder and checking the bullets in the chamber. Oscar did the same.

In any event, we now have a plan. We will tell Mr. Reeves to protect the others and will be off before Florence wakes. Our reunion was short-lived indeed, but I at least have a spark of hope that it will not be our last.

REPORT FROM AGENT CORA CHASE TO WHITE WORM SOCIETY

Date: 9 October 1882

Subject: Vellum Manuscript Taken by Henry Irving

I am sorry to report a setback in my mission. While I have managed to keep the Stokers, Wilde and the book out of the hands of Drumpf, I have now lost all of them, though I am hopeful this is only temporary.

Henry Irving took the book and secretly left sometime yesterday. Knowing of the vampire speed he possesses, I felt that pursuing him would be fruitless, so I resolved to carry through with my mission of escorting the Stokers to California in the hope that we would reunite with Irving (and the book) there.

Then Mr. Stoker and Mr. Wilde left early this morning in an attempt to lead Drumpf's bounty hunters away from the village. They left a note asking Mr. Reeves to keep Mrs. Stoker here until it is safe to leave, then travel to Lake Tahoe, where, with luck, Stoker and Wilde would join them to make the crossing into California. I planned to accompany Reeves and Mrs. Stoker on that journey.

But while I waited, I took the opportunity to investigate the green stone that the shaman wields within his staff. I had made some subtle enquiries as to the source of the stone and whether there might be more in the village or somewhere nearby, but received no satisfactory answer. So I decided to take matters into my own hands and sneaked into the shaman's wigwam while he slept. I was quite stealthy and had managed to exit with the staff, but before I got more than a few steps, it began to glow and its light alerted some nearby villagers. They descended upon me quickly, and though I tried to explain that I only meant to examine the stone and not steal it, I was soon ejected from the village.

Finding my way back in again would be nearly impossible without a guide who can see through the powerful magic.

I have made a mess of things. But the villagers returned my horse and my weapons and gave me some basic supplies, so I will persevere. All I can do now is wait for Mrs. Stoker and the others to leave and trail them in hopes they will lead me to Stoker, Irving and the book.

—End Report—

FROM THE JOURNAL OF FLORENCE STOKER, 9TH OF OCTOBER 1882

I am full of fret for Bram, Oscar and Henry, and full of anger for that traitor, Cora Chase. She attempted to steal the shaman's magical staff last night and the villagers have sent her packing.

I wish I could say I was surprised at this turn of events, but I have learned all too well how these White Worm people operate. Ever since that Black Bishop business, they have done nothing but stalk and pester us.

They know far too much about us for my comfort. At our first dinner here Miss Chase asked about Noel! Bram did not seem concerned that she somehow knew our son's name when neither he nor I had told it to her. I suppose it was in the White Worm Society report on us, and all sorts of dodgy characters now know who our son is, probably even what he looks like. It's disconcerting, to say the least, and makes me even more eager to return to him.

I do hope he is safe with the nanny. Though now I wonder: is she a White Worm operative? Was it just luck we found a nanny so quickly, who came with so many impeccable recommendations?

And who proved so capable in fending off those men who attacked us?

Perhaps I should never trust anyone again.

Though one person I do trust is Jane. "It's always the ones that smell clean that are the worst varmints," she said, and I have to agree with her. (Though I hope I also smell clean.)

In any event, Mr. Reeves has agreed to continue as a guide until we reach California. Jane will also continue travelling with us.

Shada spoke to a villager who had befriended Oscar, and he thinks he knows where Bram and Oscar went: a mining camp not too far from here. We have decided to stop there in the hopes of finding them and, if we cannot, head to the agreed-upon meeting place.

We are back in our own clothes and I have expressed my gratitude to the women I met here and to the chief. I will miss this village and its people. It is truly the most magical place I have ever been, and it makes me sad that I will never be able to find it again once we leave. But I must get back to Noel and hope that I can reunite with my husband along the way.

LETTER FROM BASS REEVES TO ROBERT REEVES, 9TH OCTOBER 1882

Dear Bobby,

I am sorry I have been away so long. I will return home soon, but first I must see my current mission through to its end. I am not sure where or when I will be able to mail this letter, so it might be some time before you get it.

I have reunited the woman I was helping, Mrs. Stoker, with her husband, but he has got himself on the wrong side of some very bad men, and he took off in hopes of keeping his wife out of harm's way. I have agreed to continue on and see Mrs. Stoker safely to California.

All of this puts me in mind of something I should have said to you long ago.

When your mama left me I did go a bit crazy, I must admit, and I took off. At the time I thought it was for the best. I thought you'd be better off without me. But when you run away from your problems, they have a way of always catching up to you, and I realize how hard it must have been for you and the rest when I left. I am grateful you were there to take care of your brothers and sisters.

You know that on my journey back into the wilderness, I found love again. I met Shada. I became her man, and she became my woman, and all was right with the world again.

But like every journey, it too came to an end. We found a village of Yahi, which has hidden itself away from the world of white men. It is a magical place where people from many tribes, and even some Negroes – escaped slaves, or the children of escaped slaves – have sought refuge. They live there in peace and work together for the good of all. I could not blame her when she told me she wanted to stay there.

For a moment I thought of staying as well, but I know my path lies elsewhere. The truth is, I miss my family in Arkansas, and long to see you all again.

I wanted to make her come with me, but that is not my right. I did not take to being owned by another human being and did not want to own her.

We wept and said our goodbyes. We said we would meet again someday, but I know that is not true. I hope she finds happiness here, and even hope she finds love again, though it also hurts to think of that.

It is hard to not feel sorry for myself, but as my friend Calamity Jane says, "Don't cry because it's over, smile because it happened."

So, when I see my charges safely to California, I will once again head back to Arkansas. I suspect I have some grandkids by now, and I aim to meet them. I have plenty of tales to tell you all, but mostly I'm looking forward to hearing yours.

Love, your father

LETTER FROM ALEJO 'LOBO' LOPEZ TO LUZ LOPEZ, 9TH OF OCTOBER 1882

Dear Luz,

My travels with the devil continue. Today we are still tracking Stoker, and this led us to the legendary village of the Yahi. Yes, it exists. Shrouded in mist and magic, it is not easy to find. The Pale Horseman thinks this is why Stoker came down this trail to seek help and hide among the Yahi.

We followed the Pale Horseman's heightened senses until the trail just stopped. He knew they had been there, and there was nothing indicating they had moved on, so we just stayed in the area, circling the valley, riding up and down hillsides. I could say we were looking for some sign, but I had no idea what that would be or if I would even be able to recognise it. It was cold, and I raised my collar, huddling deeper into my coat. My horse stopped to drink at a stream and the Pale Horseman grunted impatiently; his horse has no need of water.

Finally, as we rounded a particular outcropping of rocks for at least the third time, he raised his hand and we halted. He appeared to be listening closely. A few moments later, I heard it too: voices.

They seemingly appeared out of thin air and into our foggy surroundings. They were two white women and a buffalo soldier, riding away from us. We stayed still until they disappeared deeper into the fog and they did not see us.

"Here," the Pale Horseman whispered. "This is the opening. You wait here." He took off a pouch he had tied to his belt, which I had assumed held chewing tobacco. He poured a substance that looked like gold dust into his palm and tossed it into the air ahead of him where it shimmered. He moved his horse forward and vanished!

After a few moments, I heard screams coming from the fog. I could not tell where they were coming from as they seemed to be everywhere at once.

Then silence.

I waited in the fog for almost an hour, and then he came riding back out of nowhere.

"They came for a map," he said, handing me a piece of paper. "They are no more than half a day from us, heading for the border."

The map was of California, with an X marked on the coast by Santa Barbara.

He grinned, showing his yellow rotting teeth and fangs. "That map is the entrance to hell," he said. "Drumpf will be most pleased we have found it. Now, let's get Stoker and that fucking book."

It is odd that Drumpf calls the place Eden while I call it El Dorado and this creature calls it hell. It is as if it is all things to all people.

I feel as if I am on the edge of a great historical discovery. I am about to join the ranks of Columbus, Magellan and Cortez. This is more important than the gold or any riches we may find there. The discovery of this place will change all of mankind, just as the discovery of the new world by the conquistadors did. I only hope this change is for the better.

Lobo

FROM THE DIARY OF OSCAR WILDE, 9TH OF OCTOBER 1882

Dear yours truly,

I saved Stoker's life twice today. I have lost count of how many times this adds up to and will have to read all of your pages when I get home for the full tally.

First, I must say I am happy I purchased the waterproof canvas pouch in which to store you or your wonderful pages would be quite ruined after our latest adventures.

It was a harrowing morning. I was nearly shot, then nearly drowned, then nearly hanged. Not one word of a thank you from Stoker, mind you, but he will be getting a bill for my suit.

We left the village just before sunrise this morning, in the hopes of drawing Stoker's pursuers away from Florence and the rest of our friends, old and new. We had a head start of a good five miles as we left from the opposite side of the village from where the vampire was. At least that is what the shaman told us, looking into his magic fire.

After we had travelled a mile or so, I commented, "Well, this is certainly different from my last trip to America. I must hand it to you, Bram. You do lead an interesting life for someone so boring."

"I would like life to be a little less interesting in the future," he replied.

I reflected for a moment, then thought perhaps Bram could help me settle my own mind on a subject. "Speaking of less interesting lives," I began, then realised that might be an insensitive way of broaching the subject. "Sorry, I mean, speaking of...normal life? Married life? I don't know, the kind of life you have…. My word, I have never had such trouble starting a conversation before."

"Are you trying to ask me how my marriage is faring, Oscar?"

"Good heavens, no. Everyone knows you've made a mess of it, but it does seem to be on the mend."

"Everyone?" he asked, alarmed.

"Well, no. Mainly me. Probably Willie. Mother has probably sensed something. Henry, certainly. That exhausts our list of mutual acquaintances, so yes, I suppose I do mean everyone."

He fumed for a moment, then said, "I made a grave mistake. But I am doing my best to make it up to Florence. It will take time to regain her trust."

We rode in silence for a minute, then I asked, "But is it worth it, Stoker? Marriage?"

"Are you thinking of marrying, Oscar?"

"Yes, as a matter of fact, I am. Constance Lloyd is seemingly the perfect woman for me. But what if I hurt her, as you hurt Florence?"

"Oh, you most certainly will, Oscar."

I tried to argue but found I could not. "But will I be able to make it up to her? Or will our marriage become a source of profound regret for her?"

"The latter, without a doubt," he said lightly. He looked over and saw how stricken I was. "I am joking, Oscar. But only partly. You are a good man and a good friend. You have stood by my side through one harrowing experience after another, and I will never forget that, or stop appreciating it, truly."

"I will see that you don't."

He smiled, but then turned serious. "All that said, I do not know if you have the right…temperament for marriage." He said this with the air of someone trying his best to be diplomatic. "You are a creature of whim and fancy," he continued. "You will always do what you want to do in any particular moment. That is not the hallmark of a good husband. So often what is best for the marriage is not what one wants to do in the moment."

He averted his eyes, but not before I saw the haunted look there. I sympathised with him, even though he had all but said I am a selfish lout who never thinks of anything but his own pleasure, which is sometimes true – but wasn't I here risking life and limb for him?

I was about to say so when he suddenly sat up straighter and looked around wildly. His sixth sense had become riled. "They aren't far behind us!"

We put our heels to the horses and brought them to a full gallop!

I took up the rear and turned my head to look behind. I could see a cloud of dust in the distance!

Bouncing up and down in the saddle at full gallop made it difficult to read my map, but I did the best I could at shouting directions. Still, I must have missed a turn because we found ourselves riding full force towards a cliff, with Stoker seemingly unaware as he was not slowing down.

Before I could point this out, I heard a gunshot, and a bullet whizzed by my ear. Stoker reached the edge of the cliff and pulled the reins hard on his horse, but it was too late! The horse did its best to stop, but slid off the cliff with Stoker still in the saddle!

My steed had more horse sense and stopped hard, throwing me off with such force that I continued forward over the cliff myself! I must not have secured my saddle properly, for it came with me. (Sometimes, good fortune comes disguised as carelessness.)

It is days like this I know there must be a God and he must be looking out for us, because we plunged thirty or forty feet into a raging river. It was ice-cold and deep and swept us along in its swift current. I managed to float on my saddlebags, which had popped up like a cork. It was all I could do to keep my head above water. I caught a glimpse of Stoker, who was off his horse. Both of them were trying to fight their way to the opposite bank.

The rapids gave way to a small eddy, and the water calmed. I looked back to the cliff in time to see the vampire and his bandit turning back from the edge. With any luck, I thought, they would have to take the long way around to get down to the river.

All three of us managed to drag ourselves to the riverbank. The horse stood and shook off the water, seeming no worse for wear. The poor creature was still fully saddled. Stoker drained the water from his saddlebags and gave the horse an apple.

Luckily, we were able to salvage some food and other supplies, as well as you, dear diary, from our saddlebags.

I wasn't so sure about our guns. Could you fire them wet?

I checked our map. Using a twin-peaked mountain as a landmark

I was able to orientate us. "This way to the mining camp," I said, pointing. We let the horse rest as long as we dared, then headed down the trail on foot, leading the horse behind us. The horse must have twisted his ankle because he limped a bit, but soon was walking better.

As much as I wanted to complain about what had just happened, it was an extraordinary bit of luck. It had cut miles off our trip. Before long, we could see the smoke from the mining camp ahead of us.

"I hope you appreciate the shortcut I found for us, Bram," I said, and we both started to laugh at the craziness of it all. Our spirits were buoyed by a remarkable escape.

I should have remembered that nothing is easy when travelling with Stoker. We once again found ourselves leaving the frying pan only to enter the fire.

"Hold it right there," an unwashed man yelled, pointing a shotgun at us from behind a shrub.

Another man ran up to him through the brush. "What is it, Jeb?"

"Fuckin' claim jumpers," he spat. Literally, he spat out a wad of chewing tobacco after he said that.

"Why do people always accuse me of that?" Bram said with his hands in the air. "I assure you, we are just lost travellers."

"Let's get them back to camp," the other man said to Jeb.

They dragged us and our horse through the brush and into their camp. It consisted of a few tents and a hole in the side of a hill that I assumed was the mine. A half-dozen or so grizzled miners were sitting around a campfire, eating their lunch, while others wandered about carrying picks and buckets and other mining paraphernalia.

The other miners gathered around us and from a tent emerged a tall, moustached man who, from his demeanour and anger, I judged to be their leader. (You certainly could not tell by his clothing, which was just as rugged and dusty as that of his underlings.)

"What do ya got there, Clem?"

"Claim jumpers, Mr. Barker!"

Stoker and I both strenuously denied this.

We were still wet and probably looked most dishevelled; I could hardly blame him for thinking we were outlaws.

The one called Barker looked us over a moment and then said, "String 'em up."

Having been in the West before, I knew straightaway what he meant, and Bram had figured it out as well because he was struggling and pleading.

"No, wait!" he said as we were being dragged along by the crowd, who all seemed quite excited to attend a hanging. They were also bringing the horse along.

Are they going to hang the horse too? I thought. Then I realised the horse was to be our gallows. They pushed us both on top of the horse, took us to a tree and threw two ropes over a sturdy branch. In mere seconds there were nooses around our necks. (Are hangings a common enough occurrence in camp to have nooses at the ready? Or are nooses somehow used in the mining process? I can't see how, but then I am not a miner.)

This was all happening so fast I was taking it in as if I were an disinterested observer. My brain finally caught up to what was about to happen and the resulting panic caught up with my mouth.

"Stop!" I commanded. Stoker was in shock and I think saying a prayer to himself. "I am not a claim jumper. I am, in fact, Oscar Wilde." They all just stared at me with unrecognising eyes. Well, it was worth a try.

"You is dressed like a man I saw selling ice cream in Saint Louis," a miner shouted. His companions laughed uproariously at this, so at least I was warming them up. Humour, even at my expense, is better than murderous anger.

Bram finally found his voice. "We are on the run from a killer!" Our horse was becoming restless, and only the men keeping it in place stopped it from wandering off and leaving us dangling at the ends of our ropes. "A blood-sucking vampire is coming and he will kill you all if we don't take steps to stop him!"

Barker, who was watching the lynching from the back, pushed his way through the crowd. "Did you say vampire?"

"Yes," I said.

"Cut 'em down," Barker said. "Bring 'em to my tent."

When Stoker said *vampire*, I'd expected more laughter, but this was a much better response.

We were roughly wrestled down from our horse and brought to the tent. Inside, another man was tied to a chair. He was snarling and snapping like a wild animal. I recognised him straightaway as a vampire. He was not bound by silver but only by ropes. However, there were boxes of silver ore stacked all around the tent. This was most likely, unknown to the miners, weakening him enough for the ropes to bind him.

"One of those things turned my brother here into one of them," Barker said. "How do we fix 'im?"

"I'm sorry. I'm afraid you don't," Bram said. The man was too far gone for Bram's blood to cure him, which might have been done had the man not fully turned. "There is no cure."

Barker sat down on his cot and buried his face in his hands. "I was afraid of that," he said, his voice muffled.

His brother snarled and drooled, the effects of the silver, I suspect.

Barker raised his head and looked at Bram with sad eyes. "How do I kill 'im?"

"A wooden stake to the heart is the quickest," Bram said kindly. "Do you want me to do it?"

Barker nodded his head and left the tent.

He sent another man in with a wooden stake and a mallet. Bram did the deed and the man burst into a sludge of guts and blood, totally ruining the chair he was sitting on, most of the tent and Bram's shirt.

We left the tent and found Barker being comforted by his friends and a bottle of whiskey.

Bram informed him the deed was done, and we both expressed our condolences. Then Bram got to the point of our visit. "We would like to hide in your mine. We believe the silver will cloud the vampire's ability to track us. He is the most powerful I have ever faced and has his full strength even in daylight. If he finds me, he will attack the camp to get to me."

"He may attack anyway," I said. "He needs to feed, and according to the authorities he has been attacking settlements and turning the inhabitants into vampires."

"He already attacked the camp in Jacks Valley," Barker said. "That's where he got my brother. We'll stand and fight this murderous bastard. If you don't mind us using you for bait, that is."

Bram agreed and added, "We need to cover your bullets with silver."

"Silver is what we got plenty of," Barker said. He snapped his men into action.

We now wait, dear diary, for that monster to catch up with us. I am hoping we will have the element of surprise and can put up a good fight.

FROM THE JOURNAL OF BRAM STOKER, 9TH OF OCTOBER 1882

2:15 p.m.

Just when I am at my most fed up with Oscar Wilde, he goes and demonstrates cleverness and bravery. The man is truly a paradox.

With the Pale Horseman in close pursuit, we had no time to spare to get the miners into a defensive position. Had not one of their own been turned into a vampire, I doubt we could have made them believe us, let alone convinced them to help us.

However, they came together splendidly. We quickly surrounded the camp with boxes of silver ore. The leader of the camp, Mr. Barker, ordered his men to dip the tips of their bullets in silver and stand at the ready.

"Our weak point is this riverfront," Barker said. "The river is narrow and shallow here, no problem for a man or horse to wade across."

One of the miners approached, holding out a stick of dynamite. "We have one stick left," he told Barker.

Oscar grabbed it from his hand. "I have a wonderful idea. Let's coat it in silver."

I had to admit that might make an effective weapon.

"It won't blow up if I put hot silver on it, will it?" Oscar asked, as he and the miner hurried off towards the fire where men were melting the ore.

"I don't think so," the miner said. "Maybe?"

He came back later with a silver stick of dynamite, so apparently one can safely coat a stick of dynamite with molten silver.

Oscar practised throwing sticks across the river to the other shore to see if tossing the dynamite was feasible. He actually had quite an accurate throw, and I was happy to see he was fully confident in his ability to wield his weapon.

Finally, we had done all we could to prepare. The men took up positions behind stacked crates of silver ore, weapons at the ready.

We had finished just in time. The Pale Horseman and the human companion we had seen in the shaman's fire appeared on the riverbank across from the camp. The human looked to be in his early fifties, with long sideburns. He had a pistol in his hand, another holstered at his side, and extra ammunition in a bandolier strapped across his chest.

"Mr. Stoker," the human desperado yelled. "Come with us and give us the book, and no one needs to get hurt." I found myself wishing Henry hadn't taken the book; I might have been able to trade it for my life, or at least Oscar's life.

Barker whistled, and the miners began firing. The two bandits quickly backed away into the cover of the trees. They hopped off their horses and fired back, crouching behind rocks.

The Pale Horseman took out four miners, shooting them all in the head in rapid succession. This made the other miners take cover and stop shooting. Any hopes I had of overwhelming them with our numbers were fading fast.

The Pale Horseman was such a good shot that he could fire through any opening between crates, no matter how small.

He stopped only to reload. At this opportunity, the miners fired furiously at him and Oscar lobbed his lit stick of silver dynamite. He threw too hard, and it landed behind them in the trees.

The explosion did startle them and they froze for a moment.

Oscar had missed the gunmen with the dynamite but apparently had hit the Pale Horseman's horse. It came charging out of the woods engulfed in flames! It was an even eerier sight now, with its patches of horsehide ablaze and the exposed ribcage bathed in firelight.

It nearly ran into the vampire as it galloped full force into the river trying to find relief from the fire. It snarled and hissed, sounding more like a wounded cat than a horse. Its head was shaking violently back and forth as it tried to put out the flames.

Then it suddenly stopped thrashing. It stood up straight, its head pointed high to the sky. Its mouth opened in a scream that sounded almost human.

Though the flames were now out, an eerie red glow emanated from its body. Then what could only be described as a demon shot out of its screaming mouth. It was shaped like a horse, but that was where its resemblance to a horse ended. It was made from flames and smoke and agony. It flew in our direction, then I realised it was actually flying directly towards me! Like a drowning man grasping desperately at anything to not be pulled down, it wanted me as its next host.

To the horror of myself and Oscar next to me, it surrounded me, looking for a way into my body.

What happened next both saved and terrified me.

A green glow emanated from my very core. It pushed the red demon away with great force. For a second I could see my demon's shape. Deep down I had always known it was there, giving me my second sight and at times turning me into a beast. Like the horse's parasite had taken a horse's form, this one was human-shaped but faceless. It snapped back into me and disappeared.

The horse's demon gave out an audible scream as it was pulled down into the ground in front of me, seemingly to the very depths of hell itself.

"Noooo!" the Pale Horseman screamed in a raspy voice. He ran forward, not caring about the barrage of bullets being fired at him.

He fired wildly at us, quickly emptying his guns but not hitting a single human in his blind rage. Three or four shots hit him, but none fatally. He stumbled backwards to the riverbank and collapsed to his knees.

His companion grabbed the back of his shirt and yanked him back to the safety of the trees.

In moments we could see them riding away on the desperado's horse.

The men in the camp cheered, for we had beaten them.

Then they mourned for the men they had lost. Their anger turned towards us as the ones they blamed for bringing the vampire here.

"We weren't safe anyway," Barker told them. "You saw what happened at the camp in Jacks Valley. At least these two showed us how to fight 'em."

That seemed to quiet them for the moment, but Barker turned to us and said, "You two better get out of here while the getting's good." I could see the fear in his eyes. Not just at what we had brought to his camp but at what he had witnessed inside of me.

Oscar and I headed north with our horse.

As a reward for his clever thinking with the dynamite, I let him ride the horse while I walked ahead.

"Do you think we can make it to Lake Tahoe before he finds a new horse?" Oscar asked me. I wondered if he really wanted to talk about the demon inside me and was just using small talk to avoid it.

"I hope so," I said.

We are now bedding down for the night in a grove of pine trees. We dare not build a fire and I am forced to share a blanket with Oscar to keep warm.

"I really never saw my life going this way," Oscar said. "I was going to be a playwright and the toast of London."

I thought a moment and said, "I suppose if Irving hadn't come into my life and made me his theatre manager and a monster hunter, I would have just continued to be a civil servant at Dublin Castle."

"So no dreams as you sat behind that desk?"

"I planned to continue my writing. Maybe save enough money to travel a few times a year. Find a nice girl and settle down. I doubt Florence would have married me if I hadn't landed the theatre job, so it would have been someone else."

"I do not think that is true, that Florrie wouldn't have married you. She most likely would have turned to you after my shenanigans in any event." I thought it was nice of him to say that but didn't tell him so. It was bad enough we were spooning together under a horse blanket.

"I am not cut out for all these adventures," I confessed.

"Nonsense. It is the bureaucrat's life that you were not meant for. To live is the rarest thing in the world. Most people exist, that is all," Oscar said. "If you are going to have greatness thrust upon you, the least you can do is learn to enjoy it, or at least learn from it."

FROM THE DIARY OF OSCAR WILDE, 9TH OF OCTOBER 1882

Stoker and I have just spent hours on the run only to find ourselves at the bottom of a well. I would like to say it was the worst place I have ever been, but I have slid down the gullet of a giant snake, so it will have to settle for being the second worst.

We were walking, as our horse had turned out to be lamer than we thought from our fall into the river. The poor thing was limping along, still carrying our saddlebags. We finally took the bags off and let her go off into a meadow, as we continued on our way being our own beasts of burden. Her leg did not seem to be broken, so our hope is that she will heal in time. Perhaps she will find a nice herd of wild horses to join.

We were a way up in the hills and the water supply was scarce. To our great fortune, we found a springhouse: a shed built around a well, to keep out bugs and animals, I suppose. It was a welcome sight in the middle of nowhere.

Inside it was cool. A stone well rose from the middle surrounded by floorboards. Inside there were benches to sit on and I was happy to get off my feet.

Stoker lowered the bucket that was attached to a rope suspended from the ceiling. He pulled up a full bucket, and we drank our fill and replenished our canteens.

The well water tasted of iron but quenched our thirst nonetheless.

"We will camp nearby for the night," Stoker said. He was prying up one of the floorboards.

"Why not just sleep in here tonight?" I asked.

He hid our saddlebags under the floorboards and replaced the planks. "We would be trapped like rats in here. We need to stay where we can make a quick getaway. Not to mention they might stop here to water themselves and their horses."

I often hate it when Stoker is right, and this time he was proven right immediately, so I hated it even more than usual. We heard the unmistakable sounds of horses approaching outside!

I peeked through a knothole and saw the Mexican bandit that had attacked the mining camp. He was with three other men on horseback.

Stoker was right; we were trapped in a most ratlike way.

"Into the well," Bram whispered.

"What? I'm not jumping into a well." I looked down into it and could not see the bottom.

"Suit yourself," he said, lowering the rope into the water. He started to climb down the rope, and I had no choice but to follow.

I was worried about how deep the water was, but I didn't need to be. When we reached the bottom, Stoker and I were wedged in belly to belly with only our bottom halves soaking underwater. It was very cold and very wet. Stoker's breath smelled horrible and I could do little to get away from its onslaught.

We could clearly see out of the well above and I was now worried that they could easily see us. It would be like shooting fish in a barrel!

The bandit and another man entered the springhouse and peered down into the well. To my relief, it became quickly obvious they could not see us down in the shadows even though we could see them. I suppose if my lavender suit had not become so coated in dust and mud they may have caught a glimpse of me.

"Where's the vampire?" the other man asked.

"Looking for a new horse," the Mexican said. "It's hard to find a living one that can stand to carry him."

They pulled up the bucket, which slid past us, nearly getting caught on Stoker's elbow. He gave it a gentle shove, and it proceeded. "The horses need water," said the Mexican. "Hand me those feedbags."

I was starting to feel panicky. My palms were sweating and my breath grew short. Claustrophobia again. I closed my eyes and took slow, calming breaths as Dr. Ball had taught me. Oh, how I wished I had some laudanum! But the breathing worked, and I was able to keep the panic at bay. And oddly, having Stoker down there with me had a calming effect. Still, I did not know if I could face being down the well for much longer.

"I've never seen the Pale Horseman drink water," the Mexican said.

"Jesus," the other man exclaimed. "He only lives off blood?"

"I think so. Grab the canteens," the Mexican said, starting to lower the bucket again. It landed to the side of me with just enough room to sink. "We can camp here for the night. He'll catch up to us here when he gets a horse."

So, we were safely hidden but could not escape. And when the vampire came, would he be able to sniff us out?

I then had a marvellous idea.

The bucket was being hoisted up. I grabbed it and stopped its ascent. Stoker's eyes shot me a *what-are-you-doing?* look, as I pulled out the gourd of potion Maa'ingan had given me back in the Yahi village.

"It's stuck," the Mexican said, yanking on the rope as I poured the contents of my gourd into the bucket.

I let the bucket continue back up. I could hear them dunking their canteens into the cool water.

To our luck, they dropped the bucket down the well. To Bram's bad luck it struck him hard on the head, and he had to stifle a cry of pain.

Then they left the springhouse.

"What the hell was that?" Bram whispered. He freed a pinned arm to rub his head.

"That was the dream juice my friend gave me," I said. I told him I wasn't sure if it would work so diluted with water, but if it did, they would be off in dreamland in a few minutes.

"That's not going to work. My God, we're going to die down here," Bram said.

"If we do, Bram, I want you to know I don't blame you."

"Thanks, I guess," he muttered.

The dark, close confines must have reminded me of a confessional, because as we waited I found myself confessing my sins to Stoker, of all people!

"I have been unfaithful to Constance," I blurted out. "Twice now, and I feel awful about it."

"Like I said, maybe marriage just isn't for you, Oscar," he said in a brotherly tone.

"Yet, you survived your own moral failings," I said. I did not mean it to sound accusatory.

"Do we need to talk about this now?" he said, more than a little perturbed. "We need to keep quiet. How long does this stuff take to work? How will we know if it does?"

We then heard a man scream, something about a dragon attacking him. He started shooting off his gun in a rapid succession.

"That's how we'll know," I said.

Other disturbed voices were crying and moaning.

"I'm so sorry I left you, Marleen!"

"I'm a tree, I'm a tree!"

Within a few more minutes, the screaming and yelling subsided.

"I think they're asleep," I said.

After a few clumsy attempts, Bram climbed the rope then helped hoist me out.

We carefully looked out to see the four men curled up with each other, sound asleep.

We retrieved our hidden saddlebags and stole two horses and supplies from Drumpf's men. Our booty included a lantern, a compass and a map!

We rode quickly off in the direction of Lake Tahoe, our spirits lifted by our turn of good luck and our fists full of stolen jerky.

Luck begets luck, and we found a cave. Not the most luxurious of accommodation, but at least it was dry. It went back far enough that we felt it would be safe to light the lantern, as it would not be seen from the trail.

"Well, what do we have here?" Stoker said, rummaging through our stolen loot. He produced a bottle of whiskey. "Yes, Oscar, things are looking up."

FROM THE JOURNAL OF FLORENCE STOKER, 10TH OF OCTOBER 1882

We passed through the mining camp this morning, only to find that there had been an attack. The leader of the camp told us it was a vampire and a Mexican gunslinger, and they had fought them off with the help of Bram and Oscar.

"The fancy man managed to kill the vampire's horse," he said. "But the vampire was only wounded, and he and the gunslinger ran off. Your husband and the fancy man left right after the battle."

He told us they are heading to Lake Tahoe and then I wished we had gone straight there. But at least they are alive and that knowledge makes me very happy.

As luck would have it, a cavalry troop was passing by as we were starting back on the trail, and they too are heading in our direction. The leader, Captain Mitchell, has kindly offered to escort us to the border.

I pulled Mr. Reeves and Jane aside to discuss. "Can we trust them?" I asked. "Or will they turn us over to Drumpf if they learn I am married to Bram?"

"These men are U.S. Cavalry," Mr. Reeves explained. "They are not beholden to a weasel like Drumpf. If your husband's name was cleared on the federal level, as Miss Chase said, the cavalry will have no beef with him." (I have come to learn that this phrase means that they have no complaint against him, not that they would refuse to dine with him.)

Jane was uncharacteristically quiet during our conversation with Captain Mitchell, her hat tilted down and a kerchief tied over her mouth. "I think I may be wanted by the cavalry for something," she muttered to me when I asked about it. "I can't at the moment remember what, but it's best if I don't show my face."

Jane and I rode together. It was comforting to be among so large a force, and my spirits rose at the thought of reaching our destination safely.

Mr. Reeves knows some of the soldiers and rode with them. We could see them up ahead, catching up and laughing together.

Jane pulled her kerchief down and said, "You know, as a marshal, Reeves once had to bring one of his own sons in for murder."

I was shocked, to say the least. "That must have been an excruciating decision to have to make."

"He done did it," Jane said. "That's the kinda man he is. He always completes his mission."

I can certainly attest that he is not one to shirk his duty.

FROM THE DIARY OF OSCAR WILDE, 10TH OF OCTOBER 1882

Dear yours truly,

Our getaway did not go as planned. The only thing that got away was our luck.

Only a day after our victory over the vampire gunslinger and hiding in a well to escape the Mexican and his cohorts, we found ourselves once again under attack, this time from the entire posse!

We were making our way towards Lake Tahoe, riding along a ridge. We heard hoof beats behind us, turned, and from our vantage point could see a dozen or so men on horseback, riding fast and furiously along the riverbank. We barely took cover when they started firing at us.

We were behind a boulder but trapped. Bullets ricocheted in front of and behind us as the cloud of dust and riders got ever closer.

"They want to take me alive," Bram said. "I will go out with my hands up and you run off in the other direction."

But before I could argue, or run for that matter, we heard an amazing sound. It was the call of a cavalry bugle! I had heard it demonstrated on my previous travels in America.

The posse stopped. A bigger cloud of dust and riders was coming at them fast. The posse disbanded and scattered for the hills. You hear of this sort of thing happening in dime-store novels but you never really expect it to happen to you – we were being saved by the cavalry!

Our rescuers came to a halt, and we emerged from the safety of our rock and went down to greet them. Imagine our surprise when Florrie, Reeves and Calamity came riding up! (Oh, joy – I got to witness another tearful reunion of the Stokers.)

It seems our friends had trailed us to the mining camp, then met up with the cavalry as they resumed their journey. The leader, a Captain Mitchell, has chivalrously offered the troop's protection as they too are heading to the Lake Tahoe region.

In sadder news, it seems Reeves and Shada have parted ways.

And I was right about Miss Chase. The Yahi caught the White Wormer trying to steal the shaman's magical stick. She is no longer a member of our travelling party.

We are lunching along the river. Our hosts have supplied us with, you guessed it, beans and bacon. I'm afraid this dreadful diet has led to a constant case of flatulence and most likely will give me gout before the journey is over.

There seems to be some ruckus now between Bram and Captain Mitchell. I will go and see what it is....

It seems Captain Mitchell has the wanted poster and has taken Bram into custody. He is manacled on his horse. I hope the captain doesn't find out we stole our horses. Being labelled as horse thieves is not taken lightly in the West.

Florence pleaded with him. "Bram's name was cleared! Tell them, Mr. Reeves."

"That is what we were told," Reeves concurred.

"If that is the case, ma'am, I'm sure we'll be able to get it all sorted out once we reach Lake Tahoe. But this wanted poster is the only official information I have at the moment. I guarantee your husband will get a fair hearing."

So for now Stoker is once again a prisoner. I am sure we will work all this out when we get to California, but nothing ever is easy with that man.

LETTER FROM ALEJO 'LOBO' LOPEZ TO LUZ LOPEZ, 10TH OF OCTOBER 1882

Dear Luz,

I witnessed more black magic today.

Our pursuit of Stoker has been thwarted at every turn. The Pale Horseman is full of rage as one of Stoker's companions killed his horse, something I thought was not possible. It seems these creatures are affected badly by silver and the horse took the full brunt of a stick of silver-coated dynamite meant for the Pale Horseman. The demon that animated the horse was driven back to hell, and it fell dead again.

Later, I joined a posse that Drumpf has sent to bring in Stoker while the vampire was off looking for a new horse. But somehow Stoker and his companion managed to drug us and we were all incapacitated with hallucinations. I myself saw Mama and Papa and our childhood home, only the colours were more vivid than anything I've ever seen in real life. Then I was at my ranch, while it was thriving, and I could see a thousand head of cattle. I could distinguish every animal. I could feel the warm breeze. Then you showed up, Luz. You told me the ranch stretched all the way down to your home in Mexico, and we rode the range, trading stories and laughing.

I sank into a deep sleep, and when I awoke, two of our horses and much of our supplies were gone. It had to be Stoker. Perhaps he has some magic of his own he used against us.

Our posse rode hard after him and eventually caught up to him. We had him pinned down, but unfortunately the U.S. Cavalry showed up and forced us away.

The prophet Rayne had joined us, and we retreated to the ridge where he was waiting. The good thing about a cavalry troop is that it's easy to spot, even from a distance. We managed to trail them, and when they made camp for lunch, we watched from a nearby hilltop.

Rayne gathered us all into a circle around him. He chanted in some unknown tongue, pointing his staff to the sky. He nodded to the Pale Horseman, who grabbed one of our number, a runty gringo I knew only as Fly Speck. He pushed Fly Speck to his knees in front of Rayne and held him there while Rayne pulled a long curved dagger from a sheath at his waist.

Fly Speck's eyes were wide and panicky, and he struggled and cried out for help. The rest of the posse just looked on in horror, realising what was happening, knowing it could have been any of them, but afraid to go up against the Pale Horseman.

Rayne chanted some more, ran the stone top of his staff along the dagger, then slit Fly Speck's throat, spilling his blood into the dirt. He slammed the base of this staff into the bloody ground, and a blinding green light shot from the stone at the top of the staff into the sky.

Clouds parted. The sky for a moment turned unrecognisable, going from a bright blue to a dull red. Far in the distance was a flying creature, flapping its wings. At first, I thought it was a large bird but as it came closer, I could see it was some sort of horrible monster, more bat than bird. Still closer, it seemed more lizard than bat. It was the size of a horse and had a long beak of pointy teeth. Its talons were the size of spades and looked just as sharp. It circled us, letting out a thunderous screech. It so terrified us we froze, gazing into its merciless eyes while it lunged down for an eagle-like attack, as if we were helpless rabbits.

But Rayne held his staff high, and this seemed to bring it under control. He pointed towards the cavalry below and it obeyed. It turned back to the sky, circled once, then swooped down the hill to the valley below.

We could hear men screaming and watched them shoot at the creature and scatter for their lives.

We ran to the edge of the hill to see it attacking men, plucking them right off their horses and then smashing them on the rocks.

In the confusion I lost track of Stoker for a moment, then saw him riding away with his friends through a narrow trail between boulders where the creature could not follow.

The remaining soldiers took positions safely behind rocks and fired at the creature. Soon the barrage of bullets was too much, and the creature retreated to the sky, but it was too late. More bullets found their target, and the creature came tumbling to earth, crashing with a great thud.

Rayne had greatly overestimated his monster and underestimated the cavalry. He later told us he suspected Stoker and his gang had silver bullets in their guns, for supernatural creatures are not felled by lead bullets so easily. I remembered seeing the Negro cowboy riding with Stoker turn and shoot his rifle at the creature just before it fell from the sky, so maybe this was true. Or maybe Rayne is just trying to make excuses for his magic not working as he wanted.

In any event, Stoker and his companions were in fast retreat away from the cavalry, and we were stuck on the other side.

With the creature dead, the cavalry had nothing stopping them from turning their attack on us. We had only the advantage of high ground to slow them down. We retreated into the hills and hid. We came out of hiding only when we were sure they had turned back, to bury their dead and continue on their way.

Rayne is furious. Somehow this greenhorn keeps slipping through his fingers, and we will have to answer to Drumpf. There is no telling where Stoker and company have gone. We will head to the border at first light, as that is our best guess as to where they are heading.

Lobo

REPORT FROM AGENT CORA CHASE TO WHITE WORM SOCIETY

Date: 10 October 1882

Subject: Rejoined Stokers and Wilde

Following Mrs. Stoker has paid off. I have found Stoker, and he is once again under my protection.

Along the way, the whole party fell in with a troop of cavalry, who must not have gotten word that Stoker was innocent because I could see through my spyglasses that they put him in handcuffs. At least that would keep him from wandering off again, or so I thought.

Then the most extraordinary thing happened. A flying monster appeared in the sky and attacked the cavalry! I can only assume Rayne was nearby and had summoned it. (I will supply a sketch of the creature to the Supernatural Creatures Division for identification purposes at my earliest convenience.)

I am proud to say the men in blue made quick work of the monster and chased Drumpf's posse high into the hills.

This gave Stoker, Wilde and the others a chance to escape, and me a chance to follow.

I was not a welcome sight, to say the least. Mrs. Stoker and Calamity Jane took shots at me as I approached. Thanks to Mrs. Stoker's lack of proficiency with a gun and Calamity's inebriation, they missed me.

Bass Reeves trained his pistol on me and ordered my hands in the air. Knowing his skill, I complied.

"What in the hell do you want?" he asked me.

"Here to arrest me again?" Mr. Stoker asked.

"I am here to help," I said. "I am sorry about what happened in the Yahi village, but I assure you my intentions were good. I did not want to steal the stone, merely to examine it. I was going to sketch it, perhaps try to scrape a bit off for analysis. My first duty is to protect the world from supernatural forces, and to do that I need all the knowledge I can get. However, I assure you, my second objective is to keep you all safe from our common enemy."

"I trust you about as far as I can throw you," Mr. Wilde said. "For all we know you could be leading us into a trap. I've dealt with you White Wormers before."

"And when have we ever harmed you?" I asked.

"Well," he said, thinking. "You've annoyed me at the very least."

I held up my handcuff key. "I am here to help, and I can start by getting those handcuffs off Mr. Stoker. This key should work on U.S. Cavalry-issued cuffs."

I tossed Mrs. Stoker the key, then pulled out my pistol by the barrel and handed it to Mr. Reeves.

"If you want to help you can start by telling us the best way to get to the border," Reeves said, as he stuck my gun in his boot and holstered his own.

"If I was a betting woman, I'd lay odds that Drumpf's men will be waiting for you at the ferry in Sand Harbor," I said. "But I have a steamboat waiting in Glenbrook and I know a hidden trail to take us there."

"Lead the way," Reeves said. "But don't forget, I'll be right behind you the whole time." He patted his pistol for emphasis.

We set off and have travelled companionably enough, all things considered. I hope for my sake the steamboat is still there, and the captain is in a good enough mood to help us.

—End Report—

FROM THE DIARY OF OSCAR WILDE, 10TH OF OCTOBER 1882

What a thrilling day! We and our cavalry escorts were attacked by yet another monster, and narrowly escaped with our lives. Miss Chase rejoined us, and after some stern words from me, apologised for her earlier betrayal and offered us safe passage to California. True to her word, her guidance brought us to a town called Glenbrook on Lake Tahoe, where a small steamboat was waiting for us.

We boarded and headed off just as some of Drumpf's men caught up to us. They shot at us from the shore, but the steamboat chugged along quite swiftly out onto the lake. (Who would have thought, diary, that being shot at would become such a common occurrence for me that I would mention it so casually!)

"Fastest boat on the lake," Captain Post assured us. It was exhilarating, not only to put distance between us and certain death but to be on the open water with the cool air on our faces.

Lake Tahoe is quite a large body of water, bigger than anything we have in England, I should think. Before long I couldn't even see the shore.

Miss Chase consulted her pocket watch. "We can catch a stage in Tahoe City to Truckee, where we can get an express train to San Francisco," she said. The wind off the lake caught strands of her auburn hair, pulling them free from the stylish twist that she somehow managed to maintain even on the trail. She brushed them from her face nonchalantly. "They will expect us to take the train out of Tahoe to Sacramento, so this will guarantee we will give them the slip."

I personally was sceptical of anything billed as a guarantee, but kept my doubts to myself. Sometimes it is quite a refreshing change of pace to not speak.

"What do we do in San Francisco?" Bram asked.

"The White Worms have a hideout there. Drumpf doesn't have much power in California, but I wouldn't count him out. He has the money and bounty hunters to try to get the book and bring Mr. Stoker in."

She once again told us how dangerous it is that Henry had taken the book and pressed all of us for information on his whereabouts. We all feigned ignorance.

"Getting to San Francisco is all well and good," Florrie said. "But we need to get back to our son in Salt Lake City."

"We will put you on a train as soon as it is safe to do so," Miss Chase said. "But we need to neutralise the Drumpf threat first."

We docked in Tahoe City, and Miss Chase and Mr. Reeves disembarked first to 'get the lay of the land', as he said. After they ascertained that it was safe, and Miss Chase had secured a stagecoach, the rest of us bid farewell to Captain Post and left the boat.

I can hardly believe, dear diary, that the stagecoach ride was uneventful, but here we are, safely on a train to the only civilised city west of the Mississippi: San Francisco. Mr. Clemens said he was heading there, so perhaps I will look him up.

I am so happy to have once again rescued Bram and put that nasty Drumpf far behind us. I am equally happy that Bram and I managed to hang on to some of the whiskey we had taken from that dreadful posse.

FROM THE DIARY OF OSCAR WILDE, 10TH OF OCTOBER 1882

We have arrived in San Francisco and to Miss Chase's hideout, which, it turns out, is a house of ill repute hidden away in Chinatown; a high-end brothel, but a brothel nonetheless.

Being a worldly gentleman, I am not bothered. I have stayed in worse places for longer amounts of time, but I do worry about poor Florrie.

"Welcome to my establishment," the madam of the house said to our band of travellers. "I am Madam Ah Toy." She was a stylish Chinese lady dressed in a beautiful dress of purple silk. I could not guess at her age, but she had the eyes of someone who had seen much of the world so I assumed she was over fifty but younger than seventy. Her luxurious hair was pulled back from her face and secured with ivory combs inlaid with amethyst.

Her house is a very large mansion, ornately decorated as one would expect with oriental art and furniture. It was all quite tasteful and I might have assumed we were in the Chinese embassy rather than a brothel.

Beautiful women of all races appeared and started to fuss over us, helping us with our coats and what little luggage we had.

"Baths await you after your long journey," Madam Ah said, and before we could offer any resistance, we were escorted to bathrooms upstairs.

Calamity complained that she had already had one bath less than a week ago, but Florrie and Miss Chase persuaded her to join them.

We men were led into another bathroom. A fire blazed in the fireplace and gaslights cast a welcoming glow over golden wallpaper and crimson draperies. There were four large tubs in the room that appeared to have hot running water that came straight from the taps.

I had not seen that in the West until then and was happy to have the chance to soak away the dust and dirt from the trail. The heady scent of musky bath oil perfumed the air.

Women helped us disrobe and told us our clothes would be laundered. Bram was turning beet-red as the women undressed him. He shooed them away and finished the job himself.

Mr. Reeves and I were sinking into our hot, sudsy tubs before Bram even had his boots off. We both sighed deeply as the water warmed our bones.

We were provided with good cigars and decent brandy. Any thoughts I had of San Francisco not being as civilised as London went quickly from my head.

"I'd like to thank you, Mr. Reeves, and you, Oscar, for rescuing Henry and me, and for taking such good care of Florence," Bram said, once he was settled into his bath and sipping brandy. "I wish I'd had the opportunity to thank Shada, as well." He then looked quickly at Reeves, probably fearing he had reopened a wound, but Reeves seemed unperturbed.

I am sure the liquor was going to his head, but accepted the thanks graciously as I am known to do. I even refrained from telling him how many rescues it all added up to, partly because I no longer remembered myself.

After our baths, we were dried and dressed in clean cotton pyjamas. Not very fashionable but they would do at a pinch.

I was shown to my room, where a meal of roast chicken and golden California wine was waiting. It was quite delicious. The room is not large, but it is clean and the bed is soft and covered in a luxurious blue silk coverlet. I wish I could take it home with me.

Perhaps I have been too hard on the White Worms. Miss Chase has indeed rescued us and got us away from that dreadful Drumpf, and this particular hideout is as comfortable as one could wish. I should try to get into danger around her more often.

I will close here, diary, to begin a long and well-earned sleep. Tomorrow I will make arrangements to catch a train and start my long journey back to England.

FROM THE JOURNAL OF FLORENCE STOKER, 12TH OF OCTOBER 1882

Archivist's note: Normally we would not include such personal details in an exhibit, but this does include some important information on the demon within Stoker.

What an adventure we have had! I can scarcely believe it. Only now that we are safe can I reflect on what a thrilling time it was. We were chased by bandits, then rescued by the cavalry, only to be set upon by a monster, which we narrowly escaped. My heart beats fast just thinking about how close we came to death.

As I look back on Bram's past indiscretions during his fight against supernatural forces, I now have more understanding. He had claimed that, in part, it was just such brushes with death and contact with evil that led to his straying. "I was not thinking straight," he had told me. "I was surrounded always by danger and death. I was beset by evils that no normal person would even believe existed. It was terrifying and...exhilarating."

I claimed to have forgiven him, but I had not fully done so. I know he sensed this when he touched me. It was there, unspoken, and it kept us apart.

I did not understand, at the time, but I do now.

For a while in the wilderness, I had a sense of what Bram had gone through. It was frightening at times, yes, but I also felt fully free, like anything was possible. I did not need to lead the life of a London housewife, nor even of a stage actress. I had no use for propriety, nobody to impress. I need only follow my animal instincts. Setting off on the adventure to find Bram and Henry gave me a confidence I did not know I had.

I miss Noel and long to return to him and keep him safe, but I do not wish to lose this feeling. I cannot return to my routine life now that I have been changed.

What this means for my future I do not know, but there will be time to figure that out later.

Now we are in a White Worm Society hideout in San Francisco, California. This hideout has turned out to be a brothel.

Here is proof of how my adventures have changed me: there was a time I would have refused to set foot in a place such as this. A time when I would have been ashamed to have other people see me naked, let alone bathe me. Yet here I am. Shortly after we arrived, I was washed and dressed by prostitutes. Lovely women, all smiles and giggles and kindness. They powdered and perfumed me and dressed me in the finest of French lingerie. This certainly holds everything in place in a flattering manner but is not the most comfortable.

"Don't worry, it won't be on long," one of the girls said, looking up at me with a sly smile as she unrolled a silk stocking up my leg.

Miss Chase, Jane, and I were shown to our rooms. Jane entered her chamber, taking one of the girls in with her. Miss Chase and I exchanged surprised glances as we entered our rooms unescorted.

I should not have been surprised that Jane would seek the company of women. I was more surprised at myself for not knowing women could buy such services the same as men. I thought, then, of the kiss I had shared with vampire Lucy. I let the thought play out a while before pushing it away.

In the room I share with Bram there is a beautiful canopy bed with red velvet curtains. The gaslights have pink glass tulip shades that give the entire room a soft rosy glow.

I waited on the big feather bed for Bram, both apprehensive and excited at how he might react to me spread out on the silk coverlet.

When he entered, he was dumbstruck at first. I knew from where he stood, he could see only my legs in their silk stockings.

"Come on in, mister," I said, pulling the curtains back invitingly, revealing even more of my gift-wrapping. He turned a brighter shade of red than usual.

A nervous smile came to his face. Then it quickly disappeared behind an expression of concern and shame.

"I…I don't know if I can keep my…this thing inside of me down when I am in a lustful state."

"Maybe we can let him come out and play this once," I teased. I really had no idea where that thought had come from, but it was as if I too had something devilish inside of me.

Within moments he had shed his pyjamas and was beside me in bed. We embraced like we did when we were newlyweds. I was taken up by a desire I had never felt before. I was acting on pure instinct that pushed every rational thought out of its way.

If the demon was there, Bram was in full control of it, taking the reins and bringing it to a full gallop!

Waves of pleasure flowed over and through me again and again. I, too, was learning to harness it and take it where I wanted to go.

Not only did I not feel any shame, my shameful moments from the past evaporated. The time I touched myself after witnessing Lucy fornicating, the time she kissed and touched me, all the times I closed my eyes and said the Lord's Prayer to get through my 'marital obligations' – all that shame was washed away in sweat and ecstasy!

When we were spent, we lay there in each other's arms and basked in the afterglow.

"He was scared to come out," Bram said, breaking the silence. "I felt as though I could purge myself of it through sheer will. Perhaps that has been the wrong approach."

He told me of the Pale Horseman's horse being killed by Oscar, how an otherworldly thing had come out of it and tried to find a new host. The thing inside of Bram had almost met its match. But it prevailed, and then Bram had forced it back down and under control.

"I am its master now," Bram said, smiling. I had not seen him at peace like that in a very long time.

Everything else fell away: the danger we were still in, the worry for our friends, even the thought of seeing Noel again. There was nothing we could do about any of those things in that moment, so we simply held each other as though we were the only two people in the world. We turned out the gaslight and fell asleep in each other's arms.

LETTER FROM BASS REEVES TO ROBERT REEVES, 12TH OF OCTOBER 1882

Dear Bobby,

I am in San Francisco now at the end of my current job. I will be heading home shortly.

You will surely find it amusing that I am being put up for the night, by invitation, in a cathouse. I will not be sampling the wares, however, with Shada's departure still so fresh on my mind.

I did meet a nice girl here.

I passed a Negro woman in the hall. She was carrying folded sheets and dropped them. I helped her pick them up.

"May I ask your name, ma'am? I'm Bass Reeves." I probably introduced myself with too much smile as I am known to do around a pretty woman.

"Winnie Sumter," she said. "Before you get any ideas, I am not on the menu here. I just wash the sheets. That is a full-time job, as you can imagine."

"I made no such assumption," I assured her.

We did find each other later in the kitchen and talked about this and that over coffee and sandwiches.

She was born in Tennessee and made her way west after the war when she was freed. When I told her I was to return to Arkansas shortly, she shared with me that she has family there. She asked me to look them up and tell them she was all right.

"I would be happy to escort you there, if you would like," I told her. "If you are looking to leave here, that is."

She gave me a most skeptical look and said, "I ain't looking for a man right now." She lowered her voice. "Although, I am looking to get out of this house. Madam Ah is kind and treats all her people well, but I would like to find a more respectable job. Might be nice to find work around my kin."

"I would be happy for the company and would not expect anything from you aside from pleasant conversation," I said. "You can ask Mrs. Stoker and Calamity Jane if I am anything but a perfect gentleman and keep true to my word."

She said nothing at the time, but perhaps she did talk to the women I had traveled with. She found me this morning and, to my surprise, she agreed to come with me.

Then she told me that she had seen Madam Ah Toy talking with some men in the alley when she had gone to hang laundry. The men were looking for Mr. Stoker and even had a drawing of him. The madam sent them on their way, but Winnie thought I should know to keep my eyes open.

So, to make a long story short, I will have company on my way back home. This might delay me a bit as she needs to give notice and collect back pay and that might take a week or two.

I will write before I leave, or maybe even telegraph when I get my pay from my last job.

See you soon,

Love, your father

FROM THE DIARY OF OSCAR WILDE, 12TH OF OCTOBER 1882

Dear yours truly,

After waking and dressing for breakfast this morning I ran into Calamity in the hallway of our hideout-of-ill-repute. One of the working girls followed her out of the room and gave her a passionate kiss full on the mouth.

Calamity seemed embarrassed by this and pushed her off. Calamity had her knapsack over her shoulder.

"Going somewhere this morning?" I enquired.

"It's time I head back to the Wild West show," she said. "Now that Miss Florrie is safe and back with her mister."

She had breakfast with us downstairs and said her goodbyes.

"It has sure been a pleasure travelling with you, Miss Florrie."

"I feel just the same," Florrie said, giving her an embrace that seemed to make Calamity uncomfortably feminine for a moment. "Thank you for helping me find Bram. We could not have done it without you."

"Weren't nothing, ma'am. I owed Mr. Reeves my time for helping me out of a jam, and now that debt is paid."

"It is," Reeves said. He gave her a pat on the back, having the common sense not to hug her and make her cry. "See you on the trail, Jane."

Her eyes were glossy as she fought back emotion. I supposed it was dawning on her that she would never see Florrie again.

"Wait," I said. "I have a gift for you." I handed her my bottle of Acqua Classica cologne.

"Well, I'll be. Now I can smell as fancy as you, Mr. Wilde. I might not ever have to take a bath again." On receiving the gift she could no longer hold back the tears. She threw her arms around me in an embrace that I did not fight. Thanks goodness she had bathed just the day before.

Stoker thanked her as well, and then she was on her way.

We are off to Chinatown to buy supplies for our journey back east. I for one will be glad to get a set of decent clothes, maybe something in silk.

FROM THE JOURNAL OF BRAM STOKER, 12TH OF OCTOBER 1882

Why did I let my guard down! Just when I thought we were free from Drumpf's reach, he has taken Florence right from under my nose! I will never forgive myself if something happens to her.

Earlier, thanks to Oscar's fame, we received a dinner invitation to a restaurant here in Chinatown. Oscar knows the owner from his previous travels and seemed happy to be back in a milieu where his celebrity would once again afford him the treatment that he feels he deserves.

He also invited Samuel Clemens (better known as Mark Twain) to join us and I was looking forward to meeting one of my literary idols, as were Florence, Mr. Reeves and Miss Chase. Mr. Reeves went so far as to say Mr. Clemens is a hero, as he was a strong voice in the abolitionist movement.

We had a most delicious and happy dinner where Mr. Clemens regaled us with tales of his travels across the United States and we told him of our recent adventures, leaving out any mention of vampires or magic, of course. The only time this was awkward was when he asked why Henry was no longer with our party, and I made up some blarney about him going off to see an old actor friend who was trying to start a theatre company in California.

All was well with the world and a run-in with Drumpf's thugs was the last thing on our minds.

Then, as we were having brandy and cigars, Florence excused herself to use the water closet and did not return.

Concerned, I asked Miss Chase to check on her and she returned quickly with bad news: Florence was nowhere to be found.

"I'm afraid she has been shanghaied!" she told us.

We rushed to the water closet, and she showed us a trap door she had found that would drop the occupant straight down into the cellar onto a load of flour sacks.

We all bolted to the cellar. I was dreading the green glow that would tell me vampires had been involved, but fortunately did not see it. Unfortunately, I didn't see much of anything else useful either. It seemed but a typical restaurant storage room, with food crates and such stacked around the perimeter.

I closed my eyes and pictured the rooms above, then moved to the part of the cellar that corresponded to the hallway outside the WC. More crates.

"It has to be over here somewhere," I said, and started moving crates. A stack of them moved all too easily: a false front, nothing but a stack of empty crates on wheels.

We pulled it out and found a small room, the pile of flour sacks in the middle. Around the room were several tunnels, branching off to God knows where.

"Hold on," Oscar said. He picked something up from the entrance to one of the tunnels: a ring Florence had been wearing. "I think she left this as a clue!"

I could see a sliver of light at the end of the tunnel and immediately set off at full pelt down its shadowy length, the others following at my heels. At its end we found a door that let out into an alley where we found a comb from Florence's hair. She was leaving us clues, but the kidnappers most likely had a carriage waiting.

A small child came up to us with a note.

"Are you Mr. Stoker?"

I told him I was, and he handed me the note.

Dear Mr Stoker,

We have your wife and if you wish her to live, you will do exactly as we instruct. You and Mr. Wilde are to board the midnight train to Santa Barbara. Come unarmed and alone. We will know if Mr. Reeves or Miss Chase accompanies you.

Bring the book.

A stagecoach will meet you in Santa Barbara to bring you to us, at which point we will take you and Mr. Wilde into custody and put Mrs. Stoker on the stagecoach back to Santa Barbara.

I give you my word as a gentleman that we will let her go if you follow my directions to the letter.
Sincerely,
W.D.

"Why in heavens does he want me to come too?" Oscar said, with something of a whine in his voice, then quickly added, "Of course I will for Florrie's sake, but whatever have I done to him?"

"You killed that vampire's horse," I said.

"Oh, well, yes. But I mean, it was already dead, after all. And can't they just make another one?"

"Killing a man's horse is one of the worst things you can do around here," Reeves said.

"Did you say vampire?" Mr. Clemens asked.

"I will get my people on this immediately," Miss Chase said, ignoring him. Mr. Clemens had the good sense to see that now was not the time for further questions, but his sharp eyes missed nothing, and I suppose I owe him an explanation at some point.

"No, you read the letter – we aren't to get the authorities involved," I said.

"It can be done covertly," Mr. Clemens suggested. "They could follow you at a distance."

"I'm with Bram on this point," Oscar said. "I don't think we should risk it."

I then pointed out that I no longer had the book. Henry had taken it with him when he'd left the Yahi village.

"But Drumpf doesn't know that," Oscar said. "He most likely has never seen the book. He just knows it has strange pictures, an unrecognisable alphabet, and is written on vellum."

"I might have just such a book," Mr. Clemens said. "It's a copy of *One Thousand and One Nights* in Aramaic. I bought it last week from a rare book dealer here in San Francisco. It has illustrations and is printed on vellum. It might pass long enough to get Mrs. Stoker on that stagecoach. You are welcome to it, if you promise to come back and tell me more about this vampire whose horse Wilde killed."

What a foolish slip of the tongue on my part! But it was the least of my worries.

We all agreed it was worth a try, and Mr. Clemens went to fetch the book.

"In case someone's watching for you at the station, I'll tip a porter to slip it to you when the train gets underway."

We are now on the train. It will take us most of the night to get down to Santa Barbara. I am told it is still quite uncivilised down there and Drumpf will probably have full rein over the local lawmen.

Again I find myself putting my family in danger. This is all my fault. I pray to God for him to protect Florence. I cannot face Noel without his mother.

FROM THE JOURNAL OF FLORENCE STOKER, 12TH OF OCTOBER 1882

Such a lovely evening ruined by a kidnapping. During a trip to the water closet at a Chinese eating establishment, I found myself falling into the cellar through a trap door!

I landed with a thud, my fall cushioned by a pile of canvas sacks. The wind was knocked out of me and I saw stars for a moment. Before I could recover my senses, I found myself roughly grabbed and yanked to my feet. I struggled, but two men were holding firmly to my arms. One clamped a hand over my mouth while the other put a hand to my back, propelling me towards a dark tunnel at one end of the cellar.

Somehow, in the melee, I had the presence of mind to slip a ring from my finger and drop it at the entrance to the tunnel. I must be growing accustomed to this life of intrigue.

We proceeded down the tunnel, me struggling all the way, and emerged into an alley. A carriage was waiting. I struggled even more violently and managed to free an arm long enough to pull a comb from my hair and drop it on the pavement. Then I bit the hand over my mouth and managed to let out a short scream before I was shoved into a waiting carriage, but either nobody was near enough to hear or anyone who was there thought it prudent to stay uninvolved. The men climbed in after me, quickly stuffed a wad of cloth into my mouth and bound my hands, then thumped on the carriage ceiling. We were soon in motion, bumping over the cobblestone street.

We didn't travel long. When the carriage door opened, I saw that we'd drawn to a stop alongside a train. I was pulled from the carriage and dragged aboard. I am proud to say I managed to kick each of my captors at least once along the way.

They tossed me onto a leather chair and handcuffed me to its arm, then left without a word. I had barely been there a minute when the train started moving, quickly picking up speed. They must have had the engine stoked and ready to go as soon as I was aboard.

I had nothing to do then but look around my new surroundings. The train car was expensively decorated, the walls in velvet wallpaper and the rugs Persian. Thick velvet curtains hung over the windows, obscuring me from view of any passersby. Crystal decanters and glassware were on a nearby sideboard, secured in holders to keep them from bouncing off as the train rattled along. I would say I was in a banker's study had I not been able to feel the shaking of the train as it sped along the tracks.

I surprised myself by deciding that if I could get my hands free, a crystal decanter would be my best choice as a weapon. I felt remarkably calm and wondered if perhaps they had somehow managed to drug me. But no, my mind felt sharp. I was frightened, certainly, but not panicky. My mind was focused on learning as much about my predicament as I could, so I could manoeuvre my way out of it.

An older, well-dressed man entered. He had dark hair, going to grey, and a neatly trimmed beard. He also had my handbag and journal in his hands.

"I must apologise for the rough treatment, Mrs. Stoker," he said, pulling the gag out of my mouth and unlocking the handcuffs. "If there had been another way, I would have done it. But, here you are."

He handed me my bag and journal and poured me a glass of water from a nearby decanter. "Don't worry, I did not read your journal. A lady's thoughts are private. I am glad you had it with you, as you are going to want to write in it," he said, with a sly grin on his fat face. "You are about to witness history. You will want to record it for posterity."

I rubbed my wrists, raw from the cuffs. "And you are?" I knew who he was, of course, but I didn't want to give him the satisfaction of saying so.

"William Drumpf. This is my private train and we are heading to Santa Barbara. Your husband and Mr. Wilde will be a few hours behind us on another train, and you will all soon be reunited at the opening of the promised land." He concluded with a "Praise the Lord," though it didn't sound sincere.

My face must have betrayed me for he added, "Yes, we have a map to the location. My vampire tortured your Indian shaman to get it."

My heart sank at this. The Yahi had been so kind to us!

"If you have your map, what is it you want from us?" I said. Again I knew, but why show my cards now?

"Your husband killed my son."

"Your son was robbing a train and shooting at my husband. Bram had every right to defend himself."

"Maybe so, but I can't let something like that go unpunished. I have a reputation to uphold. But that is only secondary. I want the book. For that, I will trade you."

I turned the thoughts over in my head. Maybe I could confuse things. "Well, you can't kill Bram then. He is the only one who can translate the book."

Drumpf seemed surprised and pleased at this new information, a lie of course, but he didn't know that. Furthermore, I knew that Henry had the book and was looking for the same opening to the Realm that Drumpf sought. He might be there now and could help us!

"You can't just go through the doorway. Surely you know that." His expression told me he didn't. "There are rituals you need to perform to get the door to open. The book has instructions and my husband learned the language of the book during one of his many explorations into the Realm. That's what we call it, the Realm. If you kill him, he can't open it. He is also quite capable of casting a spell to lock it forever."

"Is that so?" He seemed genuinely curious. "Yes, I should have suspected the door would be locked somehow with magic, or people would have already discovered it."

Another man entered the car. He was dressed as what I could only describe as a wizard and he looked quite silly. He wore a light purple silk robe embroidered with a gold eye inside a gold pyramid. The robe had a collar made of peacock feathers. (Honestly, what sort of ridiculous people are we dealing with?)

But what he carried showed me he was not to be taken lightly: a gold staff that had what looked like Egyptian hieroglyphics carved into it. On top was a green stone, similar to the one I had seen the shaman use in the Yahi village. I had no doubt that this clownish man could wield magic with that stone.

Drumpf turned to the wizard. "She says there is a ritual needed to open the door, and Stoker can perform it."

The man's beady little eyes squinted in scepticism. "It's possible, I suppose. The druids tell of such rituals that need to be performed on ley lines." I was surprised to hear him speak with an English accent.

"Yes, that's what Bram called them, ley lines. There are such lines at Stonehenge," I said. "Oh, I've said too much! The White Worm Society would be quite angry with me if they knew I told you where another opening is."

"White Worm Society? Who are they?" Drumpf asked. "Why are they sticking their noses in my business?"

"They are a vast army," I lied, "put together by the Queen herself to stop people from doing the very thing you are doing. A madman in England tried to open the gateway to the Realm and a giant snake monster came out of it. My husband stopped him and that man is dead now. I suggest you abandon your plan, before the Worms get to you, too. That place is full of evil things and the doorway must stay shut."

"Lies," the wizard said casually to Drumpf. "There was an attempt that was foiled, it's true. But Wilkins was a fool, and he did not have me. I've heard tell of these White Worms she talks about. A ragtag bunch, nothing to fear."

"It makes no matter," Drumpf said to me. "We are heading to a doorway and will open it." He turned back to the wizard. "Where is the Pale Horseman now?"

"He is following Stoker and Wilde to make sure they do what they have been told."

It was then I again thought about the green stone on top of his staff. Hadn't Bram said something about the Pale Horseman wearing an amulet with such a stone?

Drumpf sent the magic fool on his way.

"We will be at Santa Barbara in a few hours. Feel free to walk about the train. Keep in mind I own everything and everyone onboard." He turned to leave, but stopped at the door. "And Mrs. Stoker? Don't think about jumping. We are moving at 50 miles an hour."

He then left me and my journal alone. I don't believe for a minute that Drumpf made no attempt to read it, but luckily it is written in the shorthand Oscar taught me. He tells me this writing is not widely taught.

I did take him up on his offer to stroll about the train, thinking maybe it would slow at some point and I could jump. At the very least, I could gather more intelligence.

The next car in line was similar to the one I was in, but more femininely decorated. A woman in nightclothes was lying on a daybed. She looked pale and ill, and was coughing into a white handkerchief stained with blood. I recognised it straightaway as the signs of consumption.

I dared not get too close. A nurse entered with a glass of water.

"You shouldn't be in here, dear," she scolded. "She isn't very contagious, but you shouldn't take the chance."

"Is this Mrs. Drumpf?" I asked.

"Yes, poor dear," she whispered. "We thought desert air would do her some good so we took her to Phoenix. But the heat just made her worse."

I then realised we had something else to trade for Bram's life. Henry could cure her! We might find Henry at the entrance as that's where he said he was going.

"When we get to the promised land, Mr. Drumpf says the waters there will cure her," the nurse said.

"Is that where we are going?" I asked.

"Oh, you must be Mrs. Stoker," she said. "I've heard him talking about you to his wife. Yes, we are being led back into the garden of Eden, where we will have eternal life and unending happiness."

Her face was full of such joy I could almost hope it was true, but good things don't come from that place.

Mrs. Drumpf stirred and sat up.

"Hello," she said, a faint smile on her lips.

"Good evening," I said, coming closer to her bed. "I am Florence Stoker."

"I'm Edina Drumpf. Please have a seat. Not too close, mind."

I sat in a chair several feet from her bed. The nurse took this opportunity to take away her meal tray.

"I am ever so sorry my husband has kidnapped you. I do hope you understand it is for the greater good."

"I am sure he thinks that to be true," I said as pleasantly as I could. "But I know this endeavour of yours to be pure folly. The Realm, this place you think to be Eden, is not what you have been led to believe it is. I fear it might even be hell itself."

"If you had seen the magic that our prophet, Rayne, has brought forth you would be a believer like I am." That must be the name of the silly wizard man.

She started to cough into her handkerchief and then pointed to a glass of water on the bedside table that I retrieved and handed to her. Beside it was a framed photograph of a young man. "Is this your son?" I asked, and she nodded. I picked it up for a closer inspection. He looked like a younger version of Drumpf, with the same arrogant smile that made me dislike him immediately. Then I felt remorse, as he could not help the father he was born to, and I was sitting here speaking pleasantly to his grieving mother. I set it down with a thud; the frame was quite heavy, though not large.

Mrs. Drumpf smiled weakly. "I can't even lift it myself any more. It's made from lead from my husband's first mine. He can be quite sentimental at times. I'm sure you haven't seen that side of him, though."

I held my tongue; speaking ill of her husband would not help my cause.

After a moment, she said, "I know I should hate your husband for killing my son. But I can understand how the circumstances appeared from his point of view and do not harbour ill will toward him. Tom should have never been in that situation."

I thought of Noel and felt I could not muster the same equanimity were I in her shoes. "Then I hope you can persuade your husband to forgive Bram. It was an accident, after all. He would not kill anyone he did not have to."

"My husband is a very stubborn man. But I think if we can see the promised land it will go a long way to putting forgiveness in his heart. If the good Lord leads us there, I promise I will do what I can to get William to spare your husband's life."

The nurse returned and made me leave. I returned to the other car with at least some hope that we still might get out of this alive.

REPORT FROM AGENT CORA CHASE TO WHITE WORM SOCIETY

Date: 12 October 1882

Subject: The Kidnapping of Florence Stoker

Mrs. Stoker has been kidnapped by Drumpf. Her ransom: Messrs. Stoker and Wilde, as well as the vellum book which, unknown to Drumpf, they no longer possess. Stoker and Wilde, sans book, are currently on a train en route to Santa Barbara.

Logic dictates that Drumpf must have a reason for taking Mrs. Stoker to Santa Barbara; if all he wanted was revenge on Stoker and Wilde, he could have had that in San Francisco. Therefore, I assume he has discovered the whereabouts of the entrance to the Realm. Logic further dictates that if Drumpf's information is correct, Henry Irving, and the book, will also be there.

And so, that is where I must also go.

Though Stoker and Wilde were instructed to come alone, I have boarded the train incognito. I am disguised as a retired schoolmarm with a gray wig and spectacles. I have had very little interaction with any of Drumpf's men and do not think they will recognize me should they enter this semi-private car.

My disguise, however, was not good enough to fool Mr. Reeves. He entered the car dressed as a porter and recognised me right away.

He slid the glass door shut. "Hello, Miss Chase."

"I thought you promised not to follow them," I said.

"And I thought you promised the same."

"Drumpf's men could recognise you," I said. He had shaved his rather distinctive moustache, but it was hardly as good as my costume.

"As soon as I put on this uniform, I became invisible to any white man. You, on the other hand...."

"This is a most convincing disguise," I insisted. "Why, a mother and her young son tried to sit here, and all I had to do was look at the boy while pulling a reading primer from my bag and he insisted that they find another car."

"Maybe so, but not everyone is afraid of a schoolmarm. You might want to lock the door to discourage anyone from getting too close."

"I will if you promise to report back on anything you learn while making your rounds," I said. He agreed, then I remarked, "You've been paid. Your part of the job is over. Why stick your neck out further?"

"My job was to reunite Mrs. Stoker with her husband. Letting her get kidnapped undoes the reunion," he said. "Besides, I am in very little danger. I can and have moved about the train freely in my disguise. Stoker and Wilde are at a table in the dining car, bickering like an old married couple. They've just spent days on the trail with me and did not even notice I was across the room. There are two men I peg as Drumpf's in the car behind the dining car and two more in the car in front of it. None of them gave me a second glance. That vampire of theirs is napping in the luggage car."

"Well, I for one am glad you're here, Mr. Reeves," I said. "I am certain that Santa Barbara is not Drumpf's ultimate destination, and I will need your help tracking them after we leave the train."

"When we get to Santa Barbara, I know a blacksmith who can lend us some horses," he said. "We can follow them to wherever it is they are going. If they are taking a stagecoach, we should be able to track them from far enough back as to not give away our position."

He then confided in me that Mr. Stoker has friends in high places: Messrs. Robert and Theodore Roosevelt. Stoker had instructed him to cable them, asking them to send help to Santa Barbara in case the ransom exchange goes south.

It is good to know that reinforcements might be on the way, though I hope they will not be needed. I hope to free both the Stokers and Wilde, foil Drumpf's plot to open the Realm, and retrieve the book.

—End Report—

FROM THE DIARY OF OSCAR WILDE, 12TH OF OCTOBER 1882

Dear yours truly,

With Stoker, it's out of the frying pan into the fire, then from the fire into hot lava. Florrie has been kidnapped by Drumpf and he is demanding we present ourselves as ransom. I fear it will be the end of Stoker and me. He killed the man's son, and I killed his vampire's horse. But we must rescue Florrie and this is our only hope of seeing her returned safely.

We were at a table in the dining car of a train, riding to our certain doom. Understandably, this had put us both in a foul mood, though with Stoker it's hard to tell the difference between foul and fair.

"None of this would have happened if I hadn't married her," Stoker fretted. "I do nothing but put her life in danger and disappoint her as a husband."

"Only one of those things is true," I said. "Still, if she would have married me neither one of us would have been pulled into the world of the occult, so your point does have some merit. But what is done is done. There is no use in speculating on 'what-ifs' at this point."

"What do you mean you wouldn't have been pulled into the world of the occult?" he argued. "Your mother studies the occult."

"Studies, yes. But we rarely interacted with it in reality."

"We hunted a werewolf at the behest of your family friend, Captain Burton."

"A one-time occurrence. I had only ever hunted birds and rabbits with him prior to that occasion."

"Your friend became a vampire and almost turned you into one."

"Yes, but had Florence married me I would have never moved in with Frank or met Derrick. We may have never even left Dublin."

"So, I am the big curse here," he said. "Every life I touch gets ruined."

"Not *every* life, surely."

"You still haven't forgiven me for stealing her away from you," he said.

"Perhaps not."

"But you would have done nothing but break her heart," he said. "What with your drinking and carousing with...unseemly men."

"How dare you say something so rude! Just because I am a libertine and a man of the world you think I am some sort of degenerate! I like beautiful things and beautiful people. It is only your smug moral superiority that keeps you trapped in your narrow little world of right and wrong."

"I'm sorry, Oscar, but I will never forget the sight of you and Count Ruthven in the wine cellar – at your own engagement party!"

"How many times must I tell you, I was under the vampire's control. I was mesmerised! Like you haven't had your own indiscretions. Need I remind you about Ellen Terry? Another beautiful woman you led astray. And there were those three vampire women."

"I was drugged!"

"You seemed to be enjoying yourself. If not for my quick thinking they would have killed you."

"You told them to eat me!"

"Because I knew your blood would make them sick, just like your attitude now is making me. How many times have I saved your life and got not so much as a thank you?"

"Once! You saved me once, and I did thank you, in person and in a letter."

I tallied them up on my fingers, "One, I killed that werewolf in Greystones—"

"I wouldn't have been in Greystones had you and your brother not dragged me there. And need I remind you that I was the one who figured out who the werewolf was."

"That was Captain Burton."

"That was me!"

"All right, but I did save you from the worm, almost dying in the process. And I killed Wotton. And mounted this rescue party that saved you from Drumpf."

"Miss Chase saved me from Drumpf, if anyone did. And I stopped Ruthven from killing you. I was the one who killed those three vampire women who were about to eat you! I disarmed the Black Bishop so that vampire could finish him off."

"Still, here we are on a train because you dragged us into the plot of another madman. You draw evil to you like Willie to a bottle of gin."

We sat in angry silence for a moment and then, catching his stony glare, I started to laugh at the absurdity of it all. He seemed affronted for half a moment, then laughed himself.

"If anything," Stoker finally said, "I think we can both agree that Florence would have been better off not meeting either one of us."

"That may be true," I agreed. "But I think you need reminding, Bram, if we hadn't been in the thick of these horrific events, it doesn't mean they wouldn't have happened. It just means they would have gone unchecked. That werewolf might still be terrorising harbour towns around the globe. The Black Bishop may still be out there, creating vampires and trying to open the gates of hell. You have saved lives, Bram. Do not write that off so easily."

He looked grateful, which was a nice change from his usual dourness. "You've saved more than a few yourself, Oscar. I would not be here if it weren't for you, and I fully acknowledge that you're a far braver, more clever and generally better man than I." (All right, I confess, diary, he did not actually speak that last sentence aloud, but I am sure that down deep he knows it to be true.) "But let us get back to the matter at hand. We need to save her. And we somehow need to save our own lives if we can."

"Right," I said, pulling out the book Clemens had given us. "I think this will fool them long enough to get Florence released, if Drumpf ever had intentions of doing so."

"And we can't rule out Henry," Bram said. "He most likely has beaten Drumpf to the opening. If he is still there, he could be of great help."

I had totally forgotten about Irving going there with the book.

I added, "I also would not underestimate Florrie's cleverness. She might be able to free herself."

"And before we left," Bram said, "I sent word to the Roosevelts about where we were going. If they do not hear from me, they will send the cavalry to the entrance. I am hoping I can use this as leverage to keep us alive. At the very least they can stop Drumpf from unleashing something from that place."

Then, to my surprise, I saw Mr. Reeves, dressed as a porter, clearing away dishes from a nearby table. He did not see me notice him, and I quickly looked away, fearing that someone might detect any look of recognition that passed between us. I smiled, knowing that we were not alone, but did not tell Bram. He had been so adamant that no one follows us that it would only upset him. I suspect that Miss Chase is also on the case. This is the first time I am happy to have those White Worms meddling in our business.

FROM THE JOURNAL OF FLORENCE STOKER, 13TH OF OCTOBER 1882

Our train arrived in Santa Barbara and we quickly boarded stagecoaches and headed into the wilderness. I was given a coach to myself, but a rider stayed close on either side, I suppose to ensure I did not burst forth and run off.

By the position of the sun, I could tell we were travelling north by northwest. The trail was rugged and rocky, but much greener and shadier than what I'd grown accustomed to during our travels in the desert.

After several hours of bumping along the stony trail, we arrived at an abandoned mine where Drumpf has set up a camp. I take it this is the opening to the Realm, what he believes to be Eden.

Men have been going in and out of the mine at all hours of the day and night. These don't appear to be miners or gunslingers of the type he has employed to persecute us, but academic men who carry elaborate instruments, and are frequently conferring over plans and papers. They seem to be working frantically at something without success, and Drumpf blusters about, frustrated and upset. I think he'd prefer to get into the Realm without Bram's help, so he'll be free to kill Bram as soon as he arrives.

Rayne the Ridiculous is trying all manners of magic. He has brought in live animals and brings them out dead, so I imagine he is attempting some sort of animal sacrifice.

Whatever he is doing in there, it is not working. Perhaps they will believe me that Bram alone can open it. I am confident this can buy us some time, but when Bram fails to open the gateway, there will be no reason for them to keep him alive.

I have not seen Henry here. Perhaps he found a way in already, or perhaps he is watching from a distance. I do remember Bram saying something about the Yahi shaman sending him to a Spanish mission nearby here, so maybe he is there.

I currently feel very alone.

In any case, I must be vigilant. The more I can observe, the better chance I have of getting out of here alive, and getting Bram and Oscar out too. I cannot rely on the vague hope of rescue from Henry, or on Drumpf's better nature winning out in the end. I paid attention on the trip here, and I saw several places where one could leave the trail and lose oneself in the surrounding woodland. If I could manage to sneak out without anyone noticing, preferably with a horse, I could be gone down the trail and into the forest where it would be difficult for them to find me. Father taught me how to survive in the woods should I ever need to, and how to navigate by the sun and stars. I am sure I could find my way back to Santa Barbara.

I will keep my eyes open and await my chance. I hope if I do escape I can take Bram and Oscar with me, but even if I must leave them behind, I owe it to Noel to get back to him if I can. Losing one parent would be bad enough; he will not lose us both if I can help it.

REPORT FROM AGENT CORA CHASE TO WHITE WORM SOCIETY

Date: 13 October 1882

Subject: Following Stoker and Wilde

The train stopped in Santa Barbara early this morning. I disembarked with the other passengers, Mr. Reeves in his porter disguise trailing behind me with my minimal luggage. We stopped on the platform and I pretended to check the train timetable as we watched what happened next. The men Reeves had earlier taken for Drumpf henchmen approached Stoker and Wilde and ushered them into a stagecoach that was waiting for them.

Two more figures emerged from the train. One was so pale and dead-eyed I knew he could only be the vampire known as the Pale Horseman, which meant the Mexican by his side must be the one called Lobo. One of the Drumpf henchmen brought them horses. The Pale Horseman had trouble controlling his steed as it was trying to buck him off. The vampire dug his spurs in and pulled back tightly on the reins, finally gaining control.

He and Lobo rode off following the stagecoach.

We acquired horses from Mr. Reeves's blacksmith friend and headed out of town in the same direction we saw the stagecoach go. We rode at a brisk pace until we could see them far up ahead, then slowed down.

Reeves and I are now following at a further distance than I'd like, but we dare not get closer or the vampire's acute senses could detect us. We lose sight of the stage sometimes, but Reeves always manages to pick up the trail again. (I recommend suggesting his name to our recruiting agents when it comes time to fully staff the American branch of the White Worm Society. He has proven most useful.)

The stagecoach was leading us northwest along an old trail that is travelled enough to have signposts and markers along the way.

"I think I know where we're going," Reeves said suddenly as we cantered along. "I know this trail. At one time it led to a mission at Point Concepcion along the coast. The mission was destroyed in an earthquake and relocated inland. Nobody uses this trail now except prospectors and miners. And I have even better news: I know a shortcut. We can get out ahead of them."

"But what if they turn off along the trail?" I asked.

He shrugged. "Then we double back and find them. They'll be easy enough to spot if we stick to the high ground. Come on, let's take a chance. If we can get ahead of them, we may be able to get the drop on 'em."

It did seem a better option than trailing behind, so I nodded and followed Mr. Reeves as he urged his horse up into the hills.

It turns out we made the right decision. About an hour later, as we crested a hill, we saw a small encampment outside an abandoned gold or silver mine. We got down on our bellies so we could watch surreptitiously from above and soon spotted Drumpf pacing about the camp.

We have counted ten white gunslingers and five Mexicans. We are not sure how many are vampires, as all of them are spending most of their time in the shadow of the hill, but I would assume at least some of them are.

In addition to his small army, Drumpf has a few other men who appear to be scholars or archaeologists, taking measurements and writing in notebooks. There are tents and supplies, and it looks like they have made camp here for at least a few days.

We have also spotted a woman I assume is Drumpf's wife, as he seems to treat her quite tenderly. She is very pale and seems to be ill and is attended by another woman at all times.

No signs yet of Mrs. Stoker, but one tent is being guarded around the clock, and we suspect she is in there.

★ ★ ★

2nd entry

Time: 6:15 p.m.

Bram Stoker and Oscar Wilde just arrived by stagecoach and have been escorted into the biggest tent. The Pale Horseman and Lobo rode into camp right behind them.

We now wait until we can figure out our next move.

—End Report—

FROM THE JOURNAL OF FLORENCE STOKER, 13TH OF OCTOBER 1882

Bram and Oscar are here!

I heard a stagecoach pull into camp and peeked out through the opening in my tent to see several of Drumpf's men take up positions around it, their guns drawn. When they were ready, one of the men yanked the door open and Bram emerged. His eyes searched the camp for me and I ran from my tent, but one of my guards stepped in front of me, blocking my way.

"Bram!" I called, and he started towards me, but stopped when he heard the cocking of a pistol.

Oscar stepped down from the stagecoach behind Bram. He gazed around, trying to look bored and above it all, but I could see that his eyes were taking in every detail and filing them away for later use.

Drumpf strode into view. He stopped for a moment and looked at Bram with an expression of pure hatred. Then he stepped forward, drew his fist back and hit Bram square in the jaw. Bram is a big man, and he boxed a bit at university; it would take more strength than Drumpf has to knock him to the ground. Still, his head flew backwards from the punch, and when he turned back, his lip was bleeding. He did not raise a hand to Drumpf, of course – to do so would have been folly. He merely pulled a handkerchief from his pocket and wiped away the blood, gazing at Drumpf with as much loathing as had been directed at him.

"Bring them to my tent," Drumpf barked. "Her too," he added, with a nod towards me.

We were all ushered to the tent he was using as his headquarters. Several tables were set up with maps and papers spread over them.

A large upholstered chair, which I recognised from Drumpf's private train, had been brought in for his use, though he was far too agitated to sit.

"Give me the book," he ordered. I feared this would be our undoing since I knew Bram didn't have it, but, to my surprise, Bram did present him with a book. I had not got a close look at the Vellum Manuscript, but I could tell this was not it. However, like that book, it looked old and exotic. Very clever of the boys to find a decoy to hand over.

Drumpf set the book down on a table and began to leaf through it eagerly. Rayne was by his side in a moment, his hands darting forward as if to pull the book towards him, but he thought better of it and merely looked on avidly as the pages flew by.

"A deal is a deal, Drumpf. You have the book and us," Bram said. "Now put Florence on a stage back to Santa Barbara."

"Not so fast, Stoker. You don't give the orders here," Drumpf said, his attention still on the book. Bram fumed.

"I was told there were maps, diagrams."

"You were misinformed," Bram replied flatly. "There are written directions but no maps as such."

Drumpf grunted in irritation. "Your wife tells me you can read this."

Bram shot me a look, and I gave a tiny shrug.

"Some of it," Bram said. It was gratifying to see how easily he fell into step with my ruse.

"Read some of it to me," Drumpf commanded.

Bram hesitated a moment, then stepped forward and pulled the book towards him. Rayne's eyes widened as the book moved even further from his grasp, but he held his tongue. Bram started leafing through it. "Let's see.... This part describes a large bird.... No, a winged serpent. A dragon, I suppose. It swoops down, engulfing all creatures who lay eyes upon it in flames." He turned the page. "Oh, and this story is about tiny men who torment unwary travellers with sharp.... Is it a stick? No, three sticks. Oh, pitchforks. I think it's describing pitchforks. And this looks like the word for water, but also foul odour. Foul-smelling water, I think is the gist of it. Or possibly a lake of fire?" I was so proud of him! We're fortunate to be Irish, both with a bit of a gift for blarney.

Drumpf grunted again.

"What's that?" Rayne asked, pointing to an illustration on a page. "That's a figure of a person travelling through a mountain pass. That looks like here."

"I don't see the resemblance, frankly," Bram said.

Drumpf grabbed the book and went to the opening of the tent, yanking back the flap. "Yes, well, this area has been mined extensively. It's bound to have changed, but yes, these are the same types of rocks."

Oscar was looking over Drumpf's shoulder by this point. "Yes, these are similarly rocky rocks," he said amiably.

Drumpf walked back to the table and set the book down in front of Bram. "Now, read me the part about the ritual."

Bram stared at him blankly. "What ritual?"

"Don't be coy, Stoker. Your wife told me this book had instructions for the ritual to open the doorway."

Bram looked at me again, with a trace of annoyance this time, I thought.

"I'm sorry, Bram," I said. "I didn't mean to spill the secret. He just irritates me so." I glared at Drumpf, which seemed to amuse him. Smug ba— (Oh dear, I almost wrote a word that Mother would not approve of.)

Bram sighed. "Yes, I can see how that would happen. Fine." He paged through the book again. "It's here somewhere. I read it the other night."

"Well, just tell me, then, man," said Drumpf. "We got the iron door open, but there is another granite door that we cannot budge, not even with dynamite."

"Yes, that is magical moonstone. It can only be opened on the night of a new moon," Bram said. (The new moon is in two days, so his lie was buying him time!) He continued, "Then I have to say an invocation from this book and the door will open."

"Tell me the words to the invocation," Drumpf said, "and I will let your wife go, before I hang you for the murder of my son. There is no need for her to see that."

"Don't believe him, Bram!" I yelled.

"I don't. He has lied to me before. I will be the one to recite it. It has to be me. And I have to keep it open for you, so if you want to go inside I need to be on this side of the door."

"And why is that?" Rayne asked, with a sceptical sneer.

Bram straightened his already impeccable posture and, ignoring Rayne, gazed unflinchingly into Drumpf's eyes. He spoke in a quiet but commanding voice. "Because I alone have the ability to discern the secrets that lie between worlds. I have a power that you do not understand. Why do you think I was called in to fight your vampires? I can sense them." He pointed to one of Drumpf's guards, a ginger-haired lad. "He is a vampire." Then he pointed to others. "That one and that one are also vampires. The man by the door is not. My power comes from the Realm that's on the other side of that door."

Drumpf was listening raptly now.

"I don't know what you expect to find there," Bram continued, "but I can tell you that it is not the 'promised land'. It is a hellscape, and I am connected to it. I have no desire to open a portal to it, yet I alone have the ability to do so. I have done it before, in England. The madman who made me open that door got more than he bargained for, I can tell you. He is dead now. I warn you, Drumpf, I have no dominion over the creatures of that land. Whatever they choose to do with you, I will be powerless to stop it."

Drumpf thought it over for a moment, then smiled. "You have no power here either, Stoker. Perhaps that land is only hell for a sinner such as yourself. Fine. We will do it your way. After all, I can't let my need for revenge override my righteous goal." He let out a sigh and told his men to lock Oscar and Bram up in the mine and return me to my tent.

FROM THE JOURNAL OF FLORENCE STOKER, 13TH OF OCTOBER 1882

Tonight I took my fate into my own hands!

Though Drumpf had promised to release me if Bram and Oscar came to him with the book, he did not keep his word. He continued to hold me captive, as leverage to force Bram to perform the ritual to open the portal.

I knew I had to remove that leverage and began to plot my escape.

As the night went on, the guards outside my tent dwindled to one. A young man, not yet 20, paced back and forth to keep warm.

My ankle was chained to an iron ball so even escaping under and out the back would prove challenging, but I did consider it. I could lift the iron ball, but the chain made too loud of a rattle to slip away quietly.

I gathered up all my nerve, for the plan I thought of brought me much anxiety. I could be putting myself in greater peril should it fail.

I called the guard into my tent and he entered with a lantern. I feel he must be new to this type of work, as he shifted about and his eyes could barely meet mine. I spoke to him kindly, asking his name.

"It's Colton, ma'am."

"Well, Colton, my name is Florence. It is good to meet you."

He swallowed. "Likewise, ma'am."

"I need a favour, Colton," I said. "I was brought here rather suddenly, as you may know, and I did not have the opportunity to gather all the supplies I would need. For hygiene."

His eyes cast about the tent, looking at the bucket that served as my toilet and a small basin of water I could use to wash. He looked back at me, confused. I tried again.

"Do you have sisters, Colton?"

His eyes widened then.

I cleared my throat delicately, then continued. "I am sorry to put you in this position. But as I am sure you can appreciate, my situation could become quite embarrassing."

He was staring at me now, squirming in horror. I felt certain that at that moment he would rather face a vampire single-handed than have this conversation with me. "I...I.... What can I do for you, ma'am?"

I pointed through the opening of the tent. "I see the light is still on in Mrs. Drumpf's tent. I spoke to her on the train, and she is a kind woman. I wonder if you could go to her and ask...."

"Me?" he squeaked. "I couldn't do that!"

I arranged my face into a crestfallen expression. "Oh. I see. Of course, I understand." Then my eyes brightened as if with a new idea. "Perhaps you could escort me there and I could ask her myself."

He readily agreed and unlocked my chain. He walked me over to Mrs. Drumpf's tent. He held my arm in a nod to his role as guard, but his grip was so weak I could have easily run off. Still, we were too much in the open and though nobody was within sight, I could not ensure a stealthy getaway.

I could hear a quiet voice inside the tent; the nurse was reading to Mrs. Drumpf from a Jane Austen novel. I rapped on the tent pole and called softly, "Mrs. Drumpf? It's Florence Stoker. Might I have a moment?"

The nurse came to the tent opening and immediately invited me inside. Mrs. Drumpf was awake, but sleepy, and merely nodded and smiled faintly at me. I explained my situation, and the nurse said she had what I needed.

While she busied herself at her trunk, I wandered to Mrs. Drumpf's bedside table, on the pretence of seeing what book she was reading. Instead, I pocketed the photograph of her son in its heavy, leaden frame.

The nurse returned with what I had come for, and I thanked her and departed. Colton was waiting for me outside. He did not even take my arm as he escorted me back to my tent this time, as though afraid to touch me while I held the offending item. Boys!

He opened the tent flap and ushered me inside, then turned to leave. This would not do!

"Er, Colton," I said. "Don't you think you should put the chain on again? I'd hate for you to get into trouble on my account."

"Oh, right," he said, coming in and setting down the lantern.

As he bent to pick up the chain, I raised the lead frame and brought it down on the back of his skull. He fell to the ground with a grunt and a thud, then lay still. I rolled him face-up, checked his pulse to ensure he was still alive – though what I would have done if he wasn't I do not know – and stuffed the pad I had got from the nurse into his mouth as a gag. (Poor boy will probably die of embarrassment when he realises.) I tied his hands with my shawl and locked the ball and chain to his ankle.

"I'm sorry, Colton," I whispered to his unconscious form. "You seem like a nice lad, and I do hope I haven't got you into too much trouble."

I heard voices outside, so had very little time to waste. I grabbed a blanket since my shawl was now in use and slipped out the front flap of the tent.

As the mining camp is in a gully surrounded by hills, I hadn't much choice but to run up one. God was watching out for me that night for it was the right hill to climb.

"Over here, Mrs. Stoker," a voice whispered from the dark. In the moonlight, I could see it was Miss Chase and Mr. Reeves, secreted in a stand of shrubbery!

I stumbled over to them and told them of my escape and what Drumpf was planning.

They had made a nice little camp among the bushes and trees. They had acquired horses in Santa Barbara, which were quietly munching on grass in a clearing behind the trees.

The two of them had followed Bram and Oscar even though they were told not to, for which I felt very grateful. I perhaps had treated Miss Chase too harshly. Here she was once again risking her life to protect us. Did it matter that she was working for the White Worms? Were they not on our side, ultimately?

"We can't risk staying here any longer," Miss Chase said. "They will send out a search party as soon as they know you are gone."

I told them that when Henry had left us earlier, he had mentioned going to a Spanish mission.

"That has to be the abandoned mission I was telling you about," Mr. Reeves said. "Even if Irving's not there it might be a good place to hide out for the night."

"We can at least get up to the roof and keep a good lookout," said Miss Chase.

We gathered their horses and set off. An hour later we arrived at the ruins of the old Spanish mission. A crumbling stone sign read *La Purisima*.

We went inside. The roof was mostly intact and inside was more pleasant than I had expected.

There was a rush of wind as something ran past us then stopped. It was Henry!

"I did so hope you were nearby," I exclaimed, giving him a hug.

"Whatever are you doing here, Florence? I thought you and Bram would be halfway back home by now," he said.

We told him about my abduction, Drumpf's camp, and Bram and Oscar's imprisonment.

"I should go rescue them," he said.

I had to tell him Drumpf had foreseen this and was holding them in the silver mine.

"Very clever of Drumpf," Henry said. "However, we may be able to trade something for their lives."

He led us deeper into the mission and we entered a spacious library through two very heavy wooden doors that creaked as Henry pushed them open.

A fire was burning in a large fireplace along the back wall, and moonlight came in through mostly unbroken stained-glass windows depicting tormented souls burning in hell. The monks had not bothered to take all their furniture with them, and the room contained several heavy wooden tables and a number of chairs. A few torches hung from the walls and Henry lit one in the fireplace.

"We still have this," he said, retrieving the Vellum Manuscript from a pile of books on a table. "I suspect they will want the book and I won't turn that over unless he agrees to let Bram and Oscar live."

"Any luck in translating it?" I asked. I could see he had many books open and was obviously using this library for research.

"Yes, I have found a Rosetta Stone of sorts." He picked up another book and flipped through its pages. "This entire mission seems to have been built here to study the opening. The monks here called it 'Boca del Infierno'."

"The Mouth of Hell," Mr. Reeves translated to Miss Chase, who was writing what Henry was saying down in a small notebook.

Henry added, "It was discovered by the Spanish in the 1700s when they were digging out that silver mine."

"How did this mission come to be abandoned?" I wondered, looking around at the once-opulent building.

"Ah, that is an interesting story," he said, putting the book down and picking up a scroll. "It says here the mission was plagued by evil spirits they called 'the Dark Watchers'. They would surround the mission and whisper evil words into the monks' ears while they slept, driving them mad. The monks eventually all fled or killed themselves and the mission fell into ruin."

"I'd heard it was destroyed by an earthquake," Mr. Reeves said.

"That's just what they wanted people to think."

"Can you really open the door?" I asked Henry. "I know how complicated it was to open the one at Stonehenge. It doesn't need Bram's blood again, does it?"

"No, nothing like that, but yes, I think we can open it. Well, humans can. Since it is inside the silver mine, I cannot enter. I don't know if that is by divine plan or just an unlucky coincidence, but there you have it." He pulled out a large ornate iron key from his pocket. "I found this key hidden here in the mission. It is exactly like a drawing in the book, described as the key that will unlock the iron door the monks installed. Then entrance can be gained by reciting an incantation to remove the lock the Dark Watchers installed on the other side."

"So, these Dark Watchers are from there? From the Realm?" Miss Chase asked.

"It appears so," he said. "They are there to keep our world from spilling into theirs."

"The White Worms of the Realm," she mused.

"I hadn't thought of it that way," Henry laughed. "Yes. I suppose they are."

"I've always wondered, Henry," I said. "Why do you think going in there will cure you? Opening the entrance at Stonehenge didn't lead to the cure you wanted, so what makes you think this will be different?"

"The Realm is where vampirism comes from. If we can find the source, we might be able to find a cure. When I was being turned into a vampire, I fell into a dream state. I found myself in another world, which I believe now was the Realm. When I awoke I was a vampire."

Bram had told me Henry was turned into a vampire a hundred years ago, but I realised I had never asked for the details beyond that.

"When the vampire king and I were prisoners of the Black Bishop, he told me that in the Realm vampires are merely parasites that feed off dragons, and it is only in our world they garner so much power over their human hosts. My hope is that the Realm holds a cure for these parasites, as we have learned to cure some of the parasites of our world."

Henry put the scroll down on his pile of books. "First things first," he said. "We have to rescue Bram and Oscar. I will go to Drumpf's camp tomorrow and see if I can strike a bargain with him."

"He seems to be holding all the cards," Mr. Reeves said. "But maybe Miss Chase and I can be your aces up the sleeve."

LETTER FROM ALEJO 'LOBO' LOPEZ TO LUZ LOPEZ, 14TH OF OCTOBER 1882

Dear Luz,

I am so close to El Dorado I can almost smell the gold!

Drumpf is angry. He had kidnapped Stoker's wife to force Stoker to bring him a book of magic he needs to enter El Dorado. But she has escaped during the night.

Drumpf has ordered the Pale Horseman and me to get her back.

I thought we needed more men, but the Horseman said he shouldn't have any trouble dealing with the woman.

He tells me Drumpf fears Stoker has sent for help that could show up any day now, and he needs my men and the other vampires to defend the entrance if they do. So, we are on our own for this quest.

The Pale Horseman sniffs at the air and we follow his nose.

I often wonder why the Pale Horseman does Rayne's and Drumpf's bidding. Even now he complains he is being sent on a task not worthy of his powers.

"One of these days I just might not come back," he said, in an uncharacteristically chatty moment. "I'll go north into Canada and create my own gang. Do you want to be part of my gang, Lobo?" He laughed, and I didn't answer.

I know not why, but I have a feeling of dread for this assignment. I have found it is often the simple tasks that lead to the greatest dangers.

Lobo

FROM THE JOURNAL OF FLORENCE STOKER, 14TH OF OCTOBER 1882

This morning I awoke from my comfortable chair in the mission's library. Henry had breakfast ready for me, a crust of bread and two hard-boiled eggs. I had no idea where he got them but my rumbling stomach was quite grateful. Henry was busy poring over books while I ate. I wondered if he had eaten anyone recently.

Mr. Reeves and Miss Chase were outside getting water from a nearby stream because the well outside was contaminated.

Henry and I discussed our plan to rescue Bram and Oscar.

"I'll demand a meeting with Drumpf and offer the book for their release," Henry said.

"But he already thinks he has the book," I protested. "If you show up with the real book, he will know Bram and I lied."

"He will find out soon enough anyway, and then there will be no reason to keep Bram and Oscar alive," he said. "I know Bram sent word to the Roosevelts, but we do not even know if they got the message. We can't count on them arriving in time. This is our best chance to free them. Once they are away, I will give Drumpf the book and invocation to open the door. Miss Chase and Mr. Reeves will be watching from the hill above should we need them."

"So he will have everything he needs to open the door. The White Worms won't like that."

"Yes. Well, I have a plan for that as well. When he opens it and all his people go inside, I have another invocation to close it."

"Trapping them on the other side of the door?"

"I promised the White Worms I wouldn't leave it open, so there you are."

I thought of all those people, trapped with no return. Young Colton, who unwittingly helped me escape. Mrs. Drumpf and her nurse. I wished there were another way, but I could not think of one.

"I will go with you," I said.

"I don't think that's wise. We should get you back to Salt Lake City."

"It isn't open for discussion," I said. "Besides, I think I can get Mrs. Drumpf to intervene on our behalf should the need arise."

"And if she doesn't, Noel will lose both parents."

He had given voice to my darkest fear, but I could not just turn tail and run while Bram and Oscar were still in danger.

"Whatever Drumpf is, I think he believes he has honour, and he will let me go, even if we don't manage to save Bram. And if we get him into the Realm, I hope he will think less of his vendetta."

Henry finally agreed that I could come. Now I pray for God to watch over us and Mrs. Drumpf to keep her word.

LETTER FROM ALEJO 'LOBO' LOPEZ TO LUZ LOPEZ, 14TH OF OCTOBER 1882

Dear Luz,

My journey to El Dorado has been delayed. Not only have we not retrieved Mrs. Stoker as we were ordered, I am no longer sure the ends justify the means.

I have ridden with evil and turned a blind eye to horrible deeds, just to satisfy my own greed and curiosity. My obsession to find the lost city has driven me mad; I see that now.

Today I saw the righteous stand up to evil, even putting their own lives at risk to do so. It has given me much to contemplate.

The Pale Horseman and I tracked Mrs. Stoker to an old mission. It was in ruins but still stirred a reverence in me. A cross still stood on the spire, and I could imagine the faithful gathering here for mass, families worshipping together, babies being baptised, couples pledging their lives to one another in holy matrimony. This was once sacred ground and the vampire I was riding with did not belong there.

He became uneasy, squirming in his saddle. As he brought his horse to a stop it began to buck. This horse was alive, as his had been destroyed by one of Stoker's men. I do not know why he even cares to ride, as he can move more swiftly than a horse. Perhaps it is a tie to his life as a human that he is reluctant to give up.

In any case, this live horse had given him nothing but trouble since he had left the stables. He was told by Rayne that the talisman around his neck would allow him to ride horses, but it only obeyed the jab of his spurs and only let him ride out of fear.

In anger at the creature's stubbornness, he leapt off the saddle, snapped the creature's neck with his bare hands and pushed it away from him with such force that all four of its legs left the ground as it was flung twenty feet away.

"Fucking nag!" he growled. Then he turned to the mission.

"Come out, Mrs. Stoker, we know you are in there!" he yelled in his raspy voice. His words were filled with bravado, but I could see by the way that he would approach then back off quickly that he did not want to enter the mission.

To my surprise, Mrs. Stoker came to the window with a rifle, squinted down the barrel and took a shot at us. I backed my horse away but the Pale Horseman just stood his ground, with bullets dancing at his feet. I was told he could see bullets coming at him and could move like the wind and jump out of the way.

"I won't tell you again. Come now or we will kill your husband!"

"Drumpf is going to kill him anyway," another voice yelled from the mission. "That doesn't give you much to bargain with."

It was Stoker's vampire.

Then, a bullet from behind took off my hat! I jumped off my horse and took cover by a stone well.

Another bullet went through the Pale Horseman's lower back and out his stomach with a big puff of dust. I could hear his flesh sizzle and knew the bullets must be silver.

He turned and returned fire into the trees. A woman was firing a Colt at us. It was too great a distance for any accuracy, but the gunfire kept us pinned down.

The Pale Horseman took shelter behind the well with me. He glared at the mission for a moment, then in the blink of an eye, he was gone. I turned to see him jump into the air towards the mission with such force and height he landed on the roof above Mrs. Stoker. He then scrambled down the wall, clinging to it like a spider, and quickly grabbed Mrs. Stoker through the window, pulling her out one-handed.

He pushed off from the wall with Mrs. Stoker in his arms, and with one more bound landed with a great thud in front of the well I was hiding behind.

"Put down your guns or I'll snap her neck," he said calmly, setting her down on the ground. He stayed behind her, using her for a shield. She fought him, but he casually grabbed her right arm and twisted it behind her back. He had her other arm in an iron grip and pulled her close, pinning her right arm between their bodies. As she began to gasp for air, the woman in the trees and the vampire in the mission threw out their guns.

From the wood to our right, the Negro I had seen with them before calmly walked out with his gun still in his holster.

"Get back," the Pale Horseman hissed. "I will kill her."

"I don't think you will. Your boss won't be very happy if you do. Without her, how's he going to force her husband to open that pesky old door?"

The Pale Horseman bared his fangs, and I could tell it was just dawning on him that we did need to bring Mrs. Soker back alive. He loosened his grip on her and she gasped in a breath. "Don't, Bass," she pleaded.

"Why don't we just settle this the old-fashioned way, with a showdown?" the soldier said, his hand inches away from his holster. "You're a Confederate man, ain't ya? I fought cowards like you in the war. I must have killed twenty rebels. Those white boys always underestimated me. They hated me because I'm black, but all of them was yellow to the core. Now, you can hide behind the woman or you can fight me like the man you once was."

Now, I can tell you this, Luz. The Pale Horseman could easily pull his gun and hit the man between the eyes before he could blink. I don't know why he didn't. Or why he didn't use his vampire strength to jump away. Maybe he just wanted to feel human again. Or maybe he just couldn't resist the Negro's needling.

He pushed Mrs. Stoker out of the way to the ground and took up the gunslinger stance. She got to her feet and made a run for the woods.

Then an odd look passed over the vampire's face. He looked down and saw his amulet was missing. He let out a guttural laugh. "Nice try, Mrs. Stoker. But I don't have to be at full strength to shoot this mongrel down."

But I could tell he was feeling the effects of the sun. His head tipped slightly and his shoulders slouched a bit.

The two gunslingers stared at each other for a moment, then in a blur, they drew and fired. The Negro was hit in the left lung just above his stomach. He cried out and fell, clutching his wound.

The Pale Horseman must have been shot right through the heart, for he instantly exploded into a cloud of foul-smelling white dust.

Perhaps I imagined this next part, but for a brief second, I swear I saw the shape of a demon in the dust cloud. It screamed at me as it evaporated into the wind and passed through me. As the dust fell down around me, I felt all the pain and sorrow this thing had collected. The feeling was almost too much to bear. I fell to my knees and prayed to God to save my very soul.

The women rushed to their fallen comrade and Stoker's vampire emerged from the mission with a blanket spread over himself to protect him from the sun. The vampire bit open his own wrist and put it to the wounded man's lips. To my surprise, he slowly got up, and the women helped him back into the mission.

Stoker's vampire came over to me. I thought his intent was to kill me and wanted him to do so as my penance. But it was not to be. "Take me to your boss. I have the book he wants – the real book – and a way to open the doorway."

So, dear Luz, I will be entering El Dorado after all. And I hope to do it as a changed man. Gold means so little to me now, but I am still curious. I have come this far and will fulfil my destiny.

Lobo

FROM THE JOURNAL OF BRAM STOKER, 14TH OF OCTOBER 1882

8:15 a.m.

Oscar and I are being held prisoner in the mineshaft. We have heard guards talking and learned that Florence escaped last night. I know not what happened to her after that – there are other dangers out here besides Drumpf, of course – but at least she is out of his clutches.

So, whatever happens to me now, Florence will not be at Drumpf's mercy.

8:35 p.m.

Henry appeared in camp today, along with the Pale Horseman's Mexican companion. The Horseman himself was nowhere in sight but, much to my dismay, Florence accompanied them.

I was with Drumpf in his tent when they arrived. The unfortunate side effect of telling him I could read the vellum book was that he insisted I translate it aloud for him as we wait for the new moon. I spent tedious hours making up horrifying stories about what we would find in the Realm and 'reading' them to Drumpf in halting faux translation.

Imagine my relief when one of Drumpf's men interrupted us with the news that visitors had arrived. I followed Drumpf out of the tent and saw Henry, Florence and the Mexican waiting in the shade of the hillside. Oscar walked over to join me.

"Lobo!" Drumpf yelled. "You've recaptured Mrs. Stoker, well done! And someone else, I see. Henry Irving, I believe? Where's the Pale Horseman?"

"It is they who have captured me, Señor Drumpf," Lobo replied. "And the Pale Horseman is dead."

Drumpf staggered back a bit at the news. I'm quite sure he thought that was impossible. His henchmen recovered from the shock much more quickly, and half a dozen pistols were soon trained on Henry and Florence.

"Tell them to put the guns away," Henry said calmly. "I have something you need."

"Oh, and what is that?" said Drumpf, regaining some of his usual bluster.

"I have a key to the iron door inside that mine. And I have the book. The real book."

Drumpf shot a look at me. There was no use denying it so I just shrugged. "You had my wife," I said. "Henry had taken the book before we even left Nevada. I had to stall for time." Drumpf's lip curled in a sneer, but he just turned back to Henry.

"Well, Mr. Irving, that's no reason for my men to put their guns away. We'll just take that book now, if you please. We already have the iron door open and don't need your key."

Henry laughed derisively. "You don't think I have the book on me, do you? It is hidden nearby. You'll never find it. I can get it in a matter of moments, though. I'm faster than I look." Here he curled his lip and let his canine teeth lengthen to fangs. I have rarely seen him display his vampire fangs like that, and I must say it was unsettling.

"Besides," Henry continued. "I know you have not yet opened the door beyond the iron one. You will need an incantation to open that one, and I alone know it."

"I've heard that one before," Drumpf muttered.

"But not from someone who has actually been there and wants to go there again. I have long sought to re-enter the Realm, Mr. Drumpf."

"Have you now?" Drumpf said, sneering at me again. "Then may I assume it is not the hellish place your man Stoker has described?"

"Oh, it was a place of nightmares, Bram is quite correct about that. But I have my reasons for wanting to enter. Unfortunately, I will not be able to pass through the silver mine, but any knowledge of the Realm will further my goals."

Drumpf narrowed his eyes. "The Realm, as you call it, is mine, Irving. I have already claimed its territory, and I have worked long and hard to get it."

Henry just waved off Drumpf's words. "I have no interest in whatever riches you think you'll find in the Realm. My concerns are more personal. You think you have worked long and hard for this? I have been seeking a way into the Realm for decades, probably since before you were born. I have consulted mystics and shamans around the world. I have studied a book like this before. I know far more about the Realm than any living person, including that fool you call a 'prophet'." Henry did not even bother to look at Rayne as he said this, so complete was his dismissal of the gobdaw.

I don't know if Drumpf was convinced by Henry's speech, or just impatient at being so close to his goal without yet crossing the threshold, but he agreed to Henry's terms – which were, of course, to release Florence, Oscar and me. And he is less angry than I would have predicted at learning that we misled him. Indeed, it seems to have bought me a measure of respect in his eyes.

He does, however, want Florence, Oscar and me to enter the Realm with him. I believe he knows that if Henry can open the door he could close it as well, trapping him inside, and he is bringing us in as insurance against that. My hope is that in his moment of triumph he will keep his word and free us, and that we will manage to get away before he realises what folly his mission has been.

So now his men are making final preparations for an expedition inside. While I would prefer to be far away from here, I must admit that after all we have been through, I do want to know what the Realm is like. I will soon find out, and I hope I live to tell the tale.

Date: 15 October, time unknown
Before we entered, Drumpf pontificated about this momentous historical event that was about to happen.

"This is indeed the most important day for America since Columbus landed on her shores," he said, as a scribe took down his words in an oversized book. "We set foot in a new world. What awaits us there, we do not know. It will be a new frontier, and we will tame it, as we have tamed this mighty land. If there be savages, we will civilise them as we have brought the word of God to the natives from Plymouth Rock to the shores of the Pacific Ocean."

His holy man, Rayne, read passages from the Bible and talked about leading the lost to the promised land. It went on for what seemed ages and many were getting restless before it was done.

Finally, we entered the mineshaft and went to the furthest point at the back where the large stone door stood, shut fast. Drumpf's men had blown off an iron door with dynamite earlier, only to find this second door they could not open, even with explosives.

The door looks to be made of a green marble or jade. There is no knob to speak of, but there is a small diamond-shaped indentation that looks as though it could be a keyhole.

"An incantation seems awfully mundane compared to the last portal we helped open, eh, Bram?" Oscar said. "Where's the blood sacrifice? A bit lazy, if you ask me."

Henry and Drumpf's vampires stayed outside, of course, due to the silver lining the walls of the mine, and several of Drumpf's human guards also stayed behind. The rest of the human gunslingers, including Lobo, entered with us as well as Rayne. A bespectacled man I had not seen before came along, hauling a camera with a large wooden tripod. A small Punjabi man was trailing behind him carrying a backpack full of photographic plates.

Drumpf's wife, Edina, also accompanied us with the help of her nurse. Mrs. Drumpf was very pale and weak from consumption, and the nurse and Florence helped her along the rocky mine floor. Florence had told me that Mrs. Drumpf believes a cure waits for her inside, and indeed she appeared to be in good spirits as she joined her husband by the door.

Oddly, inside the mine, I could hear what sounded like whispering. I could not make it out. "Can you hear that?" I quietly asked Florence and Oscar. They said they did not.

Nerves, perhaps? The sound of wind inside the mine? Or my sixth sense picking up something paranormal? There was a faint green glow about, but that is to be expected in such a place.

Then the voices became clearer.

"They are getting in! We must stop them!" the voices said in panicked hisses.

Drumpf seemed perturbed. Perhaps he was hearing the voices as well, and trying to ignore them.

"Do not do this, William Drumpf!" the whispers screamed.

Startled, I looked at Drumpf. His eyes were wide and panicked, but then he closed them tightly and recited the Lord's Prayer and the voices, after a last hiss, stopped.

We stood at the door while Henry chanted an invocation outside in an unrecognisable language. I've heard his commanding voice from the stage so many times, it provided me a bit of comfort to hear it now.

He finished the chant. Drumpf pushed on the door. Nothing happened.

"Again!" Drumpf barked.

Henry repeated the invocation, but still nothing.

It was then I noticed a green glow coming from Florence's pocket and asked her what it was.

She took a glowing stone from her pocket and told me it was the amulet she had yanked off the Pale Horseman.

It was diamond-shaped.

"This isn't working," Drumpf yelled at Henry.

"It is exactly what is in the book," Henry shouted back.

"I think we need a key," I said, putting the stone in the keyhole. It fitted perfectly. "Now, Henry, read it again."

He did. There was an almost imperceptible rumble from the marble door. Drumpf pushed on it and it gave way slightly. Then he and Rayne put their shoulders into it and the door swung all the way open, blinding us with orange sunlight.

Drumpf stood there for a moment, gazing through the door. He glanced back at his wife, who gave him an encouraging smile. Then he stepped out into the new world.

Rayne held the rest of us back, allowing Drumpf a moment alone. We could see him through the doorway, holding his arms out as though receiving the blessing of God, then he turned back to us, beaming, and waved us in. Rayne almost tripped over his robes in his eagerness to cross the threshold, and even Mrs. Drumpf seemed to be moving more vigorously as she advanced into the orange light.

I gripped Florence's hand tightly. We looked at Oscar, he nodded, and the three of us walked forward.

Now I know how Alice felt stepping into Wonderland. We spun around, silent and awestruck, trying to take in the sights, sounds and scents.

The air was moist and warm like a hot summer day after a rainstorm. A sweet smell like hay was on the wind.

In the sky were a big red sun and a second, smaller yellow sun to the lower right of the first. The twin suns bathed everything in orange light and it took a moment or two for my eyes to adjust to seeing strange, new colours. The suns gave everything two shadows, one adjacent and slightly overlapping the other.

"I have a suit that would look stunning in this light," Oscar murmured. "I will never be able to wear it again in regular daylight."

Before us was an immense field of reddish-brown grass. It was knee-high and the wheat-like tips whistled as we moved through it. One could play music just by running one's hands across the grass tops.

It was odd seeing gruff gunslingers grinning and laughing like children as they strolled through the grass, playing impromptu tunes. Florence, too, ran her hands through the grass as though she were playing a harp.

Strange birds that looked more like lizards than feathered creatures circled in the sky. A tree like a willow, but blue, with dark blue berries, waved gently in the wind in front of us.

Off in the distance was an enormous temple made of green stone. It had spires and pillars reminiscent of Turkish mosques. It was in ruins, its stones crumbling and covered in red vines.

"It's true!" Drumpf yelled in boyish wonder. "It's really true!"

We were all drawn to the temple and started walking faster towards it. To our left, a pink river wound its way through the grassy field.

We detoured a moment to see its splendour. The sandy banks of the river were sparkling with pure gold sand.

Drumpf's men ran to the banks and picked up handfuls of the sand, letting it run through their fingers.

"It's gold dust!" one man exclaimed as he started to fill his pockets with it.

Rayne carefully touched the water, then brought his wet fingers up to his mouth and tasted the water. He quoted the Bible, "And a river went out of Eden to water the garden; and from thence it was parted and became into four heads. The name of the first is Pison: that is it which compasseth the whole land of Havilah, where there is gold."

He turned to Mrs. Drumpf. "Drink from this river, my dear woman, and you shall be cured of all ailments!"

Mr. Drumpf took out his canteen and emptied the water from it, then went down the golden bank to refill it with holy water. He took a drink himself first, I imagine to see if it was safe, and said, "It tastes like honey!"

He gave the canteen to his wife, and she guzzled the water down greedily. Then she staggered back on her feet, almost falling, before the nurse caught and steadied her.

She gasped a huge gulp of air and exhaled. We were all stunned to see her pallid cheeks instantly become flushed with healthy pink. She straightened, laughed with joy and broke away from her nurse on now-steady legs.

"It's our first miracle here," Drumpf shouted. "This is truly the promised land!" His wife danced into his arms and they embraced.

Florence clapped, smiling through tears. She is quite fond of Mrs. Drumpf.

"Let's continue on to the temple," Rayne said. We all followed, Drumpf's men so weighed down with gold dust that they spilt it as they walked. Their leader, Lobo, did not have any gold in his pockets. He was clutching rosary beads and praying in Spanish as we walked towards the temple.

I, too, was starting to feel uneasy. The temple was quite imposing, and I wondered where the builders were and when and why they had abandoned it. While this place was not the hellscape I'd feared, I was not yet ready to trust it completely.

Drumpf's men were armed, and that oddly gave me some peace of mind. Should we run into a wild creature or hostile natives, we could at least defend ourselves.

We had to climb some small rubble to get inside the temple, but once we did we saw that it was dry and cool. Holes in the ceiling let in light. Small lizard birds were nesting among the beams on the ceiling and scattered out of the holes when we entered.

At the centre of the temple is a gigantic stone statue sitting on a throne. The head is missing, now a pile of rubble at the statue's base. But the body is very strange. It looks like a man with four arms, two out of the shoulders like a human, and two more that come out just below the stomach and above the waist.

Drumpf just stood there looking up at the statue. I could tell it was troubling him and Rayne could as well.

"A false god," Rayne said. "It is clear this temple has been destroyed by the true God." Drumpf nodded, then continued exploring.

It is in the temple where I have taken this chance to write in my journal. I want to record my impressions while they are still fresh in my mind.

Drumpf's people are scattered about, the man with the camera taking photographs and others making stone rubbings of writing carved into the walls. They are also filling their knapsacks with what look like gold artefacts and vellum scrolls.

The photographer was trying to get a picture of a message that was scrawled in what looked like paint. It appeared to have been written in haste over carved words that were there first.

"This is in Hindi," he said excitedly. "Raj, come here!" he called to the Punjabi man. "Can you read this?"

The man squinted for a moment, then said, "Beware the... travellers...pilgrims...settlers? It's a hard word to translate into English. 'Beware the settlers from...Barsoom, turn back now.' I don't recognise that word 'Barsoom'. But I think phonetically that's what it is."

Several of the gunslingers are collecting what look like gold bowls, vases and the like and are carrying them out of the temple. Drumpf is too preoccupied to notice or care.

I stepped outside and saw they are heading for the exit back into our world, happy with their bounty.

Florence is outside with Mrs. Drumpf. They are picking flowers and collecting plant samples to bring out when we leave. I hope that means we are leaving at some point, and soon. Despite the beauty and wonder here, my uneasiness grows. I do not feel safe in this world and I do not trust that Drumpf's lust for revenge will not rear its head again.

REPORT FROM AGENT CORA CHASE TO WHITE WORM SOCIETY

Date: 15 October 1882

Subject: Outside the Entrance to the Realm

Outnumbered by Drumpf's forces, I was unable to prevent him from opening the portal to the Realm – at least not without jeopardising the lives of the Stokers and Wilde. Bass Reeves and I observed from a distance, secreted in a stand of juniper bushes high on a hill. It provided excellent cover as I watched with my binoculars and Mr. Reeves with his spyglass, waiting for an opportunity to rescue the innocents or help contain any evil that might make an incursion into our world.

The Stokers and Wilde were taken into the mine by Drumpf and his followers. For nearly four hours, nobody else entered or exited the mine.

Finally, there was movement below. Three of Drumpf's men emerged from the mineshaft, heavily weighted down with what looked like gold relics. Their pockets were bulging with gold dust, as we could see by the quantity of it that was spilling out. They were also carrying packs filled with gold artefacts.

They were laughing and singing as they left the Realm, which I took to be a good sign that nobody had yet been eaten by a monster. The guards that Drumpf left behind appeared to be confused as to what to do. I suspect they didn't know whether Drumpf had sent the men out and would be emerging himself momentarily, or whether the men had stolen these items and Drumpf would be angry if they weren't detained.

Before anything could be determined, however, the desperadoes began screaming in pain, dropping their treasure as if it had suddenly become hot coals.

Then their pockets started to smoke and burst into flames. Some ran, others threw themselves to the ground and rolled around to put out the fire. Drumpf's guards grabbed buckets and tried to douse them with water, but it was too late.

Each man was engulfed in flames and quickly consumed.

Drumpf's men finally extinguished the flames, leaving nothing but burned corpses.

It seems that gold brought from that world does to humans what silver from our world does to vampires. (I will attempt to safely gather some of the items and submit them for testing by the Magical Properties of Objects Division to verify this observation.) The objects burn anyone who attempts to touch them.

The guards kicked dirt over the corpses and gold and are arguing amongst themselves over what to do next.

A few of the guards ran off. I suspect they did not want to see what else came out of the mine. I count only six humans left guarding the mine entrance, and this bodes well for us. However, there are also at least three vampires. Now that their sire, the Pale Horseman, is dead there is no one commanding their allegiance, which makes me wonder why they are staying. Perhaps it is only habit, or they may just be curious about what will happen next. Of course, they might just be hoping to pick off a human or two to feed on, as we are in a remote area with few dining options.

One of the vampires is an enormous Scandinavian brute, over six feet tall and broad-shouldered. Earlier I saw him working a bellows and shoeing horses so I assume he was a blacksmith in his human life. The other two vampires are wiry and very young, not more than boys. There is a red-headed one who reminds me of my own brother back in Manitoba. The darker haired one seems agitated and is often trying to pick fights with the humans, as if to test out his new strength. Mostly the two of them follow the blacksmith around and take his instructions, as though they are lost without the Pale Horseman commanding them.

I suspect Drumpf is unaware of how dangerous these vampires are with no master to rein them in. They could just as easily turn on the remaining humans out of hunger, or boredom for that matter.

—End Report—

FROM THE JOURNAL OF FLORENCE STOKER, 15TH OF OCTOBER 1882

It was only a few hours ago that I sat outside the mine, fearing for my life (and Bram's and Oscar's) as we prepared to enter the Realm. Now I am at such peace. I sit on the grass of a new world. I was told it existed and taught to fear it, but had no idea of its wonder. It is hard to comprehend even being here. Think of it, an unexplored world as far as the eye can see, under a new sky. This must be how Captain Burton felt seeing the Mountains of the Moon in Africa for the first time as he searched for the source of the Nile.

I still worry that Drumpf won't be true to his word and will enact his revenge on Bram. But as I gaze upon these new wonders, it is easy to believe that this place will lighten his heart and help him show mercy. Mrs. Drumpf assures me he is a man of his word (though he has not demonstrated this by his actions) and that she will intervene if he reneges on his promise, as there has already been too much bloodshed to get us here. "This should be a day that will be celebrated in years to come as a day of miracles. It should not be marred by vengeance," she said. I hope her words will sway her husband when the time comes.

As I write this, she and her nurse sit near me, making necklaces of flowers. They are the most intense blue I have ever seen, with an orange dot in the centre. The dark blue stems are soft like silk. One can see this plant being used to weave fabric. I wonder if a cutting would grow in my garden back home.

FROM THE JOURNAL OF OSCAR WILDE, 16TH OF OCTOBER 1882

When one sees a strange sight it scarcely seems real at first. It takes one's brain some time to grow accustomed to it. Then, the longer one is away from it, the more it seems like a flight of fancy. (The French would use the word 'surreal'.) The silver and emerald city in the Realm is such a memory for me.

We were exploring its wondrous landscape, marvelling at the unusual flora and fauna, the dual suns in the sky and the ruins of an ancient temple. I was gazing at one of the blue trees, wondering if I'd ever seen such a colour in all the art I have ever admired, when one of Drumpf's men came running down from the top of a tall grassy hill he had been exploring.

He yelled, "Mr. Drumpf!" over and over as he ran down. Drumpf came out of the temple to see what the ruckus was about, as did Bram and the others who were inside exploring it. Bram and Florence came over to where I was standing; we all instinctively knew that we were the only ones we could count on in this precarious situation.

The running man stopped when he reached Drumpf. He was winded and having a hard time speaking. "You...have to come and see this!"

He led Drumpf up the hill and the rest of us followed. Bram, Florence and I were bringing up the rear.

Bram leaned over and whispered to us, "This may be a good time for us to make a run for the exit. Let's stay back a bit and hope whatever this is offers a good distraction." I nodded, though I was as curious as anybody about what we would see when we crested the hill.

My curiosity was rewarded. Once at the top, we were too enthralled by the view before us to even think about running away.

Down in a valley was a magnificent city of green glass and silver. Buildings reached into the sky higher than any of the 'skyscrapers' I had seen in New York. Smaller buildings had enormous gardens on the roofs, with flowers and plants of every colour. My aesthetc's eye noted, to my delight, that the plants seemed to be arranged to present pleasing designs that could only be apparent from the very hill on which we stood, as though the gardener was painting with foliage.

Roads paved smooth with some unknown dark grey material weaved through the buildings and were crisscrossed by fast-moving, brightly coloured carriages that had no horses. The roadways and public areas appeared clean, with none of the mud, dust or litter that one normally associates with an urban centre.

The sky above the city was filled with silvery airships that glided along, with and against the wind. All of this industry without smokestacks or the smog that accompanies them.

We all just stared out over the city with our mouths open and eyes wide, stunned at the spectacle of it all. I longed to explore it, though it also terrified me. I have seen much of my own world – teeming metropolises, wonders of modernity – but nothing that compares to this. What power these people must have!

"What devilish enchantment is this?" Drumpf said, finally breaking our collective silence. "What am I looking at, Rayne?" There was anger in his voice, not wonder or bewilderment. How could he be angry at such miracles?

Rayne remained silent for a moment, then spoke as though thinking aloud. "There are no cities mentioned in Eden. It could be the city of Enoch, as told of in Genesis as being outside of Eden in the land of Nod. Or possibly it is a city built in Eden after Adam and Eve were cast from the garden."

"Then *who* built it?" Drumpf said angrily. "Surely not men. Angels? Demons? Who?"

"I know not," Rayne said, still looking over the city.

I thought back to Drumpf's speech about taming a new frontier and civilising savages, and could not stop myself from laughing aloud. I quickly clapped a hand over my mouth to contain the sound, and fortunately Drumpf was too preoccupied to notice. This new land would clearly be harder to conquer than he first thought. Before us was the more advanced civilisation, whether it be populated by angel or demon or something else entirely.

The photographer was frantically setting up his equipment. Other men had their sketchbooks out and were trying to draw what they were seeing.

Florence tugged at my sleeve. She and Bram were slowly stepping back, and I did the same. This would be a good time to make a run for it. I froze in my tracks, however, as I and many others spotted an airship gliding silently towards us. It was picking up speed as though it had seen us gathered on the hill and was just as curious about us as we were about it.

Drumpf and Rayne seemed to be too preoccupied with discussing the significance of the discovery to notice the airship sailing inexorably in our direction. By the time they did it was much too late, as it was swooping down right on us. Guns – I think that is what they must have been – were firing bolts of light at us! I believe this must have been meant only as a warning, for the ground in front of us was the only thing hit, sending up clouds of dirt with little explosions.

The Stokers and I turned and ran as the airship descended and landed on the ground. We could hear some of Drumpf's men returning fire as others started to run down the hill behind us.

We ran as fast as we could, being followed by the others. Soon other, louder, footsteps sounded behind us. I did not dare take the time to turn to see what it was. As we neared the bottom of the hill I tripped, and while picking myself up I looked up the hill and saw a most horrifying sight: three very large green monsters were advancing down the hill at a slower pace, firing pistols at the humans. I could not focus my eyes as I ran, but I could see these monsters had four arms and two legs!

The men behind us were trying to stand their ground and fire back but they were no match for the green creatures' bullets, which exploded like balls of dynamite on impact!

The Stokers and I made it to the entrance back to our world, hoping that Henry still had the door open. Bram pushed Florence and me in ahead of him and we stepped into the darkness of the mine. We saw the dusky light of the outside world and ran for it. By the mercy of God, we returned to our world. Unfortunately, we brought something out with us!

—The entry ends here; however, the next document from Agent Chase picks up the events that followed—

REPORT FROM AGENT CORA CHASE TO WHITE WORM SOCIETY

Date: 16 October 1882

Subject: Drumpf's Failed Expedition

A day has passed, and I have gathered my thoughts regarding the horrifying events of last evening. Here is what happened to the best of my recollection. I apologize if I write too emotionally about what I experienced.

I was observing the camp through my binoculars. The sun was setting, and the air was getting cold. Drumpf's men started a large bonfire near the entrance, lit torches and hung kerosene lamps to warm themselves and keep the darkness away.

Henry was still near the entrance with his book and removed his sun-protective clothing. He glanced up at our hiding position and subtly tapped his ear. He knew I was watching and was letting me know he was hearing something the others could not.

Then the other vampires, the two young ones and the blacksmith heard it too.

The Stokers and Wilde came running out of the mine at full pelt. Drumpf, Rayne and the others came pouring out immediately behind them. (I was very surprised to see Mrs. Drumpf running at such a pace, as from my earlier observations I had thought her to be quite frail.)

A second later, a large cloud of dust billowed out of the mine entrance, sending Drumpf's guards into a confused panic. Behind the last of the men fleeing the mine, I finally saw what was making them run; three enormous creatures emerged from the mine opening! From what I could tell, they were knocking support beams out of their way to exit, sending up clouds of shattered wood, dirt and dust.

I estimate they were easily fifteen feet tall. They had green skin and four arms in addition to their two legs. On their faces were tusks that curved up towards their eyes, and their mouths held rows of razor-sharp teeth. If I were to draw a picture of a demon, I could do no better than these things. (In fact, I have submitted a drawing of them to the Supernatural Creatures Division.)

If their size and strength were not terrifying enough, they were armed with golden pistols that shot exploding bullets in flashes of light.

One such bullet hit Mrs. Drumpf's nurse, and she exploded in a cloud of light and smoke!

Drumpf and his wife took cover behind a large wall of crates as his men protected them with a hail of bullets. The bullets seemed to annoy the creatures more than hurt them, and they swatted the projectiles away with their four hands as if they were bees. The bullets did appear to sting them enough to stop their advance.

In all of this confusion, I noticed Wilde, Irving and the Stokers had run up the hill where we were hiding.

I made our presence known and pulled them to safety in the cover of the brush.

"What in the hell are those things?" Mr. Reeves asked.

"They did not introduce themselves," Mr. Wilde said, out of breath. "But in my experience, nothing good ever comes out of there."

"They look like creatures from Hindu mythology," Mr. Irving speculated, though aside from the number of arms I myself could see no resemblance.

The barrage of bullets was finally doing some good, for the creatures dropped to their arms. By that, I mean they could use the second set of arms as legs to speed along on all fours, and they ran for cover in the trees.

Drumpf shouted something I could not make out, but his vampires emerged from their cover at great speed, so fast they were just a blur and the wind of their passing nearly put the bonfire out.

The three vampires attacked the four-armed creatures. The two younger ones ganged up on one monster, clawing and tearing away the flesh from its face.

The larger, blacksmith vampire had another creature tackled and down on the ground. This all happened so fast the third creature had almost no time to react. It fired its gun at the two younger vampires tearing into its companion, but they sped away at such a speed the bullet hit and killed its friend.

The two younger vampires then turned on the one still standing and started ripping it apart as it fired its gun wildly, hitting nothing. They clawed and snarled like the wild animals they are, eventually ripping the creature's head clean off. Dark blood spewed from its neck and it collapsed to the ground.

Meanwhile, the blacksmith vampire had his legs around the other creature's neck. I don't know whether he choked it dead or broke its spine, but it dropped to the ground and lay motionless. The vampire jumped up onto the creature's back, howled and beat his chest in victory like a gorilla.

Drumpf stepped out from hiding and looked around at the carnage surrounding him. Through my binoculars, I could see he was breathing heavily and his eyes were wild. He pulled out his pistol and shot the inert body of the headless creature several times, then screamed wordlessly in rage, waving the gun around as if looking for something else to shoot.

Mrs. Drumpf emerged, ran to her husband and grabbed him by the wrist holding the gun. She spoke softly to him, attempting to soothe him by the looks of it. Drumpf shook his head angrily, but lowered his gun hand.

Suddenly, Mrs. Drumpf swayed. Drumpf caught her and brought her to the ground. She was clutching at her throat and gasping for air. After one last gasp she was still. She had died in her husband's arms. He stroked her face and murmured to her, then screamed, "No, no, no!" He was rocking her back and forth and sobbing inconsolably.

"The cure didn't take," Mrs. Stoker said sadly, watching the tragic scene.

"Or stops working once back in our world," Mr. Stoker said.

Lobo, the second in command, emerged from somewhere. I had not seen him in all the confusion. He tripped over a mound of dirt that covered the burned corpse of one of his dead men. He looked at the man in horror, then angrily kicked away a golden cup that lay next to the body. He dropped to his knees and began to rock back and forth. I wasn't sure if he was crying or praying.

Drumpf gently laid his dead wife down, stood and raised a fist to the heavens. "I have given everything I have to get to the promised land. This is my reward?" he screamed. "This is not how it ends!"

He spun around, looking for something or someone.

"Stoker!" he screamed. "You do not get to live while my wife and son are dead. I may have lost everything else, but I can still have my vengeance! Come out and face justice, murderer!"

"This again," Wilde muttered.

"We should make a break for it," Mr. Reeves suggested.

Before we could even move, bullets whizzed by us. Drumpf had mustered what was left of his men to pursue Stoker, and one of them must have been observant enough during the melee to see where he had gone. Riflemen were down below shooting up as they walked towards us.

Lobo remained on his knees, clearly praying now, and was not part of the attack.

Mr. Reeves and I returned fire, causing the men to take cover behind wagons and supply crates.

"You go," I said to the others. "Reeves and I will hold them off."

They were all hesitant to move.

"We will follow, I assure you, but we are better able to elude them if we split up. They want Mr. Stoker so he needs to get far away from here as fast as possible."

It was too late. We had all forgotten about the vampires. One of them, the ginger-haired one, had crested the hill behind us and swooped down, grabbing Mrs. Stoker and pulling her a few feet up the hill where he held her in front of himself like a shield.

By his clothing, I judged that he had been one of the settlers who had been attacked and turned by the Pale Horseman to form his vampire army. If only we'd been able to stop Drumpf's lunacy sooner, he might have been homesteading by now, his cabin built, his farmland ploughed. I wondered if he'd had a family with him. If he had, they were dead now, more victims of a madman's quest.

"I'm supposed to use her to force you to surrender, Stoker," he said. "But the Pale Horseman is dead, and this whole scheme has gone to hell. I'm finally figuring out I don't have to obey nobody no more. And damned if I ain't hungry."

He bared his fangs and was about to bite into Mrs. Stoker's neck when Stoker grabbed my second pistol from its holster. He leapt up the hill and threw himself at his wife's feet, then twisted around, pointing the gun up between her body and the vampire's. One quick shot and the vampire fell backwards, releasing his hold on Mrs. Stoker. Bram scrambled to his feet and fired a second shot straight into the monster's heart. A moment later, there was nothing but a pile of goo on the ground.

"Quick thinking, Mr. Stoker," I said, handing more weapons from my bag to Wilde, Irving and Mrs. Stoker. "Well done."

"Quite," Irving said. "But here comes another."

With that, the dark-haired vampire did indeed appear, leaping over a rock directly at Irving, who quickly drew a stake from an interior pocket of his overcoat and plunged it into the attacker's heart. More goo on the ground. We were going to have to be careful not to slip in it if this kept up.

"Thank you for the gun, Miss Chase, but I find a stake works better at close range."

He continued to keep an eye on our rear flank for further vampire attacks, while the rest of us fired upon any of Drumpf's guards who approached from downhill.

In the heat of the firefight I lost track of the third vampire, the blacksmith. He was suddenly upon us! He had crept in from the left, avoiding Mr. Irving's eye.

I turned to fire, but it was too late. He grabbed me by the wrists and twisted my right hand until I dropped my revolver.

Mr. Irving rose, fangs fully in view, to come to my defence, but took a bullet through the chest from the riflemen below! He stumbled back, then dropped to his knees.

The giant vampire sank his fangs into my neck. I suddenly went deaf, no longer hearing the gunfire and people shouting. I could only hear my own heartbeat as the world started to fall away. My eyes fluttered shut, and I blacked out.

—End Report—

Archivist's note: See the next excerpt of Bram Stoker's journal that fills in the continuing events.

FROM THE JOURNAL OF BRAM STOKER, 16 OCTOBER 1882

Archivist's note: We have only included the section of Stoker's journal that picks up after Agent Chase's incapacitation.

It all seemed so hopeless! Six of Drumpf's men were marching up the hill with rifles and we could only return fire with six-shooters. We had plenty of bullets, thanks to Miss Chase and Mr. Reeves, but it took time to reload. We had the advantage of the higher ground, but the riflemen's weapons had superior accuracy and range. It did not help that most of our party, myself included, were not skilled marksmen.

"Vampire!" Mr. Reeves yelled. I turned my head to see the large vampire attacking Miss Chase.

We dared not fire, at least I didn't, for fear of hitting Miss Chase. I searched for Henry in the confusion; he was getting up on shaky feet and I saw he had taken a bullet. It had not hit him in the heart but he was in no condition to help.

I started to lunge at the vampire, but he stopped feeding and put an unconscious Miss Chase between him and me as if she were a limp rag doll.

"Back! Let me have this one and I'll let the rest of you go."

"I think I can get him," Reeves said calmly to me.

The vampire heard him and laughed. "You had better be sure." He pulled Miss Chase closer, protecting his chest area. He licked the blood from her neck, seemingly confident that we would let him take her in exchange for our lives.

A shot rang out close to my ear, startling both me and the vampire. The barrel of Reeves's gun was smoking, as was a hole in the vampire's forehead.

"Pretty sure," Reeves said.

Miss Chase slid out of the vampire's arms and he staggered a few steps back before exploding into a cloud of gore.

I ran over to her and found to my relief she was still alive. I tied a kerchief around her neck and checked on Henry, who was already picking up his gun again.

"I'm fine. I passed the bullet like a kidney stone and am on the mend," he assured me.

We rejoined Reeves and the others firing on Drumpf's men. To my surprise, there were only four of them left. Two lay injured or dead halfway up the hill; Oscar and Florence had managed to hit them while Reeves and I were dealing with the vampire.

Reeves hit another of the riflemen in the shoulder and he went down. The others started retreating at last.

Our victory was short-lived. What happened next was more shocking than all that had come before.

"Hold your fire!" Drumpf yelled. The men did, and we did too.

He whispered something to Rayne.

Without hesitation, Rayne walked over to the praying Lobo, took out a knife and grabbed him by the hair. Lobo had only a moment to look surprised before Rayne slit his throat!

Rayne waited a moment for Lobo's blood to soak the earth, then dropped his corpse to the ground.

"Oh, this isn't good," Oscar said. "What's he going to do with that sceptre now?"

Rayne stabbed the point of his sceptre into the ground, looked skyward and recited an incantation in some ancient language.

"No, not good at all," I said. "Run!"

A beam of light shot into the sky and seemed to part it as an enormous flying creature slipped into our world from who knows where. It looked just like the one that attacked the cavalry, a giant, winged, lizard-like beast. For me, it was also surrounded by a green glow, as if I needed that to tell me this was a supernatural creature.

Rayne pointed his stick in our direction and the creature obeyed, turning towards us with a deafening screech.

We scattered, searching in vain for some place that would provide better cover from an airborne attack. The moon was suddenly eclipsed, and I was buffeted by the wind from the creature's enormous wings. It swooped down and grabbed me by my shoulders as I ran! It gripped me tightly and I felt myself being lifted into the air. I dared not struggle for fear of being punctured by its talons. It then flew the rest of the way down the hill to Rayne and deposited me gently right at his feet.

It then hopped up onto a pile of supply crates and just perched there like a pet, its head tilted to the side as it watched its master with glittering eyes.

"Drop your guns," Drumpf yelled. My comrades did as they were told and put their hands in the air. "All of you, come down here," he ordered.

His remaining guards ran up the hill to make sure his orders were followed. As they returned to camp, one of the guards trained his gun on them and waved them over to stand by the stacked crates. Another came down from the top of the hill.

"There's another woman up there, dead or passed out," he said. "She looks like a vampire got her."

"Carry her down here," Drumpf said.

A young guard standing near Florence said, "Sorry about all this, ma'am. I'm just doing what I'm told."

"It's all right, Colton. We are all just trying to get out of this alive," she replied.

Drumpf walked over to where I kneeled at Rayne's feet and kicked me hard in the ribs.

He was about to do so again when, oddly, he stopped. He seemed to be listening to something. "Do you hear that?" he asked Rayne. His holy man just looked at him, confused. But I knew exactly what he was talking about. I heard it too. It started softly and grew in volume, but even then sounded like a chorus of hissing whispers.

I got to my feet. "I hear them, Drumpf. They are whispering to you from the shadows."

"The Dark Watchers!" Rayne said. "Do not listen to what they say! They lie. They get in your head and do the devil's work!"

"They're getting closer," I said calmly, though I had no idea if this was true.

Rayne's eyes grew wide as he looked around wildly, stabbing his staff at invisible things around them.

"Back, demons!" he yelled. "You will not poison us with your lies!"

The flying creature was becoming confused and agitated, following the staff's movements.

I took this moment to tackle Rayne, trying to wrestle the staff away from him. The creature grew frantic, and it flapped and took to the sky. I knew for sure then it obeyed the stone on the staff, not Rayne, for now it did not know which of us had control of it.

The terrifying creature flapping about sent the rest of Drumpf's men running for the wilderness. The young man guarding Florence and the others fled, allowing her, Oscar, Henry and Reeves to take cover behind the crates just as the creature soared over them.

Rayne had hold of the staff with both hands and was reciting something in an unrecognisable language. I had my hand firmly on the stone, trying to tear it off the top. As Rayne recited his incantations, the stone began to get hot. I knew I could not, would not, let him regain control of the stone, and willed myself to withstand the pain as my flesh sizzled.

"Let go of it, you fool!" Rayne said, trying to yank the stone free. "It will kill us both if you don't let go!"

I could feel the demon inside of me squirm at the supernatural force pulsing through my hand. In one big push, it seemingly poured all its power into my hand and I had the strength to yank the stone free.

I jumped to my feet and ran past Drumpf, who was still blocking his ears from unseen whisperers and seemingly unaware of the battle going on before him.

Rayne stood and pointed his staff to the sky. He waved the staff and commanded in his magic language the creature to back away. The creature didn't budge. Rayne waved his staff again. It was then, to his horror, he saw that the stone was missing.

He had time for one terrified look in my direction before the creature descended and started tearing him apart with its beak and talons, splattering Rayne's blood, as he had spilt Lobo's only minutes before. Rayne screamed in agony, but was quickly silenced.

The flying monster took to the sky once more, blood dripping from its beak and talons, and turned its wrath on Florence and the others.

I started waving the stone over my head. "Over here, you ugly buzzard!"

It obeyed, breaking off its attack and starting to circle me, awaiting instructions I did not know how to give.

"I'll hold him here while you run off," I yelled to Florence and the others.

I wanted to order it back to its own land, but had no idea how. I waved towards the sky, but it did not take the hint, and was growing more agitated and impatient by the second. If I threw the stone, would the creature chase it, like a dog with a ball, or would it take the opportunity to shred me like it had done Rayne? I had no idea, nor did I know how long I could hold it over me before it decided to act on its own.

As it turned out, not long.

The creature, growing impatient, descended rapidly, trying to snatch the stone from my hand. I fell flat to the ground, and it barely missed taking my arm off to get the stone before returning to the air.

In my fall, I dropped the stone, and it bounced to Oscar's feet.

"I have an idea," Oscar said.

"I often don't like your ideas, Oscar," I replied, as I got to my feet.

"I often don't either," Oscar said. Before I could stop him, he snatched the stone from the dirt and made a mad dash for the mine opening. The creature wheeled around to follow.

With a last burst of speed of which I would not have thought him capable, Oscar disappeared inside the mine, the creature in pursuit. Its wingspan barely cleared the entrance. Then, seconds later, dust and rubble came pouring out of the mine's opening as it completely caved in!

We all ran to dig it out, but Drumpf stepped in front of us. I did not know when he had finally risen from his knees, but here he was with one of the four-armed monster's golden pistols in his hand.

We all froze as he pointed the pistol at me. It was so large it took both hands to hold it and three of Drumpf's fingers were needed to cover the trigger. It looked like an oversized toy in a small child's hand. Up close I could see the gun had buttons along both sides and what looked like a dial on the back of it.

Drumpf's breathing was heavy and erratic and his eyes darted around madly.

"You took everything from me," he said, his voice calm now.

Then I heard the whispers in his head again.

He shook his head from side to side and yelled, "Stop it! Go away! Stop telling your lies!"

The whispers continued. He pulled one hand from the gun as though to block his ear, but quickly returned it when the weapon almost fell from his other hand.

With effort, he re-aimed the gun at me and, with a wordless shout, pulled the trigger. I braced myself for death but the gun did not fire. He took a step back, examining the gun, pushing random buttons and fiddling with the dial.

A few feet behind Drumpf, I could see the creature the big vampire had brought down. I had thought it was dead, but now noticed one of its arms moving. Drumpf had his back to it and did not see it taking in a gasp of air and stirring.

The whispers were growing louder now, and I could make out more of what they were saying.

"You have failed, William Drumpf."

"Your son died cursing your name."

"You have nothing left to live for."

Drumpf's eyes were wide and pleading as he looked around, continuing to fumble with the gun but not really paying attention to what he was doing. "Stop it!" he yelled. "You lie!"

"They are making perfect sense to me," I said, advancing slowly on Drumpf. "All they say is true. You sent your son to rob that train, and he died – because of *you*. You took your wife on this fool's quest and now she is dead – because of *you*!"

"No!" Drumpf yelled, his voice cracking. "You shot Tom. You." Every step I took towards him made him take a step back while he continued pushing buttons and periodically pointing the gun at me and pulling the trigger. "Edina was already dying! At least she had a moment of health and happiness before—"

"She might have recovered if not for you," the whispers hissed.

"I tried to warn you about the Realm, didn't I?" I taunted, advancing another step. "And you thought you could conquer that world – what hubris!" The whispers were oddly quiet and deafening at the same time. They buzzed like a nest of angry bees.

Suddenly I could see images flashing in my mind. A young boy running into Drumpf's arms. Drumpf and his wife dancing on a beach. Drumpf as a young man chopping wood with his father. Were these images being put in my mind by the Watchers, some glimpse of Drumpf's memories? From the tears pouring down Drumpf's face, I could tell he was seeing the same scenes. I could feel his sorrow crushing his will to live.

"Riches do you no good now!" the whispers buzzed.

"Killing me won't bring your son or wife back, Drumpf," I said.

Suddenly, something he pushed on the pistol worked. The entire gun lit up like an Edison light bulb and it gave off a faint whining noise. With a deep, shaky breath, he brought the gun up to fire, not seeing the creature behind him pushing itself up with the lower two of its arms.

His face hardened. "You're right, Stoker. It won't bring them back. I know I lost, but that doesn't mean you get to win!"

Before he could fire, the creature grabbed his leg with one of its upper arms and yanked him backwards with such force the pistol flew from his hands and his face slammed into the dirt. The creature stood to its full height, lifting Drumpf into the air where he dangled, upside down. With blood streaming from his face, he writhed in the creature's grasp.

I started to back away, but too late; a hand from the lower set of limbs reached out and grabbed me about the arm, holding me in place, its grip as unbreakable as an iron lock. As I struggled to free myself, the creature grasped one of Drumpf's arms with its other bottom limb. With a great wrenching motion, it tore off Drumpf's leg and arm, splashing me in blood and gore, and tossed them aside. The rest of Drumpf's body fell to the ground at my feet with a wet thud.

The creature then turned its full attention to me and I was sure I was about to meet the same fate as Drumpf. I called out to Florence that I loved her.

The creature lifted me by the leg and as I swung around my only hope was for one last glimpse of my wife.

I got it.

Florence was standing before me, the strange weapon held in both her hands, pointed directly at the monster that held me. "I love you too, Bram," she said, as she pulled the trigger.

The monster exploded, and I slammed to the ground.

Florence and the others rushed to my side.

Drumpf lay beside me. He looked up at me as the last of his life left his eyes, but I felt no pity for him. Not after all the death and destruction he had caused.

But there was little time to contemplate what had just happened. We all ran to the rubble in front of the mine and turned our attention to trying to save Oscar.

FROM THE DIARY OF OSCAR WILDE, 16TH OF OCTOBER 1882

Dear yours truly,

Once again I found myself drawn, as if by fate, into a dark hole in a foolishly heroic attempt to save Stoker. The last time it was wet and slimy and this time it was dry and dusty, so I suppose I should have been grateful for the improved conditions. Yet there I was, crying in despair as all seemed lost.

When one is trapped in a hole, in the darkness, with no hope for escape, one's thoughts turn to all the wrong choices one has made to get to that point.

Of course, I quite justly blamed Stoker for my journey on this road to ruin. However, I did quite a bit of finger-pointing at myself as well. I was about to die after all, and one needs to make one last effort to atone just in case there is someone keeping score.

I thought of poor Constance, who was waiting back in London for me. My sainted mother, who was about to lose her favourite son. My brother, Willie, who was about to lose his favourite (and only) brother. Florence would weep for me, and I suppose even Bram would shed a brief tear, knowing he only lived because of my sacrifice.

I could see absolutely nothing in the pitch blackness, and my environs felt oppressively small now that so much of the mine had collapsed. My legs were pinned under a pile of heavy rocks. I could scarcely breathe and felt as if the air was running out.

I squirmed, trying to free myself, and soon my struggles grew more frantic as my old friend claustrophobia set in again. My thoughts raced unhelpfully. I was going to die here in this small, dusty hole where my body would lie for all eternity! I would have no satin pillow, no ebony coffin, no pretty grave site beneath a flowering tree! I was breathing the last air of my own tomb! The final work for which I would ever be known was a play that closed after a week!

This was intolerable; I had to get a grip on my emotions. I forced myself to close my eyes and lie still until my breathing calmed and I could think clearly again.

I listened, hoping rescuers were in the process of digging me out, but I heard nothing so deep in the mine.

Then, the sound of whispers. They were going to find me!

"I'm alive!" I shouted.

The whispers became louder but strangely were coming from the wrong end of the mine – from the other side of the door to the Realm.

Then they were all around me!

"Who...what are you?" I asked the darkness.

"We are the Watchers. We were here when your world began and will be here when it ends," they said in unison, like a Greek chorus. "We are the guardians of this opening."

"Can you help me?" I pleaded.

"Give us the stone!" they whispered, for it was surely more than one voice. "It is not a toy to be wielded by children such as yourselves. Do something right for once in your pathetic life, Oscar Wilde. Do it before you die!"

I so rarely like to do as I am told, but in this case I had no reason not to obey. I did not want to die clutching this thing that had brought so much death and grief. Tears streamed down my face and yet I found peace as I held out my open hand, the stone resting upon it.

Though I heard no movement, I felt it snatched from my palm.

"Tell the others." One voice spoke now, no longer a whisper. "Never come here again. Never enter this world. It was not made for you!"

With that, there was a bright flash of light. I closed my eyes against its assault. Then I felt fresh air and heard the rustle of trees in the wind.

I opened my eyes to find myself lying under a tree. I stood, brushed myself off and looked around. I was on the hill where we had hidden from Drumpf's men only minutes before. The night air chilled the tears on my face, and I wiped them off with a filthy sleeve.

I made my way down the hill, still rather dazed. The Stokers, Mr. Reeves and Henry were at the mouth of the mine, pulling away rocks and rubble, trying to dig me out by lantern light. A futile gesture, but it touched me nonetheless.

Mr. Reeves put his hand on Bram's shoulder. "It's no use. We can't clear this by hand. Not even with a vampire helping."

Florence buried her face in Bram's chest, crying.

"He was a good friend," Bram said. "I should have been kinder to him. I should have told him how important he was to me."

There was genuine sadness in his voice. He fell silent.

"Well, go on," I said. "Tell me how important I am."

The others wheeled around and were stunned to see me.

Florence ran and hugged me, saying, "How is this possible? We thought you were dead!"

"I thought I was too." I explained what had happened and what the voices had told me.

"The White Worms will want to know about your encounter," Bram said. He looked around. "Where's Miss Chase?"

Ever the White Worm operative, she was awake now, moving among the wreckage of the camp, gathering evidence for the Worms to examine, I suppose. I saw her pick up a small golden statue from the Realm; she used a piece of canvas to grip it, which I thought was odd, and quickly stuffed it into a leather saddlebag. She then approached one of the large green monsters with a knife drawn, and I found it best to look away.

We did not want to spend the night here amongst the carnage, so we set about salvaging what supplies we could before setting off back to Santa Barbara. Henry was quite relieved that we would be travelling at night and he would not have to wrap himself up like a mummy for the journey.

Drumpf's horses had run off in the melee, but the steeds that Miss Chase and Mr. Reeves had ridden were still on the hill, and that would have to do. Bram and Florence would ride together, as would Reeves and I. Miss Chase would have the dubious honour of travelling on Henry's back.

As luck would have it, however, the Roosevelts chose that moment to arrive in camp with an entourage of soldiers. Better late than never, I suppose. They left some men to guard the site and we at least were all able to ride back to Santa Barbara.

Once there, Miss Chase questioned us all about our time in the Realm, and warned us to expect further questions later should the Worms need to clarify anything.

"They know where to find us," I said. "No matter how much we try to hide."

She then took her leave. It was only later that Henry, going through his bag, swore softly. "She took the book," he said.

The rest of us checked our things. "My journal is missing," Florence said weakly.

Yes, Miss Chase is a Worm, through and through.

Mr. Reeves bade us farewell, saying, "I have to return these horses I borrowed. Then I'll be heading back to San Francisco. I promised Winnie I would escort her to Arkansas." He shook Florrie's hand. "Thank you, ma'am, for one last adventure. I am hoping for a quiet life now, surrounded by my grandkids."

The rest of us are now on the train back to Salt Lake City to pick up Noel and the nanny and head back east and on to England. I have an adequate cup of tea on the table before me, and a very good bottle of whiskey for later, and tonight I will sleep on a downy soft mattress as the train bumps along and it will feel like heaven.

It is time to go home. I would like to say I will miss America. I would like to, but cannot.

REPORT FROM AGENT CORA CHASE TO WHITE WORM SOCIETY

Date: 17 October 1882

Subject: Closing of the California Realm Doorway

The mine is sufficiently collapsed to make access to the Realm nearly impossible. Furthermore, there seems to be some dark force guarding the opening, something Drumpf and Rayne called 'The Dark Watchers'.

From what Henry Irving can decipher from the writings one of Drumpf's men brought out from the Realm, the large, four-armed creatures are called Barsoomians. They are not originally from the Realm but entered like we did, from somewhere else. In addition, he says the Vellum Manuscript tells of other openings, each leading to a new world.

I suggest we do not attempt to uncover this opening and concentrate on translating the Vellum Manuscript to learn of other portals and the threats they could pose.

You will soon receive a crate in which you will find the following:

- One of the Barsoomian pistols. Unfortunately, there were no bullets left to be recovered. Nevertheless, I suggest handling with extreme caution until its full capabilities can be assessed.
- The Vellum Manuscript, similar to the one Arthur Conan Doyle retrieved on his last expedition.
- Four gold figurines of four-limbed humanoid creatures. Do not touch or look at closely without dark glasses.
- A vial of gold dust from the Realm. Do not touch or look at closely without dark glasses.
- Skin, tusk and blood samples from one of the four-limbed creatures.

- Un-mailed letters from Alejo 'Lobo' Lopez to his brother Luz Lopez.
- Scrolls and other writings from the Realm temple.
- Photographic plates, presumably containing images from the Realm.
- Eagan Rayne's scepter, minus the green stone (last seen in Mr. Wilde's hands when the mine collapsed).
- Florence Stoker's personal journal.

In any event, I think we can call the Drumpf/Rayne matter closed. We owe much to the help of Stoker, Wilde and Irving, who continue to be valuable assets to our cause. To that, I would add Mrs. Stoker, who displayed previously untapped resourcefulness under trying circumstances.

—End Report—

FROM THE JOURNAL OF BRAM STOKER, 4TH OF DECEMBER 1882

I have never been so happy to be back behind my desk and my mundane duties as a theatre manager. I missed the gloomy skies of London and a proper cup of tea.

We are in the thick of preparations for a production of *A Midsummer Night's Dream*, and the theatre is a busy hive of activity that had driven all thoughts of vampires and America from my mind.

But then Henry called me to his office and there was Miss Chase sitting in the chair across from his desk. She was the last person I thought I would ever see again, let alone in Henry's office.

"Not you again!" I exclaimed. "Honestly, Miss Chase, while I appreciate all you did for us in America, I wish the White Worms would just leave us alone. Oh, and Florence would like her journal back."

"Please, listen to what she has to say," Henry said.

I reluctantly took a seat. "I already gave your London office my records from our American adventures," I said. "What do you want now?"

She got right down to it. "We need your help in tracking down Dr. Mueller."

He was the one who had sent Henry on the wild goose chase in America in the first place, so he isn't one of my favourite people either.

"He seems to be up to no good. We have reports that he has reanimated the dead somewhere in Finland," Miss Chase explained.

"What makes you think I can help? Henry is the one corresponding with him," I said.

"We intercepted a letter he wrote to you, Mr. Stoker." She handed it to me.

Dear Mr. Stoker,

You don't know me, but I have been corresponding with Henry Irving concerning the magical properties of his blood, and by extension, yours. I assure you, Henry did not betray your confidence about your condition; that information I acquired from the Black Bishop.

I am doing important scientific work that will revolutionise medicine. I think, in time, my work could lead to the cure of all diseases and even of death itself!

I would like to buy a sample of your blood. I believe it is the key to reanimation without the nasty side effects of vampirism. If you agree to this, it can be to the benefit of all mankind.

I have enclosed the address of my solicitor and he can deliver me the sample. I thank you in advance.

Sincerely,

Dr. Victor Mueller.

"Absolutely not," I said. "I will play no part in yet another madman's schemes."

"Obviously, we don't want you to give him your blood," Miss Chase said. "There's no telling what he would do with it. But we can use you to set a trap for him. All you need to do is set up a meeting and we'll do the rest."

"Aren't there any Finnish theatre managers who could be pressed into service?" I asked.

"I understand your reluctance, Mr. Stoker, but Dr. Mueller is truly a menace. His thirst for knowledge is commendable, but unfortunately he does not feel bound by any laws of God or man in his pursuit of scientific advances."

"He's creating monsters that are terrorising Finland," Henry added. "We can't let that go unchecked."

Against my better judgement, I relented. "I will help you catch Mueller, but this is the last favour I will ever do for the White Worm Society."

"Understood," Miss Chase said. She was all smiles, and I did not like that.

FROM THE JOURNAL OF FLORENCE STOKER, 6TH OF DECEMBER 1882

Bram told me yesterday the White Worms want him to help capture yet another madman wielding supernatural power. I ask you, how many are there? Why must he be the one called upon to stop them?

I do understand why he must go – this time to Finland of all places – and am proud that he is ready and able to stand up to those who would do evil, but I worry nonetheless. I am happy, at least, that he is able to confide in me about such matters now.

"My secrecy has put you and Noel in danger in the past. I will inform you of any and all future monster-hunting endeavours," he said. "We must accept the fact I have been called up by Queen and country to use my powers for good."

He assures me he won't have to do anything dangerous and only needs to meet with the man to flush him out for the White Worms and Captain Burton. But I do not like him getting mixed up with the Worms and Miss Chase again. I do not think she or they have our best interests at heart.

I wish I could go to Finland to help, and would if it weren't for Noel. I spent too much time away from him in recent months. However, I wonder if I can get Oscar to accompany Bram on the trip as my proxy.

Sometimes I think our entering the Realm was but a dream. However, I still have the necklace of intense blue flowers I picked while there. The flowers have not wilted or faded. I hope the memories of that grand adventure, which Bram and I shared, will continue to be just as bright.

LETTER FROM OSCAR WILDE TO BRAM STOKER, 7TH OF DECEMBER 1882

Dear Bram,

It is with a happy heart I write to tell you I am engaged to be married. Having seen how blissful you and Florrie are has been an inspiration to me. My recent brushes with death have made me want to put my wicked ways behind me, and I suppose I owe you thanks for that as well.

Constance Lloyd has, for better or worse, agreed to take me for better or worse, and the wedding is to be at the end of May.

I do so hope you and Florrie will attend.

I hear you are off to Finland soon. Whatever for? I hope those White Worms aren't taking advantage of you and whisking you off to do more monster-hunting.

I myself have a strange new connection to the Worms. As you perhaps know, I met Constance through Anna Hubbard, a White Worm member. You remember Anna; she is the one who interviewed us about that nastiness at Stonehenge. We hit it off and became fast friends with our mutual love of the opera.

Miss Hubbard made my first introduction to Constance, telling me they went to school together, and I thought no more of it. Their connection seemed innocent enough; after all, even White Worm members must have some semblance of a normal life, and one presumes they have been educated to some extent.

However, now it has come to my attention that Constance's father, Horace Lloyd, was also a White Worm. Mr. Lloyd was a wealthy barrister on the Queen's Counsel by day and a monster hunter by night, just like the rest of that lot.

He is said to have died in 1874 but, in fact, Anna told me he was lost on one of Conan Doyle's expeditions into the Realm!

Miss Hubbard assures me Constance knows nothing of this or any of her father's White Worm activities, and I hope to keep it that way.

Still, one wonders if it is all a coincidence that I find myself once again tied to the White Worms, if only in a tangential way.

However, if this be fate, so be it. I am happy and looking forward to settling down to a nice, normal, boring life; it hardly seems possible for one such as myself, I know, but I shall take you as inspiration in all things boring and normal.

Yours truly,

O.W.

P.S. Please see my tailor to procure a new suit for the wedding. I will cover the expense. I am enclosing his card.